CLAIMING CAROLINE

GROVER TOWN DISCIPLINE - BOOK SIX

YASMINE HYDE

Published by Blushing Books
An Imprint of
ABCD Graphics and Design, Inc.
A Virginia Corporation
977 Seminole Trail #233
Charlottesville, VA 22901

Yasmine Hyde
Claiming Caroline

eBook ISBN: 978-1-64563-712-7
Print ISBN: 978-1-64563-713-4
v2

Cover Art by ABCD Graphics & Design
This book contains fantasy themes appropriate for mature readers only. Nothing in this book should be interpreted as Blushing Books' or the author's advocating any non-consensual sexual activity.

ONE

"Oof!" The bundle of new reins fell from one hand as the hard thump of his new saddle dropped from his other. He wasn't bothered by the falling items as long as the slight form against his chest was all right.

"Oh, gracious me. I'm sorry..." Her words ceased, as her dark brown eyes—as rich as brewed coffee, that issued a punch to his gut the same way as the roasted beans did—rose and met his.

He gripped her shoulders, feeling the thin but strong muscles hidden beneath her worn green dress, which did not a thing to enhance the beauty of the woman wearing it, but neither did it dim it for him. The unexpected contact set her body against his and he didn't regret having her in his arms. His farm and the people employed by him consumed all his effort and time. It was the responsibility for those who depended on him weighing on his shoulders that kept him from thinking of himself and the things he wanted. That want included the woman now standing in his arms at a bird-chirping early hour of the morning. Only a few businesses were even open at such a time and a handful of people were moving through the area. He didn't doubt it was strategic that Caroline Douglas was in Grover Town now.

"'Cuse me, ma'am." He couldn't help his natural male reflex to inhale and take in the soft flower scent of the soap he could smell coming from her body or hair. He gritted his teeth not to lean down and drag his nose along the side of her slender neck and take in more of her. This wasn't the time nor place. Hell, it wasn't the woman either.

His gaze must have revealed his urges toward her because she stumbled back and away from him. There was a crunching sound then a gasp.

"Oh, no!" She dropped to her knees, basket dangling from her arm, but there were three eggs, rather broken yokes and shells, staining the boardwalk between them.

Lowering to his haunches, he stared down at the mess. It was only a few eggs, but her strained expression as she wore her teeth into her bottom lip made it clear they may have been all or most of them from her basket. "Miss Caroline, it was my fault. I'll replace them."

Her head popped up and she stared at him, trying to force a smile. She widened her eyes to appear as if the destruction didn't bother her; he wasn't fooled.

She rose, readjusting the linen in the basket as if there was something else in the basket she was protecting, but the cloth lay too flat for there to be anything else within. "It's fine. I was just dropping some items off to the Russells and happened to pick up a few eggs, maybe for a cake. Don't worry yourself, Mr. Rand."

Even as he enjoyed hearing his surname from her lovely, odd lips, the top slightly fuller than the lower, he wasn't convinced. The more she talked and didn't meet his gaze, it solidified his decision to replace them. "Miss Caroline, I won't feel good about myself if I didn't make amends for my mistake."

She brushed a hand over her skirts, sweeping away mysterious dirt. Her dress was old, and more than a few of the buttons down the front of it were different colors. There was a long, jagged dark green stitch down the side, all proof she'd had to mend the dress more than once, but it was clean. "Truly, it isn't that serious of a matter." She offered him a small smile and short nod, as she made to pass him.

He placed a hand lightly on her elbow to halt her as she started to turn to walk away and felt the electric spark from the place he touched her through his fingertips and straight to his core. He didn't remove his hand as he enjoyed the soft fabric of her dress warmed by her skin. Waiting until she glanced over her shoulder at him, he kept his voice low. "Please allow me to do this."

She took in a shuddered breath as her gaze held his.

Her eyes seemed to consume him, drown him in their soulful loveliness. Garrett gave himself strict instructions not to lower his gaze to her lips, but his eager ass eyes didn't listen as they practically moved of their own accord and took in their fullness and the off-kilter size, the top one that was just a bit fuller and wider than the bottom, a captivating pair. He was standing close to her. There was a respectable gap between them but not big enough that his mind hadn't calculated the one step it would take to set his lips on hers.

Dammit. He wasn't a fool. In Grover Town, if he kissed sweet, innocent Caroline Douglas, there'd be church bells ringin' before noon. Right now, his life was headed in the right direction where his farm was concerned but too much for him to handle to even consider taking a wife. It took most of his might, but he tore his gaze away from her tempting mouth and back on her eyes.

His little nervous bunny. He saw the worry and relief that combined in her gaze when finally, she acquiesced, "If it's that important to you, I'll wait while you replace it."

His heart did a strange drop, then it soared as if he were on a horse headed face down a deep gully then coming up over the other side. There was a tug at one side of his mouth as he smiled. "May I?"

She frowned, confused at what he was asking for. When he tapped the handle of the basket over her arm, she stammered, "Oh, yes."

When she slipped off the basket and handed it to him, he saw the flood of color in her cheeks and wondered what had been going through her mind.

Was it like mine? He shoved that thought away. Caroline worked too hard alongside her pa to tend their dying farm and keep a bit of food in their mouths to be considerin' kisses at daybreak.

"Be but a minute." He tipped his hat and hustled inside of Russell's Mercantile.

"Mornin', Rand."

"Henry." He strolled up the center aisle between the rows of provisions and goods stacked and shelved on tables, crates, and barrels, and even more items displayed on shelving along the side walls. At the counter, he set the basket down.

Henry, with two thumbs' worth of salt at his temples marring the darkness of his hair, the only show of his age, looked down at it. Not something Garrett had ever carried into the store, and he was sure the older man knew it belonged to Caroline, who was standing right outside one of two large windows.

"What can I do you for this day?" the man asked, not even mentioning the woman outside.

Garrett was grateful Henry was here instead of his wife.

She was a little more than a busybody, not malicious about it, just nosey. He took a second and flipped back the top linen of the lightweight basket just to verify he was right. The basket was empty; only those three cracked eggs had been inside. "I need half dozen eggs, if you got them, and a half pound of flour and meal."

"The eggs are yesterday's. I should have fresh within the hour." He stepped over to the big sacks cinched tight with twine behind the counter.

"What you have'll be fine."

"I can get that right up for you." Henry started scooping and weighing the items.

As he waited, Garrett noticed the various jars of sourballs, gum drops, peppermint sticks, colorful gumballs, and candy sticks. Usually, they weren't something he'd paid much attention to since he was a youngster, but he thought about the woman outside, embarrassed by the meagerness of her morning shopping. He decided he wanted to give her a treat personally, hopin' she'd like it when she discovered it and even the meal and flour. He wasn't trying to shame her, or her prideful father, just help a little where he could.

"All right. All set." Henry's voice snagged his attention.

Moving back to the basket, he handed Henry the peppermint stick to place in a small wax bag. "Place it on my farm's tab. When Mrs. Copernic comes in shortly for things she needs at the house, she'll pay it with the other stuff."

"Sure thing."

Garrett covered all the small items up in the basket, then he left after a two finger tap to the brim of his hat, biddin' the other man good day.

"Here you go, Miss. Caroline."

"Oh, thank you." She held out his reins. "Here. Figured

you didn't purchase them because the boardwalk was in need of leads for a horse."

He grinned at her humor. "No, ma'am. Sorry if I delayed you today. Thanks." Garrett took the reins that he'd plum forgotten from her hand and exchanged it for the basket.

When her gaze rounded at the heft, she started shaking her head, denying herself the unseen items in it. He covered her hand, lightly gripping the handle. "Just my apologizes. Please take it with the kindness it was given."

She hesitated. "Okay. Thank you, Mr. Rand." She stepped away, breaking their contact. "I must get going. Papa will come in from the field soon, needin' his breakfast."

"I'm sure. Good day, Miss Caroline." *Lovely bunny.* He stood next to his new saddle still on the planks of wood below his feet as he watched her hasty steps take her down from the boardwalk to the nag-pulled wagon out front of the store.

Once there and in her seat, she offered him a wave and a small smile before she was tottering off on the rickety ride, the basket stationed on the seat beside her. He hoped that with such an unsteady ride before her, this batch of eggs would make it to the tiny farm. If not, at least she could make something to fill their bellies with the meal and flour. He would have liked to bring her a bucket or two of fresh milk and a pound of butter from his dairy and farm, but he knew Mr. Douglas wouldn't allow such kindness, or charity, as the protective father and farmer saw it.

Caroline Douglas was a beauty and sweet young lady. Longer in the tooth than most gals who were married by ten and six, she would make a man a fine wife if her pa ever gave anyone the opportunity.

Garrett hefted the saddle from the walkway before he slung it onto his shoulder and made his way to his horse. There was too much in his way to even consider makin' an offer. So he did what he always did, put Caroline Douglas out of his mind.

———

"WHAT BRINGS YOU 'ROUND, GARRETT?" Sam Douglas barely gave him a slight glance as he continued breaking up the hard ground with his hoe.

Fingering the brim of the hat in his hand, Garrett looked around the yard. The farm was small and the house just as little. It appeared sturdy but run down. Sam had lived out here on the outskirts of town with his daughter, Caroline for years. Everyone in town knew that Samuel and his daughter were two pennies away from the poorhouse in Topeka. Crops hadn't been good in more than a handful of years and without money to buy cattle or proper irrigation to the fields, a person could bury themselves deep in debt. However, Douglas' crops weren't the reason Garrett came around. Caroline was the reason he was here. An hour ago, he'd seen her ride into town on their weathered wagon, pulled by the old nag Douglas liked to call a horse.

Needing to speak to Douglas alone, Garrett had come rushing over. It had been two years since he'd literally run into Caroline, and since then, most things he'd done since then had set him on this course.

"If you've just come to stand around, then you'll have to do it someplace else. I'm gonna need that piece of earth your boots is takin' up roots in." Douglas continued moving backwards as he dug the hoe deeper in the ground, his Scottish brogue intricately peppering the Midwest dialect, both thick even though it was common knowledge that the older man had been in America since age eleven.

Not put off by the older man's gruff tone, Garrett took a deep breath. "Mr. Douglas, I'm here on a personal matter."

A slight pause in motion was the only indication that Douglas was truly processing the conversation. "We ain't got no personal matters between us."

Pulling a handkerchief from his back pocket, Garrett swiped the sweat from his forehead. It was late winter, but just southeast of the Great Plains of the Kansas Territory this year, things began to heat up early. "Not yet. But, I was hopin'—"

"What is it that you was wonderin'?" Stopping and leaning against the long stick of his tool, Douglas eyed him.

Garrett stood tall as he was assessed by the brown, weary eyes of the older man. Douglas' features had been carved by years of a hard life. His determined struggles had won Garrett's respect. After losing his house, wife and infant son in a twister, Douglas had never missed a beat. He cared for his six-year-old daughter alone and worked the land. Everyone in Grover knew their story, their struggle.

"I'm not gettin' any younger." Smiling, Garrett made a small attempt to lighten the mood.

Douglas didn't bite just continued to stare.

"I've been thinkin' a lot lately about settlin' down."

"Mm-hmm."

The bleating goat secured in the small pen at the side of the house communicated more than Douglas. Garrett ventured, "Look, I'm here to ask you for Caroline's hand."

"Keep away' fae mah daughter. Dinnae even think aboot it. It ain't goin' happen." Douglas' response was gruff as he gave Garrett a sharp-eyed look on the last statement as if he ensured they were communicating the same language before he began hoeing again, slammin' the tool into the dry earth with all his might, as if that ended the conversation.

Unable to let it go, Garrett questioned, "Why, Douglas? I make more than a decent living out at my farm. I can take care of her. Caroline is at least one and twenty. She's been old enough for years. Besides that, I have a feel—"

"You ain't gotta tell me about my daughter. A crofter kens his lassie better than a'body. Her place is here and that ain't goin' change." With his two dialects mangled into one, Sam Douglas raised his hoe and began his work again with more gusto as heavy rivers of sweat rolled down his tan skin. The man's face was blotchy, with red patches here and there, and the rivulets streamed from his face to his chin and dripped on his arm.

Garrett sighed heavily. He didn't know if he wanted to growl or rage. This conversation was not going as he'd hoped. "Mr. Douglas! I promise to do good by Caroline and not treat her wrong."

"I know you won't treat her wrong, cuz you ain't gettin' *my lassie*, so stop askin'," Caroline's father said without looking up. "I don't care how many of you *randy* bucks and Bellmores come round here, the answers still goin' be *na. Ye ken?*"

Garrett didn't' know if Mr. Douglas was making a play on his name or if it was true that other men in town had asked for Caroline's hand. It wasn't hard to believe others wanted her; she was a beauty. Even underneath all the old clothes and the layers of dirt from working in the field with her father, Caroline was something special.

What did Bellmore have to do with any of this?

"*Ah ken.*" Realizing that this conversation had come to a close, Garrett allowed the meeting to end. He placed his hat back on his head. "'Preciate your time, Douglas."

Grunting under his voice, Douglas continued his field work.

Shaking his head in disappointment at the old man's stubbornness, Garrett crossed the uneven, hard, dry and rocky soil and mounted his chestnut horse, King. Tugging on his reins, he steered the big horse back toward town.

It was time for him to re-evaluate his plans. Evidently, his thoughts of getting Caroline to the altar was a dream that was fading with dawn's light.

Good thing he wasn't a man who gave up easily.

TWO

Today was her birthday. But two and twenty would have been just like any other day, no cake, no celebration, nothing special, if it was not for her father's heart attack and death. A few days ago, she'd come home from the mercantile shop and having Fredricka's back hoof re-shoed and mucking the stalls of the livery to pay for it, only to find her father dead in the field, his hoe still clutched in his fist.

Caroline gazed through blurring eyes toward her father's narrow, plain wooden casket lying next to the open grave where he would rest beside her mother and her younger brother Ewan. Pastor Morgan speaking from the Bible and reciting a blessing over her father's soul, but she wasn't processing any of his words. Right now, she didn't hear anything. Her mind was filled with racing thoughts of the untilled fields, the crops that still needed to be planted before spring and harvested in the fall, and how she was going to feed the goat. They'd had chickens once, but it became a matter of feed them or feed herself and her father.

Money, or lack thereof, was something easier to think about. Anything was easier to ponder than the death of her father. Samuel Douglas was the only thing she had in this world. He'd raised her alone and had done the best he could, regardless of what the people in town believed. Her father had worked himself to death just to keep a roof over her head. She was proud of him and loved him.

"Amen." Pastor Morgan from the Grover Town Methodist Church led the closing prayer as the handful of town folk gathered at the gravesite on the side of the church chimed in after him.

Ezekiel and Amos Morgan, the pastor's teenage boys, the oldest since the other, Jacob, had left town years ago, lifted her father's pine box with Chance Spencer and Cary Brown, her childhood friend's husband, and placed it in the hole that had been dug earlier in the day. The four men seemed more for show to her. Her father had once been a tall, stout, broadshouldered man, only to wither down to skin and big bones from the work and lack of food brought on by his pride. The moment had come that she'd dreaded all morning. It was the final goodbye. The fifteen or so people who stood silently around her, waited. In the last two days, her small home had been inundated with ladies from town bringing her baked goods and preserves, permitted now that her father was not there to deny them their Christian charities. Caroline had lost her appetite and kept herself busy with the funeral arrangements.

With a shaky breath and a single one of her rose buds tight in her hand—the thorns piercing her fingers—buried deep in her thumb, the pain offered a bit of relief. It was something else she could focus on other than her father's death. She started forward and moved the steps needed to take her to the hole, her father's final resting place. He'd missed her mother, Abby, something fierce over the years and now he would be with her. Kneeling, she fisted a handful of dirt.

Closing her eyes, she said a prayer. This prayer wasn't for her father's soul. No, it was for her, the one who'd been left here alone. When she'd lost her mother and baby brother, she'd still had her father, and together, they'd made it. Now she had no one.

Opening her eyes, she allowed the dirt to sift through her fingers and watched it sprinkle onto the pine box. It was time to say good-bye.

DAWN WAS BREAKING across the horizon as Caroline prepared herself to feed the animals. The seeds still needed to be planted, and she'd need to lug the water from the weak pump she was sure would dry up by next year, to pour on the field. Hard labor for two people, an impossible task for one person. However, she had no choice. She'd scrounge up some supplies and make a few soap cakes from her rose bush she'd planted almost a year ago to the day alongside the porch. Perhaps, she would have enough to buy some onion seed, radishes, and squash. Even though her papa had fought against the harsh soil vegetables, she'd plant and raise them. When she had enough saved from them, she'd move to a better plot of land. Perhaps she could speak with Isabel's father. He may have something and be willing to work out a deal. Mr. Reynolds had tried numerous times to get her father to cut ties with Bellmore and lease property from him, an honorable and fair man.

Her papa had seen Isabel's father's offer as pity or doubt they'd be able to turn the farm around. Samuel Douglas, of the McDougals of Scotland, had wanted to believe he could be a successful farmer, crofter, as he called it. Their surname had been changed at Ellis Island, telling her *Seanair* Liam

McDougal, Grandpapa, he'd have better success on the Continent being a Douglas then anything Mc or Mac. That hadn't been true. Since, her *seanair* had died a discouraged man in the slum boroughs of New York of lung consumption, from years of work in a turpentine distillery. Her *seanair* had dragged the family around with him until he was too sick to work. Sam, her papa, had saved the money he'd earn hoeing around the trees used to tap for the product. After his papa died, Sam had shifted to less back breaking work and danger of illness and hired on in a tap bar, owned by another immigrant Scot. It was there, he'd met her mother Abby. Her mother had been a successful seamstress, a French woman, creating dresses and gowns for politician's wives in the big, bustling city. Caroline's grandmother had believed Samuel Douglas wasn't good enough for Abigail Benoit. However, Grandma Benoit could not stop the intense love of two young people. When Caroline's papa had heard the advertisements of the success stories people were having farming in the Midwest, he'd believed he could fulfill his father's dream. He'd convinced Abby to marry him and run away to the west where they could have their own land and life. Wide-eyed and in love, they'd made their way across half the Continent, working odd jobs trying to save for the perfect plot of land in the perfect place.

However, life had been hard and strenuous for them and it didn't get any easier with small mouths to feed. Her papa had met a young Mr. Bellmore, a slick talking property owner, at a trade post in Nebraska. Bellmore had sold her papa on a field of dreams, ripe for pickin' in Kansas Territory, a new, budding town with prairies of rich soil. He papa had been convinced, too young to know better than to pay for property sight unseen. He'd believed Bellmore and had followed him to the promised land.

Foolish. She loved her father; however, he'd been a foolish man. A heartbroken, stubborn man in the end.

Caroline sighed and bit the inside of her cheek hard to keep from crying at her papa's plight. Tears wouldn't do her a bit of good at the moment, when there was work to do. On the table, where they took their meals, across the small front room from the hearth, she poured water from a pitcher into a bowl to wash her face then used a rag and powder on her teeth. Removing her gown, she pulled her dress over her head and tied the most worn of her two aprons around her waist then moved toward the door. Unlatching it, she stepped onto the porch, prepared with a heavy heart to begin her work.

"Well, hello there, lovely Miss Caroline."

She wasn't expecting guests and the sight of Daryl Bellmore left her speechless. As usual, he was dressed in what most of the people in Grover Town called Sunday's best. There wasn't a speck of mud or filth on his clothes or shoes. She'd known her dress was worn and old when she put it on that morning, but now, standing before Bellmore, she might as well be wearing a burlap sack.

Supposedly, Bellmore's father had struck it rich in California, and he had been traveling through Kansas Territory. When he got to Grover Town, he'd started claiming land and using his money to start a few businesses in the town, his money dwindling, but it still kept the Bellmores in a higher station of living. After his father's death, Daryl began bringing in people hustling for a dream. Only few prospered, the rest left the town worse off than when they came.

Bellmore lounged against one of the beams holding up the overhang covering the porch as if it were a respectable time to visit. His black horse nibbled on the last few remaining grass patches in the front yard. The beam was solid, just like the small house her papa had built after the tornado had torn apart the flimsy structure Bellmore had on the land when they arrived.

She pressed a hand against her chest, feeling her racing heart. "Mr. Bellmore—"

"Oh, come now, Miss Caroline, I've always told you to call me Daryl." The wide, pearly-white smile competed with the smooth, pale complexion of his face, evidence that he spent more time indoors than out.

"You're my landlord, Mr. Bellmore; it wouldn't be proper."

He chose that moment to allow his gaze a slow glide down the front of her dress. The look in his beady eyes was anything but proper. She felt like every layer of her clothing was instantly pooled at her feet.

The urge to run the miles to the stream, dive in the water, then scrub her skin clean and wash the filth of his gaze off herself assailed her. Instead, she moved away and continued down the two stairs. She headed toward the side of the house to the tiny barn. She spoke over her shoulder. "I hope you don't mind if I begin my daily chores. Now that it's just me, I don't have time to waste."

"You know, Miss Caroline, it has always hurt my heart to see you work in these fields."

Caroline peeped back at him. Her glance caught Bellmore as he made careful steps across the ground as if he'd never walked on dirt before. She shook her head. "We all do what we have to, to survive. My papa had no sons to do it, so that leaves me." Pulling open the door to the barn, she steadied it, ensuring it didn't fall off the one hinge keeping it together. Stepping into the cool interior, she used the light from the newly risen sun to see into the dark space.

Staring into the barn as if the plague were located inside, Bellmore said, "That may have been the case when your father was alive, but now..."

Grabbing the depleting bag of oats, she scooped out a few handfuls for Fredricka, the old horse, then moved out of the aging shack and headed toward the fenced-in small corral for Driscoll, the goat. She wasn't even sure why her papa had kept the goat for so long; he would have provided more for them in a stew then a pet. If Dris had been a female, then at least they could have gotten milk from him daily. However, he was just another mouth to feed. She'd have to investigate selling him. Perhaps he would bring in enough for her to purchase some new seed.

Her mind picked up on where Bellmore's words had drifted off. "Now what? Things haven't changed. I'll still work this farm and you'll still be paid."

Whistling to Dris, she entered the fence and headed to the bucket and poured some oats into it. She gave him a scratch beside the neck and promised him some fresh water.

"In this, you're wrong, Miss Caroline." Bellmore's voice came out slightly muffled as he spoke through the handkerchief he placed over his nose to protect himself from the stench of the goat droppings and horse manure.

The smell was strong, but it was something most hard-working people got used to when the animals fed or supported their families and farms. After she'd fed and watered the animals, she'd muck out the stall and pen before she went into the field.

"Wrong? In what way?" She exited the enclosure and went to the pump on the side of the house. Taking hold of the handle, she paused and took a deep breath. She just wanted Bellmore to state his piece and go. She began to prime the pump to work up some water, praying it would be enough for the animals and herself.

Everything had been declining. Her father's death was the final plummet. She just hoped she could keep herself up.

"Miss Caroline, can you please pause for one moment?" Bellmore called from behind her.

She stopped in her tracks. Halfway to the barn with the bucket filled with water, she turned her head and stared at him. His soft blond curls glistened in the sunlight. He was always spit polish perfect. He was an oddity on her land.

Not wanting to be rude, she waited until he reached her. "Forgive me, Mr. Bellmore, but like I said—"

"It doesn't matter what you were trying to say. It appears that you have been misled in some way."

Tilting her head, she eyed Bellmore. There was something in his voice that was sending warning whistles through her ears as her heart began to thump. "If you have concern that I won't be able to keep up the farm now that my father has passed, I assure you that I can. Over the years, there were times when my father was sick, and I had to do the work."

He lifted an eyebrow at her. "Hard times call for people to make tough choices. However, women, in my opinion, are a softer sex..." He paused and his gaze roamed her form once again. "They should be treated as such. Especially a jewel as precious as yourself, Miss Caroline."

The sickening feeling in the pit of her stomach that had been there since her father's untimely death began to grow.

"I was never raised as a delicate flower." She felt a few wisps of hair slide loose from the material holding it back. She kept it shorter than most of the women in town, barely falling around her shoulders when it was down.

"You should've been." Bellmore's hand lifted as if to tuck the hair back in place.

Stepping back out of arm's distance, she reached up and shoved the hair back herself. "Life's too short to think about shouldas."

Shrugging, he continued, "It's never too late to be treated well."

It was her turn to shrug. Years ago, she'd dreamed of marrying and having children, being able to buy a pretty dress and concern herself with the upkeep of a house and cooking for her family. However, feeding useless goats and tilling hard, unyielding ground made a girl grow up fast and stop dreaming. Besides, she wasn't blind to the number of men sniffing around her skirts compared to the ones who came with flowers and candy to the door, asking for her hand.

Zilch was a number easy to count to.

"Maybe for some." Turning, she continued to the barn and filled the small trough before stroking along the old nag's muzzle then headed to the pen to set the remainder of the water down.

"I'm here to offer you the finer side of life, Miss Caroline."

Those words halted her steps. She was almost afraid to ask the question, but she had always been one to face a problem head on. Pivoting toward him, she asked, "How do you propose to do that?"

This time when he reached up, she had nowhere to move with the gate door behind her. Smiling, the winning smile that stole the hearts of all the simpering ninnies in town, he lavished her with his lopsided grin as he stroked her cheek with his thumb.

She was amazed that he would stoop to touch her after she'd been inside the goat pen.

"Be my mistress." The thumb that had been stroking her face lowered and brushed across her bottom lip. "The things this mouth could be taught to do."

The urge to shake her head to clear her mind was strong. She didn't do it, too afraid she would knock something lose because she had to be going out of her mind. Caroline did allow herself to take a step to the side and move out of contact with him.

"As unflattering as your offer is, I'm going to have to decline. I'll stick with the goat and nag."

She turned back to the pen to give herself some space. It amazed her that even though she was outside, she was feeling like she couldn't breathe, couldn't get enough air in her lungs. Angrier at his offer than she was willing to say, she took her frustrations out on the lock, breaking the rusty latch on the wood post. Now that was just one more thing she didn't have the money to fix or replace. She stood, her fist tight around one wood slat of the enclosure.

Mr. Bellmore had been so quiet behind her, she had prayed he'd taken his *fine* offer and gone back to town and his big house, where he lived with his mother. Unfortunately, God must not have been in the prayer answering business at six in the morning.

"Miss Caroline, working a farm is man's business. That's why I'm sure your father never spoke to you about finances and things."

Not giving him the satisfaction of turning around, she crossed the hardpacked dirt ground and went back to the barn. Inside, she grabbed the shovel to start mucking as she glanced over at the shelf in the back where she kept the soap cakes. There were only a few remaining for her to take to the mercantile. Her last batch, she'd had to use the funds to have an older pair of her papa's boots re-soled. They'd both needed it, but she'd gotten his done first. He'd been in the field practically barefoot; she was afraid he'd cut his foot and get an infection and die. Well, at least he'd had a nice pair to be buried in.

"If you're concerned about my arithmetic, you don't have to be. I've been handling the purchase and selling of supplies for as long as I can remember." She led the horse out front of the barn and wrapped her lead around the post there, not that she'd go anywhere. The horse was too old and too tired to do much.

Going back into the barn, Caroline started shoveling the manure the horse had left. There was no hay on the ground and none around to reline the flooring for the horse, either.

"That's all well and good," he called to her from the open door where he stood. "But unless you have the full payment that your father owes me for the loan on the farm, to include the interest for seven months of late payments—rather, no payments—then you may not have much of a choice." He called out the price in a high baritone voice that, with a nice wind, would have carried to the ears of people in town.

Her hands gripped the handle of the shovel, prepared to scoop the first pile, but not moving. Glancing over her shoulder from inside the dim interior, she stared at Mr. Bellmore as he leaned against the frame.

When quoted the amount owed, she was happy she'd been out of the rising heat of the day, because she would have fainted from the combination of an astonishing amount and the sun.

"You can't be serious," she whispered. Her head was swimming, and she was beginning to feel lightheaded. *I should have eaten.*

"Oh, but I am, Caroline." All proper pretenses had gone. "In my saddle bag, I have the original contractual agreement that your father signed, as well as the additional loan documents after the unfortunate accident when you all lost the house in the twister, and the agreement that your father signed with me when the frost stole the harvest three years ago. You will see that all came due three days ago."

Three days ago was the day before her father's death. She

wondered if the stress from believing he would lose everything and his failure at succeeding on the land was what had killed him.

Closing the distance, Bellmore stood beside her in the open stall, careful to stay clear of the horse droppings. "So, my offer still stands. Be my mistress and live your life sleeping on silk and satin. Sashay your sweet derriere along the boardwalks of town with ribbons and bows in your hair." He ran a hand over her hair, tugging at the makeshift ribbon that had come from the hem of her dress.

She swatted his hand away. "At what price? My dignity?"

He chuckled, undiscouraged, and reached again. This time, he stroked the back of her neck below her ponytail and slowly slid his hand down her spine. "Only a few kisses along your beautiful skin that your personal maid will make smell like lilies and roses. A caress here and there. Not to mention the privilege to rest between your delectable thighs." His hand dropped and took the liberty of squeezing one of her butt cheeks.

In an attempt to keep the bile at bay, Caroline sidestepped as her hands went slack and she dropped the handle of the shovel, which flipped the manure onto his high-polished boots.

"Shit! Damn blast it, Caroline!"

If she wasn't so appalled, she would've laughed at the scene he made leaping away from the smelly pile as he snapped out a handkerchief from his pocket. He started swiping at the equine fecal matter as he cursed and shuffled around.

"I think it's time for you to leave, Mr. Bellmore." She stomped out of the barn, hoping he'd follow and get.

"I'm leaving, but you'd best think long and hard about what few options you have left."

"I would show you out, but as you can see, I have a lot of work to do." Standing in the open to make sure she had plenty of space to keep away from him, she set her hands on her hips and watched as he hobbled out then flung the soiled square toward the ground without care. "Please leave all the papers on the porch."

"My pleasure. I have the originals locked away," he bellowed back as he went to his horse. "Twenty-four hours, Caroline. Then I'll be back for my money or you."

Minutes later, she heard Bellmore riding away from the property.

Stepping back into the barn, she stood in the cool interior. She took a deep breath and told herself everything would be all right. When she stooped and reached for the shovel, she noticed the tremors. She was shaking on the outside as much as within.

Her eyes were burning, and her throat was tight to the point of pain. She knew she was going to cry, but she fought her emotions. She didn't have time for tears. What she needed now was action.

Quickly, she finished the stall and led Fredricka back inside. She went to the shelf and grabbed a piece of twine scrap then went to the pen and rigged it to hold the door shut until she could get a lock.

With quick strides, she walked around to the front of the house and collected the neatly folded and tied papers from the last step. Carrying the papers inside with her, she sat at the small table and began to read. She looked for anything that would give her some time to get the money together.

Her mind began calculating until she'd come up with the sum she would bring in if she happened to sell her goat. She wouldn't come close even if she gleaned top dollar. And Driscoll was barely worth bottom dollar.

Why? The word swam around in her head so many times, she began to repeat it aloud until she was screaming. "Why, Papa?" Her question wasn't why he had signed for an additional loan or the extension loan agreements. That she could understand, but it was more important to know why he hadn't said something to her, anything. They shared everything with each other, or so she had believed, until today. She'd never known her father to keep secrets from her.

If she had known they were so deep in debt, she would have fought harder to get him to let her take a job in town or at one of the local farms or ranches. She could have aided the family better, working away from the destitute farm.

"What else didn't you tell me?" Now the tears came, and they came violently. Once again, she had lost every family member, one by one, all over again. She'd never allowed herself to cry when she lost her mother and brother. Her papa had been devastated enough for them both.

The sun had reached its peak of the day by the time she ceased her wallowing. Going to her father's rocker, she lifted the wood slats out of the grooves until the opening was wide enough for her to remove the small box inside.

This wasn't the first time she'd been in the box. Her father's funeral expenses had sent her into the small stash. Now she peeled back the worn handkerchief with its elegant A for Abigail stitched in one corner of the lace trim. It had been her mother's and in her hand, when they'd found Mama and her brother under the crumpled house.

The small amount of funds wasn't even enough for her to buy passage on the stagecoach any further than the next town. It could possibly buy a night at Ms. Livingston's boarding house, but nothing more.

Refusing to give up hope, she put the funds into her small handbag and placed her shawl around her shoulder. Her shawl was something else in need of repair. She'd sewn it so many times, it was now more thread than it was fabric.

Hitching Fredricka to the dilapidated buckboard and tying Driscoll at the back, she headed into town. She was prepared to exhaust all options before considering any offer Daryl Bellmore extended to her.

THREE

Garrett Rand flung his bedroll out beside the fire and crawled on it. He and several men from his farm, as well as two of his neighbors, had been out for days now moving cattle and he was bone tired. Tired of sittin' on a horse. Tired of eatin' beans and hardtack. Most important, he was tired of sleepin' on the ground. This wasn't even his herd he was moving, but Chance Spencer's. Spencer had helped him rustle a herd or two of his cows, so it was just neighborly to return the favor. He was thankful that Chance had a few greenhorns training with them on this trip for next year, when they would be skilled enough to lend a hand unsupervised. The three Kentucky brothers had come in from the west, where they'd flocked for the Gold Rush and continued with odd jobs. Their last job of hauling liquid explosives had ended sadly, with the death of their oldest brother. They'd been making their way back across the continent to Kentucky when they landed in Grover Town and decided to stay.

Garrett groaned as he attempted to settle himself more comfortably and rolled onto a rock he must have missed when he'd cleared his area.

Reaching under the blanket, he grabbed the rock and chucked it off to the side. He was getting too old to be out under the stars. At two and thirty, he wanted something else out of life—the next phase. Sighing, he shook his head.

"What's all that noise you keepin' over there, Rand?" questioned Lyle Joseph, his new foreman who'd agreed to come along. He had a new bride, expecting, at home, so this would be his last cattle run for a while.

"Ain't nuttin' but woman problems that keep a man up at night, tossin' and a turnin'," Jimbo Reece, one of Spencer's men, commented from his place on the outer edge of the fire, standing with his back to them on first watch.

"Or lack thereof," added Jackson, another of Spencer's crew, who was a burly and wide-chested man who whittled from his bedroll on the other side of the fire.

"A man should never have a lack with those beautiful jewels at Miss Kitty's," Phillip commented with zeal.

"That's for sure." Jimbo added a low whistle behind it.

"Y'all ever had that Diamond? Man, she's got tricks ta' make a man see stars." Lincoln, the youngest of the three Kentucky brothers, spoke next. At ten and seven, he was a virgin to the cattle trail but apparently to nothin' else.

"It's the young ones who think they've experienced something because they get a wet kiss on the prick." Carl Timmons barked with laughter.

"It'll be at least a year before he's ready to get what Ruby can show him," Jackson said, pitching a pebble, pegging Dale on the brim of his hat and knocking it off his head.

"Hey, watch your throwin', old man. You could put my eye out," Dale whined.

"Or Sapphire, for that matter." Jimbo let out a low whistle.

"Better your eye than that hangin' tail of yours you just learned to wag," Chris, Dale's oldest brother, hollered.

All the men laughed, continuing to poke fun at Dale and compare notes on Miss Kitty's ladies.

Garrett remained silent and allowed his mind to wander. Miss Kitty ran one of two brothels around Grover Town. The Harlot not only had certified clean women, but she was one of the richest people in town who wasn't a man. Miss Kitty had shown up in their town ten years ago. She had gotten off a stagecoach to stretch her legs and never got back on. At that time, she had two girls with her, Diamond and Ruby. Diamond was an ebony-haired beauty with sparkling eyes and a big smile, but she had the most talented full lips a man could ever have wrapped around his shaft. Ruby was a fair-skinned, redheaded girl, with long, wavy hair that reached beyond her backside and a full, round rear that she used in a nefarious way that gave a man a wet dream.

Most people rumored that Miss Kitty had been a whore in another town and had been run off. But Garrett knew that Miss Kitty was tough as steel; there wasn't any way someone was going to try to bully her without getting shot between the eyes.

He also knew her better than anyone else in town. Garrett had been raised by his parents not to judge people, to look at the heart of a man, not his actions. That was the main reason he didn't blame Sam Douglas for turning down his offer to marry Caroline a few weeks ago. The man loved his daughter. Douglas held on to Caroline tight, like she was his saving grace, his lifeline.

Someone's cackling laugh and a racy comment pulled Garrett's mind away from Douglas' refusal and back to Miss Kitty.

Most people didn't know that Miss Kitty's heart was just as big as her bosom and hips. One day he'd been headed into town, when he spotted Miss Kitty and her wagon with its busted wheel. She'd been on her way to the Jenkins' place with food because she'd heard the wife was ill. The Jenkins had seven small mouths to feed. He'd been on his way to church, late due to a calf being born. Miss Kitty had been going at that time, because she knew all the good Christian folk in town wouldn't be around to see her deed.

He'd given her a ride to the Jenkins' house then fixed her wheel. During those two hours, they'd talked. From that point on, they'd become friends. Even though she was most likely twenty years his senior, he still spent many a night at her place cultivating the relationship. Most thought she gave him special services. They were right; she did, by way of listening.

It had been almost a year since he'd even entertained himself with Diamond, the only jewel he'd spent considerable time with in the past. She was sweet and a little naïve with all her experience, particularly her oral talents. A bolt of heat shot down his spine with the lusty memory.

The men were correct. The voluptuous proprietor of the Harlot and the Hero knew how to pick and train the women who worked in her establishment a mile outside of town. Hell, it was one of the few places a man could bury his head after a hard day at work or long nights on the trail without getting it used for target practice from a shotgun-crazed husband. There were a couple widows in town, like sweet Mrs. Sherry Mallory.

Widow Mallory had been a beautiful woman, whose husband had died from fever. Marcus Mallory, with lucrative business dealings back east, had been an older man with a wife more than eighteen years his junior. She'd grieved for six months then began to allow several men in the county to lavish her with favors for her time. Widow Lawrence was an older, seasoned widow, discreet but still bold in her advances, but he'd not been inclined to take her up on her many hints and offers of a clandestine assignation. Her husband had also been an older businessman with a deep thirst for cards. It had been rumored that he'd owed more than a few people at the time of his passing, but nothing more had come of it, and apparently, he'd still had enough to keep his widow in high style.

Whores and kind widows had been his only vice, cuckoldin' another man wasn't Garrett's thing, so he kept away from other men's wives. A lot of damn things hadn't been his thing in a long time. As he'd told Douglas a few weeks ago, before he left on this trail, he was ready to settle down. But the old man was stubbornly holding on to his daughter, not realizing if he ever died, she'd have no one.

Shifting around, Garrett attempted to find a more comfortable spot. Pulling his hat over his face to block out the twinkling stars, his mind conjured up an image of Caroline Douglas. Too tired to fight his thoughts, he recalled the day he'd realized she'd grown up in all the right places. With the shapeless clothes her father always dressed her in, it was easy to miss all her curves and valleys. But a little over two years ago, he'd been out fishin' in the creek. It was what he liked to do from time to time just to get away for peace and quiet. It was on a Sunday when most folks would have been eatin' supper.

He had nodded off in a glen of trees and realized Mrs. Copernic, his housekeeper, was going to be quite upset that he was late. Of course, his stomach wouldn't mind missing a single one of her filling but unpleasant meals. About to rise, a small splash caught his attention. Still hidden, he peeped through the trees until he located where the noise had come from. Caroline was floating in the water. Finishing up a bath or perhaps out for a swim, he didn't know and didn't care.

Nine and twenty by that time, he was past the age of

spying on innocent females, but he couldn't pull his eyes away.

Dipping below the water, she came up and shook the water from her face. Moving toward the embankment, the upper half of her body was out of the water. Her thin, worn shift left her almost nude to his eyes. The dusky rose tips of her breasts appeared taut and inviting. Her small, pear-shaped bosoms with their large nipples captured his hungry gaze. The deep pink drops caused his mouth to water for a taste. His cock swelled in his pants as he pondered the luxury of licking ever droplet of water from her body. As she continued out of the water, more of her body was revealed to his keen sight.

Her small waist and full hips just laid the foundation to her womanhood. The hair on her head was brownish red, chestnut with a single sun kissed streak along the front. Garrett had wondered if the springy bush hiding the lips of her sex was similar. Even through the translucent material, he couldn't tell, but it didn't stop his shaft from becoming painfully erect. Sweat was rolling down the side of his brow past his ears.

He felt ridiculous eyeing a woman from afar; he was a grown man. A man who could walk into Miss Kitty's with pride and pay for a night with any of her jewels, yet he continued to stare.

At eight and ten, Caroline's form had curves, but she was also thin, too thin. The hard, sparse life she lived with her father was clear in her worn covering. It made him yearn to take care of her. His response shook his core. He'd never considered settling down before. He had an older brother who ran a dairy farm in Wisconsin where most of his father's family still resided. His oldest brother, Ian, was here in Grover, with a son, Clark, who was a clerk at the bank, with dreams and accounting skills to be bank manager one day. Clark had summered as a hand on Garrett's farm when he was in school and was piss poor at it, all thumbs and left feet.

Thank goodness, Steve, two years older than Garrett, had a wife and three boys, who could inherit Garrett's dairy farm if he passed with no heir.

When Caroline picked up the small drying sheet on the grass next to her clothes and began to remove the water from every intimate place he desired to touch, taste, and see, he felt close to losing his mind. The desire to lay her out on the grass and drink every droplet of water from her skin, starting from the back of her knees and working his way up the center of her thighs, overwhelmed him. Once he'd arrived at the center, he'd spend a great amount of time there, tracing her soft, wet skin and slippin' in and out of her until her cream of ecstasy was painting his tongue, only to start all over again.

By the time she quickly dressed, grabbed her rifle and climbed onto her buckboard, he needed relief and knew he was in trouble.

Instead of jumping on the back of his horse and expending his energy in the first willing lady at the Harlot and the Hero, he'd released the flaps and buttons of his pants and taken matters into his own hands.

Right there in the middle of the trees, he'd pumped the length of his hot, steel-like flesh. Closing his eyes, he thought of a stunning woman with chestnut hair and big dusky rose, mouthwatering nipples. When he brought himself to a spine bending climax, he'd expected to feel shame at bringing himself to the activity of a horny youth, but he didn't. He was driven and determine toward a goal. Caroline. Sweet. Kind. Loyal. Determined. Apparently, bolder than he'd realized, Caroline. What man wouldn't want a woman like that by his side? In his bed.

For four years, he'd worked hard to ensure that his farm and house were prepared and ready for a woman to desire to make a home. When he'd finally begun to turn a high profit with his business and he had an efficient and dependable foreman in place, he knew the time was right.

Taking a deep breath, Garrett calmed himself. The last thing he needed was to get himself all worked up and need a walk deep into the night to relieve his pent-up sexual tension. Caroline was the only woman who did that to him.

His mind kept telling him to chart a new course, because Caroline would never be his, which Douglas had made perfectly clear. Maybe it was time for him to take some advice from some of the women in town who hinted around at him marrying Jillian Pettigrew. She was eight and ten, sweet and soft spoken, and full of sunshine. The eldest daughter of James Pettigrew, the owner of the gristmill, he couldn't do much better. A few men had already begun talkin' about how well she'd filled out over the years and how her body was made for breedin'. There was a bettin' going at Manny's about who would ask for her hand first.

There were no bets like that about Caroline. Everyone else discussed her as 'poor Caroline' both from her lack of finances from her pa's failed farming attempts and the fact she was leashed to her pa's side for most of her life. Men said she was kinda pretty and they never made any gestures to describe any ampleness to her figure.

They didn't know what he knew about her, and that was fine by him. He'd be damned if he'd enlighten them.

Someone had written in the books that they bet Caroline would get fed up with her pa and let some sidewinder convince her to run off. That would be that.

Sighing, he firmly decided. He told himself it was time to give up on Caroline. Jillian was pretty, delicate, and sweet, and would make just as fine a wife, he convinced himself. It was settled.

His gut didn't agree.

"SO, what's it going to be, Caroline?" Daryl sat high on his horse gazing down at her. He hadn't even given her the respect of getting off his horse as he had yesterday. Today, he believed the deck was stacked in his favor.

Caroline stepped up onto the porch, so she was at a better eye level. "I need more time, Mr. Bellmore. I just found out about all this yesterday."

"Don't matter." He leaned his forearm on the horn of his saddle. "A few more days won't change the outcome."

Caroline rubbed her forehead; she knew Bellmore was right. She spent most of yesterday inquiring about a loan at the bank, but with no collateral, the bank manager was honest that he couldn't give her anything. Not to mention, he didn't do business with women without their husband's or father's approval, unless they were a widow. The only reason Mr. Johnson, the bank manager, had given her the time of day was because he felt sorry for her losing her father, but her pa had nothin' in the bank for him to even discuss with her. Not a single copper penny.

Mr. Johnson's solution had been to let her farm go and find herself a husband. But with only a few hours before Bellmore came calling with his demeaning offer, the possibility of someone proposing wasn't even slim. She sold her goat and her papa's rifle to MJ Harvey because he'd come across her headed into town. He'd paid her five dollars for Driscoll on the spot. She'd tried to get more, but Harvey, one of the big ranch owners, had been right when he'd said it would take him triple that to fatten the goat up for slaughter or to sell him to a goat farmer for breedin'.

When he'd told her he'd loan her a bullet to shoot the nag pulling her wagon, she'd wanted to show him the business end of her rifle, even if it was empty. Her father had used the last one a few months back on a rattlesnake that had been at the stairs one afternoon. She'd still shot Harvey a hard look.

He'd dragged his eyes over her body, and she saw the same lukewarm, empty look that most men in Grover gave her, casting her thin body and ragged clothing aside in a blink.

"Look, there's always a need for another cook in the bunkhouse for my workers. They'd appreciate a nice smile. Maybe one of them would be taken with you, do you a favor... you know, offer to make somethin' honest of ya."

"I'm already somethin' honest," she bit back as she climbed back onto her wagon after handing him the rope connected to Driscoll. She also knew of Milton Harvey, Jr's. ranch. He was a stingy employer, worked his people long and hard, not to mention he always hired the meanest and most despicable men who came into town—riffraff. Mostly, because anyone with any value to their heart or mind steered clear of signing on with him.

"Yup, for now." He'd chuckled. "Honest only goes so far when there's hunger in your belly and the winter nights get cold. Think about my offer."

She hadn't even offered him a response. Instead, she'd snapped the reins to get Fredricka moving. It hadn't been the fast get away she'd have wanted.

"You know where to find me iffin ya change ya mind," he'd issued as her slow wagon rolled by.

Now, this morning, as the rising sun removed the dew from the grass, she saw her options vanishing just as quickly.

"If I had time, I could plant more. Then maybe by

harvesting time, I could pay you on the loan." She'd already spent the five bucks at the mercantile purchasing tomato seeds, squash, and onions that she was going to get into the ground today.

With a lascivious smile, Bellmore said, "Caroline, is hard work that tears off the skin of your hands truly what you want?"

"It's what I have," she growled. She was getting damn tired of men around her life telling her what was best for her and what she was capable of. She clenched her fists, feeling the sting of chafed and open blisters, hating the gnawing ache of being trapped against a wall. She was cornered by the mounting problems before her.

Dismounting his horse, Bellmore made purposeful strides to her. "See, Caroline, that's where you're wrong." Slapping both his hands on the side of the house, he confined her between him and the structure. Leaning in, he whispered in her ear, "You have so much more to give than what you can provide with your hands."

"I could find employment in town." She tried hard not to cower. "Mr. Harvey offered a job just yesterday."

"Harvey." He made a sound through his teeth as a glint of shadow appeared in his gaze. Placing his hands on her hips, he aligned her body to his. "Be my mistress and I'll erase all your father's debt." He ground his hips into hers and licked the side of her neck.

"Stop, Bellmore." Clutching at his shoulders, she tried to push him away. Even with all the heavy labor she'd done most of her life, she was still no competition for him. She wished she hadn't sold her father's rifle and it was still hanging from the hooks above the fireplace.

He continued his ardent advances. Circling her waist, he grabbed her backside and pressed her against him. "Hm. As

I'd figured. There's more here than most know. The things I could do with this plump ass."

"Daryl...stop...please. *Don't* do this." Struggling anew, Caroline began to beat against his back and arms, striking at anything.

Pulling at her dress, he started to inch it up her legs. "Don't fight me, Caroline. I can make this good for you."

When he reached below her skirts and began to grope at her thighs, a red haze covered her eyes, and she began to fight with all her might. All the words of her father, telling her since she was fifteen to make sure she took the gun with her because men couldn't be trusted around a woman alone, came back to her. Biting, kicking, pulling, and scratching, she fought for the only thing that she had. What she could call her own. Her virtue. Raking down the side of his neck, she finally got his attention.

"Aww!" Bellmore stepped back from her and touched his neck. When he pulled his hand away, he noticed the blood on the tips.

Caroline stared at the two identical scrapes oozing out blood on the side of his neck, staining the stiff white collar of his shirt. For a moment, she was thankful for the jagged nails field work gave her.

Pulling out his pristine white handkerchief from his coat pocket, he blotted the wound. "Well, Caroline, you have made your point clear," he gritted out. The dark look in his eyes revealed his anger.

She had no doubt if she were a man, he'd have given her a taste of his fist. A small part of her was grateful that there had never been rumors out about Bellmore beatin' on women.

Breathing heavily, Caroline allowed a small ounce of relief to invade her form and mind. She had done it. She'd convinced Bellmore that she had no desire to be his mistress.

Now, if she could just get him to see reason on the land. "I didn't mean to hurt you, Mr. Bell—"

Shaking his head, he corrected her, "Daryl, for the last time! I think we've passed the point of formalities."

"All right, Daryl." She straightened her shoulders. She figured that if he was going to allow her the time to pay the debt off, then the least she could do is concede on this one point. "I'll get you your money, I promise. I'll work the farm or however many jobs I need to."

"You're correct on one thing. You *will* work off the debt." He smiled at her, but this time the smile wasn't flirtatious as all the other ones. No, this one appeared sly and conniving.

Her heart fluttered with apprehension at his expression. "I promise. My family always works hard to cover their debts."

"No need to promise; you have no other choice in this matter. I've consulted Sheriff Silverman. The law is on my side, the contract is legal and binding, and you'll see this debt fulfilled."

The law? "Daryl, there was no need to contact the sheriff—"

"You need to take whatever mementos you want from the house in the next five minutes before we leave."

"Leave? But you said I could work off the debt. I thought I didn't have to be your mistress."

"Have no fear, hellcat. I like my whores feisty and my mistress docile. You're not cut out to be a mistress."

She almost sighed with relief, but suspicion held her back. "Where are you taking me?" She wondered if she would be forced to be a maid in his mama's house. The thought made her shiver, chills racing down her arms, but anything was better than being at his intimate beck and call.

"Three minutes remaining."

Realizing she wasn't getting any answers now and her

time was running out, Caroline turned and ran into the house. She looked around but knew there was nothing there. She moved the floorboard and took out the box and removed her mother's lacy handkerchief. In a small burlap sack, she tossed in her nightgown and her Sunday dress. It was almost as worn as the clothes she had on, but it was the best she had.

When she returned to the porch, Daryl took her bag from her and tied it down on the side of his saddle, then he mounted. Reaching his hand down, he waited for her to grab his forearm. She had prepared herself to be swung behind him. She was shocked to find herself sandwiched between him and the pommel, the thick knob already digging into the outside of her thigh.

"I'm perfectly capable of keeping myself on the back of the horse."

"No need."

Pursing her lips at his words, she took a deep breath. It was a big possibility she'd be waiting on him hand and foot and cleaning his linens, so there wasn't much place for her to put up a fuss. "Now can you tell me where we're headed?" she inquired.

"You shall see shortly."

He kicked his horse in the side. It launched forward as Caroline stared at her family home for the last time. The red roses in the front, the last bit of life left, caused a pain in her heart as she shifted her gaze to what lay before her.

The ride was hard and fast, and Caroline knew that she would have bruises in the morning if they hadn't already appeared by the time they stopped. There was a moment of embarrassment when they galloped toward the main road in town, but she sighed with relief when, at the last moment, Bellmore skirted around town and took the back path.

When they left the main section of town, she became

even more curious, wondering where they were headed. His home was located west of town and they were travelin' east. There wasn't anything out this way depending on which way he rode, except maybe a few homes or a ranch or two and the creek. It was possible he'd decided to arrange for her to be a maid at one of the ranch houses. That would be a relief, and she wouldn't constantly have him in her sights, leering at her. If that was the case, then she would clean with pride for however many years she had to endure.

Everything seemed quiet as they followed a path through a patch of trees, then a large two-story house came into view well over a mile from the outskirts of town. At first sight, she wasn't sure whose house it was, with the black lace curtains and the multiple hitching posts out front and shutters painted as red as a harvest apple. Then she recalled one time when she and her father had stayed out at the stream fishing too long and it had gotten dark. They'd taken a short cut back to town and when they passed the house, loud music from a piano was blaring, women were laughing, and the deep sound of gentlemen's voices could be heard. Her father had told her to close her eyes. She'd obeyed for the most part, until curiosity had gotten the best of her and she'd peeped at the point they were passing the downstairs window. She'd seen women scantily dressed and men groping them in ungentlemanly ways. She'd known instantly that it was one of the whorehouses that women in town whispered about.

The name of the establishment was hung below the row of second floor windows, Harlot and the Hero. The name of the place was obscure and held no meaning to her then at ten and two.

When Daryl slowed before the house, she swallowed. "What are we doing here?"

Stopping his horse before one of the posts, he slid to the

ground and secured the animal. "*Here* will be your home until you've paid off your debt."

With her last ounce of hope fading quickly, she asked, "What will I do, cook...clean...do the laundry?"

Taking her by the waist, he yanked her down. When her feet were on the ground, he spoke softly to her. "Sorry, there's no opening for any of those positions. You, my beauty, will be one of Miss Kitty's Jewels."

Everything around her went black.

FOUR

Caroline felt disoriented. Her head was swimming with multiple thoughts, and she was having a hard time pulling herself together. She could feel a soft but firm cushion against her back and knew she was lying down and assumed she was in her bed at the farm. Taking a deep breath, she slowly opened her eyes, expecting to see the blue and white flowered print paper that graced her walls of their small home. It had been a splurge for her father when she was nine, but it had been her Christmas present. They could do little things like that every now and then before the crops started going bad.

However, it wasn't small bouquets of blue stenciled flowers held together with tiny ribbons that covered the walls but crushed red velvet. Red as ripe pomegranate juice.

Who'd decorate their walls such a color? she questioned as she sat up and looked around the room. If the wall covering didn't shock her, then the black lace curtains were really too much for her to take in. Other than windows and walls, the room appeared to be a combination lady's sitting room and a man's office, with its large desk and bookcases around the room.

In the half of the room where she sat, there was a nook with a small table and two chairs, perfect for women to have hot drinks and cakes. Caroline eyed the furniture she sat on, a long beige and gold chaise lounge. In the corner of it, where her head had lain, was a square gold satin pillow with thin black ribbon streaming from each corner. What stole her breath were the paintings on the wall, of men and women in various naughty embraces, and her cheeks blazed at the sight.

"What could you possibly have been thinking in bringing her here, Daryl?"

Caroline turned toward the voice behind the door. She didn't recognize the woman speaking, but it didn't matter, because the fog in her mind was starting to lift.

"There is only one reason I'd bring a woman to you." The suave sophistication of the male voice was like a strong wind clearing her thoughts.

She recalled everything about the past week and her father's death, but it was the memory of the last twenty-four hours that made her ill. Rising from the chair, she walked to one of two doors in the room and followed the sounds from the only one that stood ajar, as the two people discussed her fate on the other side.

"Daryl, this isn't right. That girl doesn't need to be here," the woman declared in a husky tone.

"Kitty, it was her choice," Bellmore began in his arrogant diction. "I offered her another position; however, she declined it."

Miss Kitty's voice took on a note of aggravation, "Take her back to town and find her a husband. I'm sure—"

"No," Daryl barked. "Her father has a debt that needs to be paid. What man do you know in town that would be willing to pay a substantial debt for a new bride? Times are hard enough for the good folks around here."

The scoffing sound came through the door, and Caroline imagined it came from Miss Kitty. The Bellmores didn't know a thing about the hard times of the good folks of Grover Town.

"You could let it go," offered Miss Kitty.

Daryl's chuckle came out rough.

Caroline pressed closer to the door, not wanting to miss any part of the conversation.

"Look, I'll be back in a few days to claim what's mine from her." Daryl's polished brogans clicked against the hardwood floor.

"She won't be ready," Kitty called out.

"Why not? The only thing she will require is new clothes."

"No, Daryl. That may be all that you may need. However, I'm running a business here. Unless you plan to pay me for her room and board with each nightly visit."

His voice moved closer as if he'd crossed the room back toward Miss Kitty. "Let's get one thing straight. As part owner of this here establishment, I'll not be paying for what is already mine."

"Not the controlling owner and not for much longer." There was a pregnant pause and Caroline could practically feel the tension through the door, before the woman continued. "Like I said, Daryl, I run a profitable business here. Emphasis on profitable. No charity cases. So, when you're not in use of her favors, I'll have to collect her pay through other gentlemen. You want your debt paid, don't you? For that, I'll need time. As fresh faced as she is, I'll need weeks. You may not believe this, but there's more to being a whore than a sleazy dress and knowing how wide to spread your thighs."

"Do what you must. Just don't take too long," he growled.

"One month, and I'll have her skilled better than you could imagine."

"If that makes you happy. What I'm after doesn't call for

decoration." Daryl's words were punctuated by the slamming of a door.

"Men." Caroline heard a heavy sigh follow that single word. Lighter footsteps echoed across the floor, becoming softer in the distance.

She let out a sigh of her own. Hoping the coast was clear, Caroline clutched the latch, and twisting the wood handle, she pulled the door open slowly. Peeping through the crack as it widened, the way appeared free. She didn't know how much time she had before Miss Kitty or someone else came back, but she knew she had to get out of this place. Slipping out of the room, she took a quick look around. Not taking the time to assess the décor, she located the front door. It was across the gleaming wood floor of the massive room.

Wasting little time, she began to tip-toe toward her escape. Too afraid to breathe until she could leave the house and feel the fresh air on her face, she kept her stride steady and her eyes focused.

"How far do you think you'll get before Daryl finds you and brings you back?"

A squeal of panic resounded from deep within her and filled the room. Whipping around to locate the person who'd caught her, Caroline lifted her eyes to the upper banister where a dark-skinned woman in a long cotton gown that seemed out of place in this establishment leaned against the railing staring at her. By the woman's leisure position, Caroline had no doubt the woman had been watching her the whole time.

"Some places are better than lying out in a dirty field and having a herd of cowboys running over you."

Caroline didn't know how to respond to such a claim.

"The mouse is already terrified, Marlena, without you antagonizing her."

Miss Kitty's voice drew her gaze back down to a large chair in the corner of the room that was directly across from the front door, against the wall some distance away. The older, full-figured white woman, with beautiful brown hair enhanced by silver highlights, sat relaxed in the seat. Caroline realized the woman had the perfect vantage point to watch her every move.

Rising, Miss Kitty moved toward her. "A woman who has the guts to attempt an escape even when the odds are against her is my kind of woman."

"The kind you can let go?" Caroline faced the woman who held her fate in her hands. Miss Kitty's heeled boots placed them both on an even eye level. She had grey eyes as mysterious as a summer storm. The woman had secrets brewing behind them.

"Sadly, no, Caroline."

"Every woman has her lot in life. This is ours." The brown-skinned woman named Marlena called down.

Caroline slowly shook her head. She didn't want to believe that. She was a good girl. Her papa was probably even now spinning in his grave.

"Marlena, you need your rest for tonight." Moving back toward the way Caroline had just come, Miss Kitty said, "Caroline, we have a lot to discuss. Follow me, please."

With confidence, the madam never looked back over her shoulder to see if her words were being heeded but continued on her way. Caroline glanced up and noticed the woman upstairs had left. Even more amazingly, she found herself trailing after the madam.

"Close the door, Caroline, and take a seat." Miss Kitty sat on the edge of her desk, once again in a calm pose. The older woman wore a white shirt with a high lace collar, paired with a dark blue skirt. With her hair pulled back away from her face, someone could mistake her for a schoolmarm, shop owner or a bookkeeper. It shocked Caroline how the woman appeared respectable even in such a vulgar setting.

Caroline wondered what it would take to shatter this woman's composed demeanor.

This time, Caroline chose to sit in one of the chairs before the desk, instead of the chaise.

Taking a moment to scratch some notes onto a record book beside her, Miss Kitty pierced her with her sharp gaze, assessing. "Daryl tells me that you owe him a lot of money."

"Supposedly, my father was indebted to Mr. Bellmore." Caroline still had a hard time conceiving how her father could allow himself to sink in so deep and not just let the property go. They could have moved away.

The madam nodded. "Daryl Bellmore may be a lot of things. However, when it comes to money, he doesn't play around. He got that from his mother. As absent-minded as she may seem, she's a shrewd woman. Never underestimate her." Shadows filled Miss Kitty eyes as she glanced away briefly before the storm took over, but outwardly, she remained calm.

Caroline kept silent. She'd only met Bellmore's mother a few times, and the widow had turned her nose up at her as if just a glance at Caroline would dirty her in some way. And Bellmore was a man who sold women into whoredom. She couldn't fathom this man having any admirable attributes. "I have every intention of paying what is owed to him. I just asked Mr. Bellmore for time. I'm more than capable of working our land."

"I'm sure you have the heart to give it a try." Miss Kitty looked back at the log then at her once again. "But single-handedly, no one could pay off that balance Daryl had me place on your books. Perhaps not even with an army of people, in a few months. That's probably what happened with your father, like most poor folks who get caught up in bad loans that lean solely in the favor of the lienholder."

"It can't be legal," Caroline declared. "Someone should put a stop it. I should have taken the contract to the town lawyer—"

Prepared to deny the fact she would not be able to get herself out of the financial situation, Caroline found her objection halted by Miss Kitty raising a single hand.

"Caroline, your father did you a disservice by not ensuring you were married off a long time ago. In that case, the debt would have died with your father and Daryl would have taken the land and leased it to someone else. If your father and most men did what was right, women would not find themselves in situations such as these."

Unable to argue with the madam's words, Caroline sat quiet for a moment, worrying her bottom lip with her teeth. "Things aren't the same for you. You own this place." Or at least most of it, as Caroline recalled hearing.

"Yes, I do, however, I did not start out that way."

"Did you choose to be a whore?" Caroline asked. She wondered about this sharp, confident woman in this small town running a whorehouse.

"No woman chooses to be a whore; they do it out of necessity. Necessity of different reasons." The madam was silent for a long moment.

Caroline found it hard to fathom any reason. Even now, her mind was trying to come up with various possibilities to get herself out of this web of iniquity.

Miss Kitty circled the desk and began talking again. "My father arranged a marriage for me when I was sixteen. The man was the oldest son of a plantation owner in Georgia. I was from Alabama. I lived my life by every rule that was expected of me. I was a good wife, who bore two sons for my husband. When I was six and twenty, my husband died, and since my boys were minors, everything fell to a male relative. I had no claim to anything, not even my body, I soon learned." From her seat, Miss Kitty stared off in the distance then continued, "Edward, my husband's cousin, took up residence at the manor and shortly after in my bed, telling me it was his due. I could have lived with that. After all, this was going to be the man to now provide for me and my sons and he'd offered marriage once my year of mourning was up. A week before the wedding, I became rudely aware of what marriage to him would entail. One night, he brought me downstairs hours after a party was over."

The pointed look Miss Kitty gave Caroline caused a nervous shiver to race across her skin wondering at what was to come.

"He put me on a table and held me down as, first, his out-of-town corrupt business associates had their way with me, then he let his overseer and employees he'd hired on toss a coin in a cup then have their turn with me. I remembered him looking down in my eyes and seeing the tears run over my face as he said, 'Why you cryin', gal? It ain't like you're a fresh bride'. I knew I was nothing to him. After it was over, I scrubbed my skin until I was numb. The next day, I pretended to go shopping in town with my sons. I caught the train to my parents' home. When I got there, I cried in my mother's arms and told them what happened, in as little detail as possible to spare them. My father looked at me and told me that Edward was kind enough to give me his name and I needed to be grateful. He said I could stay the night, but in the morning, he was taking me back."

Miss Kitty shook her head. "I waited until the household was asleep and I ran again, this time for my life. I left my boys in their care. They were too young for Edward to want to have anything to do with. I was penniless and hungry and soon ran out of any money I'd gotten in selling the jewelry I had on me. It didn't take me but a few towns to understand how a woman could make a living. The difference was I was in control and with that control I had power. That's what I offer my ladies here at the Harlot and the Hero."

"I don't mean to be rude, Miss Kitty, but what power does a whore have?" Caroline could hear the sarcasm in her own voice but didn't temper it. This madam was trying to make it seem like women servicing men on their back was some independent way to live.

"Oh, Caroline, you have much to learn. Except for Daryl, to whom you owe a substantial amount of money, you will be able to say who and when. Here, my girls aren't forced to lead any man to their room they don't want. Smitty and Woody are here at night and they ensure no man attempts to take what hasn't been offered."

Swallowing down the lump of disgust lodged in her throat, Caroline said, "I don't think I can do this."

"Just think about the fact that with each man, your debt will be reduced."

Caught in the motion of shaking her head and denying the madam's words, Miss Kitty's harsh, no-nonsense look stopped her.

Eying her, Miss Kitty declared, "You have no choice, Caroline. I'd steer you to marriage, but there are only a few men in this town who could marry you and pay such a debt off and you're a few years too late on most of them; they've been snatched up. The only other choice you have is take debtors' prison when the judge comes into town. As a living relative who's not a minor, you now owe, unless you know of someone who can pay the money for you." She folded her hands in her lap and waited.

This time her head shake was complete. "No."

"I didn't think so," Miss Kitty sighed as if the world sat on her shoulders. The older woman assessed her from crown to toes. Her grey gaze stayed neutral as she took in the frayed dress and worn boots. "We have a lot of work before us." Abruptly standing, she went to the corner and pulled a cord.

Two minutes later, someone knocked on the office door. An older Indian woman, short and stout with a thick long black braid over her shoulder, entered with kind eyes she set on Caroline before looking over at Miss Kitty.

"Miss Debra, this is Caroline. Our *Pearl*."

The older woman offered her a genuine smile before she greeted her.

Caroline had a hard time holding the woman's gaze, wondering what she thought about her. However, she forced a greeting out of her dry mouth.

"Please, prepare a bath for Pearl in the room at the end of the left hallway; she will be residing with us."

"Right away, Miss Kitty." The woman turned to leave as fast as she had entered.

"One more thing, Miss Debra, discard the clothes. All of them. And have Mrs. Morrison prepare her a tray to tide her over until dinner; we need to get some meat on her."

Pearl. Caroline marveled at how quickly her life was shifting. In a matter of days, she had lost her father, her home, her clothing, and her name. Her stomach tightened, then rolled. Caroline knew at any moment, she'd find herself heaving over a chamber pot whatever was left of her meager meal last night.

"LET me get two bags of flour, a sack of dry beans, a shovel and five yards of twine, to go along with those four canisters I ordered, Henry." Garrett stood at the front counter giving his order to Henry Russell, the mercantile owner.

Looking up from his logbook where he wrote down all the items, Henry lifted his head and peered at him over top of his glasses. "Anything else, Garrett?"

Taking a moment to scan his list and make sure he'd picked up everything he needed and what Mrs. Copernic had requested, he glanced around the store overloaded with barrels and shelves filled with odds and ends of things. He thought about his true purpose for coming into town. He could have sent one of the hands to pick the items, but he was on a personal mission.

"Henry, you can toss in a bushel of apples, and how about ten peppermint sticks?"

"Mrs. Copernic making you a pie? I sure would appreciate a slice of that. It's been ages. Not since Serenity Morgan up and married that preacher and moved to New Mexico and took her peach pie makin' with her."

Garrett chuckled, agreeing. "Truth be told, Serenity's pie makin' always made me wonder if I'd let that one get away."

"Most men in town are probably feelin' the same way." Henry nodded.

"That's true." Garrett didn't correct Henry. Apple pie was one of his favorite desserts, but he had no intention of taking the fruit home. He didn't truly have feelings for either of the Morgan daughters, but he would have taken them for pie makin' over his housekeeper's poor baking skills.

Henry quoted the total to him, and Garrett pulled the bills out of his pocket, passing them to the older gentlemen. Walking around the store, he collected the items and made a few trips to his wagon and loaded the flatbed.

"Good day, Mr. Rand," a soft voice called to him from behind.

Garrett glanced over his shoulder as he settled the last bag of flour. "Miss Pettigrew." He bowed his head toward her as he straightened and brushed his hands against his thighs. The beautiful, cinnamon-curly-haired girl with the gentle smile, tiny frame and eye-catching bosom stood in front of Mable's Dress Shop.

"How does the day find you?" He took the few steps that would bring him closer to her. All the time, he was completely aware of some of the townsfolks turning to stare in their direction.

"Well, thank you for asking." She lowered her eyes to her dainty hands.

This was the woman he'd decided to start courting a couple weeks ago, but he'd yet to make a move in that direction. Hell, he hadn't been to town since his return to collect Spencer's cattle. He hadn't even spoken to her father about seeing her yet. Taking a moment, he observed her round face, fine crafted curls under her bonnet and her clothes that were well-tended. Any man in town would have picked her over Caroline Douglas. Why did he hesitate? "What brings you into town today?"

"My mother and I are picking up material for a dress for the town anniversary celebration in less than three months."

"Oh, yes, Founder's Day events. I do believe that's one of my favorite days of the year," he commented. This was his perfect opening to ask her if she would consider accompanying him to the kickoff dance. But, once again, he balked.

"Jillian!" Mrs. Pettigrew called from the door of the dress shop. "We need to make our selection before all the good fabric choices are gone."

Pushing his hat back up his forehead, he waved at Jillian's

mother, who gave him a broad expectant smile and a dainty fingers wave. Yeah, Mrs. Pettigrew was with every other older woman in town who thought he would be the perfect match for the delicate Jillian. Removing the handkerchief from his back pocket, he wiped the sweat from the nape of his neck and refocused on the young woman before him.

"I should be going. Mother is on a mission this afternoon."

He held her gaze for a moment, briefly considering what his life would be with such a sweet biddable wife at his side. *Simple. Easy.* "Enjoy your shopping, Miss Pettigrew."

"Thank you. Have a good day, Mr. Rand." Turning, she headed back to the shop.

Sighing, Garrett went to his wagon and climbed on. Pulling his hat further down to shield his eyes from the glare of the sun, he made his way out of town. He didn't understand why he hadn't initiated a relationship with Jillian or shown her he was interested, and he was tired of pondering it. If he were honest with himself and admitted the truth, it had a lot to do with the fact that he'd discovered Samuel Douglas was dead upon his return. He was glad he hadn't trapped himself in a relationship, now that his way was clear toward Caroline.

When he arrived at the side road that led away from his farm and headed in the northern direction from town, he picked up his speed a little. The excitement in his veins was causing his heart to pump at a faster rate. He'd put off this ride for a week since his return, trying to be respectable. There was a small amount of guilt clouding his joy at the fact Sam never accepted his offer. Now he was attempting to pursue his agenda after the man's death. He could only hope that Caroline would be susceptible to his request. Maybe her father knew she didn't desire to marry. Or even worse, didn't want to marry him.

FIVE

After taking the narrow path miles from town, just after the main fork in the road, he arrived at the Douglas property. Things were always quiet out there, so far from town, but at this moment he recognized there was a different type of stillness. When he rounded the bend that led to the road to their house, the absence of movement was the first thing that struck him. Caroline wasn't out in the small field working the land.

Maybe she was in the house, he thought. He steered his ride toward the barn before pulling back on the reins as he brought his two horses to a stop. He gripped the lever on the floorboard and engaged the brake on the wagon. The Douglas buckboard, if one could call the weathered and rusted frame such, was parked at the side of the barn. The barn doors were wide open, one door hanging by one hinge. It was dark inside, but he couldn't even hear anything from inside, no neighing of their old horse. Had the horse finally turned up her hooves?

Garrett looked left then right, from the empty field to the bare pen where their single goat had always been corralled. He hopped down out of his wagon, leaving the bushel of apples he'd bought for her birthday in the bed of the wagon for a moment as he made his way toward the eerie silence of the house. With no horse, he doubted she could have gone anywhere, being so far away from most things in town.

It was common knowledge that Sam and his daughter were squeezing every coin to stay above water. Maybe Caroline had sold the livestock to pay for her father's burial or to take care of other debts. That thought strengthened his reason for being there in the first place.

Strutting the remaining steps to the front of the house, he saw the small, drab house, the only brightness, odd even in its appearance, was the red rose bush along the side of the porch rail. The seeds packet had been a gift for her birthday last year. He'd seen her in town and had managed to slip them onto her wagon seat. With her papa's pride, he'd figured the small gift he wouldn't deny her, and since there was no way she could return them, not knowing where they'd come from, she'd keep them. He would have loved to invite her out to dinner at the Drummonds', maybe a walk through the meadows, but he recognized the limitations over the years of what he could do for her or with her. Nothing. Over the last year, he'd hoped that the flowers had added a little joy to her day. One thing he did know was that she'd taken that small gift and turned it into a sort of business—soap.

Now, he climbed the creaking steps, badly in need of repair. He knew that even if Caroline turned his offer down, he would still bring some of his men out here and make some needed repairs. Or better yet, maybe he could convince her to move into town. It wasn't safe for a woman to live this far out alone.

He wondered for a moment if perhaps Caroline was still laid up grieving or if she was laid low with illness. The latter thought set some speed to his steps across the porch, not liking the idea of her alone and sick in there.

Rapping on the door, he waited for Caroline to answer. Moments passed with no Caroline. He knocked again then leaned toward the door and attempted to listen for sounds on the other side. Nothing. No answer, no noise from inside. He'd just come from town and she hadn't been there. Something was off; he felt it deep in his gut.

Anxiety began to tighten the muscles in his shoulder and burned up to the back of his neck. Something was wrong with the situation. He just couldn't put his finger on it. Turning the knob, he entered the house, just to assure himself that she wasn't hurt inside.

With a broad, sweeping glance, he took in the main room that consisted of a wide front room. Before the cold hearth, was a rocking chair and a small three-legged stool. In the corner farthest from the door, was a cot with a bedroll laid out on it, a crate, trunk, at the foot of it, open, with worn clothing inside. A few steps from that, was a table with two ladderback chairs. The place was small, and most of the furniture appeared faded and fragile. He knew the Douglases weren't rich, but he didn't realize how bad they were doing. Sam had always been a prideful and private person.

Shaking his head, Garrett moved farther into the house. God bless the man's soul, but he just wished the older man had allowed people to help.

"Caroline!" He moved to the closed door of the single back room. He tapped but barely paused before he opened the door.

The sunlight poured into the room from the window that faced the back of the house. Just as empty as the rest of it, he took a moment to look around, taking in the simple, delicate decoration of what he assumed was Caroline's room, with the blue and white flower pattern. He shifted his gaze toward the bed, and he wondered how she looked lying on the narrow frame. His thoughts tried to conjure what she wore to sleep in. If she were his wife, she'd sleep bare, in nothing at all. So, through the night he could run his hands along her body and feel the curves of her form tucked up against him. Shaking his head, he cleared his mind and considered the more pressing issue.

Where was Caroline?

Moving back out to his wagon, he stared at the items in the back he'd bought for her, the apples and peppermint sticks tucked among the things for the ranch. He decided not to leave them. Instead, he preferred to see her face when he gave her the items. Especially the peppermint sticks, as he'd discovered since he'd run into her in town a few years ago that they were her favorite treat. He'd had the good fortune of seeing her at the mercantile picking up a few items for her farm. She'd finished paying for her meager items and when Mrs. Russell asked if there would be anything else, she'd glanced at the glass candy jars then back at her hand. After a long moment and a few more glances, she'd handed the last two cents in her hand to the store owner and asked for one mint flavored stick.

When the shop owner handed it to her, Caroline's eyes had brightened with pleasure as she turned and exited the shop. His heart had stopped seeing the light in her gaze, and he'd wanted to do a hundred things that brought that same glow to them.

Moments later, he'd seen it bobbing out of the corner of her mouth like straw as she guided the rickety buckboard out of town.

Now, deciding to get his own things home, he settled on a plan to come out later in the day to see if she'd returned.

CAROLINE COULDN'T COME to grips with the knowledge that she was going to become a whore. One thing she did admit was that it was nice—extremely nice—to take a bath. She washed up daily, but the metal tub had rusted through over a year ago and there hadn't been enough money to buy a new one, a copper one. So, she kept the secret desire to herself and washed up discretely at the back pump daily. In the spring and summertime, she would travel to the lake for a dip and swim right before dusk, when most were home and there was less chance of anyone spying her. Now, she relaxed against the back of the tub and glanced around the room.

The room had a vanity and chair, and the table was filled with an assortment of artfully crafted creams, sprays, and face painting supplies. She assumed these were valuable items for whores. However, she knew nothing about perfumes or decorating her face. The scented rose soaps she made were the only thing she knew anything of to make her feel remotely like a woman.

Although she had to admit, she knew nothing about women taking baths with flower petals floating in the water or oils in the same bath that smelled of a jasmine heaven, a scent she'd never smelled before. She was sure it wouldn't be long before she learned other things, if Miss Kitty had anything to say about it.

There were also beautiful rugs on the floor. One by the tub, for her to stand on when she got out. It was so thick, she swore she sank ankle deep. It was more plush than the bed she'd slept on for so many years. More rugs decorated the floor in the room, one on each side of the bed and another in front of the mirror. The walls were covered with pictures of men and women in embraces she was too shy to stare at too long. Something else in the room she kept her eyes veered away from was the bed that took up most of the room. She didn't want to even conceive of the things that went on in the bed in the past, and pondering its use for the future was definitely a no-no. It amazed her how Miss Kitty or Miss Debra had managed to find everything in an ivory and so much satin and lace.

She finished washing her body and hair. Her body felt so clean, she was surprised she didn't squeak. Unsure of how much time she would be given before someone came looking for her, or even worse, some man was sent up for his pleasure, Caroline got out of the water. Standing on the rug with the drying sheet tightly around her body, she thought about what she was going to wear. When she was in the bath, Miss Debra had breezed into the room and taken all her clothes as the madam had ordered, while leaving her a tray of tea, bread, and jam. She begged to keep her boots, not willing to part with everything from her life.

Now that she was clean, her stomach growled and reminded her of the lack of sustenance. She moved the food items to the vanity and sat before the mirror. Her face was flushed from the steam of the water and gave her a healthy countenance like she hadn't had for...for never. To her, her eyes were big and the oddest shade of brown. To her, they seemed unremarkable. However, nothing was so shocking to her of her own appearance as her mouth, too full on top, almost appearing as if the upper was overtaking the lower. The odd shade of brown of her hair left little that would draw attention from a man.

It's no wonder no offer of marriage ever came my way. If it had, she would not have been in such a position.

She spread on the orange marmalade and noticed the bits and slivers of peel within. Attempting to be prudent at first, she only smeared on a thin layer. After the first bite and the buds on her tongue practically dancing with the extraordinary flavor of the sweetness and soft bread, it reminded her of her mother's cooking, before the untimeliness of her death. Her throat became thick and tight, making it hard to choke down the delectable bite. The trembling of her hands made it almost impossible for her to hold the slice. She set it down and made a concerted effort to blink away the tears burning at the back of her eyes.

Her chest became filled with both shame and sadness. Using the edge of the sheet to dab the outside corners of her eyes, she sniffed back that grey cloud of grief.

Holding the sheet tightly against her frame, she moved to the wardrobe and prayed she'd find something respectable, presentable even. Flipping through the outfits, or costumes, she wasn't sure which word was a better fit for what was inside the wooden cabinet. Things were either extremely low cut on the bodice or hemmed high at the skirt. Some of them were thin, sheer, or barely made of any material. She did marvel at the feel of the clothing. Her occasion to be in Mrs. Mable's shop had been rare, and with Isabel when her friend's mama had dragged her there, and she could have only wondered from afar of the textures of lace, satin, silk, or crushed velvet.

"I'm glad to see that you're finished with your bath. See you didn't eat much."

Spinning around, Caroline was barely able to contain the squeal that burst from her mouth at the appearance of Miss Kitty. "Um, Miss Debra took my things. I was looking for something to wear."

"It is quite all right; the clothin' is yours. Tomorrow, I'll see if Mable can spare some time for one of her daughters to come by for measurements and alterations. Right now, you're a little thinner than most of the girls who work evening houses. But, we'll get some meat on your bones. Mrs. Morrison is a great cook, as you will soon find out." Entering the room, dressed in a beautiful brown and black lace dress, the older woman was lovely with her hair pulled back in a fashionable twist. The madam looked as if she were headed to a party in town, if it were not for the fact her bosom appeared moments away from falling out of her bodice.

"Then if you will excuse me for a moment, I will find something to wear."

"You have time for that. Come here, Pearl."

There was that name again. "I prefer to be called Caroline." Holding the sheet against her breasts and in front of her legs where it kept parting, she moved around the bed to the madam.

"Well, Caroline is an innocent girl who lives on the other side of town, subject to the will and whim of her pa. Pearl works at the Harlot and the Hero and is a skilled whore."

Caroline flinched at the word whore that was used toward her. "I'm neither of those women." She pushed the words through her tight throat. For the first time since her father had left, she *actually* wanted to give in to crying. In a blink of an eye, she'd gone from girl to whore.

Miss Kitty reached out and squeezed her arm. "It will be all right. If you want to cry, this is as good a time as any."

Her vision became blurry, but Caroline blinked rapidly. She was too afraid to give in to tears now. If she did, there was no telling when she would be able to stop them. "I'm afraid, Miss Kitty, I know nothing about being a who—"

Her voice broke and she swallowed.

"Whore, harlot, strumpet, light-skirt, or lady of the evening, they all mean the same. The sooner you learn to say the word, the better off you will be." The older woman's hand lowered. "Well, you're not the first new lady I've had to train, neither will you be my last. The girls and I will get you ready before your first night. We have a month until then. So, stop looking as if any minute I'll parade a line of eager men in here." Miss Kitty gave her a kind smile.

Caroline couldn't help returning the smile, a hesitant one.

"Have you ever been with a man before?"

Shocked, Caroline said, "Absolutely, not."

Shrugging, Miss Kitty looked around the room in deep thought. "It's not unheard of." She exhaled. "Well, I will tell you, you're my first virgin harlot. That means I'm going to have to start from scratch with you."

"Oh."

"Let's begin with you moving to the mirror." Miss Kitty took hold of her shoulders and propelled her across the room.

Starting at her own reflection in the cheval mirror, Caroline shifted her gaze back and forth between her own plain looks to the madam's ornate appearance. There was no comparison. The color of their skin was the least of the differences. Miss Kitty's coloring was creamy and pale, while Caroline's own was tanned from working long hours in the sun. Caroline found herself seriously lacking in many ways.

"Drop the sheet. Let's see what you have to work with."

Clutching the wrap tighter, Caroline stared at the reflection of Miss Kitty. "Excuse me?"

Returning her stare but with a bolder one, Miss Kitty repeated the words, "Drop the sheet."

"Is this really necessary?" Caroline couldn't recall the last time she'd been nude before anyone, not even herself. As she eyed the body wrapped tight in the sheet, she could honestly say the large white cloth was only a pseudo shield. The fabric was already clinging to parts of her body, making her golden skin evident in some places.

"Either let it go, or I'll remove it from you," Miss Kitty said firmly.

There was no doubt in Caroline's mind that the woman standing behind her would do as she vowed. Loosening her fingers one at a time, she allowed the material to slip from her body. The damp sheet drifted to the floor.

Averting her gaze, Caroline refused to look at herself or even into the madam's eyes. She simply stared at a spot on the wall over the mirror.

"Pearl, the first thing you need to know about being a whore is appreciating your own body. Loving every curve, valley, rise and fall and coming to grips with each imperfection, because no one is perfect." Miss Kitty paused.

Listening to her words, Caroline was curious about her body, but she forced her eyes to remain fixed away from her frame.

"Look at yourself, Pearl."

It was that no nonsense voice again. Caroline slowly lowered her gaze, seeing her reddish-brown hair with the lighter streaks kissed by the sun piled high on her head from her bath, and then stared into her own eyes and stopped.

"Your hair is becoming in its color, all the shades of brown and the natural golden streaks, bleached from hours in the sun. Your eyes are so rich in color, clear and wide with innocence, a person can't help but be drawn in."

Caroline had never considered anything special about her eyes. They were just another brown in the multiple shades that described her, nothing special.

"Your neck is long, and your shoulders are broad from all that field work but still rounded. They will be very beguiling with an off the shoulder dress or wrap."

Off the shoulder? Caroline had never worn anything remotely revealing. She couldn't stop the fluttering of her heart at the thought of showing herself to a man. Lordy be, they'd only gotten to her shoulders.

"A whore has to know what she is offering a man. Like your breasts, they're small but nice in size even though you are thin. The men will love the large size of your nipples."

Caroline had to be honest with herself, she had not truly looked at them since the night she realized they were budding. On the farm, with all the work needing to be done and only her and her father to do it, there wasn't enough time for assessing her body. Unable to resist, Caroline gazed at her breasts. The area around the points were dark pink and they were drawn tight. The desire to reach up and touch them overwhelmed her. She denied herself.

"Very alluring, aren't they?"

She lifted her gaze to the madam's and felt as if the woman could read the thoughts that had entered her mind. Caroline refused to confess to her guilt.

"Your waist is extremely narrow, and your ribs would have been showing in another week or so. Your hips are not as full as they could be, however, they have potential, with proper meals. In the meantime, I'll show you the best way to stand and walk to display them to your advantage, so it will not matter. Besides, in this profession, they will naturally begin to expand some."

"I don't understand how that will happen." She frowned.

"That is a lesson for another day," Miss Kitty commented. "Now, look at your womanhood, sex, cunt, twat, pussy."

She marveled at the ease in which the words rolled across Miss Kitty's tongue as if they were talking about fruit at the open market exchange. Three of five words, she had never heard before. She could never imagine saying them out loud, but she played them over in her mind. They were naughty words and every time she repeated them mentally, it made her body temperature elevate as she stared at the triangle of hair at the juncture of her thighs. "Is that how the men will talk to me?" Her own voice sounded winded to her ears.

"Some of them. Others are gentlemen or just as shy as you are now. They don't know what to ask for, which is why we need to know. *You* have to know."

Caroline nodded. Her throat felt too tight to answer, unsure of how she would be able to bring herself to say such words and, surely not, instruct someone else to say them.

"Well, stare at yourself as long as you like. Mrs. Morrison will be up here with your dinner shortly and when she leaves, lock the door. I don't need any of our male guests stumbling into your room by accident. At the end of the week, you will be able to observe the activities from the upper floor." Miss Kitty headed to the door.

Picking the sheet up from the floor, she clasped it to the front of her body. "I heard you tell Daryl I wouldn't be ready for him for a month."

With one hand on the door, the madam glanced back at her. "That's right."

"So, will he be my first?" Caroline asked softly.

"Yes, he will. After all, your debt is owed to him, so he's entitled to first dibs."

"I understand." She just didn't like it. However, she knew there were no further outs for her.

Miss Kitty exited Caroline's new bedroom.

Turning back to the mirror, she dropped the sheet and stared at her image one more time. Still feeling odd at being nude, she crossed the room. She went through the wardrobe again but couldn't find anything she would feel comfortable being in, even alone in the room. She went to the tall chest of drawers and was thankful that in the top drawer she found a shift.

Even the small amount of covering made her feel more

like herself. Glancing around the room, she considered where was the best place for her to wait for Mrs. Morrison to bring her food up. She eyed the bed and quickly crossed that off the list. She would have to sleep in it later, but she would put off touching it for as long as possible. Opting for the chair at the vanity, she sat.

There wasn't much time to wait before a tap echoed on the door. Caroline moved to the door and pulled it open a crack to see a heavyset older woman with a thick, short, brownish-gray cap of curls and a large, friendly smile holding a covered tray. Stepping back, she allowed the woman to enter.

"Miss Kitty was correct; you are a frail thing." The woman walked over to the vanity and set the small tray of food down for a moment while she went behind the door and got a wooden frame. Popping it open, she put the tray on top of the mini portable table.

Unsure how to respond to the comment, Caroline just stood silent. Her mind was flooding with all the things the woman probably thought about her.

The woman's face continued to display a broad smile as she stuck her hand out. "I'm Mrs. Morrison."

Caroline took her hand. "Mrs. Morrison, it's a pleasure to meet you."

"Don't look so frightened, sweetie; everyone takes care of each other here. A woman can't always control where they end up. I'm only glad you're here with Kitty. That little saloon between here and the next town just ain't fit for no one."

Not even wanting to imagine what could be worse from one whorehouse to another, Caroline offered the kind woman a tentative smile. "Thank you, Mrs. Morrison. I'm Caro—I mean Pearl."

Winking, Mrs. Morrison released her hand. She looked

her up and down for a moment. "You remind me of my daughters, sweet, innocent, eyes full of wonder."

"You have children? Um...do they work here?" Caroline's cheeks heated at her question.

Mrs. Morrison chuckled, and her ample breasts and stomach bounced. "Oh, no. Not that, if they landed in such a place, I would look bad on them. I was fortunate there was an opening for a cook years ago." She placed hands on her hips. "My husband died about five years ago. I came to work here to keep food in our mouths and a roof over our head. Got my girls jobs, Vera at the boarding house and Rachel placed with the Reynolds family."

Caroline was familiar with the Reynolds family. Isabel, their oldest daughter, had been her best friend when she had been allowed to go to the schoolhouse and learn. At thirteen, her pa had told her he needed more help on the farm than she needed any more schooling. Caroline had attempted to keep their friendship going, but Caroline's papa made it close to impossible, working her from sunup until sundown. Isabel was now married; her husband had assisted at Caroline's papa's small funeral. Isabel was not able to attend because she was on bedrest with twins.

It made her heart sink deeper in despair as she thought about all the times she and Isabel lay in the tall, fresh prairie grass and discussed their dreams as they pointed out odd shapes of the clouds. Isabel had wanted to leave Grover Town and learn to teach, while all Caroline had wanted was a husband, a farm, and babies...lots and lots of babies. Caroline yearned for a house full of the noise of family. The burning at the back of her eyes and the tightness in her chest started again. Those dreams were better off dashed against a stone then to be in her heart, as they were no longer for her. What man would want her after her years of servitude in a whore-house, no matter how fine it was?

She had considered going to Isabel and asking her friend for a job on their farm, but she had decided against it. Her old friend had her hands full and a house full of people already on a new farm. She also was afraid that Isabel would attempt to give her the money to clear the debt, and that would just make Caroline feel worse and still owe someone else a lot of money she wasn't sure how she could pay. If she would have been able to take the train to Topeka or Kansas City, then she could have easily found employment in a big town or the state capital, but Bellmore was not about to let her out of his sight.

Mrs. Morrison crossed back to the door. "Welcome to the Harlot and the Hero, Pearl. I hope you like roasted chicken, yams and greens. The biscuits are my secret recipe."

"I do." Caroline's words were encored by her stomach's loud growl. "I love to cook too."

"Well, now." The woman's smile stretched wider. "Then feel free to come in the kitchen on your day off if you like. I wouldn't mind you being about." In a whisper, she added, "The next time you makin' biscuits, add a little bacon fat and chives, see how they turn out for ya. Don't forget to lock the door. I'll get the tray in the morning. Sleep well."

"Thank you." Caroline closed and locked the door just as she heard piano music floating up from the bottom floor. She didn't think she would be getting any sleep tonight.

SIX

Silence seeped through the walls and filled the room, a relief to the disturbing deafening echoes of the moans and groans through the night and early hours of the morning. Her body had heated, tightened and throbbed in strange places she'd never recognized before as all the grunts and cries surrounded her. She'd felt agitated and uncomfortable in her own skin. If she had not been told to remain in her room, she would have gone out to the lake beyond her window for a long walk in the cool night air to ease the tension.

Now, she lay in the center of the bed, beneath the blanket, as she watched the sun start to peak over the horizon. It had shocked her last night, when exhaustion had finally set in to a point she could not keep herself from lying in the bed, and the sheets had been soft, fresh and clean. She'd never slept on silk or satin sheets before, and the feather down duvet was so soft. The bed was firmer than she would have liked, but she didn't want to think about bed textures and the reason for the durability.

Her bladder urged her to rise. She wasn't sure what time the house rose since they only stopped entertaining men a couple hours before dawn. However, she wasn't used to lying around in bed. She and her papa always went to bed early and rose well before the sun. Pulling herself from the bed, she straightened it out then located the flowered porcelain pot behind the whitewashed wooden screen in the corner. Next to the screen, was a wide stand where a bowl, neatly folded clothes, tooth powder, shaving kit too, including dual linen and leather strop dangling from the side to sharpen the razor. She frowned at the shaving equipment. It perplexed her why in a house filled with women, there were shaving items used by men. Shrugging, she figured the women occasionally shaved their men. She had shaved her papa's beard more than a few times when he was hurt, ill, or just as a courtesy to him.

Her papa had worked so hard on the farm, mostly to no avail, but she loved him and tried to do small things that would ease the burden he carried to succeed. In her new residence, she didn't feel it was proper to think of her papa in such a place. She just prayed that he was finally at peace beside her mama and brother in Heaven.

After she completed her morning ablutions, she turned to stare at the pretty space. The room started to feel small and confining. She needed to get out. On the edge of the screen, was a silk robe. With the shift below it, she felt decent and covered enough to step out. Underneath the bed, were her worn boots, and she slipped them on. On her way to the door, she had to giggle at her appearance. She looked odd, with hair in a braid over one of her shoulders, a robe belted tight around her narrow waist and dusty boots.

Pulling the door open, she peeped out first. The hallway was wide enough for two people to stroll side by side, with a long, peach carpeted runner covering the wood flooring. All the doors down the hall and on both sides were closed. She hoped that meant all the men had left the house. She had no clue if men stayed overnight or not.

Finding the hall vacant, she stepped back into her room for a moment, grabbed the tray from the night before and went out. Halfway up the hall, she noticed the barren downstairs clearly seen over the banister. She paused and wondered what activities had gone on down there through the night. She continued, as she could not help but wonder about all the four person tables and high polished bar with the stools. There were a few blue and black velvet clawfoot loveseats scattered around the perimeter of the room too.

When she arrived at the bottom of the stairs with the tray of dirty dishes, she paused for a moment, unsure which way to go. She was promised a tour today, but who knew when that was going to happen, and she wasn't one to sit around idle. Stepping deeper into the large front room that seemed to pulse with forbidden desires and whisper wicked deeds that took place not only last night, but for years. She wasn't so ignorant not to know that women selling themselves to men was a profession that went on even back to B.C. days. The smell in the room was both sensual and pungent, a cornucopia of scents—rose, honeysuckle, tobacco, musk of both genders, and even more herbal notes like mint and chamomile.

She glanced left then right. The door not too far from the front door was Miss Kitty's office and anteroom. She knew there was a wide, plush chaise in there, but she wasn't sure if that was truly where the owner slept. Under the upstairs landing, there were three other doors along the back wall and a curtained off archway directly below the tallest part of the stairs. She could see it was some sort of private card room. Unlike the high polish of the tables in the front room, the ones in there were covered with green felt.

Deciding to try the middle door, it was without a handle

and appeared to swing. As she walked past the bar toward the back, she could smell the sweet, rich pungent scent of whisk and lemon oil fighting for dominance. The shelf wall behind the bar was fully stocked with various bottles, some tall, wide, and short that were filled with liquid that looked like water to those so dark, it appeared black. Men and their strong drink. She'd seen drunk men in town before, stumbling out of Manny's or the little saloon, making lewd gestures and comments. It made her nervous being in a place where alcohol and sex were so prevalent.

Right before she reached the middle door, it swung open wide, and two things tumbled out simultaneously. She was struck by the smell of bacon, instantly making her mouth water and her stomach growl, and children. Smiling, giggling children who, when they caught sight of her, halted in their steps.

One of the five looked back over his shoulder just as a mixed-race woman with skin as pale as her own and thick corkscrew hair bundled high on her head came into view.

"Mrs. Muriel—"

"Children, now you know we must be quiet and on our best behavior in the front room." The woman saw her and offered a kind grin. "Well, hello. I hope the little ones didn't awaken you. They can be quite rambunctious during music time."

Stunned, Caroline still hadn't moved from her spot.

"Do you think she's trying to catch flies in her mouth?" One little redheaded girl with odd slanted, almond shaped eyes, inquired to the blond boy next to her.

Caroline snapped her mouth closed, realizing her mouth must look like the opening of a beehive.

"I'm Donovan." The woman made her way around the children and held out her hand.

Locating her manners, Caroline switched the tray to one hip and hand as she accepted the other woman's right hand. "Sorry, Mrs. Donovan—"

"It is just Donovan. I was the only girl, following six boys, and my father figured I'd marry some day and wanted to make sure I never lost my name. For years, I was Donovan Donovan." She laughed. "Until I married at sixteen and was widowed by nineteen. My father sent me from Albany to the Ladies' Academy in Pennsylvania. I was headed to San Francisco to teach when I met Miss Kitty on the train. She is a very convincing woman and helped me realize my services would be strongly needed here with *these* children."

"Oh." Caroline smiled at the elegant, friendly woman. "Forgive my shock, I just never expected children to be in a who—here." She bit into her tongue and tried not to be insulting.

"No worries. It was important to Miss Kitty that the children of the ladies who work here were afforded the same level of education as the other children in town, regardless of their parentage." Donovan lifted a single brow.

Clearly understanding the woman's message, Caroline nodded. These little ones were the offspring of men who paid for their mothers' services. She didn't have to be all knowledgeable to understand that where there was sex, there would be breeding. She found it admirable that the madam who owned a whorehouse made sure the women's children were cared for and educated at such a level.

"I'm Pearl." She still was not used to the jeweled pseudonym as it slid from her lips. "Did you say music time?"

The children were standing there patiently, but they all were bobbing up and down on their toes seeming anxious to get to it.

"Yes. We start with piano in here, then out by the lake, we work on the fiddle, guitar, violin and a flute."

"And a washtub and jug," one of the bigger boys chimed.

"Those two are for pure fun and silliness. Along with my other teaching skills, I know the basics of most musical instruments, anything after that comes from a child's own inherent skills. Like this little one..." Donovan patted the head of a child, a little brown-skinned boy with short, thick, kinky hair. "He is only five but is a master at the piano. Often, Madam Kitty will let Simon Paul play in the early evening while the ladies dress but before any *guests* arrive."

Thinking about the other evening and the music playing, she looked from the bashful boy to their caregiver and teacher. "Yesterday, that was him playing as I ate my supper?"

All the children cheered.

"It was. Mr. Clay, the establishment's actual pianist, comes an hour early to offer Simon Paul a higher level of instruction that I can't teach."

"Michael is great at the flute," the little almond-eyed girl, who appeared around seven years old, professed as she stared at the tallest boy with dreamy eyes.

Caroline looked at the curly blond boy, who appeared no more than nine, as the freckles on his face were washed out by the deep blush that crept up his neck into his cheeks.

"Well, I'd love to come to one of your lake concerts if I could."

Small gasps and eyes filled with excitement as they peered up at their teacher.

Smiling, Donovan told her, "The children love to show off their skills, even in the classroom, so we'll work on a song and perhaps arrange a date soon that works in your schedule."

Donovan's subtle words reminded her that she was in the place for a specific reason, and none of that had to do with sitting around laughing and talking to children. The reality of her life and situation sank deep in her gut, even in such a lighthearted moment.

"Well, I won't keep you all any longer. I'll just get this to the kitchen."

"It's that way." An ebony-haired girl of eight pointed behind them toward the swinging door.

"Thank you." After a quick nod, Caroline continued to the kitchen as the children went deeper into the room toward the coveted piano.

With a push of the big door, she found herself in a large, fully turned out kitchen with Mrs. Morrison at the helm. There was a table filled with multiple covered dishes with delicious smells of bacon, fried eggs, toasted bread, porridge, and some sort of sweets she couldn't decipher permeating the air. As the older woman kneaded bread on a counter, Miss Debra scored a big side of pork by the stove.

Miss Debra offered her a smile as she picked up a handful of garlic cloves and shoved them deep into the cut in the meat.

Another woman, with a smooth, sienna brown complexion and her hair pulled back tightly in a braided bun fashion, sat at the table with a plate laden with food before her.

"I see you found us. Was it your stomach that led the way?" Mrs. Morrison greeted her with a smile as wide as her hips.

"Um, I wanted to return this." Caroline held up the tray, not sure what to do with it. "The meal was wonderful. I can wash the items if you show me where to put them up."

"Nonsense." Mrs. Morrison shook her head as the woman working on the meat crossed the room to Caroline and took the tray. "If you would have left it up there, Cecil and Macey would have taken care of it as they cleaned your room."

"Oh, I can do that. I just need supplies."

"Everyone has a job here, and we let them do it. Good folks gotta make a livin' the best they know how." Mrs. Morrison set a hand on her hip. "What you can do is take a seat at the table and fill your belly. Your only job right now is add more flesh to your bones." She pointed a flour- covered hand at the table.

Chastised, Caroline stopped offering to do things and sat.

"Pearl, right?"

"Yes." She claimed the seat next to the woman in the blue calico dress with yellow flowers. The dress was so modest and plain, like the teacher's, that Caroline didn't think the woman was one of the women who tended to the men. Grabbing a plate from the stack on the table, Caroline began to open the lids over the food. She found bacon, sausages, eggs, a pot of porridge, flapjacks, and potato hash. Her mouth became moist as she took in all the food. She'd never seen so much. Even when her mother, who was a fine cook, was alive, they were still struggling, and meals had to be kept simple. Not wanting to take too much with so many mouths in the house to feed, Caroline put just a small amount of a few of the items on her plate.

"You need more food than that meager amount on your plate," Mrs. Morrison demanded. "Get that belly of yours nice and full."

"I wanted to make sure there was enough for others."

"There's plenty. Don't you worry. Most of the ladies won't even be up before two hours after the sun reaches noon time."

"If you're sure."

"I guarantee it," Mrs. Morrison declared. "Mostly, I cook breakfast for the children, and they all eat twice over."

Glancing over her shoulder at the cook for a moment, she said, "I was shocked to see...there were children...here."

"If there's a brothel, there's children, even in the most cautious place like the Harlot. Other places give the babes away or sell them off. If they're lucky, because the mother wants it, or the owner doesn't allow it. Miss Kitty believes she can have a decent place for mothers to raise their children and keep the children away from the trade."

"How's that when they come into the place?" Caroline added more on her plate, filling it as she'd wanted to do before, still miniscule, only half the plate now full. There was heat in her cheeks as she piled on the food, but she wouldn't allow herself to be embarrassed enough not to eat well. Maybe if her hips and waist got too thick and they had to roll her around, the men, especially Bellmore, wouldn't want her. That was fine by her.

"Only in the day, when all's quiet." Mrs. Morrison placed her bread into a bowl and drew a towel over it. She then carried it to the counter close to the oven to rise. "This house is more than what you see from the front or even your back view of the lake. If you went out the door to the side, there's a class-room for the students to learn. There's a door that leads out to the back, and on the other side of the lake, there's a smaller house where Cecil and Macey, who are married, live, with two additional rooms where the children sleep seperatin' the boys from the girls. They never had none of their own and they enjoy lookin' after 'em."

"And Donovan?" Caroline started eating. The food was so good from the first bite, she shoved in two more, forgetting her table manners and barely hearing the cook's response.

"Her wages include a room at the boarding house." Mrs. Morrison went to the wide copper sink to wash her hands. "Nice to see you have a hearty appetite. That lets me know there's less of a chance you're ill in any way." The comment came from the woman beside Caroline.

She placed a hand over her mouth, embarrassed. Caroline chewed fast and swallowed, before she spoke. "Oh, forgive me. I must look like a glutton."

Even as she said the words, her eyes drifted down to the plate longing for her next bite of the amazing food. Caroline had always considered herself a good cook, but Mrs. Morrison and Miss Debra were outstanding.

The black woman chuckled. "Never that. As I said, means you're rail thin but heathy."

Caroline frowned as she took her next bite. The woman's comment was odd. "Are you one of Miss Kitty's...um, jewels?"

"No." A lopsided but generous smile decorated her features. "I provide care to the ladies and children here. I'm Florence Burke."

"Oh. Miss Florence, are you a doctor?" Caroline knew they were making advancement, but she'd never heard of any women doctors.

"Even though I did work and learn at The New York Infirmary for Women and Children, under Dr. Emily and Dr. Elizabeth Blackwell, two brilliant doctors sympathetic to the concerns and plight of women of all races, I'm a midwife."

"Oh, gracious. There are women doctors?" Caroline mumbled around the bite of fluffy flapjack in her mouth.

"Few, but yes. I tend to all the ladies' needs at the brothel. Anything I can't handle, Doc Clarkston will come around to assist." The woman lifted her cup of coffee to her mouth and drank. "You and I are on schedule to meet this morning. Once you're done with your meal, we'll talk about some health care things you will need to know working at the Harlot."

Nervous about what that talk would consist of with the medical woman, she ate in silence.

"After Florence and you finish up, Miss Kitty said Connie Marie, Mable's oldest daughter from the dress shop, will be over to bring you a couple of day dresses and fit you for the things in the pearl room wardrobe."

Part of her heart fluttered at the knowledge she'd get some respectable things to wear. She hadn't had anything without dirt or tears in it for so long. The other side of her heart beat fast, knowing that she'd be outfitted in some of the scandalous things in the white room.

Her life had changed, in some ways for the better...others, she didn't even allow herself to consider.

"ALL RIGHT, Pearl, you can sit up now." Florence rose from her knees at the foot of the bed then went to the bowl on the stand to wash her hands.

Caroline lay on the bed of the all-white room, mortified. She had been examined from head, looking for sores or lice, to her toes, where midwife Florence made sure she didn't have any foot fungus ulcers. When that was complete, the efficiently thorough woman had instructed her to bring her heels to the bed and drop her knees as wide as she could, only to have both the opening between her thighs and the one to her rear prodded with something slim that Caroline assumed was the midwife's finger. Unable to watch what was going on down there, she had kept her gaze locked on the white painted wood of the ceiling.

Ill at ease and shaky, never having been touched within those two areas before, she snapped her thighs together before rising slowly. Sitting there with her arms wrapped around her knees, she took more than a couple breaths to steady herself. *Men will do more to you then a quick, gentle prod.*

"Miss Kitty will be glad to hear your vagina appears clean and well cared for and hymen is intact, with way more than just the appropriate amount of moisture. Your anus is tight and untried as well." Florence smiled at her as she dried her hand on a cloth.

Moisture. Caroline could surmise what the woman spoke of. She'd felt an advanced amount of wetness on her thighs last night as she lay in bed surrounded by the sounds of sexual congress. Caroline felt the heat infuse her face at the words and the knowledge that Florence knew being in this place was disturbing her body, even if she was trying to deny and ignore its effect. "Was that...that examination necessary?"

"Yes. Miss Kitty can't promote a lie; it would put a stain on her business and her word. Men pay a high price for a woman's maidenhead and other untried areas. Men you service will expect and do a lot more than *that.* Follow the instructions Miss Kitty and I give you, to the letter, and there will be no need for myself or Doc Clarkston for that matter to probe within your lower orifices." Still holding the cloth, Florence set a fist on her hip. "The reality of a whorehouse is that women who work in them can get sick, not just with a cold or influenza, because so many men who don't care for themselves are breathing down on them. More important, some of them carry venereal diseases that can get passed on to you, Pearl."

Lowering her feet to the floor, Caroline placed a hand on her stomach. She felt nauseous and the food she had consumed half an hour ago was starting to make a return. Leaping up, not caring that she was naked—the woman had already seen and touched all that she had, thoroughly—Caroline dashed toward the screen. She just made it to her knees before the pretty chamber pot that had been cleaned like the rest of the room in her absence. With a death grip on the thick, heavy lid in her hands, Caroline emptied the contents of her stomach.

"It's all right; let it all out." The midwife held her hair back as she wiped a cool, wet cloth along the back of her neck. "Shh. When a woman truly sees the plight before her, it can be overwhelming. Everything comes up, including the emotions."

Caroline realized that she hadn't only been throwing up but crying, too. The soothing tones of Florence and her kind touch up and down her spine just made more tears run out of her. She had missed the embrace and kindness of anyone. Her papa was a hard worker and a good man, but life had beat him down, he had rarely smiled or done more than place a hand on her shoulder at times. She'd missed her mother, and her soul ached.

As if understanding the weeping of her heart, Florence knelt beside her and pulled her against herself. When the midwife's arms slipped around her shoulders and held her tight as she offered comfort and even a soft song that spoke about a balm being in Gilead that Caroline had never heard before, and would have never expected in a brothel, eased the tension inside her.

'There is a balm in Gilead to make the wounded whole.
There is a balm in Gilead to heal the sin sick soul.
Sometimes I feel discouraged and thinks my works in vain,
but then the Holy Spirit revives my soul again...'

Caroline wasn't sure how long they sat like that or even how many times the black woman holding her had repeated the simple verses, ones that Caroline had no doubt was one of the slaves' tunes she'd heard about before. Florence and others of her skin tone had been through horrors and fought to survive, and hearing it honored Caroline's heart that the midwife would comfort her now with lyrics that had given others hope.

She straightened her spine and began to feel a little

strength flourishing in her core. She wasn't a weak woman who gave in to fits of tears. She'd been strong alongside her papa, physically and mentally. Now, she would do it for herself.

"Ya gud now, gurl?"

The rich, broken dialect Florence used instead of the proper diction she'd exhibited made Caroline draw a grin on her face. "I'm good."

After a firm nod, the other woman returned her smile before rising. "Then we have a few more things to get through before the dressmaker's daughter arrives." Florence was the efficient midwife once again.

Caroline set the lid firmly on top of the pot then got up and joined Florence, who stood beside the washstand. She accepted the cloth from the midwife and washed off her face.

Moving over to the single nightstand that held one of two decorative oil lamps in the room, Florence pulled open the drawer.

Caroline hadn't opened any of the drawers, the trunk under the foot of the bed, or the small wooden cabinet at the bottom of the washstand. The wardrobe and the obscene pictures on the walls were enough to see. Florence removed a small tin box and moved back to her. The box had small green leaves painted on top.

"Here, chew this." Florence handed her a familiar leaf from the box.

Smelling the bright green leaf first, it was as she figured, mint. Caroline chewed it.

"It will not only freshen your breath, but it is good for the stomach as well. After each customer, you want to avail yourself of a leaf or the tooth powder. If you like candy, Cecil and Macey always keep a few peppermint sticks in the drawer as well."

She refused to think about why she'd need so much mouth freshening once she began to entertain men, but the peppermint sticks thrilled her. Caroline made a hesitant glance toward the drawer to see what else lay in there. However, she wasn't sure what was in all the small jars, bottles, and various shapes of tin and porcelain containers, and she didn't ask.

"I see you are curious, so we will get on to some of the other health business I'll need to instruct you on staying safe and keeping your vagina healthy."

"May I put back on my shift?" Caroline hadn't felt as naked in the last few minutes around the midwife than she did now, knowing they would be discussing things she had no clue about, sex.

"Yes. At the moment. You have to remove it when we discuss the importance and proper way to shave."

"Men?" Caroline declared.

"Your sex."

Her jaw dropped open. Caroline would have never considered that it was even conceivable, let alone that there would be a reason for removal of the hair that covered between a woman's legs.

"Close your mouth, Pearl. In a brothel, men consider an open mouth an invitation."

"To what?"

When Florence stopped in the act of putting the mint leaves back in the drawer to glance back at her, Caroline said, "Never mind. I don't want to know that answer right now." She shook her head as she walked to the bed for her shift. The midwife's laughter followed her.

"We'll talk again in a week and see how much you *know* then."

Caroline shuddered to think about the other lessons still

to come. After she was covered, she saw Florence was still standing beside the nightstand, now holding a long, rectangular tin. It was plain on top, but when the midwife opened it, Caroline noticed it was filled with what appeared to be empty sausage casing.

"Shouldn't those be down in the kitchen with Mrs. Morrison?"

"No, dear. These are what most refer to as French Letters." She removed one thin sheath from the top and held it out to Caroline. "This is meant to be slipped onto a man's cock, dick, staff, manhood, meat, wanker, and such. It will keep most diseases away, like pox and syphilis when used *every time* and tied at the base properly. Swiping your hair away will hinder anything that crawls from setting up a nest."

Caroline's ears were on fire on the outside from embarrassment and the inside because of the harsh, rapid beating of her heart in her ears. She felt as if she'd just run five kilometers up a hill, out of breath and a little lightheaded.

"I think I need to sit." She was already plopping down on the side of the bed as she still held the thin, slippery membrane between her fingers.

"Sit, but pay attention. There is a lot to go over, and we haven't much time left today before your fitting. We still need to discuss the proper way to soak and insert a sponge."

"For dishes." *Please let it be for dishes.* Caroline groaned.

"No. Your vagina. Just assume that anything we are talking about always will have to do with care and preparation of your vagina. Or anus."

Darkness attempted to seize Caroline's mind, but she fought against it. She wasn't a weak ninny. Taking a deep breath, she stood and poured herself a glass of water. Her hands were a little shaky and she almost laughed as she lifted the glass to her mouth and noticed the French Letter stuck to the side of the glass by her hand's grip. Once she started laughing, she couldn't stop.

"Good. Good. Laughter will get you a long way working in a brothel." Florence smiled up at her from the lower cabinet, where there seemed to be more than six small sponges, a few jars of various colored liquids, a bowl, and a rubber bag with a tube coming from it. "Vinegar is a whore's friend. Always remember that. We use it to soak sponges as well as a flush or douche each night after you work. Remember, a healthy vagina is a working vagina. The sooner you can right any debts, the sooner you can save money and make plans for your own life. Some women stay in the life and others decided to leave. Neither choice is right or wrong."

Caroline was back at the bed, returning the sheath to the tin. "What woman would want to continue in such a business if she could be free of it?"

Florence stood, a smile on her face and a bright sheen of remembrance and perhaps some joy in her gaze. "You would be surprised. A lot of women not only highly enjoy sex. Maybe you will as well, and they also enjoy the freedom that it is *their* choice now to stay."

Caroline had seen her fair share of animals mating and being bred, all the rutting and grunting of the male as they topped the female from behind. The females also whined and seemed as if they would rather be getting milked or eating cud. Nothing about it looked remotely enjoyable, let alone to the point of wanting to make a life of it.

SEVEN

"Any questions, Pearl?" Miss Kitty asked from her desk, where she had sat for over an hour working on her books and ordering, in a simple navy-blue calico dress with a square cut bodice. With her hair fashion in a high chignon with a few tendrils hanging at her temples, if no one knew she was the madam of a brothel, they would believe she was a clerk at one of the respectable businesses in town.

"Too many. I wouldn't even know where to start. Most of the images didn't make sense to me or they looked incredibly painful." Caroline sat a chair by the window where she had been assigned and given a sketch book of not only the female anatomy but the male. It didn't only show that genitalia that made Caroline blush several times over, but positions and such. She'd been shocked, appalled, and warm and throbbing in places she didn't want to consider why those parts of her were responding in such a way, particularly the freshly shaven parts between her thighs. The bareness had caused new sensations and she couldn't help repeatedly shifting in her seat.

The image of the manhood, as she felt more comfortable thinking of it, was interesting and she silently admitted to herself that seeing it made her heart race and sent a frisson of heat down her spine to her core. Her fingers had tingled to discover how it felt. She was scandalized at her own thoughts. Each time she reasoned she couldn't take one more image, she'd shut the book, only to have Miss Kitty instruct her to open it again. The woman had not even been looking in her direction and had still seen or known, even at the quietest of times, Caroline had brought the pages together.

Rising, Miss Kitty smiled at her. "Oh, lovely innocent, it is *all* possible." She wagged her head from side to side as she picked up the two-leather bound books she'd been working in. "A few of the positions take some time and even considerable training to get right, but you'll learn. The ladies and I will not leave you struggling alone."

"Good to know," Caroline mumbled as she stared down at the closed book in her lap, the dark binding of the collection a contrast to the pale-yellow calico with a high scooped neck. She liked the dress and felt respectable in it, which was an interesting thought to her, to already see herself somehow as not respectable that she'd have to feel respectable. She didn't have to wonder when her respectability had left her; it was the moment she'd entered this house. No, establishment, because this was a place of business—illicit business.

Here, she was Pearl. By the images in the book, Pearl wasn't expected to do respectable things. Things, had she married, her husband surely would not have expected of her.

She hadn't expected such a simple, pretty dress to wear, now that she resided here and would work here soon enough. One month, Miss Kitty had told Daryl Bellmore.

In her respectable dress as she sat by the window, staring

out over the front yard with wide open space before it, Kitty's office faced town, but at this distance, Caroline couldn't see anything. The front yard was dotted by more hitching posts then were used before most shops in town. Even though saloons didn't have but two long posts, from her view, she had already counted six. More posts, more men.

Occasionally, Caroline caught sight of two different men, big men walking the perimeter, never at the same time and not in any synchronized time that she could set a clock by either. If she saw them go in one direction, the next time she saw them, it would be a different one and he could come from another direction.

"Woody!" Kitty collected all her ledgers and moved to a painting across from her desk. The painting looked like something from the Roman Era Caroline had once learned about in school. However, the vibrant painting of a plump woman practically nude, with gauzy material draped around her body, her breasts and sex clearly seen and grapes in her hand as she lay on her side and smiled, was nothing she'd seen in her schoolbooks. The owner pushed it aside, only to reveal a safe built into the wall. Miss Kitty removed a key from her pocket before inserting it in the lock below a dial.

Caroline turned away, offering the woman privacy to get into her safe.

A moment after Miss Kitty's bellow, the door to the office opened and one of the big men, this one with black hair, neatly cut and well-trimmed around his ears, entered. He was in a fine pair of pants, looking tailored as the hem rested perfectly over polished brogans. There wasn't a matching jacket to his pants, but a white shirt that had to be made to fit such big arms, a wide chest, and a neck so thick, there was barely space seen between the man's shoulders and head.

Suspenders and a bolo tie ended the outfit. When he'd been making rounds around the house earlier, he'd been in basic brown trousers, dusty cowboy boots and a blue plaid shirt, nothing as finely turned out as this.

"Yes, Miss Kitty." He offered her a smile and a nod as he went toward Miss Kitty who stood beside her desk now. The picture back in place.

"Woody, please take the approved supply lists and drafts to Cecil and the other to Mrs. Morrison." She picked up the items from the desk then handed them over. "Anything I should be concerned with today?"

"No. Smitty had to send a man on his way about an hour ago. New to town and thought the Harlot ran around the clock." Woody shook his head.

Miss Kitty chuckled. "If he's looking for a place where the owner runs his girls down servicing gents day and night, he can mosey right to the little saloon." The older woman made a tsking sound that was accompanied by a sigh.

"Smitty gave him the directions to Manny's. Convinced him he'd be more interested in filling his gut with some quick fair, chased by a whisky, and give himself a chance to meet some folks in town before he upped and started knockin' on doors for service."

Miss Kitty laughed. "Oh, Smitty is one smooth talker."

"It's when he stops talkin', a man better watch himself," Woody added.

"Same with you. You both do a fine job of keepin' my jewels safe. I appreciate you both." Miss Kitty set a hand on the big man's thick shoulder as she offered him a brilliant smile that seemed to light the room.

Even Caroline felt the effect of it, not because it was staged, but because of the honest care in the older woman's gaze. Caroline was shocked to see the big man practically blush under it.

"Speakin' of my jewels, this is Pearl."

"I remember you telling Smitty and me about her, Bellmore bringing her over yesterday. The fuckin' jackass." Woody crossed the room to Caroline and offered his hand as if they were meeting in any other parlor, instead of the back office of a brothel.

Gasping at the words, true words, but ones she wasn't used to hearing, Caroline rose and accepted his hand. "Nice to meet you, Mr. Woody."

"Just Woody. Last name's Smith, and Smitty's last name is Woods...would you believe that?" He chuckled.

Caroline laughed for the second time since she'd arrived in the place. This man was funny and kind, and he had nice eyes that didn't appear to judge her.

"Nope. If you said it, it must be true," she offered with a small smile.

"Ah, this one will steal the hearts, Miss Kitty."

"Pure, sweet, and innocent always does. Is everyone ready?"

Woody faced Kitty once more. "Yes, ma'am. Miss Debra gave them the five-minute call not too long ago."

"Thank you."

After a sharp nod, Woody walked out, pulling the door closed behind him.

Caroline heard the beginning playing of piano music and thought about the little gifted boy on such a grand piano. "Here's your book back."

Miss Kitty took it and set it on the corner of her desk.

"You may enter my office at any time during the day to borrow it or any others, to educate yourself. If I am not meeting with someone, my door will be open. You may come by at any time even just to talk." Miss Kitty set her honest and caring gaze on Caroline this time.

"Thank you." Caroline knew she was thanking her for the invitation to talk, not to see more graphic tomes. She'd had her fill. The images were burned into her mind and would forever be stuck there. Caroline's heart lowered when she thought about how the only thing set in her mind before were different types of flowers she would enjoy planting one day and making wonderful smelling soaps with. Those days and thoughts were long gone now.

"Dinner is waiting. We don't want to be late, or Mrs. Morrison will have our heads," she teased as she moved to the door ahead of Caroline.

"Beautiful. Simon Paul, if you continue to play so well, I'm sure some conductor from the big city will show up in town and snatch you up before you're ten, to play in his orchestra." Miss Kitty winked at the child as they went past him and a thin older man who sat on the piano bench beside him offering instructions.

Caroline saw that the child didn't look up from the sheet music, but he did grin so wide that the absence of his two front teeth were revealed. That gap-toothed smile made it clear for her to see that the madam's praise meant a lot to even such a small boy as it had to a grown man.

Who was this woman who owned a brothel but freely poured out kindness on others? When one was poor, Caroline knew what it was like to be snubbed by those in town who felt themselves better than she. However, this whore, just a truth of Miss Kitty's profession, was humble and compassionate to all around her.

She followed Miss Kitty through the door on the left of the front room, on the other side of the swinging door. When they entered, Caroline froze. She could not have been more shocked if they had mysteriously entered an entirely different place altogether.

"Good evening, Jewels, children." Miss Kitty continued into the room without pause toward the head of the long, formal dining room table, even as Caroline still stood rooted to the floor at the entrance.

It wasn't only the decoration of the room, with its oil lamp chandelier overhead or the ornate high polished oak hutch that matched the chair backs and table legs of the twelve person table, but how nice and conservatively dressed all the other ladies were, and the children. With the multiple bowls and platters of food laid out along the runner in the middle of the table, it looked like Sunday dinner or a holiday dinner, Caroline had only been at one when she was younger and still in school. She'd been invited by Isabel to have Easter Sunday dinner at the Reynolds' home. She and her papa never had anything as fine as this; a pot of rabbit stew was as good as it got.

"Pearl, let's not allow Mrs. Morrison's meal to grow cold after she worked so hard at preparing it." Miss Kitty was settled at the head, placing a cloth napkin in her lap.

"S-sorry. F-forgive me," Caroline stumbled over her words, feeling like a ninny as she made her way to one of two empty seats. A striking, petite Asian woman directed her to one on the other side of the little redheaded girl with almond shaped eyes. She could see the resemblance between the two with them sitting next to each other.

"I'm Sarai." The girl beamed a smile at her. "I like Mrs. Morrison's green beans, do you?"

Caroline returned it with a smile of her own. "I'm Pearl. Green beans are one of my favorite things, too. So, I'm excited to try these for the first time."

The little girl wiggled a little in her seat, joy bubbling from her.

"Who would like to say grace tonight?" Miss Kitty looked around the table.

"I can do it!" The blond-haired boy patted his small chest twice as he sat beside a lovely woman with blonde hair that looked like sunshine, complemented by a set of blue eyes as brilliant as the sky. The woman was gorgeous.

Her beauty made Caroline uncomfortable. She'd always seen herself as plain, and across from a woman as arresting as the blonde, she felt like the cream unadorned wallpaper around the room.

"Jared, thank you." Miss Kitty smiled at him.

The music changed in the other room just as the door opened, and Simon Paul entered.

"Perfect timing, sweetheart." A stunning, dark-skinned woman, who wore a blue silk ribbon along the edge of her thick coils, patted the seat beside her. When the talented little boy sat next to her, she kissed his cheek.

As everyone bowed their heads, a short prayer was uttered from Jared that not only thanked the good Lord for the provisions before them but also for their mothers and a fun day with Mrs. Muriel. The other children snickered, making Caroline believe they must have a secret that all the little ones were in cahoots on. It made her remember her own childhood in school and the pranks some of the boys would play on the teacher and other children, most of them harmless antics.

Caroline stared at all the food that looked so good, and even though she had eaten a big meal that morning, her mouth was still salivating with excitement. She could tell her appetite was increasing. At home with her papa, they only had an egg or day-old biscuit for breakfast and some kind of stew for dinner. She had learned to live on miniscule amounts of substance to sustain her.

"Before we find out what silliness the children have wrought on Donovan, we'll have introductions." Miss Kitty picked up the platter with the roasted pork and started the food being served and passed around. "This is Pearl. Some of you may have seen her yesterday when she arrived. Pearl, tell everyone a little about yourself."

Caroline wasn't sure what all she should say about her situation. She took a moment to get her thoughts together as she scooped up green beans and onions onto her plate, before passing the bowl to the vibrant redhead beside her. She claimed the bowl of roasted potatoes from the little girl on her other side.

"I'm Caroline. Pearl. I've been in Grover Town since I was little. I came with my papa, mama, and little brother. Not too long after we moved here, a twister came through and took my mama and brother's lives." She shrugged as she passed on the bowl to the next person. So much had happened to her in a matter of a week, she'd gone numb. "It was my papa and me for a long time, until he died last week. I don't know if he wasn't a good farmer, but the land we rent on never yielded much of nothin'. After he passed, I found out just how bad things were. Now I'm here. The debt has to be paid."

As she accepted the bowl of biscuits with more bits of goodness in it, Caroline noticed that the smiles and gazes from the other women seemed kind and understanding.

"It can be rough to find yourself without anything, penniless and feeling hopeless." That came from the black, svelte woman sitting beside Miss Kitty. "I'm Marlena. Simon Paul is my son." Love filled the woman's light brown eyes as she helped him place slices of meat on his plate. "I go by Onyx." She added meat to her own plate and handed it on. "I'm originally from back east. I was raised and educated in Maryland. My parents worked for a rich family all my life. I fell in love with the youngest son, who was expected to marry someone else. He wanted to end his engagement. His family was furious, and they paid my family to send me away or lose their jobs, with no reference, and their house on the property. I got a one-way ticket west, workin' and cookin' on a wagon train. When it was discovered I was with child, I was kicked off in the middle of nowhere. Miss Kitty found me lying out on the road when her stagecoach happened by. We've been with her ever since." Onyx's tone was so matter fact, Caroline could tell she didn't regret how her life had turned out.

"It's nice to meet you and Simon Paul. He's exceptionally talented." Caroline cut into the tender meat.

"He is." Onyx smiled with pride. "I'm going to use my savings when he gets old enough, to send him to a fancy music school in Europe. He'd be accepted better over there."

Caroline wasn't a fool about life for some in the world.

"I'm Katy-Lynn." The woman down the table drew her attention as she wrinkled her nose and went on. "It seems so strange to refer to myself as such, because no one ever calls me that anymore, besides my son." She lifted the free hand of the boy beside her with sunshine curls and kissed the back of it. "This is my Jared."

The boy blushed and bit into a biscuit, but his smile was still evident behind it.

"I'm known here as Sapphire." The beautiful blonde with captivating, deep blue eyes the color of her moniker continued, "I was on a wagon trail with my parents, who are missionaries. A month into our trip, I was taken during an Indian raid. I was with them for weeks before my parents were able to sell most of their goods and buy me back. Except, once I was returned, the rest of the *devout* believer party would not allow me to stay." A perfectly arched blonde eyebrow bowed high. "I was considered soiled. I ran away, so that my parents wouldn't have to make the choice. Miss Kitty found me in some podunk town, in a trashy saloon, and persuaded the owner to release me. I've been with her since."

Caroline noticed as she listened and ate that even though the women were sharing more than she would have thought appropriate before their children, they were still conservative about what they shared.

"I will go next." The Asian woman on the other side of the little girl to Caroline's right spoke. Her accent was thick, denoting her culture as her features did, but her speech was clear. "You have already met my pride and joy, Sarai. My story is simple. I was Ling. Jade is my name. I was brought to Kansas from a mining camp in California. The man convinced me he cared for me and would take care of me and I would never have to work in the mines again. A couple days after we arrived, my man was shot in town when he was caught cheating in a poker game. I was sleeping in a tent, six months with child and nothing but the clothes on my back by the Kansas River, when Miss Kitty found me. I was out there alone doing...what I could just to have a little food. She offered me a place here and let me stay for months without working until Sarai was born and two more months after." Jade reached over to Miss Kitty and covered the back of the older woman's hand. "I am grateful to her."

Caroline recognized the pride and loyalty these women had to the owner. She wasn't just running a brothel for men's pleasures, but she was giving them a family and an honest place to raise their children without shame. Her core tightened and her heart thumped against her chest as she sat in the mist of the warmth filling the room. The children here, even if they didn't fully comprehend yet what their mothers did in the rooms upstairs for their care and survival, one day they would, but they would know it was done out of love and determination to see them succeed. Caroline understood her own father a little more sitting there. She was still angry at him for putting her in the predicament to even end up here, but she knew he had given his blood, sweat, and eventually his life to try to give her something she could be proud of. Only difference was that these women had succeeded where he had failed.

"I'll go next." A woman with flamin' brilliant red hair as deep as a ripe apple, with vivid green eyes and skin so pale and creamy, there wasn't a single freckle marring it like most redheads, spoke from the other end of the table. Her accent was thick, cultured, and smooth, with a little flare at the end of each word.

Caroline was fascinated, but unsure where the dialect was from.

"I'm Diana. Ruby to most. I've been with Miss Kitty from the start. I may have been much younger than she, but I taught her in the beginning. Only thing is she was way smarter than me. She is sharp, with a mind for business." The woman, whose thick accent seemed to be some sort of combination of southern and French, paused, the romantic tenure of her sultry voice drawing all in even as she glanced around at the opulence of the room before continuing. "You see, Pearl, I am the daughter of a...woman of such an establishment." She winked at Caroline.

Caroline understood Diana was the daughter of a whore. For a moment, she thought about Sarai and the other little girl who sat to the left of the redhead. One day, would they believe this was the employment they were supposed to take on because their mothers did it? She prayed not.

"My mother was a beaut and knew how to charm a man.

However, she never liked competition, not even from her daughter. One morning, when I was fifteen and garnering male attention and questions, my mother came to me and said it was time for me to make my own way somewhere else. I hopped on the first stagecoach out of town, not sure where I was headed, when lo and behold, who was on that coach? A wide-eyed but determined Miss Kitty. We hit it off as we traveled around from town to town talkin', laughin', and figurin' things out. I know this is the life I'll live until I can't anymore and maybe one day soon Miss Kitty will be in need of a second establishment somewhere."

Ah. Caroline reasoned that this was what Miss Kitty meant when she said some women enjoyed the occupation and did it for that reason alone.

"Save the best for last, I always say." The woman had a thick, southern accent to match her thick black tresses that were slick to her head with the ends in curls that hung over a single shoulder. "These two are my youngins, Jessup and Liddy Belle." She gestured to the boy on her right and the girl, who appeared to be the youngest of the children to her left, next to Ruby. "My ma and pa called me Shannon. But since I met Miss Kitty and Ruby, I've been Diamond. On account of my eyes and smile sparklin' and all." To prove her words, the woman offered a wide smile and batted her large, round eyes.

Caroline had to admit to herself, the girl's features did dazzle a room when she smiled with her even white teeth and pale blue eyes.

"I was headed west with my family from Alabama. My pa heard there was gold to be had there. It was just us, 'cuz Papa said he didn't want any claim jumpers along. A month in, and every one of them got sick, the ague. I cared for them each until they gave up the ghost." Diamond shrugged one of her shoulders then the other. "A preacher came along. I didn't know he was a fake one, though. He offered me a ride with him but claimed my virtue as cost for the travel, and along the way, others paid him for the same benefits. When I got a chance, I escaped. Just took off one night while he was sleepin' and just ran until I couldn't run no mo'. Miss Kitty found me dehydrated and near death on the outskirts of Grover Town. I'll keep doin' this until a man wants me to wife and we'll raise a big family together." She placed her arms around her two children and drew them into her.

Taking a moment to glance around the table, Caroline offered a smile to each of the ladies and the children. "I thank you all for sharing and making me feel comfortable and welcome with your stories. I look forward to getting to know you all. I have a lot to learn and I'm sure there are things each of you can teach me." She swallowed a thick knot coiled up in her throat. She truly didn't want to learn the skills these ladies had cultivated over the years, but she also knew that she didn't have much choice if she wanted to pay her debt off as quickly as possible and get out, before she settled in.

The women murmured some 'you're welcomes', 'any times', and some 'we're here to help'.

Lifting her last green bean to her mouth, Caroline looked over at Sarai. "You're right; they are incredibly good. I think these green beans are the best I ever had."

Sarai giggled. "I could eat a whole plate of them."

"Me too."

The staff came in and began clearing away the dirty dishes and empty platters, as Mrs. Morrison came in carrying a large, silver platter with slices of a chocolate cake on it. The cook started at Ruby's end and offered a slice on a small plate to each person.

"While dessert is served, children, tell us of your day." Miss Kitty glanced around at the little faces that were way more interested in getting their cake than talking, but they still chattered on in between bites.

Caroline ate her cake slowly, only half paying attention to what the children reported about their day. Her mind whirled as she considered each woman's tale and how there were small fractions of each of their honest accounts she could identify with. It was true she had never had a mean husband or bad parents or a disloyal preacher to contend, but she knew what it was like to be dependent on a man, hungry, poor, and left to fend for herself. Even with all the confidence the women exuded, Caroline was terrified of the moment she had to take her first customer to bed. Even though she knew it would be Daryl Bellmore, she still wasn't looking forward to him bedding her, nor the scores of strangers, or worse, familiar faces that would come after him.

She sent up a silent prayer. An empty prayer, because she wasn't even sure what to entreat. So she uttered the only words that came from her heart—*Lord, help me.*

GARRETT FOUND himself at Mrs. Livingston's boarding room. He'd returned to the Douglas' land two more times, and there was no sign of Caroline. He was starting to get worried. He'd checked the depot to see if she had taken the train or stage, but Lowell had confirmed Caroline had not left town by either travel route he managed.

"I'm sorry, Mr. Rand, but Caroline Douglas is not on the registry." Vera Morrison stood behind the desk at the front of the boarding house and dragged a slim finger with short nails cut neatly along the book, as she scanned the entries.

Mrs. Livingston wasn't in now, and Vera had kindly agreed to delay her afternoon outing to check the guest journal for him. Silas, the clerk from Reynolds Property Management, stood at the door patiently waiting to escort the pretty young woman to the Drummonds' for lunch.

"Thanks for checking." Garrett could feel the tightness in his shoulders, practically a burning from the tension that had resided there for almost a week. It didn't make any damn sense.

"Thanks, Miss Vera. I'll allow you your afternoon now."

"I didn't mind, Mr. Rand." She rounded the desk as she stepped closer to Silas, who tipped an elbow in her direction for her to take. As she smiled at him and slipped her hand around the bend, she murmured, not truly paying much attention to Garrett, all eyes for Silas, "When Mrs. Livingston returns before evening meal, I'll be sure to inquire for you."

"Much obliged." Garrett gave a nod to the besotted couple and exited the boardinghouse a few steps before them.

He decided to make his way to the mercantile shop and pick up a few supplies, but more importantly, if anyone in town knew anything about Caroline's absence, it would be Mrs. Russell. It wasn't that the store owner's wife could be called a busybody; it was just that she *was* a busybody. She was kind and sincere, but she was nosey and listened or paid attention to all gossip and conversation that went on in her store. There wasn't much of anyone's business in town she didn't have information on.

He started across the road when someone stepped in his path.

"Well, Mr. Garrett Rand, my day has just brightened." Widow Lawrence, with her big, light blue eyes and her even bigger bosom, concealed by expensive satin and lace but still well displayed on her small frame, stood before him as she came out of the millinery shop with a hat box in hand. Her thick, ebony hair was artfully dressed in perfect twists and curls and cascading over one shoulder.

He would have sworn that her maid had created the bottom ringlet to curl perfectly over the area of her bodice where a man would suspect the widow's nipple would be under her clothing. It drew a red-blooded man's gaze right to that point. Garrett was no monk, but he didn't allow himself to speculate any further on what lay beneath her silks, like the color of her areolas.

Meeting her eyes, seeing the beguiling smile on her painted red lips, he cleared his throat. "Ma'am." He tipped his hat. "Sorry, I almost knocked you over there."

She took a step toward him, keeping a decent space but close. "Mr. Ra-a-nd..." She dragged out his name in a seductive, breathy tone, in a way that he knew if she were coming and calling his name, it would sound just like that. "There are worse things to happen to a woman than to find herself flat on her back before you."

He cleared his throat. "S'pect there is. If it's all the same, I'd not like to be the reason such a thing happened to you."

People moving along the wide boardwalk nodded and smiled at them; a few greeted, and they replied in kind.

"Well." She lifted her shoulder and lowered it, an easy, sensual move. She placed a hand on his forearm arm, properly, if not for the subtle curl and pressure of her fingers on the back of his bicep. "I'm still waiting on you to accept my invitation to dine. You know I'm one of the best cooks in this here part of Kansas."

Rumor had it that before the widow married her husband, a businessman who had his fingers deep in the new oil businesses that were being discovered around the country and did more than dabbled at cards, Daniella worked as a cook in a restaurant and he'd eaten a meal she prepared one night and married her on the spot. Shortly after they'd arrived in Grover a few years ago, the man had kicked up his boots with a failing heart. Supposedly, it had happed during the night while they slept and the young widow had awakened to her husband cold in bed, too late for Doc Clarkston to do anything to revive him.

Being a young woman with needs, she discreetly entertained a few men occasionally at her home. To his knowledge, she wasn't looking for another husband, just companionship. For him, sleeping with a proper lady in his own town was too personal, and he preferred to satisfy his needs where there would be no entanglements or misinterpretations.

"Sorry, Widow Lawrence, but my schedule is real tight at the moment; the farm is growing fast, and calving season and all...and it takes most of my attention." When he was not devoting every available moment to searching for Caroline Douglas.

"I wish you'd call me Daniella." She pursed out her thin lips, making them pouty, in a 'kiss me' fashion. "I understand, but I'm going to hold you to visiting me once things slow down. A holiday dinner would be nice. I'm sure you can spare a lonely woman a few days then."

This time she did step too close, practically pressing her ample breasts against him. He stepped to the side and away, making her drop her hand.

"Perhaps. I must be goin'." He tipped his hat again and rushed across the busy road in a diagonal fashion to get to the mercantile.

It was Saturday afternoon, and he swore everyone was in town. This was his half day off and he'd wanted to find Caroline and spend it with her, possibly start courting her and see if she'd agree to be his wife. However, he couldn't do any of that if people kept getting in his way. He took the steps closest to Russell's. When he went by the tanner shop, he encountered Roy Benson and James Reynolds. He shook both the men's hands and agreed to a poker game at the back of the Tanner Shop midweek but continued making his way. The men in Grover Town had Chance Spencer to thank for bringing the game of chance and skill to the area when he returned from making his money working the gambling boats of Mississippi and Louisiana. Manny's saloon as well as the smaller rot-gut saloon were good for rowdy games of poker or billiards, but a few of the business owners in town played privately at the Tanner Shop on occasion.

Garrett was on a mission and wouldn't be derailed.

"Rand!"

Dammit.

Garrett halted two steps from the mercantile door at the sound of his name. Before he turned, he knew who had called him. It was Ian Silverman, the sheriff of Grover Town, his older half-brother. Their mother had been made to marry at fifteen, by her pa, to an old man, Magil Silverman, who died from an intestinal infection four months after they married. When Garrett's pa discovered she was widowed and pregnant, he offered to marry her. They'd been in love while at the schoolhouse, even though she was a few years younger than he was. However, her pa had married her off before he had been able to ask for her hand. Their parents had three boys and a daughter. Their baby sister had gone off to school in Boston, only to meet and marry a young up and coming shipping merchant within a few months. For four years, she'd been happy and living well as part of the Boston elite wives.

Turning to face his older brother, Ian, as he crossed the street from the Sheriff's Office, darted before a two-horse wagon, and drew closer to the boardwalk where Garrett stood.

"Ian, everything all right?" He originally thought perhaps

his brother was just offering out a brotherly howdy-do, but when they were standing face to face, he saw the strain around his brother's familiar blue eyes and the furrow of his brow.

They embraced after a clap on the back, and afterwards, Ian shook his head. "Not so much. I'll be damn glad when the new deputy arrives in a few weeks. I don't have enough men to handle a fast-growin' town with death comin' knockin' too often. Unexpected like."

Rand understood his brother's issue. He'd heard him say more than a few times over the last few months that trouble had come in on the train or by horse, chased out of the frontier in the form of cheats, riffraff, and con men. Sherriff Silverman was stern, broad-shouldered, leaner in the body than Rand, who took after his own father in size, but strong. His oldest brother didn't take any shit in his town. Ian and his two deputies had run more than a few bad apples out and the jail had plans to be expanded, fortified and moved from the center of town.

"I'm sure you will."

"I hate botherin' ya." Ian had snatched his hat from his head and dragged a hand through his black hair, his father's coloring, unlike the dark brown of their mother like Rand. However, Ian had lost all his Wisconsin accent, same as Rand.

"You know I'm here for ya, brother." Rand usually didn't mind offering his services, but today...of all days.

"There's another body found. Deputy Nelson's going to see about that while Deputy Dilbert holds down the town. However, there's a family of brothers, some lowlife who moved in one of the old farmhouses on the west end of town, and they've strung a line of bull long enough to stink up all Kansas. Cheated more than a few businesses and roughed up others, in self-defense, of course."

"Of course."

Ian situated his hat back on his head just as a sun ray connected with the eight-point star on his breast pocket that read sheriff, making it shine even brighter. "I'm sure they won't be goin' kindly. So, I'll need a few extra bodies as a show of force, to get them down to Topeka. With the jailhouse expansion still being worked on, I don't have the space to keep them. 'Specially after the brawl at the little saloon in the wee hours. Six men are still sleepin' off all the bad whisky in the cells.

The little saloon, that never had more than Saloon carved into the sign, was much smaller than Manny's place.

"Not sure why the mayor doesn't shut that place down." Rand shook his head.

"Cause Ringo has founder's rights. You know it was the mercantile, sawmill and him that started this town with a few farmers. Russell's doubled as the post office until we got the government to declare us a town and we got a real one. Hell, and you know, Ringo was the boarding house too, until Livingston built the one now."

Dropping his voice, he said, "Now, he runs unkempt whores out of those rooms. I'm just waitin' to hear some guy's part rotted off after being with one."

Ian chuckled. "True. You just keep your parts safe from there, little brother."

"Ain't no way I'd darken the door on my worst and horniest day with both my hands broken." Rand laughed, then sobered up. "What time you thinkin' about roundin'em up?"

"Right before sunrise. Before they can get out of their dusty beds. Harvey and Spencer are going to provide a couple hands as well. Harvey swears the Unger Boys are responsible for a couple heads of his cattle that have gone missing. I've been 'round the Unger property and didn't see anything but two mangy mutts. Most likely it was those boys we arrested around Christmas doin'."

"All right. I'll meet you at your office around four. Work for you?"

"It does. You sure with calvin' season going on, you can spare the time?"

"I'm sure, with Lyle solid in the foreman position for months now. The days it'll take us to get them down there, settled and tried, will be time enough for him to show and prove himself to the rest of my men."

"Thanks." With a firm pat to Rand's shoulder, Ian strolled down the road on his rounds.

Rand sighed. That only gave him a few hours to locate Caroline and make an offer to her of courtin' before he had to get back to his farm, pack his horse and get some rest before he had to meet his brother.

With all hope, he pulled open the mercantile door and entered.

"Well, Mr. Rand, welcome." Mrs. Russell paused in her sweeping of the hardwood floor and smiled at him. "Henry delivered your new canisters yesterday. Was there a problem with them?"

"Oh, no, ma'am." Rand removed his hat and offered her a grin. "Those canisters are just fine."

He took a moment to glance around the store and was thankful it was empty of customers now.

"Perfect. Are you here to pick up some things again for Mrs. Copernic?"

He swallowed. There wasn't a proper way for him to ask about Caroline, but he couldn't worry about appearance right now, when he felt deep in his gut something was wrong and it was possible she needed help. "I'm here about Caroline Douglas."

With the tip of her head as she leaned into the wooden handle of the broom, she met his gaze, her eyes bright, interested. "Miss Douglas. Do tell."

His brow drew down. "I was hoping you'd be able to tell me if you know where she's working...living?"

Mrs. Russell placed a hand over her heart. "It is truly a shame that her father passed. It was bad enough he kept her working that farm like an unpaid hand, now..."

Rand wasn't going to fault the man for having his daughter help him on the farm; families did what they had to do in order to survive. Same as Mrs. Russell working in their family store, work was work, simply different for some. "Do you know her whereabouts?"

She glided a hand up the back of her immaculate hair, perfectly coiffed. "I do occasionally hear things about people in Grover...and you know people like to confide in a kind ear." She smiled at him, her eyes wide, unimpeachable. "However, it is curious that I haven't heard a single word about her. Well, that is besides her coming to town to sell a few stray bars of her rose soap. It's been almost three weeks since she collected the few dollars that was on her books, thanks to Isabel buying them all out in a single sale before her wedding. I also hear tell that Harvey bought that old useless goat of hers. But nothing else." She cleared her throat softly. "Do you know more?"

"I don't. You haven't seen her in town in the last few days?"

"No. I assumed she's been hard at work trying to get that small farm to turn some kind of profit. Which is a shame—"

"Now, children, you can have one sour ball each and a peppermint stick." The new Mrs. Hemming, formerly Widow Marks, the organist from the town church before she married the widower with small children. All of them had smiles and appeared as a happy family.

"You have customers now. Enjoy the rest of your day, Mrs. Russell." He moved toward the door.

"B-but—" Mrs. Russell stuttered.

"Good day, Mrs. Hemming." He placed his hat on his head then tipped it.

"Mr. Rand." The organist and new mother of four grinned as she went to her children at the counter who were chattering away, excited about all the jars of candy.

Rand continued his way out of the store. He needed to get to the ranch and speak with Lyle and the other men, before getting things together and trying to get some shuteye. He crossed the road to the post where King was tied in front of the boarding house. This trip into town had been unproductive, clearly a waste of his time. It seems that Caroline had vanished into thin air. No one had seen or heard from her. He was still on square one.

He brushed a hand over his horse's flank and whispered into the animal's ear, as he ensured King was hydrated and had consumed enough water from the trough below the hitching post. The days were getting longer and hotter, and he believed in taking care of his animals, just like he did the men and women who worked his farm and dairy house. The next few days would be long ones and he'd need King in top shape to carry him to Topeka and back.

As he vaulted up into the saddle then steered him out of town, he recognized the war going on inside of him. His mind told him just to let her go, give up and make an offer for Jillian. At the same time, his gut tightened as he thought of Caroline and urged him not to give up.

He'd been listening to his gut over the last few weeks since he'd returned from the trail; it was what had guided him into town today searching for any crumb that would lead to her. It had gotten him nowhere. He had to face facts that it was beyond time for him to give up. He'd ride out with his brother, take the time to get Caroline out of his core, and align himself with the sense in his head. If no one had started courtin' Jillian, she'd be his.

Caroline Douglas was for sure a long way from Grover Town by now. Just like in a poker game, it was important for a man to know when to fold and count his losses, walk away.

EIGHT

Caroline stood at the railing across the hall from her room. It had been the same position she'd held for almost three weeks. She leaned against the wall at the end of the banister and tried to keep most of her body in the shadows as she stared down at the evening's events in the front room. The music coming from the piano was upbeat but classic. Caroline couldn't identify the song Mr. Clay was playing. His selection choices were proof that he should have been playing in the famous Boston Music Hall instead of in a small town like Grover, where most, like her, could barely appreciate his music.

When she'd made such a comment to the slender man in the top hat and coat with tails, he'd told her that some play for fame, while others play for love. She originally thought he'd meant love of the act of playing the instrument, until she'd seen how he gazed at Miss Kitty, and when the evening was over how he'd escorted the owner to her room on the other side of the office as if he were returning her after a night out at some fancy ball and stayed. It didn't escape Caroline's notice that Miss Kitty glanced at the pianist with the same admiration in her eyes.

More than one man looked up at her, as they did every night. Caroline could hear their inquiries about her, and what was the price. Miss Kitty would only tell him her name was Pearl and that she would entertain soon enough, but for them to be patient. Then she would guide them over to one of the other Jewels, who teased and flirted with them, and the elusive Pearl was forgotten for a time.

Caroline ran her fingers over the edge of the veil that half covered her face, ending at the tip of her nose. It was another way Miss Kitty kept the layers of mystery surrounding her. Everything in her wardrobe that she was allowed to wear while viewing the evening activities in the house was white or cream in color—denoting her moniker. Just like the other ladies wore salacious gown representing their own names, red, blue, black, yellow, and, green, her dress wasn't any different.

She marveled at how sexy and painted the women were now compared to the way they were dressed and clean faced with the children each night at dinner. It was such a dichotomy to see most of the Jewels go from mother to whore.

Over the last couple weeks, Miss Kitty had hand-picked each of her dresses and garments she would wear as Pearl, each more bolder than the night before. Even now, Caroline's hands itched to reach up and tug at the deep bodice, but that was a no-no. The first couple days she'd been on display at the high banister, she'd fidgeted and yanked at her apparel, only to be given one sharp look after another from Miss Kitty and a lecture in sensual decorum of all things. So, she simply tightened her grip on the high polished, carved birch wood banister.

The cut of the pearl-white, satin dress she'd donned tonight was cut low and offered more of the swells of her small breasts than had ever been seen by any one before. The other days, it was one shoulder out or both, maybe a dress that was high collared but bunched high at her thigh with a bow. She'd tolerated that because she'd worn high garters that covered most of the bare skin, but not tonight. Her core was tight and quivering, but her nervousness could not be told on her face. No. Miss Kitty had instructed her how to tilt her chin at a saucy angle and how to purse her lips just a little and smile so that it drew men's minds to her lips but kept them from the secrets and thoughts hidden behind her eyes. So that was how she set her face as she watched what was going on below.

Days ago, she'd passed, shocked after seeing the men who came to the establishment nuzzle Ruby's large breasts, which the woman always kept on daring display and corseted so high, they looked as if they would pop out at any moment. More than one man smacked, pawed, or pinched Onyx's round, plump derriere. Each of her fellow housemates laughed, smiled, teased, and cajoled the men with such grace and each, whether the men were young and so nervous about being in a whore house or an old wiry and sly man. They didn't even seem to discriminate on looks. Caroline watched as one after another man was led up the stairs to the lady's rooms for a time then left with a smile and more than one naughty comment and a little lighter in coin. Caroline had been taught about pricing and how each man would pay before services were rendered. If any of the women had an issue with a client, which Miss Kitty told her they called them, all they had to do was alert Woody or Smitty about the situation.

The two were gentle giants to all those who resided within the Harlot and the Heroes walls, but they were bruiser and order keepers to everyone else. If a man got too aggressive or handsy in the front room or the gaming room, they escorted them out, never making a scene inside.

Her fellow Jewels usually escorted the men to their door,

a signal to the house guards that they were all right, then Caroline knew they would hide their coin until the end of the night when they paid a portion to Miss Kitty and freshened up. Both those things Caroline was too familiar with now, as well as other skills she'd been trained to perform over the last three weeks.

The thumping of a bed against the wall and the groans from men, accompanied by the fake, theatric moans of her fellow Jewels made Caroline's body shake with cold chills. The loud piano music by Mr. Clay barely drowned much of it out at her post upstairs. Caroline stared over the crowd and tried not to think of the fact that in less than a week, that would be her downstairs and upstairs through the night, with a different man thrusting between her thighs. Bellmore came around at least three times a week, sat at the bar and stared at her for an hour or so. The heat in his gaze made her skin crawl with the thought of him touching her. After a couple drinks at the bar, he'd wink at her before he claimed one of the other ladies, showing no difference to any of them. It was clear to her that the Jewels were familiar with his attentions. They rarely questioned him but only greeted him with one of sala-cious, facsimile smiles they gave other men they took to their rooms. When they would pass where she stood by the railing, he barely acknowledged her, but shortly after the door closed, the woman would seem extra loud in her cries and groans of passion. Caroline wasn't sure what kind of skills Bellmore had and she refused to inquire but got the impression the exuberant noise was all for her benefit, a warning of such. When he left the room, he would pause briefly behind her and chuckle. "Soon," he'd occasionally say. At times, he'd whisper something to Miss Kitty on the way out.

Her feet pained her in the high kid boots that her employer told her would lift her backside becomingly. Her boss made her walk the front room and the stairs for an hour each day, to train herself to move in them without toppling over as she did the first few days. She also made Caroline recite all the various erotic names of male and female genitalia, so she would be comfortable in saying them without blushing or giggling. Now she could strut in the boots smoothly and utter each word mindlessly without a pause.

She was thankful that, tonight, he was absent from his perch. The evening was almost over, and in a little over an hour it would be dawn. Most of the men had already spent themselves in women, on booze, or cards. When the door opened an hour before the evening was done, Caroline's feet were aching and her eyes felt gritty from being up so late. Even after the weeks she had been there, she still had not gotten used to staying up through the night. She forgot all that when she saw the man who entered. He met Smitty, who was monitoring the front door now, eye to eye. The man still wore his black cowboy hat, like most of the men there who were courting the Jewels. She'd discovered that etiquette was different in a whorehouse—men kept their hats and boots on, always.

This man, with his broad shoulders and biceps and chest that posed a threat to the seams of his faded red shirt, with dusty grey britches that hugged hips and thighs and other male places she still felt too uncomfortable to stare upon, was a specimen like no other. It wasn't simply because he wasn't wearing his Sunday best or dressed up like a dandy like a lot of the men who frequented Miss Kitty's place, because the owner demanded a certain level of decency from the patrons. This man seemed to buck all that tonight.

'If I'm requirin' my Jewels to give you their best in dress and skill, then you can bathe after havin' your hands buried in dirt, animals, and shit before you come into my place.' Caroline thought of the bold woman's words she usually had to repeat at least twice a night, mostly to newcomers or those out of towners. It had shocked Caroline to discover that men came from miles around to spend time flirting with or a few moments in the bed of the Jewels of the Harlot and the Hero.

The man continued to speak to Smitty as he nodded occasionally to both the men and the ladies who greeted him around the room. When his gaze landed on Miss Kitty's, who was speaking with the bartender, the owner's smile broadened as she held up her palm and let him know she'd be right with him.

The man nodded, patted Smitty on the back as he stepped to the side of the door, not entering any further. Smitty said something to him as he passed and the man chuckled, his chin tipped up and revealed most of his face under the bright, flickering candlelight of the massive crystal candelabra that hung over the room.

Garrett Rand.

She would recognize him with sleep-hazed eyes or not; the man always made her heart flip. Even when she didn't want to have a response to him, her body tingled and heated in her intimate places. This man could make her body hum and throb, making the pulses she often felt being bombarded with all the sexual sounds that filled the upper level of the brothel seem like a mild purr of a kitten. Just one look at him, made her insides come alive. Nervous that he would spot her, she moved to the side by the wall. Not completely hiding herself, no, because when she'd done that the first two nights, she'd been instructed to stand at the upper banister. Miss Kitty had sashayed up the stairs and explained to her that if she were having trouble keeping her wares on display upstairs, then maybe downstairs in the center of the room would be easier.

Caroline had fully comprehended the threat and had rooted her feet to the floor for the last two weeks. Right now, she'd take her chances with the warning and at least try to place herself mostly in the shadows of the light caused by the three rooms in the back hallway. Her own place of employment, as she thought of her room since she'd been made to stay out of it to draw higher bids and more customers, was only a few steps behind her, across the thick carpeted runner. If she dashed backwards into it, how long would it take for Miss Kitty to realize she was missing from her post? Perhaps by that time, Garrett Rand would already be gone or in one of the other women's rooms.

That latter thought caused her heart to sink into her belly like a boulder at the bottom of the Kansas River. Where her body had once throbbed, it ached to think of him doing the things she had been studying and practicing with another woman.

She tugged at the veil again and made sure it was as low as it could go, even though still barely clearing the tip of her nose. It seemed that no other male from Grover Town who frequented the establishment recognized her, and she thought herself a ninny for even being worried Garrett Rand would. Her interactions with him had been few, precious. With all the ladies she heard, more than once, who milled around in the mercantile shopping and placing orders, going on about him and the lovely Jillian Pettigrew, she didn't stand a chance catching his eye or holding his interest. Now, once it was discovered she was employed in this place, he'd only ever see her as a whore. She'd be lucky if, once she'd done the deed with Bellmore, if Garrett Rand would pay a few coins to toss up her skirts.

Her throat became thick, tight and the muscles around her neck filled with pain as she fought hard to suppress emotions that shocked her even as they rose from her core and surrounded her heart like a fist. The shame and loss she was now feeling disturbed her; it was more intense then when she had awakened from fainting and realized her future was tied, for the foreseeable future, to this place.

Still standing half in the shadows, she continued to watch the man as he leaned against the wall between two windows, not too far from Miss Kitty's office door, appearing to patiently wait for the owner. She wondered what he would need to speak to Miss Kitty about. However, her mind never had a chance to continue that path as she spotted Diamond strutting boldly toward him, her inky locks shining as they spilled around her bare back and shoulders. The pale-yellow satin of her dress glimmered from the multiple tiny crystal beads and sequins adorning the bosom and hem of the gown with each sway of her full hips.

Men she passed were letting out low whistles, and a couple of them tried to catch her hands to halt her journey and tempt her to them. Diamond flirted and flitted away from them in a taunting, yet clever escape, offering promising words about her return.

Even though Diamond was across the room from Garrett, and the woman had a way to go to reach him, Caroline, from her vantage point, could clearly track where the Jewel was headed. She shifted her gaze back to the man the other Jewel had her sights set on, and she'd been fascinated. Garrett still stood by the window waiting patiently on the madam as Miss Kitty made rounds, checking on both patrons and Jewels, and then he tipped his head up. Caroline's lungs seized. Her breath became trapped in her lungs when her gaze all but collided with Garrett's. She started to step back, moving deeper into the shadows, but she doubted if he could tell from the distance and the veil who she was; no other visitor had.

Even with the gulf of space between them and her height advantage, the intensity of his gaze caused her belly to quiver and heat to swell so large there, it consumed her entirely. Her fingertips trembled along the high polished banister she gripped. She licked the seam of her top lip in her nervousness, and she swore he tracked the movement. One after another image and picture played in her mind that she had been forced to study over the weeks, but now those sketches had real bodies and real faces—hers and Garrett's.

It was him on top of her, behind her, touching her, licking her in places no man should place his mouth. Her mind was whirling, and her body was on fire, her imagination taunted with her own moans and whimpers that weren't manufactured or fake as the Jewels could do on cue and Miss Kitty rehearsed with her. No, every vibration in her body told her they would be real. That lying with Garrett would be true pleasure and he'd hold and caress her skin like she was his world.

This is ridiculous. She was starting to talk like Diamond, who always chattered on about a man sweeping her away from the life of whoredom. Caroline chided her body on its response as her heart raced so fast, it took her several deep inhalations to get it to calm even a fraction. When his gaze dropped to her small, pert breast hoisted high above the edge of the bodice by design and cinching of a tight corset, it was easy to brush Garrett's ardent attentions to the same corner as all the men who had taken a shine to her.

Garrett Rand only saw a whore before him, whom he wanted to possess for a fee.

GARRETT WANTED TO POSSESS HER.

Fuck. He rose to his full height and started away from his spot by the wall to do just that when Diamond stepped before him.

"Evenin', Mr. Garrett Rand," the lovely Jewel with the big bright eyes whispered his name in a sultry tone, as she always did, a way that constantly made him feel as if she was trying it on for size. But instead of his name, it would be hers.

The times they had spent together in the past, she'd asked him to call her Shannon, but he never did. In his mind, she was always Diamond. However, not wanting to offend her, and expecting it was what she said to all the men who paid for time in her bed, he just never addressed her by name; darlin' worked well enough.

He lowered his gaze from the woman at the railing above, to the pretty one who had been his favorite for a time. Even though it had been more than several months since he'd been with her, it wasn't in him to be cruel to a woman, even in the slightest. "Hello, Diamond, you're radiant tonight as always."

She smiled at him and coyly slid her gaze along his body and back up. "Why, thank you. It's been so long since I've had your company, I didn't think you'd noticed me anymore," the deep, southern texture of her voice teased as she seductively rolled a bare slender shoulder back, a gesture that somehow made her back arch and her gloriously plump breasts sit up higher.

There were times before that, such a movement would have had his mind fixated on baring her tits before him in her yellow room upstairs. He was a breast man, and Diamond had quite the pair, but tonight, it didn't even stir his blood. For well over a year, he'd been after a little more than a warm body in bed. Hell, what he was after was a little more than fifty feet away from him.

"Not notice you. That's impossible, darlin'. You light up this room more than the chandelier above."

Diamond giggled, a coquettish sound that ended on an artistic moan, meant to set a man's cock to risin' with one goal in mind, making the woman do it again as he was buried inside of her. "So, is there something I can do for you tonight, Garrett Rand?"

When she stepped toward him and placed a hand on his bicep as she stared into his eyes, kohl outlining hers, his body recoiled inside. His response shocked him. This was sweet, vivacious Diamond, who had brought him to pleasure with her superior talent more times than he could count on both hands, but it was as if now that he was mere feet from someone else he'd wanted for so long, his body was rebelling against any other.

"Sorry, darlin', not tonight. I've only got a few minutes before I'm ridin' out of town to assist my brother. Reason I ain't even dressed properly to make a house call here." Let her down easy. During the times he'd spent with Diamond, he knew she had hopes that one day she and her two children would be accepted and cared for by a man and she could be a full-time wife and mother. What he also knew was that man wasn't him, and he never led her on to believin' it would. It wasn't even because she was a whore, but more to do with he'd already had dreams of another woman in that place in his life.

"You sure you can't be tempted? A man shouldn't have to be out on a lonely road unsatisfied." She licked her lips, making the paint that colored them red as an apple glisten. "It'll only take a moment, I promise."

He knew exactly what she was offering, and his rebellious cock did jerk once; it was semi-erect now, but not because of Diamond. He could be a horny son of a bitch when it came to sex, like any other man, but he made it a point not to drive into one woman while he thought of another. Even a whore was worth more than that.

"If I did, I think Carl would flay me." He had seen the man behind Diamond to the right of her shoulder. The tall, lanky, bowlegged man, who had about seven years on Garrett, was gripping his hat so hard in his hand, it would most likely only be fit to hold water.

Diamond must not recognize the significance of a man who removed his hat in a whore house, especially before a specific woman. Carl, a good man, who worked out at Chance Spencer's ranch, was more than a little besotted with the Jewel.

The woman beside him turned and looked at the man perched on a stool in the bar staring at her. "He's a bit long in the tooth. But nice. Always more generous than most to me. Not just in his tips, you know."

Yes, he knew what she meant but didn't want to think about another man's actions in the sheets.

"Well, I think Carl'd be more worth your time." He patted her hand as he drew it from his arm.

"Garrett, that took a minute. Didn't mean to keep you waiting." The madam of the Harlot and the Hero stepped before him. "Diamond, honey. Go show Carl the way out of his misery. I'd hate for Smitty to have to toss out a paying customer because he attacked poor Garrett."

"I was just goin', Miss Kitty." Diamond giggled again, offering Garrett a mischievous finger wave before she sashayed away.

Garrett exhaled.

"What's got you up so early, or so late? You're not my usual last call crowd." Miss Kitty set her hand on her ample hips, as she tilted her head to the side and assessed him.

"No. But I'm headed out shortly with the sheriff. He's got a situation and needed an extra set of hands."

"That s'plains your timin'. What's got you lookin' all twisted inside?" Her steady gaze held his. Miss Kitty was a wise woman who knew men, and it had been a relief to have her as a trusted friend who, more than once, had allowed him to unburden the weight on his shoulders with her. He was aware most thought something more was going on between them, but it gave them both a twisted pleasure to let them think it. Even though Rand and those at the brothel knew that Mr. Clay was the only man who'd shared the madam's bed for years.

"May we?" He gestured toward her office.

Her full lips curled into a beguiling smile as she slipped an arm through his and whispered in his ear as they walked, "You know this is driving the other men wild wonderin' what Garrett Rand is wieldin' in his britches to win over the head whore of this place."

He purposely let out a loud chuckle as he planted a kiss on her cheek for all to see before they stepped into her office then closed the door.

Miss Kitty laughed, a husky, clear sound, as she patted his arm then moved away. "Can I get you a scotch or whiskey?"

She had some of the best alcohol shipped in for her clients, just like she trained the best women. Miss Kitty was a savvy businesswoman, with one woman too many, now.

"No. I haven't had much sleep for a while now, and the alcohol will just steal the few remaining wits I have about me."

He stared down at the floor instead of his friend, attempting to select the right words because he could feel the roar of emotions going on inside of him and he was trying not to unleash them.

"What's eatin' at you, Garrett? You look as if you're about

to come apart from the inside out." Leaning back with her hips against her desk, she waited.

"Answer me this, BethAnn." He knew he was one of two people who used her real name. Before she'd had to run away from a sadistic in-law bent on fostering her out to every male coming to deal on the failing plantation, she'd been BethAnn Donnellson, a widow and mother of two.

The observant owner arched a brow, picking up on his agitated tone.

"What's she doin' here?" He held her gaze.

"You can't be talkin' about Diamond. I know she's hankerin' for a man to lead her out, but as far as it appears to me, you don't have no arrangement with her." She folded her arms under her ample bosom, the stance forcing them high in the deep valley of her black and rose striped gown. "So who specifically are you referrin' to?"

"Caroline Douglas," he growled, snatching his hat off then shoving a hand through his hair.

She didn't move. Didn't say a thing for a long moment.

Garrett was pretty damn good at waitin' someone else out. In this situation, his friend had a lot to answer about. The jolly music from beyond the door filled the space.

"Was she under your care?"

He held his arms wide. "Does that matter? I never figured you for a spoiler of innocents."

"You wait a cotton-pickin' minute..." Rising to her full height, her gaze hard, the top of her breasts flushed with the anger that filled her voice as she aimed a finger into her own chest. "I ain't never allowed no woman's virtue to be taken under my roof against her will. That goes for Pearl or any other of my Jewels."

He leaned in with his hands fisted on his hips. "I thought not. But how do you s'plain Pearl?" he spit the name out, the salacious moniker meant to make men think of a woman's pure virginal body, ashamed just saying it in reference to Caroline made his come to attention some. "She wouldn't have come here on her own."

Would she? He said the words, but he had to admit not to truly knowing her. Caroline Douglas wouldn't be the first to fall on hard times and seek out such employment; brothels were full of women for mainly that reason.

"You sure?" she tossed back.

That was the damn thing that branded him in the gut; he wasn't. It was easier to accuse his friend than consider the other. "Honestly, BethAnn, I don't know." That took some of the wind out of his sail. "Perhaps she didn't think she could handle the strenuous work that farm needed alone."

He glanced to the side and stared at the wall where a man held a naked woman in his arms with her head thrown back and a look of contentment and pleasure on the woman's face as the man pressed his lips against her ear. The painting, he'd seen more than once and was both sexual and intimate. The faces in the portrait shifted and became his and Caroline's. He'd wanted to be the one to care for her, but would she want that now that she'd experienced the independence of working in a whorehouse?

"She possibly could've decided that, Garrett, but she didn't have much choice in the matter." Miss Kitty sighed.

Those words snapped his attention back to his friend. "What do you mean, she had no choice?"

"That farm of theirs that you mentioned, Bellmore owns it."

"Yup." He shrugged. That was common knowledge. "Bellmore rents lots of property to folks. Most of the land ain't worth shit or the person don't have the know how to run the business venture." If the man wasn't one of the prominent members of the mayor's town council, Bellmore would've been brought to answer for the state of the lands he sold to poor folk. Most of them went belly up financially within a year of movin' to Grover Town with high hopes, only to be gone after the first good winter. It was a testament to Sam Douglas that he lasted out there all the years he did.

"True." She moved around her desk then settled into her seat. "What you may not know is just how deep in debt her land was. I doubt Caroline knew how far in that hole her papa had buried them. I'm sure he loved his girl, but he sho' didn't do right by her."

Dammit. It was worse than he thought. Garrett shook his head. "If she didn't come here on her own to raise the money, how'd she—"

"Bellmore. He's a silent owner here. I told you he backed me years ago, for what I didn't have. Hopefully, not for much longer." She rested her elbows on top of the high polished desk as she linked her fingers below her chin. "But he brought her here. Her debt, a large one, is on the books for him. She could be out of it in a year if she didn't take any of her nightly share."

"Motherfucker!" Garrett slammed his fist into his palm, wishing it was the slick, rich man's face.

"That he is," the madam confirmed.

"What's she owe? How long's she been here? Workin'?"

"A few weeks." She leaned back in her chair. "I'd have to get the ledger out of my safe to give you the exact figure, but Pearl owes somewhere in the field of two hundred and eighty dollars. Give or take another fifteen for all the garments and fittings she needed. The girl didn't even have a decent dress on her back."

He stepped forward and gripped the back of the chair across from her. Garrett tried not to calculate the cost of the acts in the place, which at one point in his life, he was all too familiar with, and think about all Caroline would have to do over the next two years to be paid in full. And that was if she gave a hundred percent of her earnings toward her debt. "After three weeks, is that what's remaining or where she started?"

"No, Garrett. She ain't even started yet." When his head popped up and he stared at her, she continued with a chuckle. "You men just think a woman lies on her back and spreads her thighs and figures out all she needs to do under a man. That may be right, down at the little saloon, but as *you* well know, my Jewels are highly trained professionals. Pearl was in need of a lot of training before I even let Bellmore start with her."

He claimed his full height at hearing that. "What? Bellmore hasn't had her yet?"

"Hell, no. And I told him I'll be takin' her full maidenhead price out of what's owed him, even if she does keep her portion," Miss Kitty declared.

"I'll pay."

"Look, Garrett, as much as I'd like to sell her virginity to you, Bellmore's already—"

"No." He sliced the hand still holding his hat through the air, cutting her words. "The whole debt. Three hundred flat should cover the back payments on the farm and the wardrobe, which most of it, you can keep."

She stood. "What are you about, Garrett Rand?"

He smiled at her. "I'm about to have me a wife."

The world-wise whore's eyes stretched wide. Garrett was pretty sure it had been too many years to count since she'd been shocked.

"Well, I'll be." Miss Kitty chuckled. "Now, we may be confidants and all, but I can't take no I-Owe-You on this one.

Bellmore will want to see cash money when I tell him his Pearl has already been plucked."

Garrett chuckled too. He knew his friend didn't doubt that he was good for it; his farm and dairy were more than successful. He'd ensured that was the case with his years of dedication and hard work, but business was business, no matter the kind. "Give me a piece of paper. I'll make a draft you can take to the bank first thing tomorrow."

Keeping one eyebrow arched high, she pulled open a desk drawer and passed him some parchment and a fountain pin, then a bottle of ink.

Moving closer to the desk, he picked up the pen and filled it. He then took only a moment to turn the paper into a bank draft with the agreed upon amount and his signature. Once he was done, he stood then passed the paper to her.

She looked it over briefly then nodded. "After I clear this at the bank tomorrow, you can come collect your bride."

"I'll need her to stay. Just until I get back if you don't mind."

"You sure you don't want her moved over to the Livingstons'. Save her reputation?"

"Trust me. Her reputation is secure. No one knows she's even here." He didn't tell her he knew this because he'd spent weeks combing the town for a hair of her, with none found, until now. "You've kept her face pretty well disguised."

"You figured it out?"

"I did." That was all he was going to say on the matter.

Her head tilted to the side as she assessed him. When he didn't volunteer any further information, she said, "I'll get one of the boys to bring her down, so we can tell her."

He held up a hand, halting her start around the desk. "I'd rather do it once I'm back." He fished a couple coins out of his pocket and set them on the desk. "That should cover her for food and board for the week."

"What do you suggest I do with a non-whore in a whorehouse for a week?" She slapped a hand on her hip as it shifted off-center and stared at him.

Backing toward the door, Garrett settled his hat back on his head. "Maybe keep on with that trainin' you was goin' on about." He winked at her before he turned and reached for the door.

"You're one lucky man, Garrett Rand, to be takin' home a virgin whore in a week."

Whistling, and feeling his chest finally releasing all the tension that had been around it for weeks, Garrett strutted out of the office. When he got to the door of the brothel, most of the patrons cleared out, and only a few echoes of grunts competed over the final tunes of Mr. Clay at the piano. He cast his gaze skyward toward the upper floor one last time. Pearl, Caroline Douglas, was no longer there. He didn't despair, knowing he'd come to claim her soon, and she'd be his.

NINE

"Jasmine." Holding the stopper with its short glass wand that glistened with oil beneath her nose, inhaling again, Caroline allowed the sweet, intoxicating notes to fill her senses. *Sweet. Exotic.* Those were the two words that came to mind as she sat at her vanity and took in the unique floral scent. This was how she spent her Sunday evenings in the brothel, the only day Miss Kitty closed the place to customers.

'Even whores can respect the Good Lord's day of rest.' The madam was constantly shocking Caroline with her words or actions. If anyone had ever told her that an owner of a brothel, a woman who openly talked about the years she'd spent beneath all types of men as if she were describing various teas, would still hold a belief in the Lord, or run a small private school for the bastards of whores, or value family time, she would have been shocked. Yes, this place was a house of ill-repute, but Miss Kitty never allowed the people who worked under her, in whatever capacity, to feel as if they were so morally corrupt, they didn't deserve favor and decency, or to give charity to those less fortunate. Just last

Sunday morning, the madam had Jewels and the children putting together care baskets filled with jams, jerky, and aged cheese to be delivered to a few families who had fallen on hard times. Smitty, Woody, and Donovan took the items around to people, to keep it respectable like, with a simple message that a neighbor in Grover Town was thinking about them. They never let on that it was Miss Kitty, the whore-house owner.

Caroline would have appreciated such thoughtfulness and well wishes with her papa, but unlike the anonymous baskets, there was no secret in town about her papa's staunch refusal of handouts, like he could do for himself. She'd always smiled and agreed with his prideful rants as he turned one person after another away who just wanted to help them in one way or another. However, in her belly, she would bemoan his words and actions because they had needed the help and goodwill of others. It was why she'd shamelessly accepted the replacement of eggs and the flour and meal she'd discovered in the basket on her way home two years ago. She'd hidden the packet of rose seeds someone had left for her in the wagon on her birthday a year ago, too, that had grown pretty roses and given her the idea of making soaps from the petals.

She wondered if it still sat next to the porch of their small old home or had Bellmore had them dug up and torn the place to the ground? There was no value in the house or land, just memories of her papa's blood and sweat and her silent tears. She'd been miserable and lonely there, but it had been her life. Sitting at her vanity now, in a beautifully decorated ivory room with multiple bottles of oils, creams, and powders before her, she felt ashamed that in some ways she'd been happier since she'd come to the Harlot and the Hero, no matter what circumstances had brought her here, or what she was expected to do within the spacious walls. She'd gained friends and a bodacious group of aunts of sorts in Miss Kitty, Mrs. Morrison, and Macey. Each of the older women was apt to drop one pearl of wisdom or another to teach things to Caroline that her mother never had a chance to do.

"Come in." Caroline opened her eyes and called out to the knock at her door, just as she replaced the stopper into the small vial to write down her impressions in the journal she kept with her ideas, her mother's handkerchief hanging from the back binding. A week after she'd been consigned to the whorehouse, she'd realized what she would save her share of her profits for. She planned to open a small perfume shop, where she could sell the soaps she made and various oils she could order from around the world. She knew she'd have to move to another town far away after years in the brothel of Grover Town. The townsfolks were accepting of others, even turned a blind eye to the thriving brothel on the outskirts of town, but them extending that acceptance to a reformed whore was beyond any amount of Christian charity, she was sure. Besides, she would want to be in a place where no one knew of her past sins. It was the reason she never went into town for any purpose like the other ladies did, dressed in the conservative calico and gingham dress. People in Grover Town knew her, and they would ask questions and begin to suspect when she couldn't come up with a plausible place of employment or quarters to lay her head at night.

She didn't know if she'd ever feel comfortable going into town again before she'd saved up enough to leave it.

"It smells like one of those French perfumeries Ruby always goin' on about them havin' on the bustlin' Bourbon Street in the heart of New Orleans." Dressed in a yellow satin and lace wrapper, Diamond waved a hand before her face as she attempted to mimic the creole accent of Ruby, but she failed miserably since her own sweet, backwoods country drawl mangled it.

It smelled wonderful to Caroline, who smiled at the mother of two. "Sorry about that. I got a little carried away today and forget how overpowering the smell can be to others when I keep my window closed. I'll open it."

Caroline did that because she had learned since being there, it was easier to not be distracted by other scents in the air competing with the one she was smelling and detect the notes. She rose and made to go over to the window and open it to allow in fresh air.

"After you open the window, Miss Kitty is askin' for you to join with the others of us down in the main room."

At the window, Caroline frowned and asked. "Did she say what for?" It was rare that the madam needed them for anything most of the day or night on Sundays. It being each of their days off, she let them do as they wished. Even house meetings were done on Saturday afternoon, an hour before dinner with the children.

"Aha, she did." Diamond's face lit up with a smile and there was a twinkle in her overly bright, big eyes. "So come quick; it'll be fun."

Caroline watched the other woman dash away with unbridled excitement, the yellow hem of her wrapper billowing up in a wave behind Diamond, caught on the breeze of her movements. She shrugged then slipped her hands under the edge of the window and pushed it up higher and allowed the balmy evening air to enter and decrease the oily scents that permeated the air. She took a moment to pop in her last piece of peppermint stick into her mouth, close her journal then return it to the nightstand beside her bed. The tray of oils she'd return later to Macey's supply closet, where she used them to place requested droplets into the bath waters of the Jewels each morning after the last customer left.

Not wanting to keep the people waiting for her long, she pulled on her own ivory, satin wrapper over her simple cotton shift she'd worn under her purple calico dress earlier then left her room. As she walked past the banister on the upper level, her usual viewing spot, she glanced down at the main room and noticed all the women were there like a naughty rainbow of colors as they sat in circle with their own designated shade connected to their moniker. The only time the Jewels were not in specific colors was at 'family' dinner, when they went into town, and during the day on Sunday.

Miss Kitty caught her gaze as Caroline made her way down the sweeping staircase. "Pearl, you're here. Come, come, so we can get started." In the one of four large chairs that normally peppered the area for the male clients to use, most times with one Jewel or another in his lap teasing him, the owner patted another of the seats that was still empty beside her.

Reaching the bottom of the stairs, Caroline turned and walked into the circle of laughing, giggling women. She would have thought she had joined a knitting club if it were not for the satin, silk, and lace wraps, or the wiggling eyebrows and naughty smiles of jeweled comrades. "What's going on?"

"Oh, you're going to love it." Onyx winked at her.

"Tomorrow, will be a big day for you," Jade teased in her heavy oriental-accented voice as she smiled.

"Me?" Caroline settled deeper into the soft chair, frowning, until it dawned on her what they were talking about. As she had been locked in a trance and smelling her scents, she'd blocked out the fact that tomorrow would place her here for a month and it would be the day Bellmore would come and claim his rights. The excitement she had felt and fed off in the room from the other ladies deflated inside of her and became a heavy weight in her core. She felt nauseous, not because she would start being a whore tomorrow—she had come to grips with that fact—more because it would be Bellmore who touched her first.

Why couldn't it be someone like Garrett Rand? She hadn't been able to stop thinking about him over the last week since he had come into the place. The kind, big, strong, ruggedly handsome man had been floating from the back to the front of her mind every day and filling her nights with vivid, erotic dreams. They always started off so innocent, like the two of them walking in a field of fresh prairie grass or sitting at a picnic along the river, but they quickly became erotic, causing her to wake in a panting sweat, damp and slick between her thighs.

'A whore rarely gets a choice on the clients she serves.' Another lesson from Miss Kitty.

That was for sure.

"Yes, love. Here, take this." Miss Kitty handed her a white, wooden box with flowers painted around the sides and over the lid and PEARL in a delicately slanted cursive in the center. "This is a gift from me and the girls."

Caroline set the box in her lap. It was wide but not as heavy as she would have believed when she saw it. She knew by the skill of the design who had painted it as she lightly slid her fingers over the artistry. "Jade, this is lovely. Thank you."

The Asian woman had a shy smile on her lips as she shrugged one small shoulder. "It is nothing. A woman should always have pretty, decorated things."

"Perhaps you're right." Sadly, Caroline mused, the only nice things she ever had were the items she'd gotten since coming to the Harlot and the Hero.

"Well, we can't let you start your sexual experiences

without your own personal box of accoutrements." Ruby's accent and sultry voice made everything she said sound like she was in a parlor giving tips on how to bake the perfect bread.

"Oh, of course not." Caroline was too nervous to open the box yet and she just let it sit in her lap. These women had freely discussed their escapades with her. Often, one or two of them would come into her room after the night's activities and tell her about a very randy customer or a difficult one. Rarely, one of them would talk about the man who, for a few moments, made them feel as if they were somewhere else, treat them like a lady and not a whore. They'd worked with Caroline on various techniques and skills, too.

"As you know, Pearl, all of the ladies service the men who come here, in common acts of sex, but each Jewel has perfected a certain skill they are notorious for within the house and several towns over." Miss Kitty crossed her thick thighs and tugged the edges of her purple wrap over them, covering the paleness of her bare legs. The collar of her apparel was adorned with a black animal fur that beckoned a person to reach out and touch it as the lapels ended in a vee at her breasts.

Frowning, Caroline glanced from one woman to the other. All their faces held secret smiles and gazes filled with gleeful naughtiness. Her nervousness increased, but so did her curiosity. Unable to restrain herself any longer, she unhooked the golden filigree latch keeping it closed then lifted the lid. She gasped as she stared inside, shocked at all the items within. Some of them, she felt were clear as to what they were for while others, she was perplexed. There was even a bundle at the back, wrapped tightly in white, delicate tissue paper with a thick, bold red ribbon cinching it closed.

"Remove whatever item you would like first, and the

woman responsible for placing it there will tell you about its use. Save the parcel for last, please," Miss Kitty instructed her.

Caroline swallowed; her finger trembled as she reached for a small glass jar with a dried leaf adhered to the top of it. It seemed safe, so she held it up.

"That is from me." Diamond was on the couch that had also been dragged from its usual place against the back wall to add to their circle. She was curled on her hip, with her feet tucked beneath her bottom. She smiled and clapped her hands, clearly excited that Caroline had selected her item first.

"What is it?" Caroline tipped the jar left and right as she eyed the thick, clear substance clinging to the side even as it rolled the other way. "It looks like syrup."

"That is what it is too. Mint syrup. Men enjoy oral stimulation and some like their cocks to be sucked to completion." She pointed at the jar. "Before you begin fellatio on any of the clients, stick your middle finger in the jar and place it all the way in your mouth, as far back as it can go. But don't swallow."

"Isn't that part of your art and skill?" Onyx teased the ebony-haired woman from the other end of the couch.

"Why, yes, it is." Diamond flicked her dark locks over her shoulder and giggled. "What you don't want, Pearl, is for most of the syrup to end up down your throat and then you're stuck with tasting a lot of the sour sweat and salt of a man, before he gets to the end, which can be an acquired taste." Diamond licked her lips, not seeming repulsed at all.

"Won't the man wonder what I am doing? Be suspicious?" Caroline unscrewed the jar and took a sniff. It smelled minty sweet and opened her nasal passage some.

"Oh, honey, you just tell him that you're simply givin' him a treat for his treat. To be honest, the mint may mask the taste a lot for you, but the coolness will give him an experience as well. Use your tongue to coat your mouth, then coat him."

She placed the jar back into the box then met the other woman's eyes across the room. "Does it taste like the trainer?"

"Heavens, no. It will not." Diamond looked appalled. "But like that rubber trainer Miss Kitty is fond of, most are at least wider than that narrow thing if not longer." The woman wiggled three fingers in the air.

All the other ladies and Miss Kitty laughed. Caroline blushed. She'd only seen the men in the drawings, and she wasn't sure how accurate the pictures were in size.

"You want to take it slow. Remember, Pearl, you control how fast and deep the man starts out in your mouth." Diamond gave her instructions about where to place her hand on the man's shaft. "Breath through your nose and stay relaxed." Diamond ran a hand along her throat as she tipped her head back. "It's easier to start out if you are lower than he is or leaning over a bed with your head upside down. Over him in a bed, will be more difficult if he thrusts too deep and your gag reflex kicks in, so keep that fist tight." She went on about tongue placement and movement for maximum stimulation. "Practice humming with something in your mouth; that drives them wild."

"Okay." Diamond's blatant instructions already made her feel as if there was something stuck in her throat. She had to swallow three times before the sensation went away. Miss Kitty had made her suck on a long rubber instrument one day until she had stopped gagging and choking every time it touched the back of her throat. She'd been thankful that Mrs. Morrison had made her a hot cup of tea with honey when she'd heard the raspiness of her voice. *Breath through the nose.*

"Choose the next item," Miss Kitty told her.

Caroline spotted a small box. She took it out and opened

it. Inside, nestled in crushed blue velvet, were two glass marbles about the size of a peach pit but smooth and round. When she was in the schoolhouse, boys had pitched marbles in the dirt all the time, but they were never as big as the two balls she held in her palm now. She glanced around the room as she wondered what they were used for.

"Those are from me." Sapphire sat with her legs crossed in a high back chair and her robe split high up her thighs, with the long length of her limbs revealed, brazen in her sexuality. "Once that pesky maidenhead of yours is gone," she waved a hand in the air as if she were shooing away a fly, "you will insert those balls into your pussy...all the way up."

"They will fall out more than a few times," Diamond sighed. "Especially because they shift against each other inside of you and make you wet, and the next thing you know, they're rollin' around on the floor."

The other women laughed at Diamond's description.

"Have you gotten them to stay yet, Diamond?" Sapphire twirled a lock of her beautiful blonde hair around one finger.

"Once." Diamond pouted. "Suckin' em off is easy. And trust me, Pearl, once they're in your sex, a man just keeps pumpin' away so fast, he can't tell if you can do nuthin' fancy around him no how."

"Oh, he can tell." Sapphire shook her head as she leaned in. "You learn to control your most important muscles, the vaginal walls, in the bedroom around a man's shaft, squeezing and flexing like you're milkin' teats on a cow, and you will have him seein' stars and singin' your praises. Running to you at every chance for you to do it again."

It was the way Sapphire was holding her gaze so intensely and talking about the area between her thighs, Caroline actually felt those muscles clench and release multiple times, making shivers travel up along her spine. She bit the inside of her bottom lip to suppress the sensation.

"All of you ladies get accolades for your talents." Miss Kitty's voice was still filled with humor as she calmed the small disagreement then encouraged Caroline to continue.

The balls went back in, and Caroline took out a leather covered wooden paddle with thin leather thongs around the handle of it. With a stomach full of trepidation, she stared around the room searching for the woman who had given her such an item. She wasn't a complete fool. Standing close to the rooms each night, she'd heard the smacking sounds coming from different rooms on occasion. One in particular, Jade's.

The small Asian woman's feet dangled a foot off the floor as she sat in one of the high backed chairs. Her small mouth pulled into a wide smile as she wiggled her toes at the end of her legs as they scissored below the knee, causing the hem of her green robe to dance. "Those are from me. Most men, even if they don't confess it, enjoy tying up a woman and having their wicked way with her if given the option."

"Don't that scare you? I mean, you wouldn't be able to escape if you don't like something." Caroline stroked the edge of one of the butter soft straps between her fingers. The binds most likely would not hurt or leave a mark, but they would hold tight.

"I'll warn you, it's all based on trust," the woman declared in her broken dialect. "Some of these ranch hands, I wouldn't let bind my pinky finger to a grain of rice. It is my job, so I give Smitty or Woody a signal." She paused and brushed her delicate fingers over the edge of her ear then dragged that same finger over her chin. "They know then to watch out for how long I am in the room with them. If too long, they come in. If, when they leave, I don't come out with them to let them know

I am okay, then they take the man for a walk and set him straight."

"None of my Jewels are mistreated under my roof, as we have spoken about before. They may be whores, but they *will* be respected in this house." Miss Kitty was usually calm and controlled until situations occurred that threated the safety or livelihood of the women.

Caroline had seen at least once a week a rowdy man, usually someone new to the town, get escorted off the property, without making a scene inside the house.

"I can figure out that the paddle is for spanking." She'd seen illustrations of such acts as well, and Caroline didn't think she'd enjoy such an act at all.

"Oh, yes." Jade's almond complexion had a tinge of red as she fanned herself. "Just the right amount of pain can be pleasurable. Some of the men who come here are good at it. Very. Consider *yourself* lucky."

There was something in the other woman's dark, almond-shaped eyes, as if she were trying to communicate something significant to her. Caroline smiled but was shaking her head inside. *Lucky. Not likely.* Her only luck was that she had ended up at the Harlot and the Hero and not the little saloon.

Miss Kitty cleared her throat. "What else is in there, Pearl?"

There was a small brown vial inside that she removed then opened. Instantly, Caroline recognized the dual scents. "Sage and lavender."

"Very good. It's all about the hands." Oynx sat on the other side of her, held up her hands and waved her fingers in the air. "It's all about how you touch a man. The men who come here work hard in their various trades, and being able to close their eyes for a moment and let a naked woman rub all over those tired muscles, and one excited muscle, is Heaven to them.

Sometimes you can get them to the happy ending without you wearing all their sweat when it is over." She let out a peel of laughter and shimmied her shoulders.

The other ladies joined in.

Caroline couldn't help smiling. She took one more sniff of the oil before screwing back on the top and putting it back in. "If I come by your room after this. Do you mind showing me a few techniques?"

"It'd be my pleasure."

"Thank you." It was one skill Caroline hadn't had a chance to practice, and she was happy it was something that didn't seem so intimate. Looking in the box once again, she saw an item wrapped in a red silk cloth beside a short jar. She opted for the short, stout, white jar with the unmarked silver lid. It seemed safe. She figured it was either something else to eat or rub on herself, like a night cream.

"The wrapped item and the jar of cream go together." Ruby spoke up.

"Oh." Caroline hadn't expected that. She reached in with her other hand and carefully began to unwrap the item.

"It's for your derriere, backside, bum, rosebud...your ass." Ruby was nothing if not blunt.

"It goes where?" Caroline stared at the woman sitting on the other side of Miss Kitty, across the room from her, as she held the small, phallic-shaped object, about the width of her thumb and length of her pointer finger, with a wide flat base.

After all the education the Jewels had given her, this one was the one that shocked and appalled her the most. Caroline licked her lips trying to figure out just how the combo would work. "Do I rub the cream on my bottom?"

"Not if you intend for him entering you to go easy." Ruby's smile was broad, with her lips bare of paint, but they still held a red stain from the years of coloring them. The bodacious redhead was dressed in a silk, wine rapper, cinched tightly at her impressively small waist.

Caroline felt flushed and hot just trying to make out what the older woman was getting at. There were several positions in the illustrated journals she'd seen more times than she would have liked. "In the drawing, it looked like the man was always...you know..." She set the items back in the box, feeling like they burned her fingers just holding them, but she stared down at them. "Going into her sex."

"As a whore," Ruby began.

"Even as a wife," Miss Kitty added.

"A man likes a little wicked pleasure. He enjoys knowing he has access to all of you. Trust me, lovely innocent one, putting that wood cock in for a couple hours a day will make the going of it all a lot easier on you," Ruby advised.

Speechless, Caroline nodded. Just as her sex had tightened with Sapphire's discussion, the muscles surrounding her rear hole drew in with a snap, not even able to conceive such an act. They remained clenched for a moment, as her mind was swimming, heart was pounding, and she was both feverish and sweating from the conversation. She felt hesitant now in the remaining item. The wrapped bundle appeared so innocent, but as she'd just learned over the last hour, nothing was ever innocent in a whorehouse, including her, by tomorrow night.

"Pearl." Miss Kitty placed a hand over hers.

Caroline didn't realize she had been clutching the carved wood of the arm of the chair until the tension began to leave at the madam's touch. She forced herself to relax her grip as she glanced beside her.

"It's all right to be apprehensive about it all. Sex is always more of an undertaking for us women then a man ever must deal with. None of us, not even Ruby, didn't experience anxiety their first time and many others."

Caroline nodded as she took in a calming breath. The overwhelming tension in her body released some and she was able to feel herself relax all over. She reached inside of the crowded box of eroticism and withdrew the last thing. She practically let out a sigh of relief, not because she figured out what it was, but it was the possibility that this tutorial session would end soon. Hopefully.

Carefully, she undid the precious silk, red ribbon from around it. The bundle was wrapped tightly but was still as long as the box it was in. She could feel that whatever was inside of it was soft and pliable in her fingers as she held it in one hand. Pulling away the layers of tissue paper around it, she spotted the most delicate of material. Her first thought was that it was some sort of handkerchief. It was both lacy and gauzy. It was ice white, reminding her of the shocking hue of the chunks of ice Henry Russell and his hired hands cut out of the frozen lakes in later winter to fill the icehouse for the town to purchase for use through the other seasons.

She set the open paper in the box aside, then, with ginger fingers, she lifted the creation and quickly realized it was much longer than a handkerchief. It was the length of a curtain panel that covered the room windows. It took shape and she gasped.

"It's b-beautiful," Caroline stammered, because it was the loveliest nightgown she'd ever laid eyes upon, but it was utterly transparent. The sleeves were long and lace, an intricate floral pattern, most likely made in Belgium somewhere, with the hem of the apparel embroidered in the same material. However, the longest section in between the lace, the part that would cover most of her body was a gauzy, flimsy, delicate organza. The single layer fabric was often used for a woman's wedding veil instead of something to sleep in. Nothing would be hidden behind it.

Her mind conjured up an image of her standing before Bellmore in it, and it took all her efforts to hold down the simple meal of cheese, cold meat slices, and bread she'd consumed two hours ago in her room. Swallowing once, twice, and holding her breath for a five count before she slowly exhaled, allowed her to not only keep herself together, but to smile, a real smile of gratitude.

"It's the loveliest thing I've ever owned." Which was saying a lot, since her wardrobe and dresser upstairs were filled with many silk, satin and lace things. However, the gown she was now folding and returning to its wrapping was breathtaking, in so many ways and only hers, not previously worn by anyone else.

"I'm glad you like it." Miss Kitty patted her knee and returned her smile. The perceptive madam held her gaze and Caroline had no doubt she wasn't fooled over the false cheer.

If it weren't for the items, women, and place, Caroline could have imagined this gathering was one of those rumored bridal shower events she'd occasionally heard discussed by women, in the mercantile or out on the lawn after church service, offering invites. It was a custom that came over from England that a few of the more affluent residents of Grover Town began locally. However, it wasn't the case. No new bride got the education she'd had not only today, but the month leading up to it.

"We'll talk more tomorrow."

"I have tea and cakes, Jewels." Miss Debra pushed through the swinging door that led into the kitchen, with a large copper tray in her hands. There wasn't really a place for the tray so the short Indian woman made her way through the chairs then paused before each of the ladies so that they could remove the saucer, selecting cake and a cup of tea.

By the time she arrived before them, Caroline had placed the closed wooden box on the floor beside the foot of her chair. She was grateful for the hot tea, hoping it would warm her inside and settle her nerves. She chose only two tea cakes, loving how pretty the small white iced confection was decorated with candied bits of oranges along the top.

"Thank you, Miss Debra."

"Don't fear tomorrow; it will come anyway. Never let the mind shape the story before it has even happened." The woman's soulful brown gaze held hers for a moment, causing the mystery and wisdom of her words to set in on Caroline.

"I'll try." It was the most honest thing Caroline could say. She wasn't sure how she was going to put aside her thoughts and fears of the next night, but she would work hard not to think about it until she had to.

After a small nod that barely moved the older Indian woman's head, Miss Debra stepped away and headed back to the kitchen.

"You don't want anything?" Caroline asked as Debra never offered anything to Miss Kitty.

"Mr. Clay and I got a few plans. It seems there's an anniversary of sorts between us."

As if on cue, the front door opened, and Mr. Clay came strutting in carrying a brown paper wrapped parcel and a box with twine around it. He greeted the ladies in the room but didn't move deeper into the space. When his gaze moved to the only person he had eyes for, he smiled.

Miss Kitty's ample frame rose with a smooth elegance Caroline could only imagine she'd be able to achieve one day.

"Good night, Jewels," the owner called out without turning toward them as she continued her sultry glide toward the thin, older man. When she reached him, he held out an elbow for her to take.

Caroline's heart swelled as the two walked in step together toward Miss Kitty's office door that would lead into her room on the other side. Watching them, Caroline surmised that no man had ever escorted a woman with more refinement on a date.

He loves her.

Seeing such clear adoration made her heart sink. She had always wanted love from a husband, but unlike Diamond, Caroline closed herself off to such a ridiculous hope. Who would want to marry a whore?

Assuming the situation must be commonplace, because none of the other ladies paid the situation much heed as they nibbled and talked loudly with each other, Caroline turned back to the other ladies and took in the rambunctious conversation around her. She was happy to hear that the discussion had moved away from sexual acts and now focused around the day's activities of mothers and children, or what the women had done on their Sunday off.

Barely offering much to the conversation at hand, Caroline sank her teeth into the small square and enjoyed the orange marmalade nestled between the two thin layers of cake. Her mouth filled with the sweet taste and she stifled a moan as she savored it. She'd never tire of having sweets to eat. The strong bite of the warm black tea helped her relax and ponder how much her life had changed in a little less than four weeks. It wasn't all the sexual things she now had a better understanding of. No. She looked around at the laughing and teasing going on among the other women. It was the camaraderie and friendship. She hadn't experienced it since she was in the schoolhouse and had a friend whom she could talk with. There was more than a handful of them now.

She still missed Isabel Reynolds, who was married with children now. However, that relationship was over. Caroline's father was no longer hindering the friendship by working her to the bones, but her employment now made associating with a respectable woman an impossibility.

Caroline's heart sank with the thought, but she didn't allow her mind to stay there. Instead, she joined in on the conversation around her. Tomorrow, was time enough to worry about what was and what never would be again.

TEN

"There you go, Marigold. Nice work." Garrett was in the stall on one side of the cow who lay on a bed of dried stalk, while across from the massive girth, was Lyle, his new foreman, in the same hunched position as they watched the calving moment. It was her first calf and he and his right hand had been out there for hours with her, making sure she didn't have any trouble.

"The head's out now." Lyle's voice was as steady as his own as the foreman poured more fresh water from a bucket he'd filled at the ranch well into the shallow bowl, before the cow. It was important that the cow stayed hydrated during the birthing.

Outside of that, if nothing went wrong, the first-time mother wouldn't need anything else from them. They were both close but kept their distance in the wide stall. Cows were docile creatures for the most part, but still big beasts, and even an accidental kick during a contraction could knock a grown man on his ass. The impact could take out a few ribs, kneecap, or leave him unconscious, only to walk away senseless if it landed against his head.

Garrett had acquired the new mother right before last Christmas to help a new family who had moved to the area and couldn't farm a plot of bad land and were headed west before the weather turned bad. Another property of Bellmore. The jackass. Garrett's purchase of the two-year old heifer from them helped sure up the family's funds for their journey. They had kept the two goats to provide milk for their small children, more sturdy animals for the long journey. Now, he couldn't help but smile as the new life came forth, even as the sac-covered, wet, narrow-legged calf slid from his mother. There was a gut clenching stench that permeated the hot air around them, a combination of bovine sweat, soiled hay, and blood. However, it was all still wonderous to him.

His mind couldn't help thinking about what it would be like for another mother, his soon-to-be wife, to birth his child, a son to carry on his name or a daughter as beautiful as her mother.

He hadn't bred Marigold at the time he'd taken the bull to the others, because he wanted her to be comfortable in her new surroundings.

Now that the head was fully out, Garrett, at the back end of the cow above the pine, reached out with a firm but ginger hand to puncture and remove the film covering the calf's face. The slimy, thin membrane came away with a gentle tug as amniotic fluid poured out from it and saturated the ground. The heavy odor that accompanied new life became stronger around them. He rubbed a sure hand over the nostrils and muzzle, to ensure all the tough film was completely cleared from the face so the newborn could take a clean first breath. If too much of the mother's fluids got into the air passage and lungs, it could spell trouble, a risk Garrett did all to avoid.

Marigold continued with low, throaty moos through a few more contractions as she brought forth her little one. The small, coal eyes opened as the calf began making small sounds and wiggling on the ground. Once the last of the calf was out, Marigold sprang to her four hooves and turned to it and started licking along the newborn's wet fur. She comforted and greeted the calf as her tail swung back and forth, flinging her switch from left to right, a show of excited maternal pride.

"You son of a bitch, Rand!"

Jerking his head right at the vehement outcry, through the thick slats of wood that made up the fencing of the stalls in the barn where he kept the cows when it was close to their breeding time, Garrett spotted Bellmore. The angry, immaculate form came through the wall that two of Garrett's ranch hands had made to keep the man from moving any deeper into the barn.

Rising slowly, he took in the tailored black suit, starched white shirt, bolo tie, and Bowler hat with a small jade green and indigo feather fastened along the white ribbon that went around it. Garrett wanted to laugh at the man's get up. Bellmore stuck out like a sore thumb before the two burly men dressed like Garrett and all the other men on the farm in plaid shirts, dark britches, dusty cowboy boots and a well-worn cowboy hat to finish it off.

"There's a pile of cow shit on two legs," Lyle uttered, louder than they'd been speaking around the cow before.

Garrett chuckled in agreement. He stood after a sharp nod to Lyle, signaling his foreman to take over with Marigold and the unnamed calf. He walked to the stall door and unlatched it then exited, keeping an eye on the angry, slim man the entire time.

Catching his gaze, Bellmore ranted more. "Your ass had no right."

"You on your way to some ball, Bellmore? Why the extra shine of your normal get up?" Sauntering up the aisle between the row of stalls toward the front, Garrett couldn't help taunting the pampered, crooked property owner. Garrett was pretty clear on the reason behind Bellmore's rage.

He stepped between the opening of the big shoulders of his workers to get them to part ways so Garrett could step before the angry man, not giving two shits about the excrement still dampening his hands. "I got this, boys."

"Let us know, boss," one of the men stated as they both headed back out to the fields where Garrett grew the corn, alfalfa, and oats for the feed for his cows.

"Don't act ignorant with me, you milk soaked fuckin' goon." Bellmore shoved a finger about a foot away from Garrett's face.

Garrett arched a brow as he stared into the deep red face and bulging blue eyes of the Grover Town dandy. He'd allow Bellmore this one pass, knowing just what the man had lost that had him in such an uproar. However, if he approached him ever again on the subject, Garrett would lay him low. Caroline was his, and Garrett had always protected what was rightfully his and she fell under the same awning, even though he'd yet to make her his wife.

"You're unsettlin' the work on my land. State your piece, then get off my property, before I have your ass tossed off it."

"Caroline Douglas," Bellmore hissed the name as he lowered his hand and balled it into a fist along his side like the other.

Garrett almost wished the man were ballsy enough to take a swing at him, so he could let his fist fly into his face. There was no love lost between him and Bellmore, but they usually had no dealings, so it was easy for them to skirt each other. Samuel Douglas' loan was just the kind of sneaky deals Bellmore managed, always just a hair shy from criminal conduct.

"What about her?" Garrett folded his arms over his chest as he widened his stance, preparing himself just in case.

"She's mine," he grumbled as his top thin lip turned up in a sneer. "I've waited for weeks because Kitty whined about her needing training. And on the day set for me to claim her, I get a note delivered to my office inviting me for a meeting. When I arrive at the whorehouse, Kitty hands me cash money while informing me I'm welcome to come tonight and be entertained by any of the other ladies, but Pearl is *no longer available.*" The last three words came out in a low, menacing whisper.

The sound may have sent shivers along the spine of a weaker man or one of the hopeful, hapless saps who bought into the weaved dreams Bellmore sold them, but Garrett was another thing. Unfazed, Garrett offered a smile even as he kept a sharp eye on the man. "You heard the madam; choose another."

Garrett wasn't shocked to discover that Miss Kitty had promptly informed Bellmore that their deal surrounding Caroline Douglas was off. He'd returned from helping the sheriff during the wee hours, and at daybreak, he'd sent one of his young workers over to the brothel with a letter to inform the madam he'd be there at the work day's end to collect his bride. He'd have thought the brothel owner would have set Bellmore straight the next day when she cleared the draft at the bank, but she'd kept Caroline safe at the house for over a week, so he wasn't going to hold that against the older woman.

"You had no right to her." Bellmore's arms jerked down as if he were slamming his fists into the ground.

"No," Garrett growled as he leaned forward just enough to place less than a foot between their faces. "You've no right to her. Caroline is mine. I won't repeat that to you. So, keep away from her."

They locked eyes as Bellmore's chest rose and fell high from his rapid breaths.

Then as quickly as a maid could wash away heavy soot from a window, Bellmore's face shifted into a cunning smile. He glanced down and plucked at the white cuffs of his sleeves, adorned with jade and gold cufflinks that were sticking out at the bottom of suit jacket sleeve. "You know what. All coin is fair when dealing with whores. I wanted fresh, but that's only something that lasts but a moment. Virgins have a custom of being tepid bores as fucks anyway. What do you say you give me a heads up once you tire of her and I'll benefit from the nights of your uncouth randy attention putting all her book knowledge to actual practice?"

Hearing Bellmore's words, Garrett didn't move more than to cock his head to the side. "That'll never happen."

"Why not?" Bellmore's eyes were wide, filled with curiosity and trouble.

"I'm takin' her to wife."

Silence.

There was no sound between them, but around them, the work of the Rand Farm continued as men shouted, cows mooed, and the women's songs rang out from the dairy house.

Bellmore gaped mouth showed the level of his shock. "You can't be serious."

"I am. Mind you keep your tongue about where she's been since her pa's death, and I won't inform the Town Council about how you treat innocent, grief-stricken women."

Bellmore's mouth snapped shut. Garrett was sure it was that threat that would surely ruin Bellmore's reputation in town and send him and his snotty mother fleeing. For a moment, Garrett considered saying something anyway, but he knew it would hurt Caroline more if people discovered where she had been. They would speculate about the month she'd been under the roof and no one would believe she hadn't been on her back all that time. It didn't matter a hill of beans none to him, but he'd do everything in his power to protect her, much better than her pa had.

"A whore is a whore is a whore. Even a virgin one. She knows and has seen too much. She won't ever be satisfied with just one man." He offered a sly smile. "You'll see; this isn't over."

"But it is. Now get off my fuckin' property." Garrett took a step toward the other man and felt the tension in his shoulders, drawing his arms up. He wanted to beat the shit out of him. Bellmore was an asshole but apparently no fool, as he shuffled away quickly. Garrett growled and considered chasing the man down and unleashing his fury on him for putting Caroline in such a position for his own lust.

Without another sound, Bellmore turned and stomped away to his horse. One of Garrett's young workers had led the horse over from wherever Bellmore had left it.

"Turn loose my horse." Bellmore snatched the reins from the boy, then he quickly mounted and galloped off.

Timmy, a fourteen-year-old whose pa worked out at the Spencer Pride Ranch, strutted back toward the barn, where he'd muck and lay down fresh alfalfa hay for the afternoon milking. "That's one fine horse."

"But a jackass of a man ridin' him." Garrett gave the boy a pat on his shoulder as he walked by.

Timmy laughed as he continued into the barn.

Garrett turned toward his south pasture instead. He knew that Lyle would have Marigold and her new calf in hand, so he'd help the men get the calves separated in the field and start leading in the cows toward the paddock. As he walked past the dairy where he could hear the women inside laughing and talking now, the singing for a moment over, he thought about Caroline. He wondered if Caroline would want to manage the dairy, be inside the whitewashed house with the red painted roof. Earlier that morning, he'd sent Timmy on more than one errand, all in preparation for him claiming his bride. Not trusting Bellmore, he had the urge to go get her now. However, he'd been gone long enough from his farm helping the sheriff and he needed to see about things here first. One thing about dealing in livestock, some processes couldn't be rushed, like milk. The more hands available, the faster things would get done.

No matter what, before nightfall, Caroline would be his wife, in his bed.

THERE WAS a knock at the door. Caroline had been expecting it for over an hour, ever since Miss Kitty had come up and told her she needed to pack a bag, that she would be leaving the house that night, but it still startled her. The woman hadn't elaborated, and when Caroline asked more questions, the madam had simply stated she'd learn more when the gentleman arrived.

Caroline didn't understand all the mystery. They both knew that Bellmore was the one coming to claim her, but what she didn't understand was why he was taking her from here. She'd refused to be his mistress, although, in hindsight, she wondered if it would have been better to service one man instead of many. Perhaps that was the reason he'd have their first time together somewhere else, to feel as if he was still getting what he wanted. Hopefully, it wouldn't be a permanent situation until she'd paid off her debt to him. For many reasons, she didn't want to be stuck under the same roof with Bellmore, his mother being the main one.

After a deep breath, Caroline rose from her seat before the vanity in her room. She hadn't been looking at herself, just staring at the paisley pattern of the carpet bag on her bed. The madam had handed her the bag when she'd come up. Caroline had no clue what one took to have sex with a man who was buying her favors. Not knowing what to expect, she put in the box the women had given her, a soaking sponge in a jar, and her other day dress. She had on the light blue calico dress with a square collar. It was cut lower than the yellow one in the bag, but nowhere near as deep as those of the gowns in the wardrobe. Her old boots surrounded her feet like gloves. If she were meeting him here, she'd already picked out one of her many salacious satin gowns and high kid boots, but since they would not be at the brothel, she was not going to prance around Bellmore's house before his mother looking tawdry. The old woman already stared upon her with her nose turned up, an indigent no one. Widow Bellmore was the reason Caroline had always gone into town at first light, once the mercantile opened, to avoid running into the supercilious woman.

Once the night was over, she'd work at convincing Bellmore that it was best for them to conduct their business at the Harlot and the Hero. Not able to put off the night any longer, Caroline grabbed the bag then went to the door.

"Madam sent me up here to see if you're ready." Macey stood in the hall smiling at her.

The bright expression seemed odd to Caroline. It was the same expression she'd received from Mrs. Morrison, Miss Debra, and the midwife at breakfast. Even after a month of staying up all night, she still was unable to sleep late and ended up in the kitchen to break her fast. She looked forward to time with those women, just as she would miss having dinner with the children in an hour.

However, knowing how the house schedule worked,

Caroline surmised it was better for her to be gone before the children arrived to eat and before the men began to line up outside. She was sure it was only because it was Bellmore that she was even being taken from the establishment, Miss Kitty was very protective of the women who worked for her, and she would not want to give other clients any ideas about getting the Jewels to service them away from the house.

"Yes." *Since I have no choice.* She kept the other words to herself as she followed Macey down the stairs.

At the bottom, Macey pulled her into a tight embrace. "Cecil and I wish you well."

"Th-thank you," Caroline stammered, shocked by the older woman's uncanny declaration. She wanted to remind the housekeeper that she would only be gone for a night, but the supportive embrace felt so good, Caroline simply received it.

Soon, Macey was headed to the kitchen and Caroline went in the direction of Miss Kitty's office, one hand fisted around the handle of the carpetbag, sweat pooling between her fingers.

The door was opened at the same time she arrived before it and was prepared to knock.

"Thanks for being prompt. We've been expectin' you." Miss Kitty's smile was as wide as her bosom. The madam was dressed in a cream-colored shirtwaist with an impressively high collar and a dark green skirt. The woman's curvaceous bulk filled most of the gap in the door, keeping Caroline from seeing any of the room behind her.

"I got some things ready as you requested. Hopefully, you all were not waiting long." Caroline really did not care if Bell-more waited until the cows came home, but the woman before her now had not only taken the time to educate her, but she had given her a home and a sense of confidence in herself.

"Come in." Miss Kitty stepped back, pulling the door wide as she moved.

With a quick exhale, trying to let out some of the anxiety that had her stomach twisted, Caroline walked past the owner and into the room.

"Hello, Caroline."

Frozen, Caroline stared at the man leaning against the front side of Miss Kitty's big wooden desk casually, with his polished black-booted ankles crossed. *Garrett Rand.*

Her heart thumped hard, dropped, then soared, and beat fast. Confused and unsure of her own eyes, she glanced away from the strikingly handsome big man to Miss Kitty, who had closed the door but was still beside it.

"What...why...what?" Swallowing, Caroline tried to get her mind and mouth to work together.

"Expectin' someone else, are you?"

It wasn't Miss Kitty who answered her jumbled questions, but the imposing man. Caroline still couldn't bring herself to look at him. When she stared at him, her body started acting in strange ways. She ached and throbbed in places somethin' fierce when he was around her, making her feel as if she would pass out or lose her mind. Now that she had been in this house, she knew what that heavy pulsating feeling between her thighs was. It was need, lust, sexual desire. Other men she'd spied from the upper level had been handsome or had a certain quality she found attractive and her heart had done a flutter or two. She wasn't blind to others' looks or build, but never had they caused the spine-tingling response Garrett did. When she'd seen him a little more than a week ago, her body had practically vibrated with need. There'd been a quiver so low in her belly, she'd pressed her lips, thighs, and clenched her fist to try to stifle it. Nothing had worked. Mostly, because of all the lusty sounds going on around her in the other rooms. Her mind had raced, drawing image after image, replicating the sketches from the madam's naughty journals, with her and Garrett's faces.

She'd fled from her post early; she'd had to. In her room, she'd removed all the face paint, hair pins, and sensual garb then opened the window, hoping the night air would offer her some relief, but it hadn't. So, she'd lain on the bed and tried to count sheep, and when that didn't work to stop the intense feelings echoing through her, she ran the different oils through her mind in alphabetical order. It had distracted her for a time, but as the moaning went on in Onyx's room beside hers, Caroline had discovered her fellow Jewel had been entertaining a cowboy named Stan. As the rich, brown-skinned nymph continued to call out with the thumping of the headboard and groaning of the bedframe, Caroline's mind filled in the blanks as it chanted 'Rand, thump, Rand, thump, Rand, thump, *Rand...*'

Her own internal torment had forced her to draw up the simple cotton shift she always slept in and slip her hands between her thighs. She'd been drenched, her wetness coating her fingers. The glide of her own fingers had felt so good, she'd pressed in further between the swollen puffy flesh guarding her inner secrets. She had never caressed herself in such a way. During the times Miss Kitty and Florence had made her inspect herself with a hand mirror to see and know the parts, she had ensured she didn't touch herself there more than she needed to see. However, as she lay in the center of her soft bed, she'd run a finger over the tight nub at the top of her sex a couple of times. The sensation had been too intense and the tension in her belly wound too tight. She wasn't ignorant of where all that buildup led to; living in a whorehouse, a woman learned things fast. A climax was the end of the culmination of sensations. It was what they learned to get their client's to as fast as possible and something the woman rarely got.

The lust in her body and thoughts of Garrett Rand had been too overwhelming, causing apprehension of her own response. She'd not only been unsure of herself, but she had doubted a man like him would ever want someone like her. Not that she hadn't heard the women discuss his sexual prowess, always led by Diamond. The ebony-haired beauty had a thing for him and had serviced him solely for months before he began to keep his visits brief and only with Miss Kitty. If Diamond and her oral talents couldn't keep him interested, she surely didn't have a chance with a man like him. Those subjugating thoughts had her body cooling as she pulled her hand away. She'd rolled to her side and slipped her folded hand beneath her pillow, forcing herself to sleep as the house began to quiet down and her own musk taunted her.

Now, here he stood, a strong presence in the room, drawing out all the air around her, making her slightly light-headed. Was it possible that somehow Garrett had won the first night with her? Maybe over a game of cards or billiards? She'd seen more than one man swearing at a loss in the back-room while another cheered, sometimes over money won, but often in the whorehouse, over a particular Jewel. Caroline couldn't see Bellmore giving up anything, especially his claim to her innocence. Then this had to do with something else, and Bellmore would arrive shortly. Miss Kitty was too honorable to allow some other man to sample what another had paid for. Technically, Caroline owed Bellmore, and it was that large price that would allow him to claim everything from her in full.

Her throat tightened to keep the bile rising in check. She didn't know how she would keep herself together with the man she hated most on top of her that night.

Miss Kitty smiled, arched one slender brow as she pushed away from the door, and moved toward her desk. "I'm sure you know Mr. Garrett Rand."

Licking her lips, she skirted a quick glance at him, feeling the immediate draw of her nipples, then away. "Yes."

Even with a swift look, his intense eyes were cobalt blue, just as she'd recalled them from over a year ago, when he'd replaced her eggs and gifted her and her pa with flour and meal. When her papa had asked her how they had corn cakes with their eggs for breakfast, she'd lied and told him she'd made a little extra on her soaps. She hadn't regretted the lie, and shamefully, she'd eaten her food and thought about Garrett the whole time, categorizing everything about him from the brief encounter, not really expecting to have a reason to be around him again. Now, here he was before her.

"You'll be leavin' with him today."

"What?" Shocked at the madam's words, she took a step forward, closer to her desk, closer to him. Garrett hadn't moved, but she could see—feel him—watching her, from the corner of her eye. "But Mr. Bellmore is coming today. He'll be furious if I'm not available to him. The last thing I need is him tackin' on more money for the slight."

She liked the women, friends, here, but she didn't want to be in the brothel longer than she had to, in order to survive.

Kitty set a hand on her ample hip and looked at her, a small smile on her painted lips. "It's all been settled."

"Settled," Caroline mimicked. What her employer was saying didn't make much sense, as the reason she'd been in this place had been because of Bellmore, and the training had all been to serve him.

Then she felt it, the shift in the air in the room. Garrett had moved. She still had not allowed herself to glance in his direction, but now she could feel his large body as he crossed the space, getting closer to her. She knew what a rabbit felt like in the sights of a bobcat; the smaller animal would not even have to hear the elusive predator make a sound yet and still every fiber of the rabbit's being would be on alert, reacting, knowing it was in sight and would be captured soon. The closer he drew, the more she was sure she could not handle this man, handle the intensity he would bring to the bedroom. It would consume her very soul. She would not walk away unscathed.

"You don't owe Bellmore or anyone." The rich, baritone of Garrett's voice reminded her of some of the island rum Miss Kitty had at the bar.

She'd given her a taste after she'd instructed her to look in on Ruby and a client one night. The man had been behind her, taking her so hard and rough, while Ruby's body stayed low and she rotated her hips into his with each thrust, Caroline had become hot, flushed, and lightheaded at the sight. She'd closed the door and pressed her back against the wall to keep from sliding to the floor. Woody had been there with a small glass half filled with the rum. 'Miss Kitty said to drink it all,' he'd told her.

Ashamed of her weakness, she'd gulped down the liquor. It hadn't burned, as she'd expected. Instead, it had been smooth but warmed her body instantly as it hit her stomach and radiated out to all her limbs. That same effect Garrett's voice was having on her now.

"I've paid your debt in full," Garrett continued.

She faced him now, caught him standing less than a foot away. He was too close, and she wanted to take a step back but held her ground. She forced her chin up and her eyes to meet his cobalt ones, deep-set under a strong brow that gave him an intense look. "So, now I'll have to work off my bill servicing you?"

Garrett was a better man, but she'd still be trapped in a whorehouse.

His hand lifted, brushing callused fingers along her cheek before he cupped it. "As my wife."

What? The word never left her mouth as her throat locked up around it. *His wife*?

There was a banging sound in the distance, and night moved in quick as stars began to twinkle in her eyes, as she thought about narrow possibility, she'd be any man's wife, Garrett Rand's wife.

"Breathe, bunny."

It wasn't until he commanded her, Caroline realized that the white lights blinking before her face weren't stars in the room, but evidence she was about to faint. She took in a deep breath as Garrett's rich tone came in muffled through the tunnel, covering both her ears.

"Inhale nice and deep for me." His other hand was gripping her waist and holding her tight against his chest as he spoke. His callused thumb brushed down and up along the side of her throat. "Come on; give me another one."

She followed his instructions, her mind and body responding helplessly to his direct orders. When strength returned to her limp arms and legs and her mind righted itself, she became aware of every place their bodies touched. Her breasts were nestled against his chest, her belly pressed against the rock-hard plane of his abdomen, and her pelvis rested on his as the lower part of him, a thick bulge, sat situated at the seat of her sex. She also became aware her feet weren't touching the floor, but Garrett bore all her weight in his hands.

A shiver of heat raced through her. "I'm fine. Please put me down."

He held her for a moment longer, and she wasn't sure he

was going to do as she asked. His intuitive gaze caressed her features first, as if he were assessing for himself that she was all right, then he lowered her down his body. Since he was still holding her tight, she more or less slid down his frame.

Her sensitive nipples, barely covered by the material of her day dress and shift, tightened as they dragged along his broad chest, causing her body temperature to rise and her sex to clench. The man was too potent, if she was responding so strongly to a simple touch, one he'd only done because she was about to make a fool of herself and collapse at his feet.

"Should I get you some water, Caroline?" That question came from Miss Kitty.

"She'll be fine," Garrett answered for her. "It's been a long day for me, after a long day of travel. I'd like to get things done and get home before nightfall if we can."

Caroline stepped back, startled as Garrett bent at the waist. He caught her hasty movement and glanced up at her, holding her gaze locked in his.

She waited, unsure what he was about, until she realized he was picking her bag up from the floor. She hadn't even recalled dropping it, but at some point, it must have slipped from her numb hand. Her cheeks heated, embarrassed. This man, and her response to him, made her jumpy. Bellmore may have owned her life from the debt, but she wasn't afraid of him. He didn't cause the same overwhelming response in her mind and body that Garrett did. Handling the businessman once a night would have been easier. It would have required her to yield only her body; however, with Garrett, she was sure it would cost her so much more. As his wife, there would be no escape; he'd take everything from her.

"Makes sense." Miss Kitty came around her desk.

Caroline turned to her. "I owe you so much, for your kindness and generosity."

"Stop that. You owe me nothing; your company has been refreshing and delightful." The older woman pulled her into a warm embrace. "I want you to enjoy your life. Garrett is one of the best out there. He'll be good to you."

Holding the woman, who had been a surrogate mother of sorts, tight, Caroline said, "I'll try. I didn't get a chance to say goodbye to everyone. They'll be curious when I'm not at dinner."

Miss Kitty leaned back, holding her shoulders. "They already know you're leaving. Last night was their way of saying farewell."

That shocked her. "All those...things."

The madam winked at her. "All brides need their own trousseau. It's just the kind we give out at the Harlot and the Hero." She laughed.

Caroline's cheeks flamed. Blushing, she couldn't help but think about all those things now in the bag Garrett carried being used for him, by him.

"Oh, gracious," Caroline uttered low. "I'll stop by sometime."

Kitty shook her head violently. "It won't be decent. Garrett's given you a chance to hold your head up in the town you love; don't go ruining that."

Caroline understood the stigma the women were under because of their occupation, but after being here a month, she also knew the kindness of the women inside the walls. She wouldn't allow herself to be judgmental and snobby. "It's not fair."

"Life rarely is. When you see any of us in town, just offer a nod; it'll be enough."

"And a small smile." Caroline held up a hand with her index and thumb an inch apart.

Miss Kitty laughed and stepped away, but not before Caroline saw the glassiness in her eyes.

Feeling just as emotional, Caroline turned toward the door where Garrett stood in the open frame.

"You 'bout ready?"

She nodded at his question, not able to say much else.

With her bag in hand, he led her out of the whorehouse. She was happy to see a wagon waiting out front with a lovely chestnut horse harnessed to it.

"This is King." At the wagon, Garrett strolled over to the horse and stroked him along the side. "I got him as a foal from my pa when I bought my land here in Grover."

Caroline thought about her family nag, old when her father bought it off someone else. She and Garrett had such different lives. "How old were you when you moved here?"

"Nineteen." He moved back beside her when she began to get up into the wagon, placing a hand on her arm. "Let me." He set her bag down on the hard-packed dirt ground that too many men and their horse's hooves had trodden, getting to the women in the house.

She held a hand out to him, thinking he was simply planning to steady her as she climbed up into the box seat.

"Oh!" She gasped when he placed his big strong hands at her waist and hauled her up in one swift movement. She felt dizzy by the contact and the smell of him, something heady, warm, and intoxicating, but she would need a moment longer to take it all in. The hand she had moved toward him had bumped against the center of his firm chest then slid up to rest on his shoulder as she stared down at him from the seat. His hands were still on her waist as he gazed up. There was something in his stare that she couldn't decipher, and it made her unsure of herself as things began to flutter in her core. She removed her hand. "Um, thank you."

"My pleasure, Caroline." Her name came out on a soft timbre as if on a prayer. As if he'd lain awake at night thinking of her, praying for her.

She shook her head at her nonsense thoughts. It had only been her father. Yes, the people of Grover Town cared and tried to help them for a time but then all went away, and she doubted anyone gave her much thought. *Then how is it Garrett Rand came to purchase your debt?*

She wasn't sure, but it was one of the things she needed to discover. "My bag, please, Mr. Rand."

"Now, none of that. Mr. Rand is a neighbor or employer, not a husband." Even as he denied her label, he stepped away and stooped to pick up her carpet bag then handed it up to her.

"Well, right now, you're neither." She claimed the bag and set it on the seat beside her, not because it was filled with any kind of valuables, but she needed something of a barrier between her and the utterly senseless attraction she had toward this man.

Garrett chuckled as his lips tilted in a side-smile that made her heart flutter. The man was just too stunning.

"You're right." He strutted around the front of the wagon, caressed King's muzzle as he went by, and soon he was climbing up beside her and unwinding the reins from the hook. "I do believe it's time we take care of that."

"You're going to let me work on your farm so I can pay you the money back?"

He made a clicking sound with his mouth before he snapped the leads and started the horse trotting away.

Caroline glanced over at the house. The windows at the bottom had the curtains still drawn. They would be that way for the next few hours until Miss Kitty was ready for them to be open for business sometime after dinner. She spotted

Woody coming around the side of the house, doing his first property check, ensuring no men had tried to get into the house early. She knew the next hour, Smitty would make the rounds. Miss Kitty kept her house running like clockwork. She'd miss it.

Smitty glanced her way and saluted. She waved back as Garrett led his horse on one of the side roads away from town. It was a similar route to the one Bellmore had taken that had brought her here. Except, instead of at the fork taking the road that went farther away from town, the long stretch that would go past the Spencer Ranch and eventually would lead to her old family farm, he took the one that ran two miles perpendicular to town.

They got nods and tips of hats by a handful of ranch hands on horseback and a couple walking along, finished with the day's work as they headed to town, for dinner, drinks, gambling, or eventually a stop at one whorehouse or another. If not for Garrett, she would have possibly had to entertain one or two of them after Bellmore left for the night. If he left.

He leaned forward with his elbows resting on his knees, the reins slack in his hands as King kept up a steady cadence along the well-tended dirt road. It probably held that the wagon had well-oiled springs and joints that kept it bouncing and groaning smoothly. It was much different than the one that went to her home, or what was her home, that was rough and worn, and their buckboard...was more like timber on rotted wheels.

Garrett's silence frayed her nerves, causing her mind to race not knowing what he was thinking. Bellmore had griped and grumbled about her papa and him not being a good steward, and had taken advantage of his kindness, and how she should have been more grateful for his hospitality of allowing them to stay in the house for so long when he had a right to sell it right out from under them at any time after the first few months of late payments.

"You know, there's no reason for you to...marry me." She licked her lips and kept her own gaze locked on the road, nervous to see his expression. "I'll still provide the same service to you as I would have to Mr. Bellmore. As a whore, I'm trained not to complain, you know?"

ELEVEN

He pulled the reins, and King came to a halting stop.

Jerked back then forward, not expecting the fast movement, Caroline gasped. When she glanced over at Garrett, his blue eyes were practically dark as coal as he stared at her, his brow knit tightly.

"Don't," he growled as he began popping up one finger, "ever refer to Bellmore's sorry ass again as it pertains to what he was tryin' to do to you." His middle finger joined the index. "Never call yourself a whore again. I don't care if you'd slept with every man in this town, you're goin' to be my wife and that's how you'll be treated from here on out. Got it?"

He was so furious, she couldn't do anything now but nod. She assumed he was most likely concerned that others would know her prior occupation and it would cast shadow on him.

As the wagon rolled on, she sat there, trying to figure out the man beside her. The only thing she knew of him was the little she'd overheard about his dairy farm and the few times she'd seen him in town, struttin' proud and talkin' neighborly to others. It was common knowledge that the sheriff was his older brother, even though the two men didn't look much alike.

"What kind of man would I be, Caroline, if I brought you under my roof but didn't take you as my wife?" He shook his head.

She lifted a shoulder in a shrug. "I'm sure it happens more often than not. From stories I heard from the Jewels, not all housekeepers working for a single man or a husband whose wife can't do her duty because of sickness or something, just only cook and clean."

"That's true. But that ain't me. You'll meet Mrs. Copernic and *all* she does is cook, clean, and wash for me during the week."

That bit of knowledge shocked her. Those were jobs of a wife. "If you already have an efficient woman to run your house, what do you need me for?"

If someone could have harnessed the heat of the sun and placed it into his body, it was Garrett, because the blaze that caressed her from his eyes scorched her everywhere his gaze touched—face, lips, breasts, and hips. She was on fire.

Quickly, she shifted her gaze back to King's sleek chestnut form and concentrated on the move of the horse's powerful muscles as they shifted and played under his coat. She didn't need him to answer her ill thought question. His look had brought up images she'd seen and studied before.

"I wouldn't dishonor your pa by not takin' you to wife."

Those words came out low, but she heard them clearly. It choked her up. She'd tried hard not to think about her papa in the days she'd been at the Harlot and the Hero. He would have been shamed by the way her life had turned out after his death. Part of the reason she didn't let her mind think of him was because she was still angry at the fact he never allowed her in on the true state of their problems. She could have helped more.

"Why would you concern yourself with my papa? Did you know him?" She never recalled seeing Garrett around the house, and her father surely never spoke of him. He didn't speak much of anyone, besides her mama.

"Not really." He fell silent again.

"Oh." She figured he was done speaking and she sat in the humid warmth of the early evening and played her fingers along the handle of the bag, a bag filled with a single day dress and box, as her only possessions. Her life hadn't really increased at all in a month.

"If the Good Lord blesses us with children, a daughter, I'd protect her with my life. Just as your pa did. I'd run down and through any man lookin' to do her harm."

Stunned at his words, she looked at him, considering him with fresh eyes. Garrett seemed to be the man of honor people in town spoke about. It was true he was making assumptions about the reason for her father's restrictions on her, but she knew, with all her father's financial faults, he loved her. Garrett's words caused her belly to tighten at the thought of carrying his child. When she was younger, and she and Isabel went to school together, she'd talked with her friend about her dreams, wanting a farm of her own and working it with her husband and raising children. Was it possible that those hopes had returned to life and would come to pass for her?

It was too soon for her to put faith in another man. The last two men who had charge of her life, her father and Bellmore, hadn't cared to ask her what she wanted for her life. Instead, they ordered her about to follow their will. Time would tell if Garrett did the same.

When they turned off the main road, into the lane that led to the Grover Town Methodist Church, she saw the big single-story wooden structure with the extension on one side, which was the children's church they had added some years ago. Church had been the only time she and her papa weren't working the farm until their hands bled. She'd found a peace within the hallowed walls. She'd allowed herself the respite from work but never offered a single prayer on her own behalf. What did a girl who had nothin' and had seen nothin' even pray for? Nothin'.

Pastor Morgan was sitting on the top step before the open double doors, with one of his boys, David, the youngest, beside him, and at the bottom of the stairs, stood a dark-haired woman beside a man Caroline didn't recognize. She figured the strange man must be the owner of the black and white horse beside one of the oak trees with a sack tied below his muzzle, a makeshift feed bag. As they drew closer, she realized she did know the woman with the swollen belly. It was Rachel Morrison, the housekeeper who worked for the Reynolds and her friend Isabel, who was married and who had most likely delivered her twins since Caroline had been at the brothel. She and Rachel had occasionally exchanged a greeting in the early mornings when they ran into each other in town. Rachel was also the daughter of Mrs. Morrison, the head cook, who managed the Harlot and the Hero. Caroline's stomach pitched.

Garrett slowed the wagon before the church and pulled the brake, locking the handle in place at the front side by his foot on the outside of the wagon. "Don't get down, Caroline. I'll come 'round."

She heard the command in his voice, but she wanted to tell him she hadn't even thought about getting down; she was way too nervous. Pastor Morgan had been her spiritual leader for most of her life. He'd performed the eulogy for her father's makeshift funeral just over a month ago. Now, here she was before him, expecting him to perform a wedding. It wasn't because of the haste she was anxious, or maybe it was. She was afraid the pastor would ask her where she'd been all this time, and because she couldn't lie to a minister, she'd tell him the truth. She doubted he'd believe that she'd spent a month in a whorehouse and hadn't already been doing the job of a whore. The older man was staring right at her with his all-knowing gaze. She felt sick.

Garrett had paused at the front of the horse to say something to the stranger at the stairs.

Caroline put her hand to her stomach and felt it flippin' and turnin', and it didn't seem at all inclined to stop. Not thinking, she jumped from the side of the wagon and ran.

"Whoa, there. Where do you thinkin' you're headed off to?"

Before she could drop to her knees, Garrett's arm was around her middle, a vise holding her against him.

"Put me down!" she groaned as she squirmed, afraid of what would happen. She gritted her teeth, fighting against the onslaught of bile rushing its way toward an exit of her body.

"I'm not gonna let you go so you can try to escape again." His other hand took hold of her jaw and began to pull her face to the side, toward him.

"No. No! I think I need to—"

"Dammit!" Reacting quickly, he pitched her body forward to allow her to spew all the contents of the light fare she'd eaten that came shooting out of her mouth.

She cried and retched. More and more wetness covered her cheeks as she heaved everything inside of her out on the ground less than a foot away, for all to see.

"Let it all out. It's all right." Garrett hadn't released her, one of his arms still held her waist while he rubbed her back with his other hand, firm strokes up and down, then circles along her spine.

His considerate touch caused her to wail even where there was nothing remaining for her to throw up. The tears stopped and her voice was now hoarse from the burning bile that had scorched her vocal cords on the way out. She found herself turned in big, strong arms and heard a man's voice cooing in her ear, as if she were an upset baby. "It's all right." His words rumbled through his chest as he held her tight against him, one side of her to his chest, her body secured against him.

Her mind raced around to every corner of her mind as the tears poured out of her like someone had turned on a spigot.

"Come now. What's this all about? Am I that much of a scary guy to be hitched to?" He chuckled a little, but there was sincerity in his low tones.

Still crying and soaking his nice light blue shirt with black stripes with the moist salt from her eyes, she couldn't even take a breath to tell him it wasn't him. It was everything. She hadn't allowed herself to cry when her papa died because there was work to be done, to continue to survive. Then when she'd ended up in a whorehouse, she had held in her fear of having to live a life lying beneath so many men too, and now the shame of the minister seeing her with a man she barely knew who'd plucked her fresh out of a brothel.

"Caroline. Stop crying." His hands stilled, and his voice dropped an octave with his order.

Her crying ceased, but she just stood there, smelling cedar, fresh cut grass, and male musk. She could always smell the sourness from her own mouth after throwing up, making her more embarrassed. A whimper or two came out, but she could feel herself settle some. Unsure of whether it was the direct way he'd spoken to her or the fact she'd had enough of her own antics, she sniffed then tried to step away.

He held fast. He slipped a finger beneath her chin, curling it slowly, in a way that caused warmth to spread from his touch, then he tipped her head up toward him. There was dusk all around him now as she looked up at him.

"Tell me what's all this about." His dark blue eyes traveled along her features, accessing her.

Slapping a hand over her mouth, to keep him from smelling her foul breath, she shook her head.

"Talk to me, Caroline," he insisted. "Or I'll pull you over my knee right here and now."

He had to be kidding. Jade had discussed how men liked to spank women before or during the sex act, but here, before the church and the man of God...that was just absurd. Not knowing Garrett well enough to know if it were a threat or the truth, she mumbled, "I'm fine."

"Take your hand down, my lovely bunny. A little spittle won't bother me none. Just this mornin', I stood before a cow giving birth with all the smells and slime that comes along with it. A little ripe breath won't bother me."

She vacillated but finally lowered her hand to her chest. He was holding her so tight still, she could only move it so far.

"I'm fine. It was just nerves. I woke up this morning and didn't see my day turnin' into all this." She tipped her head toward the people who now gathered beside the wagon and noticed another man had arrived at some point. From the distance, and with the sky darker now, she couldn't make out who the man was.

Garrett stared at her, holding her gaze. One thick, sable brow arched, and his hard look said he wasn't convinced, but he nodded. "If you're sure."

"I am. I wasn't running away. Just was aimin' for a little

privacy to..." She made a small hand gesture, small circles by her mouth. "You know."

He chuckled.

She enjoyed the sound and feel of it.

"You don't ever have to hide nothin' from me. In sickness and in health, we're about to pledge. You understand?"

"Yes. I'm sorry for embarrassing you in front of the others."

"Nothin' to apologize for. You could never embarrass me." His arms went slack. "How about gettin' this arrangement legal and let everyone get on with their night?"

She nodded. "I'd like that." She realized that was the truth. She still didn't know Garrett Rand any better than she had a little over forty minutes ago when they left the Harlot and the Hero, but she trusted him. That feeling she stuck in her mental bonnet to examine later.

He took hold of one of her hands in his big one, then stepped away and turned and practically plowed into a small woman.

His quick actions helped him stop quickly and avoid the collision.

"Gracious." Startled, Caroline had even missed the tiny redhead standing a few feet behind Garrett, Gretchen Spencer.

"I figured you'd want somethin' to settle your stomach." There was kindness in the woman's gaze.

"I'll leave you two alone and speak with Pastor Morgan." Garrett squeezed Caroline's hand before he released it. "Caroline, you come along when you're ready. Gretchen." He offered the other woman a small smile and nod then walked toward the men. Ian, his brother, who came riding up, and Rachel stared at her as she rubbed a hand over the small swell of her belly.

"I've been in your same situation, and it can knock the

wind right out from under you." Gretchen held out a mason jar filled with liquid toward her.

Caroline took it. The woman's words shocked her. She'd met this petite mother of two a few times when she had ridden over to get cattle bones and fat from Spencer after a slaughter to boil and mix with ash for her rose soaps. "Thanks, Mrs. Spencer."

"Gretchen, please."

Caroline drank liberally from the jar but couldn't stop her gaze from tracking the swagger of the man who would become her husband in a matter of moments. His gait was sure, smooth, his shoulders rolling with confidence, carrying that smooth, shifting movement through to his hips tipped left then right, just slightly carrying him along. She could watch him walk all day and never tire of it. Her pulse quickened, and she sighed. Discovering he wanted her as his wife hadn't stunted the attraction and feelings she experienced around him, but intensified them. Her mind could not help but bring up thoughts of the two of them later that night. She sighed.

"I guess the drink is to your likin'? It's my own blend of mint and orange syrup." Gretchen's voice brought her around.

Lowering the glass, Caroline blushed. She hadn't even really considered the taste, just drank, too focused on Garrett. The man was all-consuming. "Um...it's good. Thank you."

Gretchen laughed. "No need to lie. I know a licked woman when I see one." The shorter woman leaned in toward her. "Chance does the same thing to me. Makes my head a twister and my belly feel like nothin' but gelatin."

Caroline's face was flaming now. "It's nonsense...I don't even know him."

"It's a mule kick in the head; you're right about that. But once your heart gets lassoed, you might as well give in."

She heard the other woman but refused to believe that

love was in the future for her and Garrett. For some reason, he had felt compelled or sorry for her being in the brothel. She assumed it was because, somehow, he'd recognized her a week ago. Since she was from Grover Town, unlike the other ladies, and everyone knew how she and her father lived, he had taken pity on her. She hated that his benevolence would link them together for life, but she would do her best to be a good wife to him, as she'd been a good daughter.

When Garrett looked over at her as he spoke with the pastor, nodding at something, she figured it was time she started on the path of being that good wife.

Screwing the two-piece lid back onto the jar, she handed the half empty glass back to the owner. "Thank you, Gretchen."

Gretchen placed a hand on her arm, stilling her with a maternal look. "Are you feelin' better? If you ain't, I can get Chance to have Garrett postpone the nuptials."

It seemed that everyone in town saw her as fragile and someone in need of coddling. She'd have to show them all she had more than enough strength to care for herself, see things through. Straightening her back, she smiled down at the five years older, but short woman. "I'm fine. Just ready to get this all over with. Stopping it for a day is still going to have it before me."

"If you're sure." Those curious green eyes still held hers.

She stepped away from Gretchen's kind touch and went toward the man who wanted her as his wife. "I am."

"I DO." Caroline held her chin high but kept her gaze fixed on his chin as it had been for the entire short service.

He assumed it was her nervousness and the haste of the

wedding that kept her from looking into his eyes. He didn't fault her for it. How could she be expected to pledge herself wholeheartedly to a man she didn't really know, who had plucked her out of a brothel? It would be his job to assure her she could trust him, that his affection for her was sincere.

When she'd come walking into the church, carrying a simple bouquet of roses that he'd had Gretchen and Chance stop by Caroline's old house and get, his breath had caught in his chest. The red flowers had made the blush in her cheeks more pronounced and the natural dusky rose of her lips contrast with it, but in a beguiling way, that even now had his eyes lowering to her mouth, her full lips, with the top more plump and slightly wider than her bottom one. In a moment, he'd be feeling those lips beneath his own, sealing her to him forever.

He wondered if she could feel his stare, because her pink tongue darted out and licked along the upper half.

Before the groan that started to rumble in his chest came to fruition, a loud noise drew his attention.

"Ahem." The pastor cleared his throat a second time, as Garrett glanced to the side at him, curious. "Garrett. Again, I ask, do you take Caroline Douglas as your lawfully wedded wife?"

The few who were gathered to bear witness of his union to Caroline snickered or chortled from the front rows of the pews.

He realized, he'd been so fixated on the beauty who would become his wife, he'd missed his own cue. No embarrassment even grazed his shoulders. Caroline was a sight to behold and he cared deeply for her. She had been a distraction in his mind for a couple of years. Now she was going to be in his life and his bed permanently. "I do," he declared boldly.

The older man smiled. "Do you have a ring?"

"Yes." Garrett glanced over at his brother.

Ian stepped forward as he unwrapped tissue paper and handed him the ring. He'd sent a message to Ian, asking his brother to stop by Russell's and pick it up from the few they kept locked up in the back of the store. There wasn't time for Garrett to order anything special, but if Caroline didn't like this one with the small leaves carved all the way around it, then he'd let her pick something else.

Holding it out, the multiple candlelight from sconces around the church reflected off the gold band.

"Oh, my..." Caroline gasped softly.

Gretchen, Spencer's wife, walked up and removed the flowers from Caroline's stiff fingers.

Garrett watched Caroline inhale and wipe her hands along the skirt folds of her blue dress. He tried not to think about how her slim figure looked in the blue dress. It was modest, compared to what she had on a week ago, standing disguised on the upper banister of the brothel. However, the square cut of her bodice was just low enough for him to view the top swells of her breasts and a small shadow of the crevice between them. Standing in the Good Lord's house, before the man of the cloth, was not the place he wanted his mind to roam on thoughts of his fiancée's small but plump breasts.

"Take her left hand and repeat after me, Garrett."

When he did as instructed, Garrett felt the coldness of Caroline's fingers. Even in the warmth of the late spring evening inside the church, the bed of her fingernails had a blue tinge to them. He couldn't help but take her hand in his and squeeze, hoping to provide a little warmth. Lifting his eyes, he met her soft brown gaze, filled with worry. "Everything will be all right. Trust me."

She gave him a wavering small smile but remained silent.

Not expecting more from her, Garrett looked over at the pastor and gave a firm nod for him to continue.

"With this ring, I pledge my affection. I join my life with yours in loving kindness and compassion. I join my life with yours in faithfulness. All that I have, I will use to care for you, protect you, and provide for you. You are my beloved, and you are my friend." At the last line, Garrett settled the ring in place then gave her hand another squeeze, with two hands this time, feeling the slight tremor there.

Pastor Morgan stepped up and placed a hand on Caroline's shoulder. When she glanced over at him, the minister said, "I'm sure your father is smiling down from Heaven, Caroline, seeing that you are wed to a good man as Garrett."

Caroline's eyes began to glisten and fill.

Garrett was nervous that the minister's words may start the crying from earlier, but Caroline gave a simple nod and whispered, "Thank you."

Moving back to his original place at the center of the altar, Pastor Morgan declared, "I now pronounce you husband and wife. Garrett Rand, you may kiss your bride."

Still holding her hand, Garrett tugged it, until he had pulled her against his chest. He stared down into the brown luminous pools of her eyes surrounded by thick, dark lashes that captivated him. Instead of dropping his gaze to her lips as he tipped his head and leaned down toward her fascinatingly odd lips, he remained steady on her eyes. This moment, for him, wasn't about lust; it was about him assuring her that she was his. That he knew who he was marrying, and that this moment was not a fluke that he'd crafted just to have a warm body in his bed.

"Caroline," he uttered her name on his last breath before he brought their lips together. Her lips were soft, as they yielded beneath his. There was warmth there too, unlike her hands, which let him know she may be nervous about their wedding, but there was some affection or maybe simple attraction for him. Either, he'd take at the moment; they had years to build on the former.

When her lips began to part against his, he stepped away. He couldn't allow the kiss to deepen. He was only hanging on to his need for her by the thinnest of threads and he didn't need, nor want, it to snap with others around.

"I am happy to present Mr. and Mrs. Garrett Rand," Pastor Morgan announced to the small group gathered.

Lyle let out a whistle that Chance and Ian joined in on as the two women and David clapped. Garrett thanked Pastor Morgan with a handshake before he led Caroline from the church.

They stood around for a few moments, taking in the adulations from their witnesses. It was dark out now, but the light coming from the open double doors of the church, where the pastor and his son were still inside, helped illuminate the little group.

"Well, little brother, I need to get home. Been at the office all day." Ian pulled him into an embrace, then whispered, "The missus and I are happy for you. You needed this."

"'Preciate you, Ian." His brother was the only person he'd shared with about his feelings toward Caroline. Ian knew he'd gone out and asked Douglas for her hand and had stewed for some time after being rejected.

Ian stepped to Caroline and placed a kiss on her cheek. "Welcome to the family. Ma is going to love you. So make sure you give Garrett a little feistiness to keep him on his toes."

Caroline's cheeks tinted, but she gave Ian a shy smile as she nodded. "Thank you."

Moments later, after a quick wave to the rest of the crowd, the sheriff was saddled up and gone.

"I made you all a wedding cake." Gretchen presented a metal cake tin to Caroline.

"Thank you, Gretchen." Caroline smiled at the shorter woman. "I'll get the tin back to you as soon as I can."

"No rush at all. When you bring it back, you and Garrett must come for dinner," Gretchen offered.

"Um, we will." Starring down at the tin, Caroline shook her head softly. "What don't you think of?"

Gretchen shrugged and smiled. "I'm used to keepin' busy, and I enjoy doin' for people. It ain't much. Just a small spice cake, with dried fruit and nuts. I didn't have one for mine." She cut her eyes to her husband, but there was only love in her gaze, no malice.

"But I gave you so much more, darlin'." Chance stooped down and kissed his wife on the cheek and whispered something in her ear that made Gretchen giggle and blush.

Seeing Chance and Gretchen so happy, after their own impromptu wedding a year ago, made Garrett hope that things would turn out well for him and Caroline.

"This is Lyle Joseph, my foreman out at the farm," Garrett introduced the slim man and his pregnant wife.

"Ma'am. Glad to see my boss finally takin' a little happiness for himself. He's always worryin' about doin' for those who work for him. Now, he'll have someone concerned 'bout him." Lyle patted him on the shoulder. "This here is my wife, Rachel."

"Yes, we've met a time or two." Caroline offered a smile to the brown-haired woman, who was her height, but slimmer in form, except for the small, round belly.

"I also know what it is like to have a hasty wedding. Mine was on Christmas Day. The Drummonds allowed my mama to use their restaurant dining room for a small breakfast gathering and ceremony."

Just like Gretchen, Garrett watched as his foreman's wife offered his wife compassionate words, letting Caroline into a sort of sisterhood of flash weddings. He appreciated their kindness in letting Caroline know there was no shame in them tying the knot quickly. However, he knew that the rush of the nuptials wasn't truly the bother, it was where he'd gotten his bride from that day.

"I picked you up a few doilies in town. I wasn't sure if Mr. Rand's house was like my Lyle's. Not much in place that looked like a woman lived there." Smiling, Rachel handed her a soft parcel wrapped in brown paper and twine. "Maybe I'll see you in the dairy sometime this week, Caroline. I've only been there since Lyle and I married on Christmas, but you'll like the women in there. They're friendly," Rachel informed her.

"Thank you for the gift. I've a lot to learn, and I look forward to learning from everyone." Caroline's answer was non-committal.

Garrett didn't mind. He hoped his wife would find interest in the farm and dairy he'd built, but he wouldn't force her and would give her a chance to settle in and find her space.

"Mrs. Morrison spoke often of you and your sister. Spending my mornings in the kitchen with her was one of my favorite parts of my day," Caroline confessed as she took hold of Rachel's hand.

The smile on Rachel's face grew wide. "Mama is where I learned how to be confident and independent. She always told my sister and me, after our pa passed, that women could find a way to succeed in life as long as they put their mind to it and looked beyond their current situation."

"She still imparts that same kind of wisdom to other young

women." Caroline stepped away, moving back to Garrett's side.

"Well, I think it's time we head to the house and let you folks get on with the rest of your night. Thanks for coming out and helping me get this wedding together." Garrett offered nods and a round of thanks before he led Caroline to their wagon.

"Rand," both the men called out to him as they escorted their wives away.

Garrett tipped his hat in thanks for coming and the things they had done to make the moment special.

At the wagon, Caroline paused, looking perplexed. She lifted one foot then the other, trying to figure out how best to get into the wagon while holding both the parcel and the cake tin. She rolled her bottom lip in her mouth as she started to turn and set the items in the back, he was sure, until she climbed into the seat then claimed them again.

"Wife, if you take another step, I promise you the first thing I'll do is redden your backside as soon as we're home."

She whipped around to him, looking from left to right at the others not paying them a lick of attention as they assisted their wives and prepared to leave. It didn't matter to him if they all had been still standing right beside them, as he knew his foreman and friends, most likely even the pastor, believed in a disciplined household.

When her gaze met his, her eyes were wide and her mouth agape. He'd shocked her. "You can't be serious," she whispered. Leaning closer, she added, "How can you think to bring such a...a bed sport out now. The situation doesn't call for it."

"Bed sport...hm." It was moments like that, he was reminded that his wife would know a lot more than most new brides, after spending a month in a whorehouse. Taking a step, he moved closer so that his tone could match his wife's, without him whispering, to ensure she clearly understood how things would go. "You can trust that if I have to give you a lesson in obedience and mindin' my words, you'll find no fun in how soundly I administer the discipline, *wife*." He held her gaze and let those words sink in, with the reminder of her status in his life now.

She inhaled a deep breath then swallowed, as she lowered her eyes to the center of his chest where she was eye level. "What *dis-o-be-di-ence* are you claiming I did?"

He smiled at her tart division of the word. He kept it to himself that such a tone would also get her ass smacked. It was their wedding day and he'd allow her the grace, this time. "I told you and showed you at the Harlot, when I'm around, I'll assist you into the wagon. When we arrived here, I told you directly not to get out of the wagon. I'm willin' to forgive that you were unwell and filled with emotions, so you didn't do as I told you. Then there's this moment. If your memory keeps a slippin', there's only one way I can see makin' my words stick."

Caroline gasped.

Out of the corner of his eye, he saw the other wagon and the black and white horse carrying two riders heading off.

"My own papa didn't even spank me," she declared, her voice filled with indignation.

"I'm not your pa. I'm your husband, and I'll have order in my household." Taking his wife by the waist, he brought her eye level with him, holding her there. She was taller than most women around town, but still slight in size compared to most. "Kiss me, wife."

He could tell by the press of her lips and the fire showing in her brown eyes at his words, she would rather not. But she did. The kiss was quick and loud, almost something a parent would give to a child. He chuckled as he sat her on the seat.

Caroline was a fast learner, but he was going to enjoy instructing her on what true o-be-di-ence was and what it was not.

As she settled herself in the seat beside her bag, with the cake and parcel in her lap, Garrett went around to the front of King, stroking his muzzle a couple times. "Take us home, old boy."

Once he was in the wagon and had the reins, King didn't need any other encouragement to bring the wagon around and start a trot toward home.

"Any children who come along between us, I'm goin' expect you to help me make sure they're well-behaved, so I don't have to take the strap to them often."

"Children," was her only comment that she'd heard him.

Garrett didn't miss the way she'd moved a hand to her belly as she stared off into the dark road before them. It was the first thing he knew that Caroline wanted, and he'd make damn sure she got a whole passel of them. And find great pleasure in doing it.

TWELVE

"Tomorrow, I'll introduce you to the men and Mrs. Copernic, my housekeeper. By now, she'll have gone home." Garrett had his wife's bag in one hand as he led her up the stairs.

Kyle K. was already walkin' over from the bunkhouse to get King and the wagon settled in the horse stable. Usually, he enjoyed tending to King, but his employees knew he was bringing home a wife, and he appreciated them lookin' out to help.

"Don't you tell your missus that tall tale, Garrett Rand." Mrs. Copernic, a small salt and peppered, pale-brown-skinned powerhouse who lived in a small house with her husband by his south pasture, pulled open the front door before he could. "There ain't no way I'd have gone home until I'd seen for myself that you'd convinced some woman to marry your bossy self."

Shaking his head, he stared at the woman who did more bossing of him and his men than he could ever attempt to achieve. "After all these years, I should have known better."

"A hard head makes a soft backside."

"Is that what Mr. Copernic has had to tell you?" He winked at the older woman who'd been a mother-type to him, since his mama lived states away.

Her withered cheeks bloomed a tinge of pink, which it always did when he talked about her husband to her. "It ain't right for a young man to speak on grown folks' business."

"You're Mrs. Copernic? His housekeeper?" The words seemed to tumble out of his wife's lips as her gaze was fixed on his housekeeper.

The older woman beamed a smile at her as she slapped a hand on her hip and shifted her stance to the side. "I am. Were you expectin' someone else?"

"Um, I-I..." At the direct question, Caroline stammered as her face pinkened around her neck and cheeks, showcased in the rays of light coming through the open door.

Garrett frowned, not understanding at first his new bride's confusion.

Mrs. Copernic was faster on the draw. "I see. Because Garrett is a handsome, strong, strappin' type and without a wife for way *too* long, you thought Mr. Rand had some pretty young thang doing his chores and maybe offering him some services too." She cackled.

He stared from one woman to the other. Mrs. Copernic was practically bent over with laughter, while Caroline's face became the color of holiday poinsettias as she shifted a shy glance at him then away from them both.

The smile pulled up at the side of his mouth and he didn't even attempt to hide it. He liked the fact that his new bride had been thinking about who warmed his bed, because that meant she'd had him in bed in mind, and he was looking forward to her joining him there. "Well, you at least got the pretty right." He winked at his housekeeper.

"Oh, shush now." Mrs. Copernic waved him off with a hand as she exhaled, getting herself under control. "Now, bring this pretty girl in. She's got to be tired."

"Yes'm."

Garrett reached into the door and set the bag against the wall. He then took the tin and parcel from Caroline and handed it over to the housekeeper. He was happy to see that Caroline hadn't made a move to enter the house. Scooping her up in his arms, he crossed the threshold with his new bride.

Her cheeks colored in the oil lamp lights filling his front room. "I didn't expect that."

"Why? It's tradition." He held her gaze, enjoying having her in his arms as well as his home—their home. "Besides, if I hadn't, I'd have never heard the end of it from Mrs. Copernic."

"Darn tootin'. Now, put her down, so I can meet her proper."

"Yes, ma'am." Doing as instructed, he set Caroline back on her feet. "Mrs. Copernic, this is my wife, Caroline Rand."

"Oh, you are a beauty." The older woman nodded as she held the items and took Caroline in from head to toe, then tipped her head to the side, squinting. "It was Douglas, right?"

His bride licked her lips. "Yes, ma'am."

"I remember meetin' your mama on the day y'all came to town. You were knee high to a grasshopper. She was buying you a new bonnet in the mercantile. She said you would never keep one on for long and had flung it off the back of the wagon somewhere enroute."

"My papa used to tell me that. I don't remember very much of my mama." One of Caroline's shoulders shifted a little, not really making a shrug. "I still don't like bonnets to this day. They make my head hot in the sun."

"That's why you've got such a nice goldenness to your

skin. You keep it moisturized at night and you won't be a wrinkled old lady like me." Mrs. Copernic glanced between the two of them. "Well, I'll take care of this stuff while Mr. Rand shows you the house. I'll get the meal on plates for you two then head home. I'll be around tomorrow so we can talk about the care of the house." She stepped close to Caroline and placed a hand on her upper arm. "It's good to have you here. Garrett's been needin' a wife, and I'm glad it's you."

His wife's lips parted a little, but she didn't respond.

Stepping to him next, Mrs. Copernic waved him down. When he stooped to her short height, she kissed him on the cheek. "Well done, my boy. See y'all sometime in the mornin'. The farm will keep if you don't get to it before sunrise."

"Yes, ma'am." He took his marching orders as he straightened up and watched his housekeeper's brisk pace into the kitchen.

When the woman was out of earshot, he moved so that he was standing before Caroline. He reached out and cupped her face, tilting it up so she met his gaze. Once her brewed coffee brown eyes stopped shifting nervously around and stayed on his, he informed her, "Let's get somethin' out the way. I'm not only not sleepin' with my housekeeper, but I also don't dally with any of the ladies in my employment, and that includes those who work in the dairy. It's bad for business my gramps and pa always told me."

"Women talk."

"In town?" He arched a brow at her, urging her to continue.

"In brothels," she whispered.

"And?" He cupped her face with both hands, ensuring she didn't look away.

Finally persuaded, she let out a sharp exhale. "Diamond, who had a strong tender for you and who probably would have made a more experienced wife and children's mother for you, commented a couple times how you used to come at least twice a week to...to...for services of the ladies, mainly her. Several months ago, you only started coming to see Miss Kitty. Since everyone knows that Miss Kitty flirts with the men but only has eyes for one man..." her voice trailed off.

"The chatter is that I must be getting' my shaft tended to by another woman or women somewhere else?" he filled in. "Besides my staff, anyone else tossed in?"

"Widow Mallory was tossed in, but mainly Widow Lawrence. More than one of the Jewels said they saw her arm linked through yours when they've been about town."

He didn't dignify the last rumor with an answer. Even though he hadn't taken Widow Lawrence up on her many offers, he had been a randy buck, with a reputation for business and with the ladies, never overstepping with innocent ones. His time with Widow Mallory had been brief and discreet and he would not besmirch the sweet woman's name, especially since she was now married again. However, now that he was married, he'd make sure how he conducted himself around other women, to keep any shadows being cast over Caroline. Focusing his attention on his bride, instead of gossip, he caressed the sides of her face, tracing lines from her temples to her neck, and enjoyed the shiver he felt race through her body. "Everyone's got a past. Just know that my future is you, Caroline. You're the one I chose; you're the only one I want to slack my pleasure on. We clear, wife?"

"Yes." She licked her lips.

He claimed them. At the church, he'd kept the kiss light, chaste. Now, in his home, with his bride, he showed her a glimmer of the intensity of his lust for her. Her lips were pillowy soft beneath his as he moved over them. Still holding her about the neck, he applied enough pressure to tip her head to the side as he ran his tongue along the seam.

She gasped, parting her lips and allowed a wisp of air out.

Garrett swallowed the breath in as he drove his tongue into her mouth. There was no teasing or coyness in his kiss. He wanted her to know his desire for her was barely leashed and at any moment, it could consume them both. Her mouth was warm and wet under his, her soft tongue bowing beneath the commanding force of his. He felt the fluttering movements of it under his own, tickling the sensitive skin below, and he groaned.

She was moaning and her hands settled along his side, clutching his shirt and gripping his flesh.

Heat rose in his body; his cock was swelling, thick and hard in his trousers at her taste, her touch. It took Herculean effort not to lower his hands to her breasts or ass. He yearned to discover the shape and size of them both and grind his eager shaft into the juncture between her thighs and let her know what waited for her. One corner of his mind remembered that his housekeeper was only a couple yards away in the kitchen, and he didn't want her to find him on the first available surface located balls deep in his wife. His wife deserved a better first time than that. He wouldn't disrespect either of them that way.

Ending the kiss, he stared down at her, his breath ragged and his need great. "I believe I'm supposed to be showin' you the house."

Her eyes were glazed and unfocused for a moment. She licked swollen lips, this time gliding her tempting pink tongue over the bottom then slowly across the thick top, as if tasting what was left of him there.

Instantly, he let her go and stepped back. He couldn't continue to touch her and not take her.

She stumbled from his quick release but caught herself as she settled a hand to her stomach.

"I'll get your bag." He turned back to the door, shifting his aching cock to a more comfortable position in his pants as he went.

"It's amazing...big."

Gripping the bag and practically coming at her words, he turned and realized that Caroline was looking around at his house, taking in the front room and upper level. *Get your mind out of the outhouse, she wasn't speaking of your cock.*

"It's our home now. And thank you." He crossed to her. "My pa and Ian helped me build it, when I first arrived with my six cows. It was just this front room, the kitchen and the three rooms upstairs. I always knew I wanted a big family like my parents had."

He watched her walk through the great room as she took in the large, cold, empty hearth, with the two rocking chairs before it. Chairs he'd always imagined he and his wife would sit in during the winter months, talkin' and sharing stories of their day as their kids slept. She glided by the long table before the couch then ran her fingers along the base of the font glass and brass oil lamp on the end table.

He enjoyed the vision she made standing in the space, feeling it all out.

She turned slowly and took it all in. "Is the dining room through there?" She pointed to another open passageway on the side of the room to the right of the hearth, opposite of the archway where Mrs. Copernic had disappeared.

"No. That was one of two additions a couple years ago. It's my office. There's another door that leads into it, so you don't have to worry about the men traipsin' through the house when I'm workin' their part of the day. You can thank my house-keeper for that. She said if I was ever plannin' to have a wife, I needed a space to run the business side of the farm that wasn't the kitchen or the front room table." He chuckled. "I think she actually got tired of my fuss about her straigntenin' up my mess. I couldn't find a darn thing every time I came back to it."

She nodded. "My papa didn't have many things that required him to have a place to keep it and write it down, so he just kept it all in a crate at the corner of his sleeping area."

"Most family farms don't require much."

"Especially if it isn't successful." Her face was expressionless, her tone matter of fact.

Not wanting to send their wedding night into conversation that may depress her, he directed their next path toward the stairs with a jerk of his head. "How about a quick tour of the rooms and we get somethin' to eat?"

"Okay."

"Anything you want to change or add in the house, you can. Besides the doilies and all." He thought about the gift from his foreman's wife. It never struck him how simple his furnishings were until he saw his lovely bride standing in the middle of it. "It's your home."

"I feel like a stranger." Her voice sounded distant.

He wondered if she was thinking of the house she'd lived in with her pa. "Well, do whatever you need to make yourself comfortable here. I'll do my part."

"I'll try."

"All I'm askin'." He held a hand out for her and waited for her to circumvent the furniture back to him. When he took her hand, he felt the shiver that ran through her as sparks ignited up his arm and started heating his blood. He pulled her along beside him up the stairs and wondered if one day, the powerful sensations he experienced every time she was near him or he touched her would abate, if they would just become so comfortable around each other that the fire would go out. He thought about the Reynolds, Copernics, Morgans, and his own parents. Nothing about the calf eyes and heated glances those couples exchanged seemed to state the blaze would die down. Heck, one of the older couples he thought of was the town pastor and his wife. He'd been around them more than a few times and seen Pastor Morgan whisper something to his wife and her face blush, and they'd raised six children, two of them with husbands of their own, and a grown son who was out travelin' the vast country.

Garrett wanted it to be that way between him and Caroline.

"We have three bedrooms and a bathing room installed up here." He gestured to the two open doors down the hall. "Nothing but a bed and dressers in both."

She nodded as she glanced down the way but showed no inclination to go that way.

"A bathing room. I've been in the one at the Reynolds' house when I was younger. I believe after the Russells, they were the first family to have one in Grover. They even beat the Bellmores and Pettigrews getting one, which Mrs. Russell was not happy about, as I recall."

"It's not practical when there are two floors, to lug the water upstairs to fill a copper tub. Especially when it's a large one for a big man like me."

He didn't miss the side glance she took from his shoulders to his feet. He liked her looking at him. He was sure she hadn't missed that he wasn't a slight man in height or girth. The men in his family were pretty wide across the shoulders and chest.

"Do you get your shirts made at the shop in town? I couldn't imagine you finding your size on the mercantile shelf." She stared into his face now as they arrived at the top of the stairs.

"I generally get some made by the handful every couple of years, when my housekeeper tells me they're fallin' apart in the wash. The haberdasher in town usually will take my measurements and I place an order to some company through the mercantile."

"I can make you some shirts. I've made my papa's since I was young. The first few I did, weren't very good and uneven mostly, one sleeve longer than the other and the material bunching at the buttons. I got better over time and Papa never complained about my inexperienced mistakes." She reached out and ran a finger along the seam at his shoulder.

The one he wore now was of two he kept nice for Sunday service and special events. There was nothing sexual about her touch, but it didn't stop the blaze along his skin that traced the path of those fingers of her free hand as they went over the top of his shoulder then journeyed over the stitching that went to his collar.

He clutched her hand and drew her closer to him. Her eyes widened as their bodies made the slightest contact. When she glanced up at him, her eyes darkened.

"Wife, I'm tryin' real hard to make your weddin' night special and not happen in a flash, but you keep runnin' those slim fingers over my chest and I'll take it from there," he growled. He needed her to know he was on thin ice when it came to his desire for her and the river was ragin' beneath the surface.

She snatched her hand away and stepped back so quickly, he had to drop the bag to take her by the waist. He steadied her, ensuring she didn't go topplin' down the stairs. "Whoa there, lovely bunny."

"Why do you call me that?"

"Lovely?" He frowned.

She shifted her gaze away.

Seeing how uncomfortable she appeared at his question about his use of lovely, he wondered if she didn't understand how pretty she was. Caroline Douglas had been one of the beauties in town, even with her slim form and her worn apparel. Sam Douglas had done well to keep her close at his side. Garrett had no doubt it was why Bellmore had wanted her under him so badly. He was just shocked the man hadn't wanted to keep her solely for his own purposes. Why take her to a whorehouse where she'd have to service other men? The dandy had even mentioned that Garrett should make Caroline his mistress instead of a wife. He wondered why Bellmore hadn't done that.

Garrett wouldn't want to share Caroline with anyone else.

"No. Bunny." She moved away from him again, this time in a safer direction and he let her hand go.

"I once saw the loveliest wild brown bunny in the woods by the lake. The sight of it took my breath away."

"Jack rabbits are so common in these parts. What made that one so special?" She moved into the first door.

He picked up the bag before following her into the largest bedroom in the house, their room. He didn't have to tell her that the bunny had hopped less than a foot beside him on the same day he'd seen her bathing. He'd taken it as a sign. Since then, every time he thought of Caroline, she'd been his wild bunny. "It wasn't a jackrabbit. Their fur is more multicolored, with brown, grey and black. This rabbit was plumper and lower to the ground instead of tall, and its fur was the color of chocolate but golden where it was kissed by the sun. It was rare, unique."

He stared at her hair as it sat pinned up and back at her nape. He wanted to see it down around her shoulders again as she'd been that day. "Does the endearment bother you?"

"No. I guess not." Her cheeks looked a little flushed as she looked at him then around the room. "I hope your bunny friend didn't end up in someone's stew." She stopped at the foot of the bed. Unlike the front room, she didn't touch anything in this room. Her hands were clasped before her, her fingers twisting around each other.

Oh, his bunny had ended up in one hot pot after another, but he was determined to save her from any other dangers. Chuckling to himself, he set the bag next to the second wardrobe he had put in. He'd heard stories from other men about how many dresses, blouses, and skirts their wives liked to have and he wanted Caroline to have space to buy as many things as she'd like.

"This is for you to put your clothes in. I'll use the one to the left." He pointed across the room to the chest of drawers between the wide oak wood washstand, unlike the small marble-topped ones that were in the upper rooms of The Harlot and the Hero. The ones he had placed here were wide enough for him to keep his shaving kit to one side of the basket his housekeeper had insisted he keep his brush and tooth powder tin so he'd stop tossing the items on the space beside the wide, shallow porcelain bowl. "I moved my things into the bottom two drawers of the tall chest; the other three are yours."

"Thank you. But just the top one will be fine. I don't need a wardrobe to myself. I only brought my other day dress from the..." Her voice faded away.

He was all too familiar with the type of apparel the Jewels wore, and he was glad she'd left those dresses there. They weren't appropriate for a farmer's wife. "That's fine. At the end of the week, I'll take you into town to Mable's, and you can have made whatever you'd like."

She dragged her hands down her skirt. "That won't be

necessary. A room full of dresses is wasteful. I'll make do with what I have."

He crossed the room to her, then he took her by the shoulders, keeping his tone low because he understood all Caroline had done her whole life in Grover Town was make do, with a pa who'd never garnered the means to provide for more. "I'm a pretty well-off man. I've worked for years to make my dairy farm a success. I plan to use a good portion of that to spoil you, wife. I want to see you in pretty dresses and shifts that just make me want to take it all off you." He lowered his lips to her and whispered in her ear, "Not that I'd need any incentive to see what's hidden beneath your clothes."

Her breath caught.

He felt the breathy sound like a shot to his core that sent his blood back into his cock. He wanted to hear her make all kinds of sounds just like that and to make her scream in pleasure. Inhaling, he took in the sweet, floral scent of her then blew softly along the bare curve where her shoulder and neck met.

She gasped again and shuddered.

It would only take a step to bring her down to the large bed behind her. His hands tightened on her arms as he warred with himself.

"Food...you said we were going to eat."

Taking a moment to place a kiss on that same spot, he then stepped back and dropped his hands at his side. "I did. Come, wife; let's see what Mrs. Copernic has for us."

She let him lace his fingers through hers before he led her out the room.

"Cake. We should have some of the cake Gretchen made for us, too. You may not even like sweets?"

He escorted her down the stairs, in the same way they had journeyed up, side by side. "You will discover, lovely bunny, that your husband has more than one sweet tooth in his mouth."

"I like them too, when I could have them."

When they arrived at the kitchen, it was empty; his house-keeper gone as she'd said. On the long wood table with eight ladderback chairs around it, were two plates filled with stewed chicken, potatoes, and green beans. His housekeeper was a decent cook but not the best. This dish was one of the five staples she made during the week, and she couldn't bake well at all. The iced cake sat uncovered in the center of the table with a knife resting on a white cloth napkin and two small plates beside it. A porcelain pitcher of water and two empty glasses were also on the table, close to their plates.

"Hope you like stewed chicken," he offered with as much enthusiasm as he could muster.

"It smells good. Can I pour you some water?" She stepped to the side seat and left the chair at the end of the table for him.

He wondered if that was by chance or if she was settling into traditional family customs. They had to be ones she'd seen elsewhere, because he'd been inside the small home she and her father lived in and there wasn't much of a table in there and not one with a head of the table. He claimed the seat after she sat. "Please."

Caroline reached for the pitcher and began filling the glass. "Your kitchen is almost as big as the front room. Our house could have fit in here." There was a wistfulness in her voice that had been missing from the bedroom. "That door on the other side of the pantry, does that lead somewhere, the cellar?"

"There is a cellar, or storm room door, in the floor of the pantry." Garrett ladled some stew onto her plate. She held up her hand after the first one, but he added another. She was still thin and he wasn't sure if it was genetics, never having seen her ma, or the lack of food from so many years with her pa. "The other door is the other addition I made, about a year ago. I figured if I were lookin' to marry and have children, that'd take up most of the rooms upstairs. I wanted my ma and pa to have a place when they visited."

"H-how often do they come to town?" Her voice wavered, but her expression was hidden because she had her head bowed over her plate that she'd added a heaping of green beans but only a couple potatoes.

He filed away that his wife really liked green beans, and he'd let Mrs. Copernic know to serve them often. "They usually come once a year, around the end of summer, and stay for about a month or so into fall before headin' back to Wisconsin. My two older brothers run the dairy farm at home. It's more than twice the size of mine here, especially the dairy, and they make more profit from cheese than milk. Steve and Gil takin' over allows my parents the freedom to get out and see about their children and be home through the colder months."

"It must be nice." She ate and remained quiet.

Garrett felt like a heel, going on about his family when Caroline had none. Reaching under the table, he covered her hand in her lap and discovered it was balled in a tight fist. He caressed along her knuckles. "I wasn't thinkin', didn't want to make you feel bad about your family and all."

She glanced down at their hands then up at him. "I like hearing about your family." She shrugged. "I'm going to be sad sometimes, but I don't want you to feel like you have to be on eggshells."

He pulled her hand up and kissed the back of her fingers, now more relaxed. "Now they're your family, too, cuz you're my wife. So, if I'm not around and you need anything, you go to Ian."

She nodded. "I can see how you're brothers, now. You have the same eye color, you're both bigger in the shoulders than most. And you walk the same."

His brows tightened. "Walk the same?"

"Yea, like 'no one better mess with you' swagger."

Tipping back his head, he hooted out a laugh. He knew his brother would like hearing that; Ian prided himself on being a bad ass lawman. "That's one I've never heard before." Meeting her gaze, he asked, "So, you've been watchin' me walk, have you now, Mrs. Rand?"

Her face went flamin' red as her fork clanged against the side of her plate when she dropped it. She tugged at his hand, trying to pull away, but he held fast. "Well...um...well. People walk; it's not hard to see it."

By her reaction, he was sure there was more to it. His pretty bride had evidently been eyein' him when he wasn't lookin', and he liked knowin' it. He planned to be a bad ass husband that she couldn't keep her gaze away from. Hell, if he was smitten with the sight of her, he wanted her feelin' the same about him. The urge to sweep her up and carry her upstairs and bury himself deep inside his captivating bride was rippin' him apart. But he held fast; he needed to have a care for her first.

"Eat, wife," he instructed.

She picked up her fork and began eating.

He went back to his own food but kept hold of her hand, needing to touch her.

HE STOOD ONCE they had finished their meal and the deliciously sweet cake.

Quickly, she reached for his empty dessert plate and stacked it with hers on top of their larger ones.

Placing a hand on her shoulder, he waited until she lifted her chin and met his gaze. "I'll take care of rightin' the kitchen tonight. You get yourself ready upstairs."

"Oh...all right." She glanced away and rose from her seat.

When she pushed her chair forward, he noticed the slight tremors in her hands where they rested on the wood slats.

"Would you like a bath first? I can show you how to work the tap." He scooped up the plates and waited. He was anxious to make her his wife, however, he wanted to ensure she knew her needs came first to him.

She shook her head, still not looking at him but at a spot somewhere beyond his shoulder. "No. I had one before I got dressed to meet...you."

He knew she was going to say Bellmore; the slickster had been the man she had been expecting. Did she want the other man? Was there a part of her that was disappointed it had been him downstairs instead of Daryl Bellmore? His mind played images of Caroline allowing the other man to kiss her, touch her, draw her beneath him, and his blood heated with rage. His fingers tightened on the plates and he knew he had to shove the thoughts away before he had to explain to his housekeeper why there was a pile of them in the bin.

"Upstairs. Now. I'll follow shortly." He heard the harsh words from his mouth, but there were so many emotions blazing through him now, he couldn't temper them.

Caroline let out a small gasp before she fled the kitchen.

He didn't go after her, even though he felt the pull in his body the farther she moved away from him. Strutting to the sink, he set down the dishes then gripped the copper edge of the basin. Staring out the window into the darkened night on his property, he could see the lights of the bunkhouse off in the distance. He knew his men who were there sat around singin', jawin' and playing rounds of various card games. Some, who were married, were home with their families, while others were already in town, dividin' themselves between Miss Kitty's and the little saloon, while Garrett was here attemptin' to get his ass under control. His jealousy and agitation over Bellmore placing a claim on Caroline first had him wanting to rush the stairs and waste no time in stamping there, but his would be permanent. *Let no man put asunder.*

Caroline deserves better than that. And she did. She wasn't some whore they were fightin' over like two bulls over a heifer in heat. *She's your wife.*

As his wife, he'd made a vow to treat her well and protect her, and right now, that meant from himself. He grabbed a cloth and dampened it before he wiped down the table and moved the empty bowl and pot into the sink. He made himself rinse off the dishes instead of just leavin' them in the sink for his housekeeper, anything, just to slow himself down, give Caroline time. When everything was straightened and the tin lid back over the remainder of the cake on the table, he turned down the wick of the four sconces then started upstairs, dousing other lights in the front room on the way.

His barely banked urgency wouldn't allow him to take the stairs less than two at a time. At the top of the stairs, with a darkened house behind him and the only remaining light in the room where Caroline was most likely smothered under quilts and sheets, preserving the last vestige of her maidenly virtue, he took a deep breath.

He started forward into the open door, where he could first only see one side of the bed, where it was empty. When he entered the room, he saw that the other side was vacant too and the linens weren't even turned down. He glanced right then left, wondering if she'd hightailed it out of there.

Garrett froze. Caroline stood between the two curtained windows on the other side of the room with her multi-shade brown locks down around her shoulders, in a gossamer gown of bright white as if fresh snow had fallen around her body. With her hands at her sides, nothing was concealed from his sight, even though a satin ribbon was laced through it at the top and tied in a bow at her collar. With any other material, the gown would have been modest, virginal. But there was nothing innocent about the apparel or the confidence of the woman who stood there in it.

As he consumed her with his gaze, a frisson of heat licked down his spine, spreading through his core and straight into his trousers. His cock became harder than the wooden stakes around his property securing the fencing to keep his cows in boundaries. Only the material of his pants was keeping in his hard shaft. His bunny had always had this effect on him, since the day he'd seen her bathing in the river. He wanted her.

Her breasts were small but perfectly pear-shaped, with dusky rose nipples that were taut and large. He wondered if their tightness was because of the coolness of the night or if she felt the heat that brewed between them. He continued to lower his eyes down along her narrow waist. She was thin in frame, but her ribs were not prominent as he had suspected from her years of meager eating. Where her waist dipped, he found himself captivated by the indention of her navel—he wanted to lick around it and see if she was sensitive there. Hell, he wanted to discover every place on his wife's body that made her laugh and sigh.

He paused as his eyes roamed lower and he discovered that the dark thatch of hair he'd seen years ago showcased through her wet shift was no more. Now, she was bare, every strand removed, and only the pouty, plump lips of her sex were revealed behind the sheer gown. His hands tightened as desire slammed into him. He wanted to reach out and part her thighs to see how pink her center was. Was she wet? Aching? She would be. He'd ensure it.

"I didn't know what side of the bed you preferred."

Her voice, soft but steady, drew his gaze to her face. There he frowned. Something was off. In an instant, his brain formulated what he was seeing and what was wrong. "Take it off," he commanded.

Lifting her hands, she grasped the ends of the ribbon.

"No, the lip paint and kohl," he instructed. "That enhancement may be expected at the brothel, but not here. Not in our marriage bed." He wasn't averse to her using a little lip coloring when they were out at a town function but didn't want any falsehoods when they were together.

"Oh. I was sure...didn't know." She dropped her hands and began wringing them before her belly.

The tremors were back in her voice and Garrett could have put a boot to his own ass. He wasn't trying to scare her or make her unsure of herself, but he needed her to know that some things she'd learned at the Harlot would be welcomed, while others would not.

Making haste, she took the steps past him to the washstand. In the small mirror mounted there, she picked up a damp cloth that had been hanging on the ring, one she must have used when she'd come upstairs, then she opened a jar of cream and smeared it on her face before applying the cloth in circular motions to her face.

As she stood with her back to him, the sight of her pale, round, upturned, heart-shaped ass made his balls fill and draw tight below the base of his cock.

"Fuck." The word was more of a growl than actual words.

His mind played with thoughts of all the things he'd like to do to her sweet ass, things that would make her cry out and moan. He was a hungry and needy man who enjoyed bedding of all kinds, his wife would soon discover.

It only took a moment before she faced him again. Her fresh face resembled once again the woman who had captured his interest years ago.

She stood there with her hands behind her back now. He was sure it was to hide her nervousness. She'd been so confident moments before and he'd ruined it with his boorish tone.

"Come to me, Caroline." He'd wait no longer.

Without hesitation, she moved with light steps and a sensual sway of her hips that drew his eyes to the fluidity of her form. Her breasts bounced just enough to shift her nipples along the diaphanous material. Her soft sigh flowed before her across the room. The innocent wonder in her darkened brown eyes made her more beautiful than a houseful of Kitty's whores. Caroline was lovely and special. It was her inner strength which had carried her through years of struggle and survival with her pa that made her this preserved treasure.

He didn't touch her yet as she halted before him. Holding her gaze, he ordered, "Show me your breasts, lovely bunny."

Again, she reached up, and this time he didn't stop her from untying the ribbon. The light fabric parted instantly, only held up by that satiny strip. She shimmied and rolled her shoulders just enough to aid the gown's descent.

Still staring into her eyes, he could see the rapid rise and fall of her pert breasts in his lower peripheral. He continued to hold her gaze, enjoying watching the anticipation of his bride as she stood before him. When her lips parted in an inhalation of air, he allowed his gaze to drop to them, but still, he went no further. It was delicious torture for them both.

"Kiss me, wife." He wanted her as a part of this night, not

simply giving herself as a willing sacrifice of her own freedom. He needed her desire for the act, him, what he could give her and what they shared to burn in her blood the way it did in his.

Caroline leaned in, placing her hands on his sides for balance, to steady herself as she set her lips on his.

THIRTEEN

He didn't move, refusing to aid her in this moment.

Barely able to do more than drag her lips lightly over his, she took one step, then the final one that brought her breasts against his chest and closed the gap between their mouths. He felt the shuddered breath she took in as it entered his mouth, and she guided her tongue inside. She may have known what to do from his kiss earlier and her training, but she was a novice, completely. Her teeth clinked against his more than once. Her tongue darted in and out of his mouth instead of caressing and stroking along the hidden sensitive spots inside. But she kept it up, deepened the kiss, flicked beneath his tongue to coax him to come play with her. Her inexperience was still a turn on, an erotic teasing that made him groan.

When his tongue entered her mouth, she wrapped her lips around it, drawing it deeper by sucking on it. She sucked along it, turning her mouth left then right as she bobbed along the wet appendage.

Shit. Fuck! The words exploded in his mind as he thought about her doing that same action to his cock. His straining cock must have thought of it too, because it miraculously hardened even more. If he didn't undress and get inside of her soon, he knew several buttons would pop off from his pants soon.

No longer able to be a bystander, he cupped the back of her head and took her mouth. He wasn't gentle or kind; he allowed the years of pent up craving for this woman to come forth and claim her. Her moans vibrated from her mouth to his as she took and gave back in the kiss.

He tore his mouth away. He enjoyed the feel of her pliant mouth beneath his and could spend hours kissing her, but he wanted so much more of her tonight. As he gripped her waist, he felt the shivers coursing through her. His gaze traveled along the slim column of her neck, over her collarbone, sweeping from left to right, then he went lower until he set his eyes on her breasts. Beautiful creamy breasts, dark pink nipples swollen with need. From across the room, he'd seen that her nipples were large, distinct, but he hadn't realized they had a little length to them as well. He knew one day they would be ripe and perfect for feeding their children, but now they were a treat for her husband. Lifting a hand, he swept a knuckle just beneath one lower swell. It was warm and softer then the finest silk.

She quivered against his hand.

Sensitive. He did the same action to the other breast.

His wife moaned this time.

When he rose to her face, he saw she was biting deep into her bottom lip. "It seems my bride enjoys havin' her breasts played with. That's good, because I like to play with 'em."

He bowed his head and dragged his lips along her throat, nipping her satin flesh, not hard enough to mar her soft, golden skin there. Inhaling, he took in her sweet scent, unsure of what floral notes combined with the headiness of her musk. What he *was* sure of was that it wasn't the rose of the soaps she'd sold at the mercantile. He'd lifted them a time or two to his nose under the guise of searching for the something woodsy, only to use the time to imagine the rosy scent had been on her skin while she bathed at the river. He hadn't been close enough to smell her, take her scent in for his erotic dreams. He could now, and the reality was so much better than anything he could have fantasized about.

At the curve of her neck, he swept along it, it gave way to her shoulder, then returned into the valley above her collarbone to trace patterns.

"Oh...Garrett..." Caroline tilted her head away from him, giving him more access to the area as she moaned.

The responses she made were natural, real and unrehearsed. There was too much wonder and surprise in her sounds, as if she was discovering her own body even as he did.

One kiss after another, he walked his lips down her chest until he reached one of her breasts. He wrapped an arm around her waist to lift her up and hold her against him, her feet barely grazing the wood floor.

Garrett kissed around the round globe, drawing the skin along the inside valley between her breasts into his mouth. Pulling at it firmly, he felt her clutch at his shoulders and whimper. When he pulled away, there was already a dark purple mark that had bloomed there. He'd marked her. Before the night was over, he'd place one on the inside of her thighs and another on her sweet ass. No one else would see it but the two of them. And he wanted that every time his wife dressed and undressed, she would know and remember who had placed them there, who she belonged to. It would be her first lesson in knowing her husband was possessive as fuck about what belonged to him. Caroline Rand was number one on that list.

His tongue traveled under one breast to the other, and he

tasted the saltiness of her scent and the beads of sweat that collected there. Every new taste and smell of her set his teeth on edge with desire. He made wide circles in a figure-eight pattern, each path narrower as he moved closer to her nipples. Finally, he arrived at the first stiff peak as he circled the tip of his tongue right at the edge of the deep, pink flesh around her needy tight center.

"Garrett..." she whispered his name as she arched her back, offering herself to him.

He knew she needed him to calm the ache he'd created in her body, and he planned to do just that and then some, but he would do it in his time. Shifting his gaze up, he watched her face as he took one of her nipples into his mouth. He sucked on it, groaning to himself as the stiffness jabbed into his tongue. It was the berried center that was the width and size of the tip of his smallest finger. Being a breast man, he knew nipples and his wife's were larger and longer than most, a succulent treat. He could feast on them all night. Sinking his teeth along the side, he flicked the sensitive center.

"Oh...oh...Garrettttt..." She was writhing her delicious willowy form against him.

Instantly, he could tell she was susceptible to his oral tutelage, and it made him draw on her stronger, harder. He felt her finger plow into his hair, fisting it, holding him against her as she moaned. The sharp sparks of pain along his scalp made him give her more. Moving from one breast to the other, he played with it in the same way. Her cries of pleasure and the bucking of her hips against his erection made him groan. Swirling his tongue over her tip, he intermittently sucked and flicked it mercilessly, giving her no quarter.

Sliding one of his hands down along her spine until he was cupping one supple ass cheek, squeezing and stroking it through the thin fabric, his ears picked up on her sighs and the soft murmur of his name from her lips. Opening his mouth wide, he took in as much of her breasts as he could, so that he was pressing her hard peak to the roof of his mouth from the bottom only, to swipe over the center as he drew.

She was now quaking, her body bucking, thrusting her soft pussy against his rampant hardness. All the signs she was giving off showed that she was on edge, on the verge of sensual madness.

Lifting his other hand, he cupped her other breast then pressed her nipple between his fingers, compressing the tightness.

Her short nails dragged along his scalp to the base of his neck before her world split in half. "Garrett, ah, Garrett, Garrett...ahhh..." she screamed.

Garrett heard his name come from her lips as a chant of the ultimate satisfaction as she came, twisting, thrashing, and crying out her pleasure. Amazed to discover that his wife could climax from having her nipples stimulated, shot heat through his body and made his dick weep with joy. He wanted inside her, to know the feel of all the glorious tremors that wracked her body now. He continued to ply her breasts with teasing pain, until she settled, with intermittent quivers.

Allowing her nipple to pop from his mouth, he stared into her face, seeing her features flushed, her eyes wide with wonder and shock.

He was pretty damn sure it was a new experience for her. "Was that your first climax, lovely bunny?"

She licked her lips and shifted her gaze from him as she nodded. "The other Jewels talked about it what it felt like, but..." Her voice drifted away.

"But you had no reference for their experience?"

"No."

"Well, there's more, darlin'. So much more." He turned

and walked her over to the bed, before he set her down on her feet.

Caroline's brow knitted into a crease between her eyebrows. "More. How? What?"

"As much as I want to tickle your ear and tell you about the ways I plan to make you come tonight, it's better to be shown."

"Okay." She was clutching the gown at her waist, keeping it up while not covering her rosy, damp, sensitive buds.

"The nightdress is pretty, but I don't want anything keeping me from having access to all of you. Drop it," he told her. "Lie back on the bed."

When she let it go, the light material floated to the floor around her feet.

Garrett let his gaze caress all the skin now available to his sight, even though the transparent gown hadn't really hidden anything. He still just wanted Caroline naked before him. Taking hold of her shoulders, he felt the warm silk of her skin then pressed her down to the bed. Once she was sitting on the side, he guided her to lie back along the light green counterpane. It was something his housekeeper had placed on his bed. He hadn't really paid it much attention, but seeing how the soft green made the pale golden glow of Caroline's skin stand out, he liked it.

Lowering himself to the floor before her, he reached out and parted her knees until they rested as wide as his shoulders. He could see the evidence of her desire and the residual of her climax. The lips of her sex were swollen and glistening.

When he reached out and slid a finger down along the wet seam, Caroline sat up and stared along the length of her upper body. Her eyes connected with him. "What...are you doing? Don't you want to just have sex, reach your pleasure now?"

"Pleasing you...is my pleasure." Finding her clit, he circled the firm bit of flesh.

"Oh." Her hips tilted up then away.

He marveled at how his wife's body was like a garden of delight, ripe for him to pluck and turn her inside out. "Relax; let me take care of you."

Her eyes flashed, and she hesitated, looking unsure of what she should do. He was sure she was debating the training she had learned. In the house, it would have been all about the paying male client, however, he would show her that the rules of Kitty's house didn't have any precedence in their home.

"Caroline, don't make me repeat myself."

She shifted her arms, so she plopped back on the bed and stared up at the ceiling, as she let out a heavy sigh.

He smiled at her response. There would be plenty of time in their marriage for her to give his body her undivided attention, but now was not it. Placing both his palms against her thighs, he pressed her legs wider. He took in all her glistening, smooth skin. There was so much cream coating her on the outside of her pussy, his mouth watered. He couldn't wait to taste her. From the distance, he could smell the rich, warm scent of her essence. The floral fragrance of whatever soap she'd used mingled with the intoxicating nectar of her natural musk. It was an aroma he would never tire of smelling. He wanted it painting his hands, face, and his tongue. Leaning in, he set the fingers of both his hands at her lips and separated her juicy, full labia.

Her dark rosy center, the engorged nub, and the tiny opening of her entrance was before him. Licking around her tight center, he took his first taste of her, and her sweet, heady flavor bloomed along his tongue. He felt her small crevice flex against his tongue as the room echoed with her gasp. Slowly, he swiped up along her delicate, savory inner folds until he reached the underside of her hooded clit.

Caroline's moan was loud.

He did it three more times and smiled to himself as her thighs relaxed and widened. When he reversed his action, going from her clit to her entrance, only to go back up and circle her tip, tremors ran through her.

"Please. Please, Garrett."

He loved her vocal begging. Not stopping, he continued to lick her all along her wet skin. He even sampled the cream covering her inner thighs. She was so wet, he could only imagine how she was going to feel once he buried his rampant cock inside her tight, wet pussy. When he finally latched onto her eager button, drew it between his lips and gave it the same devotion he had paid to her nipples, the room filled with her pleas and moans.

Caroline tried to draw her legs closed, pressing against his forehead and trying to push him away even as she thrust her sweet pussy against his mouth. She was a dichotomy of lust. Even as she wanted him to ease away and cease the assault, her body needed him to persist. And persist he did. He licked, sucked, and drank of her erotic liquid like a man lost in the desert for years and finally before an oasis. His wife was his fantasy come to life. Digging his hands into her supple thighs, he kept her just how he wanted her, available to his torment.

Flick. Flick. Flick. Flick. He goaded her toward an orgasm. Garrett refused to stop until he had her cum dripping fresh from the source.

Then it happened, his name reverberated against the walls of his room, the house, as she came hard and loud. Beneath his hands and mouth, his wife was bucking violently.

Unrelenting, he pushed her further, taking her to the next cliff until she dropped off and one orgasm became two.

"Garrett...please...no...please...oh, oh...Yes! No! Yessss...." She was crying and whimpering as her body took over and followed his lead.

Reaching up, he captured her nipples then squeezed and plucked them, knowing the pain along her sensitive buds would push her toward another release. He released her clit, only to drive his tongue down her slit and into her snug passage. In and out, he fucked her orally.

So damn good. She was so wet, her cream coating his tongue and satisfying his hunger for her even as it incited it. When she was shaking and started the climb for the third time, he drew out, then he dipped lower, past the small, fleshy area until he could titillate the puckered rosette.

"Garrett!" Her voice rose as she shifted away from him.

He chuckled as he moved away from her. Not tonight, but one day, he'd discover how far her training had gone at the house. He looked forward to showing her all the nefarious things they could do that catapulted her into bliss.

Turning his head, he set his lips into the tender skin of one of her inner thighs, already showing reddened scrapes from his beard as she'd squeezed and thrust against his face. Just like he had done to her breasts, he placed his mark there as he continued to roll her nipple between his fingers. Finally, moving away, he rose to his feet as he stared down at his wife. Her thighs were wide, flushed.

"Too much." Caroline's voice and body were both quivering as she rolled to her side, watching him. She curled her body in, as if attempting to ward off the shudders coursing through her.

"Never enough, bunny." He meant that. He'd never get enough of pleasuring her. He wasted little time in removing his own clothing. Toeing off his boots, he kicked them to the side, not caring where they ended up. His shirt went next, buttons practically ripped from their holes before he was snatching the cotton from his pants then letting it flutter to the floor behind him. He attacked his belt and the fastenings, keeping the flap of his trousers closed.

Golden brown to midnight dark, Caroline's eyes reflected then snuffed out the flickering lamp light. Garrett marveled at the heated glow of his wife's gaze tracking every movement of his hands as he stripped off the layers separating him from aligning his naked body with hers. Once he'd shucked his pants, he stood there and allowed her to take all of him in.

She sat up in the bed. Bringing her knees up to her chest, she shook her head as her gaze locked in on his hardness.

He arched a brow at her. "Not what you were expectin', darlin'?"

Her throat moved up and down as she swallowed, still staring at him. "It's nothing like all the—"

"Wife. I'm going to need you to finish that sentence," he growled. Jealousy's green-eyed head rose and sank its teeth into his core. "What other man's rod have you seen?"

It must have been his tone that shot her eyes up to his face. She licked her lips. "All the wooden ph-phalluses and the sketches. Kitty and the women gave things to me so I could learn, so I would know what to do to please the men."

Some of the tension receded from his shoulders at her words. "The only man's cock you're goin' to concern yourself with pleasin' is mine."

She nodded. She lowered her sights again to his shaft then back to his face. Shifting, she moved on her knees to the end of the bed. She reached toward him. "May I touch it?"

Taking hold of her hand, he grasped it inches from his hard length. "Not now. Later." He lifted her hand and kissed her palm. "I'm on edge as it is. If your hands take hold of me, I'll lose all that I'm holdin' back."

She sighed and curled her fingers into his face, caressing the short hairs of his beard.

Encircling her waist, he brought her body to his and held her there, just enjoying feeling all her soft warmth against his. Caroline in his arms, this was peace.

He brought her body to the bed, shifting them back so they were stretched out along the mattress. He kissed her, not deep and hard as before, just licked and shifted his lips over hers. He loved how she settled beneath him and returned his kiss. Insinuating his legs between hers, he pushed them out until he was situated in the space. Her wetness was coating his length as he rested it right on her swollen sex.

Ending the kiss, he looked down into her face. He took in all her unique beauty as he ran a finger along the side of her face until he brushed it over her lips.

Her dewy lips parted, and her warm breath fluttered over his digit.

Continuing down, he slid it down her neck, between her pert breasts, then journeyed down along her ribs and caressed the valley of her navel. When he got to her sex, he took hold of his hard shaft. He pumped once down his length before he brought the head right through her slick heat.

She shivered and her eyes darkened. He was intoxicated on the intense coffee brown color gazing up at him. At her entrance, he pressed forward.

"Garrett?" She tensed beneath him.

Stopping with just the bulbous head inside of her, and bringing his hand up, he laced his hands in hers as he brought their linked fingers above her head. He kept her from bearing all his weight yet by shifting most of his lower body as his knees dug into the mattress beneath them.

"Wrap your legs around me, lovely bunny."

Even the smallest shift of her body shot through him, from

the tip through the shaft and into his core. He groaned but kept himself still until she was positioned right.

As she brought her legs up around him, the action caused her pelvis to tilt and her thighs to widen and give him more room.

Once her ankles had crossed at the small of his back, he lowered his head, bringing his lips against hers and locking his gaze with hers, then he whispered, "I take thee, Caroline, as my wife." He drove forward.

He felt her body jerk as he broke through the barrier of her virginity and pushed through her tight walls.

Her eyes flashed and liquefied, becoming bronze crystals as she cried out at his claiming.

He refused to silence her scream with his lips. Instead, he listened and felt each shudder from her, drawing in the pains of her loss of innocence. Stroking his thumbs over the delicate skin of the inside of her wrists, he remained still, waiting.

Finally, her breathing resumed in a more eased rhythm out of her lips and her legs, which had a vice grip on his hips minutes before, began to relax. The walls of her sex flexed around him, taking him in another inch.

"Lift up to me, wife."

Her brow furrowed, concern darkening her gaze. A tremor went through her.

It would be easy for him to sink his length farther into her tight sex, leading them, and he would, but right now he wanted to give her the chance to adjust, accept the act.

"All right." Her tongue darted out and ran over her upper lip as she concentrated on what to do.

He groaned at the sight but stayed in place, even as sweat beaded along his spine from the urge to dominate her.

Tentatively, she moved not even an inch and took him a little deeper.

Tremors of heat went through him, causing his cock to flex and jump inside her.

She gasped and met his gaze.

A lopsided smile tipped his lips. He wouldn't apologize for his cock responding to the slick slide of her sweet pussy along it.

Bravely, she arched up more, inviting his length farther in as she whimpered then sighed. She kept going gingerly until the mouth of her sex touched him. "Ahhh."

"Mm. Now down," he gritted out. Shit, his whole body was tight, shaking as he restrained himself.

Caroline pressed her hips back into the bed, leaving just his crown inside her.

"Up." His head was spinning from the erotic sensation.

Following his directive, she rose again, this time not stopping until she had most of his shaft inside of her. "Oh...it feels...feels—"

"Fucking good. Again," he demanded.

She did. Now there was no hesitation as she slipped him out.

"Up. Down. Up. Down," he instructed.

Their moans and groans echoed each of his commands as they began a cadence of pleasure.

"Ahh, yes...oh." Caroline began moving without his direction. When she arched up, she flexed her tight, wet pussy around his cock as she swiveled her sweet hips at his base, the fetters holding him in check with patience torn apart.

"Stay with me, bunny." He pulled out only to drive deeper, harder than even she had taken him.

"Oh! Garrett!"

He buried his face in the side of her neck as he started working his cock in and out of the sweet haven of her pussy. He was pushed by a madness of pleasure he couldn't fight, didn't want to fight. His body needed her; he had to have her and claim her, take her body over and make sure every area of her channel would be carved out and shaped by his shaft. With every thrust, he was painting his hardness with her cream and sculpting her walls with the tool of his cock.

In and out. Over and over again, he was loving her, claiming her, fucking her. His pumping became harder and harder. He was pulling all the way out and driving back in to his base while kissing the mouth of her sex. Her swollen lips flattened, stretching wide and tight around him.

"Oh...yes. Garrett...ahh oh." Her hands were squeezing him as tightly as her sex as she dug her nails into his knuckles. Whimpers and moans tumbled from her lips as he rocked her hips under him.

"Just like that," he encouraged as she tipped her head back and arched her middle against him as he pushed back in, swiveling his hips to stroke over the right spot.

"Oh. Oh. Oh...please." Her face was shadowed by the bewilderment of the act as she yielded her body to him.

Training had nothing on the actual act.

Placing kisses up the side of her neck until he got to her ear, he nipped at the lobe then sucked it into his mouth. Licking around the shell of her ear as he rocked into her, he whispered, "Tell me to fuck you."

She moaned as his knees inched a little higher up his sides. Her sex was drenched, creaming around him, and soaking them both. She was close.

His balls were drawn tight below the base of his cock; he was barely holding his release back. "Fuck me. Say it, Caroline," he ordered.

He refused to allow her to hold back anything from him. He would command her completely. His body needed it. His mind demanded it.

When he looked into her face, her eyes were closed, her face constricted and twisted in passion. As if she could feel his gaze, she turned her face from him, as if her own hunger shamed her. He'd allow her the small reprieve only.

"Caroline," he growled. Keeping them both on the edge, he pressed into her, fusing his pelvis to hers as he ground against her clit.

"Ah!" She shuddered under him as a single tear rolled from the corner of her eye. "Fuck me. Please."

Her plea was his undoing. Pulling one hand from hers, he cupped her chin to turn her mouth toward his and sealed them. His kiss was as hard and deep as his hips drove into her. Going deeper than he had before, he gave neither of them mercy. He pistoned forward, driving his full length into her in the same tempo as he thrust his tongue into her mouth then sucked her tongue into his, forcing her to accept his claim even as she took what she needed from him.

The big bed rocked beneath them, the carved wood headboard slamming into the wall from the force of his momentum.

She went over first, her release almost violent in nature as her body quaked, vibrating around him from her channel to her lips. Her cries roared into his mouth as she drove her heels into the back of his thighs, arching into him, her sex constricting like a fist around his length.

The orgasm ripped through his soul as his entire body filled with a dizzying heat that stole his breath and went from the tail end of his spine up to the base of his neck and spread out into his fingertips and lower limbs while the fire of his release shot from him, filling his wife's sex, bathing her womb. He stayed deep, his cock impossibly still hard until her clutching passage wrung every drop from him.

His kiss softened, his lips a mere whisper as their lips

moved lightly in their touching. He shifted, withdrawing, and felt her shudder. A satisfaction as he'd never known before with any other woman settled around him like an early morning fog, blinding him to everything else except Caroline. He shuddered and rolled to the side, both of their bodies covered in sweat, their exertion palpable in the room. Her wince was evident in the pinch of her features and the small hiss she attempted to control as she rolled her bottom lip in to stifle it. He should have felt like an ass for having taken her so forcefully, but he couldn't pull that emotion out after enjoying being inside her so thoroughly.

Silent, he pulled her against him, his lips pulling up into a small grin when she curled in along his side. He stroked the damp hair away from her face as she rested her head on his chest. The contentment he experienced in that moment told him that no words were necessary, so he just held her. Sated, heart pounding, he stared up at the ceiling with his wife in his arms. He wasn't sure what life would bring their way, but he knew he wanted a lot more nights just like this one.

His mind reminded him how close he had come to losing Caroline to another. However, he knew he would have moved Heaven and Earth to have her in his arms, any other man be damned.

"Darlin', you all right?"

Quiet greeted him, and he knew that his wife had fallen asleep. He was aware of the weight of her slight form and her heavy breathing. He stifled his chuckle at her forceful breaths that fluttered along his chest.

Staying that way for a time, he allowed her to get the rest she needed. He wasn't sure how long he held her in his arms before he got up, slipping from the bed to go to the washstand. Pouring water into the bowl from the pitcher, he wet a fresh cloth then returned to the bed. Caroline hadn't moved; she was still on her side, with her hand on the empty spot where he had lain while her other hand was under her cheek. Stepping over to the bed, he guided her to her back.

She didn't even awake when he cleansed her, gliding the moist cloth between her thighs, removing his seed and her virgin's blood. A small whimper was the only sign her body responded on some level to his ministrations. Once that was finished, he returned to the washstand to wipe himself down.

Back at the bed, he turned down the lamp on the nightstand then crawled into the bed, maneuvering the top spread from under her body before pulling it over them. Under the blanket, she rolled to her side and snuggled deep as he curled his body behind her, stretching his length along hers. Thankful, he closed his eyes and followed his new bride into sleep.

FOURTEEN

"Sleep."

That single word had been the only thing Caroline had been aware of when she came awake. For a moment, she felt disoriented, unsure why the sun was so bright in the room. She had always been an early bird, but there was so much sun in the room, she knew it was well beyond sunrise. Inhaling, she took in the heady warmth of woody, honeyed overtones that made her aware of Garrett. Intoxicating, soft cedarwood was what his scent made her think of. It was one of the oils Kitty had among her collection.

Garrett's smell did something to her, gave her a sense of peace and protection that she couldn't explain. She hadn't been able to identify his natural scent when she'd run into him a few times in town, but now she had a name for it. She thought about writing notes on him in her journal, as his own natural male musk combined with it made it unique. At that moment, she recalled she had never taken her journal from the brothel.

Groaning, she shoved her hands through her hair and rolled to her back.

"Ah." The throbbing soreness between her thighs made images of the night before come flooding back. Garrett had pleased her in ways she had only attempted to imagine. Nothing compared to actually having the man touch her, kiss her, everywhere, all over her body. She'd climaxed so many times, to the point of physical and mental exhaustion. She wasn't even sure how long she'd slept before she found herself awakened and rolled to her stomach.

Her new husband had kissed and licked along her spine to her buttocks. There, he had stroked his incredible tongue between her legs again. By the time he'd finished there, she'd been begging him to bury himself inside her.

Blazing heat infused her face as she thought about all the things he had coaxed, rather demanded, her to say to him. Naughty things he'd growled in her ear as he thrust deep while he slipped his hands beneath her and cupped her breasts, pinching her nipples.

She moved a hand beneath the covering and palmed one of her breasts, feeling the tenderness there. She moaned.

Not wanting Garrett or Mrs. Copernic to think that she was lazy or thought herself too good to get up before noon since she was married to such a successful livestock owner, she flipped the cover back and wiggled her body to the edge of the bed. The pain shot up through her sex from the over stimulation and avaricious attention from Garrett's manhood, both long and wide, something she had not been prepared to see or receive. It still amazed her that it had all fit within her body. And she was now paying sharply.

Rising, she grimaced as she glanced around, but didn't see her gown anywhere. Garrett's clothing from the night before was no longer scattered around the floor where he'd tossed them. She took a few steps to one of the two windows and pulled back the drapes a little to look outside, to see what time of day it was. The windows faced the front of the house. There was a flurry of activity going on. Some men stood along a gate and a narrow corral, just wide enough for a big cow to move though, that led to the barn where only a single door was open. Three other men were on horseback behind the cows, leading them toward the narrow fencing. Most of the men, she didn't recognize, but her gaze was drawn to one tall, broad-shouldered form on the back of a chestnut horse. King. Garrett. She couldn't help admiring the pose of his seat and his fluid movement. He controlled both the big animal he rode as well as the barrel-bodied black and white beasts moving in mass around him.

He controlled you just as well last night and in the wee hours of the morning.

Flipping the drapes back in place, she then turned and made strides across the room, no longer looking for her sheer gown. Not needing it, she moved over to the washstand. Taking a moment to examine her body in the wide looking glass behind the bowl, she stared at her nudity and wondered if she could see a difference in the woman who stood there now compared to the one in the brothel just yesterday. There was a rosiness to her skin, a few abrasions in places over her body from her husband's short beard. She gasped when she saw the deep purplish-red mark at the inside of one of her breasts, a stamp or claim.

She blushed to the roots of her hair as she thought about other places he'd sucked her. Parting her thighs, she saw the second mark there. Her sex throbbed, recalling just how rampant his mouth had been on her, driving her to a mindless climax. She turned and saw another on one of her rear cheeks, low at the bottom curve. She refused to ponder why the visual evidence of his brand made her core clench and her heart throb, the response bewildering.

Shaken, she glanced away. When she started to reach for the pitcher, a small piece of vellum caught her eye. She picked it up and read the note.

TAKE *your time in coming down, lovely bunny. Take a bath. Your body needs the soaking. I will see you at noontime if you don't make it down to break our fast.*

Your husband

A SHIVER RAN through her body and she blushed again at his mention of why her body would need a good soaking. She set the message down, then took a moment to use the soap and razor to remove the new growth from between her thighs. The scraping of the blade's edge made her press her lips together as it glided across her tender pieces, but after a month of performing the act, she was both quick and efficient. Once that was done, she went to the chest of drawers and pulled open the first one, the only one she had put something in, and removed her cotton shift. Dropping that over her head, she went to the wardrobe where her two day dresses hung and her carpetbag rested. She removed her jasmine oil from it and a cake of soap. The box that was inside it, she had placed in the cabinet beneath the washstand. She didn't think she'd have use of the other items, since she would no longer be working in the whorehouse.

She didn't want to discard the items since the ladies had given them to her, so, shrugging, she went out the door to locate the bathing room.

Less than thirty minutes later, with a nice warm bath to draw out some of the aches in her body, she was dressed in her other dress and headed downstairs.

"Morning, Mrs. Rand," Mrs. Copernic greeted her with a wide smile when Caroline entered the kitchen. The housekeeper, a woman of color, was at the stove stirring something in a pot that appeared extremely thick and opaque. "Didn't 'spec to see you up and down so early. Mr. Rand said you might sleep in, due to the long, excitin' day you had. Weddin' and all."

"Good mornin'. I'm usually up with the dawn or before." She shoved away the thoughts of just why she'd been so exhausted. "Is there anything I can help with?"

The older woman eyed her as she lifted the spoon from the pot, the gooeyiness oozing down the spoon to land back into the bubbling pool with a plop. "How's your cookin' skills?"

Caroline smiled. "Pretty good. Cooking for myself and my papa, I had to make sure the small amounts we had was the best; we couldn't afford the waste."

"I've always hated cookin', and my husband is a real simple man and just likes a handful of things, like chicken stew." Mrs. Copernic placed a hand on her hip. "Mr. Rand hired me as housekeeper and asked if I'd be willin' to prepare his meals at least mornin' and evenin'. If you don't mind, I'd 'preciate if I could still keep the house and laundry together if you'll feed your man."

"That's perfectly fine by me."

"Phew." Mrs. Copernic banged the spoon on the side of the pot then set it on the counter. "Then if you don't mind makin' something edible out of this, Mr. Rand usually don't take his breakfast until after the mornin' milkin' is done. Should give you about an hour and half. He likes something hearty that sticks, cuz he usually don't eat again until supper." She removed the apron covering her white shirtwaist and grey skirt.

"My pleasure." Receiving the apron with a light heart,

Caroline switched places with the housekeeper. She had been concerned how she was going to fit into the farm life that already ran efficiently, and now, she at least had her space in the kitchen until she figured out what came next for her.

"If you don't find what you need in the pantry or on the shelves, then make a list and I can go into town and get it for ya."

"I'm sure I'll be fine." Caroline took hold of the cast iron pot handle with a kitchen towel and moved it to a trivet on the counter. She promptly put a lid on it. She would decide later how to repair the damage to the overcooked oats.

"I'll leave you to it then." The housekeeper started out of the archway then stopped and turned back to her. "Garrett needed someone to care for him, a wife. I'm glad you're here."

Caroline knew that the right thing to say was that she was happy to be there and his wife as well, but so much had happened to her in just over a month, she'd have to see how she settled in before she could claim that. "I'd spent so many years caring for my papa, I've been feeling a little out of sorts, so it seems to have worked out for us both."

With a nod and a smile, the older woman walked away.

CAROLINE FELT his presence in the house before she saw him in the kitchen archway. Every nerve ending in her body began to fire off, more than aware of him. She ached in places she'd soaked more than an hour ago, and now she pulsed all over, her body throbbing with each heartbeat. She wondered if women felt this way around any man they'd lain with and if the sensation would go away after a while. "I hope you've brought your appetite."

"I did."

The two words came out deep and husky as he reached her from across the kitchen and caressed her aware skin. She turned with a bowl of eggs in her hand, freshly scrambled, and froze at the sight of her husband.

Garrett's height and wide shoulders filled the entrance as his intense blue gaze took all of her in, from head to the hem of her skirts. Nervous under his perusal, she brushed a hand over her hair, ensured it was pinned back and in order as she rushed over to the table and set down the bowl in her other hand.

He moved deeper into the room, still not looking anywhere but at her, even though there was a table filled with food she'd prepared. "I didn't think you'd be up already."

She held his gaze briefly before turning and going back to the stove. "I'd slept long enough. I like to be up and doing things early, before the heat of the day sets in." She was babbling because Garrett made her nervous, unsettled. She picked up the carafe she'd just brewed then began to fill a mug. "Coffee. I made you coffee. Assuming you drink it. I actually don't know much about the things you like."

"You. I like you."

His breath whispered along the back of her neck. Her body quivered. She hadn't even heard him move. How a big man could be so light on his feet, she didn't understand. Her father had been a stomper, bringing down all his weight with every step, and he hadn't been as robust in size as the man behind her.

"How are you this mornin', wife?"

Coffee in hand, she turned to him and smiled. She gripped the hot mug like it would provide her with some form of stability or protection from her reaction to the man before her. Her husband. "Fine. As you can see, I made you enough food to keep you going through the day. Mrs. Copernic said you like a big morning meal."

"I do. And I'll get to it shortly." He took the cup from her hand and set it back on the counter behind her. He didn't move his hand back, so he had her boxed in. "You sure you don't need more rest? The farm will survive another day without you."

His words stung. A reminder that she really didn't have a place here. She didn't have a place anywhere if not on her back in a brothel. Her papa had at least needed her.

Lifting her chin, she met his gaze. "I know you had a successful farm and dairy before you needed a wife."

He frowned as she gave his words from the other night back to him. "No," he growled. "Because I don't want you to feel like you have somethin' to prove by being here or push yourself if you need time to adjust."

"I'm made of stern stuff, Mr. Garrett Rand." She slapped her hands on her hips and jutted her chin out to him. "I can do whatever needs to be done on this farm anytime."

Dark eyes stared down at her as if really seeing her for the first time. People in town always tiptoed around her as if, just because they were poor and struggling, she'd break if anyone placed an obstacle before her or challenged her.

She felt pretty darn good standing up for herself. He'd see, and if he had any employees who had doubts about her being here, she'd show them.

"Prove it."

"I will." With a nod of her head, she took a step to get past him, but he didn't move.

Instead, he blocked her in completely, by placing his other hand on the counter. The new position brought him lower and placed his handsome face right before hers. His scent was stronger this morning, carried to her by the sweat coating his skin from his early morning exertion. The normal warm intoxication of him now had an earthy, peppery spice to it, but it still did strange things to her insides. All the varied smells that accompanied the breakfast items on the table could not compete. She wanted to lean against him and feel his strength and warmth as she had felt them surrounding her through the night. His face was clean of any dust, and she assumed he'd washed away some of it before he came into the house.

She exhaled to clear her head.

"You'll need to move, so I can show you I can milk a cow. It can't be much different than milking a goat," she said, even though her family goat was male and was more for show and sentiment. She hadn't ever milked anything, but she'd seen her mama do it when she was really young. With her baby brother gone, milk hadn't been a necessity when she and her papa were trying to keep the farm up and running. Her father had sold their only cow one day when she was at the schoolhouse, for money for more seed and food for their belly.

"Right here." His mouth shifted into one of his breath-stealing, lopsided smiles.

It was her turn to frown. "Here?"

"There's plenty time later for you to show your stuff on the farm. What I want you to show me is the only thing *you* can." His gaze darkened and his head tipped to the side. His light brown locks were flat and a little mussed from the hat she'd seen him in earlier, most likely on the peg at the door.

She wanted to reach her hand up and feel the silky dampness of it. She remembered the cool, soft feeling of it in her hands last night as he'd been buried between her thighs, licking and sucking at her most private place. Her sex throbbed at the memory and she pressed her thighs together, trying to stop the ache, only to be shocked at the feel of the slickness of her inner thighs. *What is wrong with me?*

Tipping her head, she felt a little lost on his play on words. "Then what am I supposed to be proving to you in here?"

"That you're fine. I believe that was my original question. So, undo those tiny little buttons not made for a man's hands, and show me those lovely breasts of yours, Mrs. Garrett Rand."

His words reminded her of her role in the house.

If a goat had headbutted her in the backside, she would not have been more knocked over. She'd never truly had a chance to practice the flirting she'd learned in the brothel with a man. Unfamiliar with flirtation between sexes or the teasing that went on between husbands and wives, she hadn't realized the road Garrett was leading her down. So, she had no way to avoid the pitfalls of conversation that would lead to her baring herself in a kitchen in broad daylight.

She swallowed and placed a shaky hand on her quivering belly. "It's not right. Mrs. Copernic could walk in here any moment."

"The housekeeper is pole deep in a boiling lye cauldron out back, working on the wash." He leaned in and placed a light kiss below her ear. "Are you going to open your bodice, or are we going to add an extra dress to the ones I'm already buyin' you?"

Gasping, she clutched at the buttons, afraid he may ruin them before she had a chance to unfasten them. "Wait, wait. I'll do it."

He leaned back, giving her enough space to work them, but not more than that as he followed the movement of her hands.

She was trembling from her own nerves of what she was doing, this being only the second time she'd bared herself to a man, several hours ago being the first. She also admitted to herself that the butterflies fluttering around low in her belly were set off by her own response to the man before her. Garrett always had the most unsettling effect on her. Often, when she'd seen him in town, even though she never let on that she was looking at him, she'd drive all the way back home categorizing everything about him and enjoying the hum in her blood. The man was kind and arrestingly handsome. All the women, married and single, murmured about him. Of course, it was never said to her, because most of the women in town just offered her polite pleasantries when they saw her or asked about the health of her father, because Papa never went into town. All his waking moments, except Sunday service, were spent in the field.

She slipped the last button through the hole. Now that she knew what Garrett looked like nude and aroused, she'd never be able to keep that image far from her mind.

"Now the shift." There was a tension in his voice she knew from the night before was lust.

Once she'd reached up and pulled down the cotton layer, the only thing shielding her from her husband's smoldering gaze, since most women in Grover Town didn't wear corsets. The only ones she'd worn had been at the Harlot. In a brothel, the stiff undergarment took on a whole new meaning. When she started to adjust the cap sleeves of her dress and shift so that she could remove her arms, Garrett placed a hand on her shoulder.

"No. Leave them." His strong fingers squeezed her, holding firm.

"But I can't move them." She wiggled around, attempting to work the tightly drawn fabric down to her elbows, where she could bend them and free herself.

"Exactly." Garrett began to trace along her collarbone,

leaving tingling in his wake. He then danced his fingers down, toward her breasts.

She was imprisoned in her own clothing, and she realized it was exactly her husband's aim. She was at his mercy.

"You are beautiful, Caroline." The way he always said her name when he was touching her, was wistful, filled with longing, as if he didn't believe she was truly before him.

In some ways, she identified with that sentiment, because she'd had to pinch herself more than once in the bath that morning to ensure it all wasn't a dream. That any moment she'd awaken, and she'd be back at the brothel waiting for Daryl Bellmore to claim her, or worse, at the farm alone after her papa's death, too prideful to admit she was scared.

Gingerly, he brushed the pad of his thumb over the inside slope of one breast. "Do you know what it does to me knowing that beneath your clothes, you wear my marks? That secretly, you can feel me on you even though I'm not touching you. Could be yards away."

Swallowing, to moisten her dry mouth from the shock of his words, she thought maybe he saw her like one of his cows, a brand to signify something that he owned.

"No." She could hear the bite in her own words. Men in her life always thought they owned her, could control her. Garrett, even with all his kindness, was apparently no different.

Cupping both her breasts, he met her gaze. His hands flexed, palpating her breasts, pulling them from the fullness and squeezing them down to the tips. He did it two more times.

She gasped as she felt the pressure from her nipples to her clit, both areas throbbing, aching for more of his touch.

"It fuckin' knocks me on my ass. It's not just that you're

mine, it's that you're *mine*." His voice was rough, fierce, as if it took every ounce of his strength to hold back his emotions.

Feelings? What did this man feel for her, she questioned silently as he stared down at her. The darkness in his deep-set eyes made her feel as if he were trying to communicate something to her, but she wasn't sure what.

"Mine to touch, protect...to..." He paused, glancing down at his hands on her with a scowl on his face, as if they belonged to someone else. "...to care for. I care about you."

She heard his last words, but for some reason, they didn't seem to be the words he wanted to say. Not sure what he would have said and a bit dizzy herself from the possessiveness of his touch and speech, she said the thing that would place them both on a footing they had navigated already, sex. "Well, my body is yours, Garrett, by law and the good Lord. Take it."

He shook his head but still lowered his lips to hers and kissed her mouth. The kiss was intense like all the others, but there was a gentleness there this time. As his tongue glided slowly into her mouth, teasing her, she felt the air on her thighs as her skirt was lifted.

The kiss continued in a lazy fashion as one of his fingers of one hand circled her nipple and the other slipped into the slit of her drawers and cupped her sex.

She moaned around his tongue as she parted her legs and allowed him more room for his titillating touch. With her hands trapped, she could only grip his hips. When he parted her sex, circling her needy bud even as he caressed the taut tip of her breast, her sex was drenched. She could feel it around his fingers as he slipped between her labia.

Clutching his hips, she tugged, trying to bring his closer. After a night of him thrusting inside her, she knew what she desired—to silence the throbbing of her center. But Garrett stayed, his bulk not budging even as she tried to urge him forward, showing him she was willing to let him take her here, now. Right in the kitchen, where Mrs. Copernic could come walking into, no matter that Garrett had said she wouldn't.

She was burning up inside; she needed him, wanted his thickness pumping into her.

Around and around, he went, not giving her what she wanted but building the pressure inside her higher and higher.

Tearing her mouth away, she whimpered, "Garrett...please."

He laid light kisses on the corner of her mouth, her chin, and the side of her neck. "Let go, lovely bunny."

"What? No...I can't...wait!" she called out as his skilled touch continued its insistent orbiting of her twin peaks. Shaking, she felt the knowing fire heating her core and setting fire to her body. Even though her insides heated and tightened, she tried to fight the delicious orgasm racing through her body up toward the summit of pleasure.

She wasn't even sure why she didn't want him to take her over right there in the kitchen with gentle caresses. It was too much. Evidence that she was at his will no matter how much she denied it. That his control over her could have her yielding everything to him, and that scared her, more than the prospect of being out on her family farm alone for the rest of her days.

Regardless of her fight, her mind was bested by her body. She was coming hard, her cries filling the kitchen as she shuddered violently between the strong man before her and the counter.

Still trembling, she leaned away from him, giving her weight over to the counter instead of the man who had destroyed her sensually. Her skirts dropped back over her legs as Garrett removed his hand. She turned her face from him, couldn't pretend she didn't know what the musky scent and wetness was being painted around her nipple that had been left unattended.

"Beautiful."

Garrett was smearing the evidence of her release all over her breast. Before she could pull up her top and cover her humiliation, she felt the warm strength of his mouth as he suckled her, his swirling tongue cleaning off every layer of cream he'd placed there.

Her rebellious body started to heat all over again.

Only once he was done, did he tug her shift and bodice up and over her aching breasts. He bent to her and kissed her lightly on the lips, her scent on his breath as he moved away.

"Let's eat, wife. There's work still to be done."

Turning away, she jerked the sides of her clothes together and redid the buttons. "Your housekeeper said you didn't usually slow down for noon meal, so I wanted to make sure you had enough to tide you over until supper."

Finished straightening her clothing but still more than a little out of sorts, she turned around with his mug of coffee, praying the trembling in her hands wouldn't cause her to spill it. She found him standing at the seat she'd sat in last night. "Why haven't you started eating?"

"I'll always wait until you're settled, wife." He patted the top of the ladderback chair.

"Oh." She walked the steps that would carry her to the chair he stood behind, setting down his drink, tepid now, she was sure, but she lowered herself to the chair as he settled it beneath her. She inhaled. It was things like this that had her heart swelling in her chest around Garrett. If she wasn't careful, she would be falling in love with him.

Yes, he cared for her, but could he love her? It was easier

to think of the food than the heart of the man now seated in the chair beside her.

"Is there anything you don't want on your plate?"

"Nope. It all looks great." He poured fresh milk from a glass carafe on the table into a glass for her then pushed it in front of her as she served him.

When the plate was full and the bowl filled with the boiled oats she'd added a few things to, to make it more palatable from the blandness Mrs. Copernic had created, she set it all before him,

"Potatoes, sausage, eggs and porridge? Everything looks great."

"I hope it tastes the same." She placed a sausage, a few eggs and potatoes on her plate. She didn't miss how he eyed the meager servings. "I'll have more later. I'm still not used to eating a lot at one meal."

He nodded. "Then I'll try and be on time for noon meal."

"But you don't do lunch."

"Not before. But I enjoy your company. So, anytime I can get it, I'll take it." He winked at her and began eating.

She didn't miss the groan he let out or the way his eyes closed with each bite. She smiled but kept her head bowed and ate her own food.

"I knew if I was a good boy, I'd be blessed." He looked over at her as he held a link before his mouth. "Havin' a wife who cooks as well as you do, is more than I could have ever prayed for."

Her face became warm under his adoration. "I like fiddling around with herbs and things and seeing what goes together. Now that I have more than a few things..." She glanced over at the spice rack and pantry then shrugged.

"Thank my ma for all that. She loves cookin' too, so after my home was built, the next year she came down with Pa, and stocked the place with dried herbs she brought with her." He leaned toward her, conspiratorially, and spoke low. "Mrs. Copernic didn't mess around with any of it. She'd always say the Good Lord gave us salt and pepper and we don't need more."

"And I stand by that too." Mrs. Copernic breezed right into the kitchen and headed to the pantry.

Caroline gasped.

"Well, now that I've got a wife, Mr. Copernic can suffer alone." Garrett spoke around the bite of sausage, teasing the older lady.

Too shocked to speak, Caroline kept her head down, eating to cover the color she was sure was in her face. How long had the older woman been in the house? Had she heard or seen what they had been doin'? She thought about how Garrett had brought her to a screaming orgasm. The housekeeper had to think Garrett had married some hoyden.

"He's been suffering for thirty years of marriage; a few more years won't kill him any sooner."

Garrett chuckled. "Pretty sure you're right."

"I am right." She paused to give them a wink, swiped a sausage, then with a bucket, a bottle of lemon oil and a rag, the housekeeper went out just as fast as she'd come in.

"Garrett, you said she was out back," Caroline whispered.

Garrett slid a finger beneath her chin and tipped her face up. When her eyes met his, he said, "You're my wife, and this is my property. Ain't no one goin' tell me when and where I can touch you if I feel like it." He leaned in and kissed her deeply, intensely. When he pulled his mouth away, his blue gaze was dark. "Not even you, lovely bunny."

She took a deep breath and felt her pebbled nipples graze the cotton of her shift. She choked back a moan. The man was cocky enough, without him realizing how quickly he had trained her body to respond to his attention.

"As you said, we need to eat. There's plenty of work to be done."

He chuckled again but resumed eating.

FIFTEEN

Garrett rode King around the paddock and through his herd, keeping them from bunching up, trying to get into the narrow passage toward the barn. It was the late afternoon milking time. He glanced over and saw his pretty wife standing by the barn door with wide eyes as she watched one after another bovine prance by her, anxious to be relieved of their full udders and chew on the special feed his team gave them while they were being milked. He'd enjoyed having Caroline up on his horse settled before him as he took her all around the farm. He showed her not only the three pastures they moved the cows between, the area where the men sterilized the milk to prepare for shipping out, but the boundaries of their property. Everything had amazed her. When he'd taken her down off King and introduced her to the new calf that had been born the day before, she dropped to her knees in the dirt, not caring a mite about soiling one of her only two dresses. She petted the small animal and made a sound only a woman around babes of any kind.

It made him think about how she would be with their children. He doubted their night last night had her conceiving already, but he couldn't help the swelling of his chest as he thought about her belly round with his child.

When they walked through the fields on the other side of the property, he got to show her the crops they grew to provide for all that his cattle needed—corn, hay, and oats. He let her know that they still picked up grains and supplies at the mercantile for cooking in the house and bunkhouse.

"Why would you purchase things in town when there seems to be so much here?"

Holding her hand, he strolled through a path in the high stalk, for shade against the strong afternoon sun heating up the land as it shone down on them. He wore a hat, but Caroline didn't have a bonnet. "Two reasons. First, cattle consume a lot, but milkin' cows require even more to keep their supply up. The second reason is to keep up the Grover Town motto of the community providin' for one another. It's how this town started. I know that my purchasin' grains, meats, and vegetables from my fellow ranchers provides for their families. Just like they purchase their milk, butter, and cheese from me."

"Oh. That makes sense." With her head tipped back and the sun shining down on her, it made the chestnut of her locks show off all the browns and sun-bleached streaks in her hair.

Garrett wanted to pull out the pins that held her hair back and see it tumble around her. He also wanted to strip her down and admire the soft, golden glow of her body. However, he needed to keep his mind on work now. If he gave in to his desire for her, he'd have her cryin' out in the maize for the rest of the day. It had been hard enough for him not to bend her over the kitchen counter and bury his cock deep, but she'd been untried last night, and he'd not held back his passion for her the two times he'd taken her. She needed time before he was drivin' into her again. At least a few more hours.

Leading her back out, he finished explaining about the

crops they raised. "The stalks, we use for straw on the floor of the barn, for bedding of the cows. Straw is removed with manure and ground into fertilizer for new crops. Now, the alfalfa we grow, we use for seed and hay in the winter."

"Gracious. This is quite the farm you have here."

"*We* have. It's important that we have our own crops for our livestock. My family has never messed with that rancid, distillery swill, like farms around New York were doin'. Shame all those babies lost their lives because some greedy ass businessman wanted to cut corners. That's not how I was raised to do things back in Wisconsin." Garrett's face was tight as he shook his head in disgust. "I'll raise our children to tend it and appreciate the livelihood it brings, just like my pa did to my siblings and me."

"It's been so long since I thought much about having children of my own."

They headed around the house, nodding at the workers he'd already introduced Caroline to as they passed them. He drew her hand into the crock of his arm. "You do want them, right?"

She stopped and faced him, her lovely eyes staring up at him. "Yes. I want a house full of them. It was just my papa and me for so long, things got lonely. Sometimes I would wish that he'd find another wife, maybe someone in town who already had children, so I could have some siblings." She sighed and shook her head as she glanced around the farm. "My mama and brother's passing damaged his heart too deep to ever consider there was anything else. I think he worked the fruitless land so hard because he blamed himself for taking mama away from the city, from the prosperous life she could have had if she'd married a gent. He wanted to prove he could have provided for her, that her death wasn't on his hands."

He heard the thickness in her voice, the emotions locked inside. It surprised him to see the strain it took on her, to hold it all inside. Garrett recalled how she'd fallen apart at the church and now knew his wife was just as stubborn as her pa. She was determined to prove she was all right and she wasn't affected by life's challenges. However, no one could always stand so strong without support. He had his brother, his parents, and a whole community that looked out for him, as he did them.

"And your papa's isn't on yours."

Quickly, she turned her head to him, her gaze unreadable. "I never said it was."

"Nope. You didn't." He ran his hands up her arms and up to the curve of her neck. "However, these tight shoulders of yours tell a different tale."

Her shoulders tensed more at his words, but she remained silent.

"A man's got to work out his own soul salvation however he deems fit. Don't let your pa's battle become yours." He drew her to him. "You're not alone, darlin'. I'm here."

When she still didn't respond, he placed a kiss on her pretty lips before he took her hand and led around the front of the house. Inside, he made sure she ate more of the great breakfast she'd prepared. He wanted to make sure she was not only fit, but healthy. He finished off the sausages and eggs then took her back out to the pastures.

With no time to think about the thoughts going on in his wife's head, Garrett shifted his thigh against King and guided him toward the other side of the big animals.

Once the first eight were in the barn, Garrett moved over to the gate. He shifted in the saddle, calling out to Lyle, also on his black and white horse. "I'm takin' a spot on the milkers. I'll send Rud back out."

"Got it, boss." Lyle knew that meant he was in charge of the pasture.

Ryan, one of his young workers, pulled open the gate once Garrett and King got to it then quickly closed it again, keeping any cows from escaping.

Galloping over to Caroline, he enjoyed how she turned immediately and looked at him. He wondered if she found her body tuned to his whereabouts as his seemed to be for her. She moved close and stroked King's muzzle as he dismounted.

"You ready to milk a few cows, bunny?"

"You sure know how to say the sweetest things to a girl, Mr. Rand." Teasingly, she batted her sooty lashes at him, dust covering her face but not diminishing her beauty one bit.

"It a skill of mine, darlin'." With a hand on her back, he led her into the barn.

They strolled down the wide aisle, stalls to the left and right, the place filled with masculine chatter and mooing.

"Gracious. I think this is the biggest barn I've ever seen. I thought your stables were nice."

"They are. I couldn't have King just anywhere," he jested. "Besides, my workers keep their horses there too. If you want to learn to ride, I will get you a horse."

She stopped and looked at him. "I've never even considered riding. Can I just use the wagon for now?"

"Bunny, you do whatever it is you please."

She smiled and his heart skipped a beat and lifted.

Shaking his head, he curved his hand low on her waist and directed her to the last stall. "Rud, take the paddock with Lyle."

The short stocky man who'd just started to close himself in with the cow turned. "Sure 'nuf, Rand."

Garrett caught the stall door as it swung out.

"Ma'am." Rud tipped his hat toward Caroline as he walked by.

Stepping to the side, Garrett let his wife enter the stall before him. "Always remember to latch the gate behind you. If something happens that spooks the cows or all the ones in the barn, last thing we need on our hands is a stampede. They are gentle animals, but hundreds of pounds of flesh that can hurt slammin' into a person." He placed a hand on the withers then along the back of the black and white spotted female as the cow ignored him for the most part, too happy to be eating. He looked at Caroline, who stood right in the stall but hadn't come any closer. Having been around her all day, he knew she wasn't afraid of the bovine, just respecting his workspace until he instructed her to do something.

He walked over to a corner and grabbed the items he would need. "Come over here, bunny. I'm going to talk you through what you need to do."

"All right." She slipped her hand into his and let him pull her to the short, three-legged wooden stool he had set down.

"Timmy and Ryan, the two young boys I introduced you to, handle makin' sure that each of the stalls has the supplies needed for milkin' twice a day. If you ever come into a stall that is missing something, those two are the ones you go to. If it happens more than once, make sure you inform Lyle; he gets them straight. We have too much to get done through the day, to be chasin' down things that should be in place."

She nodded.

Squatting beside her, he pointed out the things he brought next to the animal. "Your bucket, a damp cloth. There's another bucket with warm water, so you can rinse it between each cow." He set the cloth in her upturned palm. Pointing on the other side of her, he said, "You have a canister to fill with the buckets."

"Why is there a cloth over the canister?"

"The cheese cloth is the second way we make sure the milk is clean. If it isn't, we'll never hear the end from the women in the dairy." He chuckled.

"That's where Rachel, Lyle's wife, works."

"It is. Tomorrow, you can spend the early part of the day in there. They get in sometime after breakfast and are gone shortly after the noon meal. Most of them got families to tend to."

"It's nice that you provide a place for them to help out their family."

She didn't say much else, and Garrett knew, along with most of the town, that Sam Douglas didn't allow his daughter to pick up work anywhere. It would have helped the stubborn man and probably Caroline as well, to have others around her instead of only her pa. Garrett would have provided her a place here if she'd ever come asking.

"How do I do this?" There was an eagerness to her voice.

He smiled, shifting around so he was squatting behind her with his knees wide at her side. "First, use the warm water to wipe off the udder and around the teats to clear off debris, manure, and anything else. The warm cloth also stimulates the udders and begins the letdown of milk. You can also give a firm rub up and down and around the udder, pressing gentle that will cause letdown as well."

"Like this?" She followed his direction perfectly.

"Yes. Just like that. Now set the bucket under the udder. You're going to fill the bucket then pour that milk into the canister. That way, if the cow kicks over the bucket, which happens more times than you think, you won't lose all your milk."

She moved the bucket where he told her. "Can I give it a try now?"

"Yup." He watched her pull and squeeze at one of the teats, but it only produced a few drops."

"This will take you all day. How can you do all the cows out there?" Her brows were tight, and her voice was strained with frustration.

"Here, let me show you." He leaned in so his chest was pressed to her back as he slipped one of his hands around hers and his other around her narrow waist, holding her into him. He inhaled, finding her scent amidst the pungent odor of the bovine. "You need to test the milk first. Give it a few squirts onto the cow's hoof, to check it is flowing smoothly and there are no clumps." He was careful to apply enough pressure around Caroline's fingers to cause the effect he needed with the cow but would not crush her delicate fingers. Setting his lips at the shell of her ear, he spoke low, calming his wife even as he instructed her. "Use the thumb and index finger to grasp at the top of the teat, pinching it off, holding all the milk in the teat canal. Take the other fingers and squeeze. No tugging or pulling, be firm but gentle." He could feel the quivering in her stomach as he whispered the words to her. It had never crossed his mind that teaching someone to milk a cow could be so erotic. He was soon learning that everything with his wife was a test in restraining his lust.

"It's working." There was amazement in the breathiness of her voice.

"Yes, lovely bunny." His cock was hard, but he didn't make any further advances. They were in the back stall, but they weren't alone. "Use your other hand so you're working two teats at a time."

"Okay." When she shifted forward to grab the second teat, it set her lush ass right at the perfect angle of his hard cock.

He swallowed down a groan.

"How much do you need?"

"We need to make sure to get all the milk out so the cow continues to produce a lot of milk, also so mastitis doesn't develop. Another reason we milk them twice a day."

Once they were finished, Garrett rose, moving away from the temptation of his wife to get the lid. He showed her how to lock it in place on the canister, then he hauled it to the side of the stall, away from the path of the animal.

"Ryan!"

"Here, boss." The shaggy haired lanky boy jogged down the aisle to them with a rope in his hand.

"Daffodil's ready to go," Garrett told him.

"I'm on it." The boy made his way into the stall then looped the rope around the bovine's neck before leading it away.

Caroline had taken the rag to the bucket in the corner and rinsed it out.

"You want to do the next cow, or you think you've had enough?"

She rolled her bottom lip in, her white teeth sinking into the plump flesh. "Would it be awful if I wanted to get started on supper?"

He shook his head. "No, wife. In fact, my stomach would be much obliged if you did."

She laughed. "Then I'll see if I can find Mrs. Copernic's recipe for roast pork."

Steppin' toward her, he said, "As long as you improve it like you did the oats, I got no complaints." He winked at her, then swatted her backside as she left the open stall door.

She squealed. "I'll see what I can do."

Garrett didn't even try not to watch the swaying of her hips as she walked out of the barn.

"WIFE, I thought you would have already been asleep in bed."

"I was, but I forgot something." Caroline set the white box back into the cabinet underneath the washstand as she heard her husband enter the room. She stood, holding the small vial behind her back to keep it out of sight.

Garrett glanced from the rumpled bed to her with a slow arch of his brow, moving deeper into the room. He was semi-dressed in a fresh pair of britches and shirt. The shirt was open, revealing the bare muscles of his chest.

She enjoyed looking at him, no matter what he was wearing or not wearing. The man caused her mind to think of all sorts of naughty things. Earlier in the evening when he had been giving her directions in the proper way to milk a cow, feeling his massive body and his strength behind her, all around her, had made her breathless. When he'd cupped her hand and guided it up and down the base of the udder and along the teat, all she could remember was how his hands had worked along her bare breasts in the kitchen, priming her, and milking an orgasm from her. It had taken all her willpower not to beg him to come back to the house with her and not care if his men knew why they were leaving. However, she'd recalled the housekeeper was still in the home and she'd possibly already embarrassed herself once today.

Preparing the roast pork with apples and chatting with Mrs. Copernic, whom she liked, had been a great distraction.

"What did you forget, bunny?"

The way he used the endearment always made her nipples tight and caused a deep ache within her body. She smiled and took her time crossing the room. At the brothel, she'd learned how to seduce a man, how the slow, subtle movements of her body could cause a man to lose his wits.

As Garrett's eyes trailed along the simple white shift she'd put on after her bath before his, watching her hips swaying from left to right, she knew her husband wasn't immune.

"Lie on the bed, please, Garrett." She stopped about an arm's length away. If he wanted to reach for her, he could, but she liked that he was allowing her some leeway.

"What are you up to?" He began lowering himself on the bed as he kept a curious eye on her.

"Wait! Undressed, please." She licked her lips, more than a little nervous with taking the lead.

His eyes tracked the movement of her tongue.

Heat spread through her body as she thought about his fascination with her odd mouth. She wouldn't deny she liked the frequent kisses he gave her.

Resuming his full height, he shucked out of his shirt. "I don't want to be the only one undressed, darlin'." He stared pointedly at her shift.

With a crimson hot face, she lifted the cotton over her head. Bare as the day she was born, she shivered. Even though the night was warm, there was barely a breeze coming from the open windows. The drawn drapes weren't even moving. It was a hot Kansas summer night. "N-oow, you."

"For the record, when we come to bed, no need for covering that I'm just going to remove." His pants were on the floor in a blink.

She gasped at the leashed strength of his body that was before her. His form was filled with bulging muscles and thick rope-like veins that created a map of deliciousness she wanted to follow not only with her hand, but her mouth as well. It was the sight of his long, engorged shaft that made her tremble and her thighs slick with her own moisture. She would have said it blushed from the deep reddish-purple tint of it, but she didn't think the man or his cock were ever shy. It stunned her, made her breathless that something so large could fit inside her.

"If you keep staring at him, lovely bunny, he's going to want you to touch him."

Biting her lip, she glanced away then forced herself to look up at Garrett, not wanting to lose her boldness. "Well, maybe later. For now, he'll just have to wait."

His chuckle was deep and robust.

She enjoyed the sound of it, but she liked hearing whatever came from his mouth.

"On the bed, please, boss," she mimicked his men and how they spoke to him.

"I think in this situation, at least for now," he clarified, "you're the boss." Garrett sat on his side of the bed.

"That's true." She made a spinning motion with her hand. "Onto your belly, please."

This instruction made him pause, and he glanced at her hand that she held clenched at her side. He didn't move. "Wife, I'm sure they may have taught you a lot at Miss Kitty's, some things that some men like, others don't," he growled, holding her gaze. "If you don't want this night to end with a spankin', I suggest you tread lightly on what you got planned."

At first, she wasn't sure what Garrett was referring to. What it was that he could possibly think she was planning to do with him on his stomach and nothing but his broad back and backside available to her. "Garrett, there's nothing I can do to your back—"

Her words dropped away, and she gasped as memories of sketches in one particular book Kitty had given her to review came back to her. It had shown some alternative cuppling, some of the same genders and other sketches had a woman with a fake shaft in her hand and a man bent forward.

"No, no." She waved her hands between them. Opening her closed fist, she showed him what was in it. "I just wanted to give you a massage. Onyx said men like them. I figured since you've had a long day, I could treat you with one."

His lips tilted in a smile. "Ah. Then my body is yours."

Without any further hesitation, her husband moved to the center of the bed, onto his front.

Sighing with relief, she climbed onto the bed with him. She would have preferred to remain at his side while she rubbed it on his back, but the brown-skinned beauty had told her that the best position and the one men loved the most, was the feel of a woman's body straddling him, the heat of her sex against his skin. Once she got beside him, she brought her legs over him and settled onto the backs of his thighs. She was a little embarrassed as the air made contact with her wet inner folds. There was no doubt that Garrett could feel the evidence of her response to him.

Shoving aside her anxiety, she uncorked the small bottle and dribbled a line down his spine. If she had thought her plan out better, Onyx had told her it was even better if she submerged the bottle in hot water first. If Garrett liked the massage, she'd do that next time. Pressing the cork back in place, she set the bottle on the bed then used a finger to glide a design over and along his spine.

Garrett's body seemed to relax with just that light touch. She flattened her hands at his lower back and smeared the oil around as she added more pressure with her palms. Around and around she went, and when she dragged the heel of her slick hands back to work into the top of his firm buttocks, she heard him groan. She worked them harder, his muscles there so thick, she knew it could take the added pressure.

Her papa never complained about his back and the strain the labor took on it, but she'd catch him secretly rubbing his back and would at least take a warm compress when it was really bad. Garrett was her husband, and she would see this

act of massaging his body as one of the things she was responsible for on the ranch, keeping him as healthy as possible, for
as long as possible.

She never would have considered, when Onyx had shown
her the techniques for sensual pleasure, that she'd feel so
compelled to use it to also care for a man. Her man.

Up her hands went, slipping through more oil as she
spread her hands up to his shoulders. Those bulging muscles
were just as knotted as his backside. She squeezed and
pressed, rotating her thumbs and fingers into the base of his
scalp, his hair, damp from him washing it in the bath, swirled
around her fingers before she lowered back into his broad
shoulders. He was much longer than she was, and to reach all
of him, it required at times that she lower her torso against
him.

She made use of all her body, flexing her thighs at his hips,
grinding her pelvis into his round backend, and shifting from
left to right so her breasts stroked him. Her clit was swollen
and aching, and every time it bumped against his heated flesh,
she had to bite back the moan. She inhaled, taking in the soft,
relaxing scent of the lavender and sage in the oil. The aroma
mingled with Garrett's own natural male musk and made her
want to bury her nose along the side of his neck and fill her
lungs with as much of it as she could take in.

The sound of Garrett's groans vibrated through his chest
and titillated the tips of her breasts, drawing her nipples taut.
She knew he could feel the poke of them in his back. The
sensual massage was doing things to her as she continued.

She pushed aside her own response, using all her efforts to
really tend to the man beneath her—the man who had
thought enough of her not to just make her his mistress but
take her in as his wife. She was in danger of caring for this
man on a level that scared her. It wasn't that she believed he

would put her away one day, no longer want her as his wife, but maybe he'd regret the burden of her. She had nothing to offer him, nothing to give or contribute to the world he'd built.

On the sexual front, she had barely been coming into her own knowledge when he'd taken her away. Would she be enough to satisfy him? She couldn't help but think about the sensual beauty and talents of the Jewels. Garrett would have been better off marrying someone like Diamond or Sapphire, who already brought him a family to fill the empty rooms of his house but would also have the skills to please him greatly in the bedroom.

"Ah!" she cried out as she found herself bucked. Now she was staring down into her husband's quizzical gaze. She was straddling him now, her bottom on the flat washboard of his abdomen.

"What are you thinking about, bunny?"

"What?" She lowered her gaze to his mouth, trying to get away from his discerning eyes. "Nothing, just concentrating on pleasing you...with the massage." She grinned, broader than was necessary, and asked, "Are you enjoying it?"

"I always enjoy your hands on me, wife." The arch of one of his brows told her he was not convinced.

"Then lie back and let me finish, please." She hoped he didn't hear the tremor in her voice, her emotions still caught up by her own dejected thoughts.

He flexed his fingers on her thighs where they rested, and she could feel the bulbous head of his cock resting along the crease of her backside. The touch of it burned, and part of her would have much rather wiggled back and taken him inside her, allowing him to assuage the ache there, but she stayed still, waiting.

His hands slid up around her hips and clutched her ass, as if he were trying to decide what he wanted to do. Finally, with a sigh, he dropped his hands back to the bed. "Have at me, darlin'. Tread lightly, because there's an angry beast that wants to devour you."

Her smile was real this time, as she exhaled. Moving off him, she located the vial that had bounced to the edge of the bed. Settled at his side this time, she poured a pool of oil into her hands. When that was done, she reached out and set the bottle on the nightstand beside the lamp, as she wouldn't be needing it anymore. If Garrett's beast didn't take her soon, she'd take him. Her sex clenched on the empty space, and she yearned to feel his thick shaft driving into her. She rolled her bottom lip in and stifled her giggle.

"Whatcha think 'bout?" He tapped her top lip.

She blushed at being caught in her own naughty thoughts. "Mr. Rand, you're supposed to have your eyes closed."

The heat in his gaze reflected her own, but he lowered his lids. "The stuff smells nice. There's a softness to it, but I won't be walkin' around my men smellin' like one of those flowers in Gretchen's garden."

The short redhead did have an amazing garden. Caroline would love to talk to her about using some of them in soaps. However, she wasn't sure if that was something Garrett would ever allow her to make again. She let the giggle at his words come out, focusing there instead of what she couldn't do right now. "The oils at the Harlot were bought with the male clients in mind."

"That Kitty is a smart lady."

"I agree."

She shifted her body until she was settled on the tops of his thighs. Then she tipped her hand and let the substance run from it to his chest and down to where she set her hand, right beneath his cock, hovering above his navel. His skin was hot, firm, and trembling beneath her palm. She liked knowing that she wasn't the only one affected by this act. With her free hand, she started rubbing over the front of his shoulders, down along his bulging biceps and up again. As she skated along the ridges of his chest, she admired the deep tan of his skin and thought about how many hours he'd had to work out in the sun with his shirt off to get it so rich and golden. The flat disc of his nipples were brown and smaller than hers. She knew from her lessons that men could be just as sensitive there. With the tip of her finger, she circled around it. She marveled at the sight of it drawing tight, into a tiny bud.

"Bunny, you're feedin' the beast."

Sighing, she moved her hand away and continued to his other arm. When she was back at his chest, applying firm pressure into his pecs, she let her other hand, saturated with the oily substance, slide down to his thighs. She worked her fingers into one thigh, then the other. She was purposely giving him sensations from both ends. Up and over, one hand went along his shoulders and chest, while down and around, she moved the other. When she slipped her hand up the inner part of his thigh, cupping his sac briefly before encircling the base of his cock, her other hand was squeezing his bicep.

"Shit!" he barked, his body jerking.

She kept her focus. His shaft was too wide for her fingers to close around it as she had done to the carved piece of wood she'd practiced on, but she didn't let that stop her. As she gripped and stroked up and down his hard length, avoiding the head for now, she also went up and down his bicep from shoulder to elbow.

All his muscles that she had worked hard to relax were tense under her hands. She loved touching him, knowing that she could drive his body wild like he did to her just by walking in the room or giving her one those heated glances no matter where they were. Her body responded.

"Fu-uck!" he was growling, and his hands were fisted at his side, clenching the sheets.

Up and down. Up and down. Up and down. She worked his muscle harder, faster, as she kept her gaze fixated on the one in her right hand that was now releasing a small pearl at the tip. The bead swelled until gravity forced it to run over the dark head and drip onto his taut abdomen.

Too tempted, she couldn't resist the taste. Bowing her head, she swiped the clear, glossy substance, his essence. Even as the musky, salt, and strangely sweet taste of him bloomed in her mouth, she barely had a moment to savor it before she was on her back.

"Enough!" The beast was unleashed. Her husband was a wild man.

Garrett's mouth claimed hers, his kiss fierce and deep as he dragged her body beneath his. If ever a kiss could be called oral fucking, this was it. He drove his tongue far into her mouth, to depths she didn't even think were possible. He took over her mouth, claiming her.

"Suck it," he commanded, then he was inside her again, shoving in and out.

Adhering to his directive, she drew her lips tight around the firm, wet appendage and sucked it as if it was his cock.

His rough growl vibrated into her mouth as he drove in and out, almost choking her.

She didn't care; she wanted the unbridled lust of this man.

Shifting, he pressed his knees wide, forcing her leg out until her joints were pulling at the hips. Then she felt it, the swollen head of his cock pressed against her swollen clit. It circled her then a second time before sliding down her wet slit.

She was sopping. The evidence of her own desire was coating her smooth sex, her inner thighs, and even made the area between her bottom slick. She moaned around Garrett's tongue as the need in her body caused her to quake.

At her center, Garrett thrust forward. There was no pause or ginger gliding as he had done their first night. No. He was giving her the no holds barred animal of lust that lived deep in his core. He went from tip to base in one move.

She whimpered. There was pain in his entry. Her sex tried but was still not used to takin' in such girth and length. However, she didn't want him to stop. She enjoyed knowing that she had brought him to this point, that it was her he wanted. She was his bunny, and the wolf in him was devouring every ounce of her.

The novice part of her wanted to cry out that it was too much, he was too big, that it wasn't possible for her to take all he had to give. But the vixen in her, one she didn't even know until Garrett was inside of her, silenced the denials. Moaning, she wrapped her arms around his big shoulders then dug her nails along his spine.

Thrust. Retreat. Thrust. Retreat.

He gripped her hips, angling her up then down, showing her how to meet him, take him. He groaned. Pulling his chest away from her, he stared down the length of their bodies. "Damn, you're so fucking lovely. You're swollen, tight pussy's so wet, spread so wide around my fuckin' cock." He squeezed his eyes shut briefly as if the amazement of the sight was too much for him to take in. He swore.

She watched the expression of rapture darken his face and relax his features, as if he'd found some earthly haven. It took her breath away, because she was experiencing the same thing.

He continued to thrust hard, rocking into her deep.

"Look at us, darlin' bunny." He balanced his weight ono

one elbow as he slipped his other arm beneath her shoulders so she could have a clear view of them.

In this position, she almost didn't recognize herself. Her legs were splayed wide over Garrett's thighs as her hips arched and shifted beneath him eagerly, a participant in their actions, not a bystander.

Garrett's cock was glazed in her cream. She watched, even as she felt him pull all the way out, showing off his bulbous head before he propelled forward, hammering back into her, the thick, blush lips of her sex stretched wide and tight around him. Her desire increased from both the vision and the feel. White-hot light flashed in her eyes, obscuring her gaze as her channel clenched around his driving length. She cried out as her body shuddered beneath him and the orgasm rocketed through her core.

He didn't stop driving into her, and she didn't stop coming.

"Fuck, that's it. Your pussy...so fuckin'...tight." He lowered his chest to her, wrapped his arms around her, and thrust harder. He said words to her, erotic words that he groaned into her ear that she'd only read about in the naughty journals, telling her how she felt around him as he ground deeper. His crown stroked along some sensitive bundle of nerves along her walls.

"Garrett...oh, Garrett." It was like Garrett had become a part of her, and she understood what it meant to become one with another person. She screamed as she came apart again.

She was delirious, feeling outside of herself as he pulled away from her. She clutched at him with her hands, not wanting him to leave her. He shifted away. She didn't even realize he'd taken one of the pillows from beside her until he thrust it under her hips.

"What are you—" She never got a chance to finish her

question before Garrett had lowered himself between her thighs.

"I want to taste your next orgasm, darlin'." His breath fluttered over her sensitive sex as he spoke.

"But I can't." He'd wrung two orgasms already from her.

"You will." Then his mouth was on her. He was licking around her slit. He sucked her lips into his mouth, before clamping around her clit.

"Oh...oh." It was impossible, but she could feel the heat begin to swirl again, low in her belly.

He alternated between suckling the peak to letting it pop from his lips, only to feast on it again. The skills of his clever, dexterous tongue was fucking delicious, making her delirious. She was writhing and whimpering her pleasure.

When he glided his talented tongue down her swollen, achy sex and thrust it into her channel, she was a mad woman. Garrett gave her pussy the same passionate deep kiss as he'd wrought on her mouth. Just like her lips, her walls tightened around his thick, long tongue and sucked him in farther. His fingers bit into her thighs as his hands held her wide, keeping her open as his mouth fucked her sex.

Fisting his hair in both of her hands, she bucked against his face, grinding into him, seeking the satisfaction only he could provide. She worked herself on his tongue until she was coming again. He curled his tongue up inside of her and did something wickedly delicious as he flicked it right along those receptive nerves, spinning her out of control.

"Fuck me...Garrett. Garrett...please."

Then he was there, inside her, his length driving hard. His chest pressed into her taut nipples as he kissed her, fed her on her own pungent, sweet cream as her musk coated his face and beard.

The pillow, still beneath them, placed her at a different

angle that allowed him to go deeper, thrusting against the mouth of her womb. He wrapped her in his arms, holding her tight as he covered her walls with his seed.

As he bucked and shuddered, his body giving over to a release that seemed to steal his breath, she took over the kiss. Yet, her kiss was soft, gentle as she rocked her hips slowly against him. She slipped her tongue in and out of his mouth in a sensual movement, showing him the only way she knew how that she was there for him, that her gentleness would comfort the beast that raged inside of him.

"Oh, love, I don't believe I'll ever get enough of you." He groaned even as the last shudder ran through him and he rolled to his back, taking her with him.

Love. Oh, how she wished he was confessing his heart instead of using it as an endearment. Her heart ached. She found herself sprawled over him with his semi-erect cock, still quite a significant size that wasn't easily ignored, buried inside her. She began to shift off him, to her side of the bed.

His grip was firm on her hips, holding her in place. "Not yet, bunny. I need a moment to recover."

Her cheeks heated as she gasped. "I-I wasn't trying to start anything. I was just moving. It's been a long day and I didn't want to fall asleep on top of you."

"But that's where I want you." His head was back on the pillow with his eyes closed.

"I'll be too heavy."

He was already stretching one of his eagle's wing long arms out to turn down the wick of the oil lamp.

She stared down at him as the light dimmed. He hadn't even opened his eyes to reach the nightstand, telling her that there'd been many nights where he'd fallen into the bed exhausted and had accomplished the same move. Proof, as she'd witnessed herself, her husband worked hard to build and maintain his farm.

"Never. Shhh." When that hand returned to her body, he cupped it around one half of her backside, his fingers so long, they curved in right along her crease and settled against the side of her tender stretched sex, as his other hand stroked slowly up and down her back.

It was a wicked position to sleep in but choosing not to struggle and fight him to get away, she rested her head on his chest and allowed his heartbeat to lull her into dreamland.

SIXTEEN

Caroline couldn't stop blushing as she crossed the property with her husband the next morning. It had been hours now, the cows had already been milked, and the two of them had shared another hearty breakfast and discussed the day with Mrs. Copernic, but she couldn't stop thinking about waking up to her husband's thrusts. She had first awoken, surprised that she had slept soundly splayed over Garrett's body. Then she became aware of the benefits of being in such a position as she became aware of Garrett's hard, thick shaft gliding along her wet walls. Not fast, just a ginger rocking of his hips.

She realized it had been her own moans of pleasure that had brought her out of the dream state, or rather entered the reality into her dream. But, having sex with him had been exactly what she'd dreamed about all night.

"Morning, wife. Are you awake now?" He whispered a throaty growl in her ear.

"Yes," she sighed. "How can I not be with what you are doing to me?" She gripped his biceps and moaned.

"Me? Bunny, you still must be sleep, because I'm not the one doin' the doin'," he growled.

His words found their way through the fogginess of her brain. "What? But you're..." Even as she said it, she realized that, yes, both Garrett's big hands were cupping her ass cheeks, but it was her hips that were doing the moving. She was arching, lowering, and rotating her hips, riding his length.

"Oh...oh, gracious," she whimpered, embarrassed. She started to move. "I should—"

"Don't you fuckin' stop," he growled as his grip tightened on her backside, spreading her cheeks wider. "You take what you need, lovely bunny. Satisfy that hunger inside you."

He was right; it was a hunger, a deep-seated ache inside her that was gnawing for a release. She ground down, stimulating her clit in the curls at the base of his shaft. A broken moan came out; she needed more, needed him ramming his hard cock into her. "I don't know how."

"No time like this mornin' to learn." He shifted his hold to her hips then guided her body up into a sitting position. "You're about to have your first ridin' lesson."

She gasped as she settled down on his length. Garrett's cock was so deep inside her now, she could barely catch her breath. "Oh...yes."

"Oh, yes," he echoed her. "Now, spread your knees out real wide as you rock that sweet ass, just like you were doin' before."

She followed his instruction. Her breath caught in her throat as the intense sensation caused frissons of heat to spiral from her core to the base of her neck.

"Use your thighs to rise up and down my dick at whatever speed feels good to your sweet pussy."

"But what about you?" She stared down into his gorgeous face, his eyes hooded in pleasure in the pre-dawn light, but she could feel him watching her.

"Anything you do, bunny, will feel good to me too."

Taking him at his word, she placed her hands on his wide chest for balance, then lifted and lowered herself on his cock. The sensation was thrilling, spine tingling, so she did it again, and again.

Up and down, she went, under her husband's encouragement. When the slow pass was just keeping her on the edge of the cliff of pleasure, she thought about how Garrett took her and began to move faster, slamming herself down to the base of his cock where he stretched her wider. Harder and harder, she rode him.

"That's it, darlin'...fuck me." His hands were tight, his fingers digging deep into the plumpness of her ass, but he allowed her the lead.

Tossing her head back, she didn't care what she looked like as her breasts jiggled and her ass slapped into the pools of her own cream collecting down on his groin and balls. It felt glorious and erotic.

Then her world was spinning out of control and she was coming, bucking against him and stroking the head of his cock just at the spot inside her channel that felt oh, so good.

Garrett didn't let her come down from the first climax before he slipped his hand around the front of her hips and began circling her clit with his thumb. The pressure flared from the tip to her core and she was mindless again, seeing stars in the morning.

Then she felt the tremors rush through Garrett beneath her before her sex was filled with the hot jets of his release.

This time she collapsed on him, burying her face in the pillow at the side of his neck, as wet as a limp blade of grass pounded flat under a summer storm. She felt beaten, yet gloriously refreshed.

"Oh, darlin' bunny, feel free to wake me up anytime," Garrett sighed, his hand light on her back, still trembling.

Her giggle came out weak as she had allowed herself to snuggle in close and inhale his warm, earthy scent and their mingled musk that saturated the air around them like a heavy blanket, comforting and erotic.

Shortly after, they had roused themselves enough to clean up, dress and head downstairs, her to the kitchen and him out the front door, a hot, toe-turning kiss parting them.

Now, as she walked the packed dirt that paved the way from the house past the barn and to the porch of the dairy house with its apple red rooftop, she couldn't stop her mind from returning to the bed. This man was turning her into a wanton woman, not able to go more than a few hours without him touching her or inside her.

"Bunny, if you don't stop smilin' and makin' those little purrin' sounds," Garrett pulled her close, his hard body aligned with hers as he whispered, "I'm going to take you behind this house and ruck up your skirts and give you something that will really make you purr." His tongue swiped over the shell of her ear.

She shivered. "You wouldn't," she sputtered, shocked at his words.

He leaned back so she could clearly see his face below his black hat, his eyebrow hitched high and his cobalt eyes flashed, heat radiating from them. His expression said, 'try me', but she was too nervous to tempt the wild beast.

She pushed away from him as she pressed her lips together to keep all sound in her mouth.

He chuckled as he knocked firmly on the door.

She wondered, if this place was his, why he'd knock instead of walkin' right in.

Moments later, the door was opened by Rachel, the foreman's wife, who stood dressed in a white calico dress, white apron, white bonnet, white stocking feet, and no shoes.

When she saw it was them, she smiled broadly but kept the gap of the door narrow. "Hello, Garrett, Caroline; it's good to see you. What can we do for you?"

"Mornin', Rachel. Was hopin' Caroline could spend the day with you ladies here and y'all can show her the ropes, let her see what goes on here."

"Oh, we'd enjoy the time to get to know your new bride and get an extra hand on the churns." The dark-haired, expectant mother's face lit up with genuine kindness and joy.

Caroline liked knowing that the friendship the woman had offered at the wedding had been real. Rachel and her family had moved to the area after Caroline had already left the schoolhouse at thirteen and she had never really gotten to know her. She seemed nice and Caroline could use a few more friends.

"I'm glad to help. Mind you, I've never worked in a dairy before, so you may have to start from the basics to teach me," Caroline admitted. She knew about farming, cooking, making soap, and ways to please a man, but that was about it.

"Oh, none of us had any true experience, but we've learned together. Take off your shoes and we'll get you a bonnet and apron."

"Well, you're in good hands." Garrett pulled her in and gave her a quick kiss on the lips. "I'll see you at the house for noon meal. We'll be out getting the cows moved to the east pasture today. If you need anything Rud will be close by and he can come for me."

"I'll be fine, Garrett, stop fussin' like a mother hen," she teased but gave him a pleading stare. She didn't want these women to think she was weak and helpless, in need of Garrett to always hold her hand. Before he was in her life, she worked the small field alongside her papa like a son and travelled into town alone. She would have continued laboring on the same plot of land by herself if not for Bellmore whisking her away. She knew that he was only coming out of the field to eat midday to ensure she had eaten. The man was obsessed with feeding her; he always stared at her small portions with a concerned eye.

He made a clucking sound and winked at them before he walked away.

Caroline shook her head as she removed her boots. She now saw the row of boots aligned against the wall of the house. She pushed hers right next to the last pair, making it five in all.

"All right." She held her hands out, waiting for her next instructions.

"Well, come on in, Caroline. I'll introduce you to the other ladies." Rachel stepped back, widening the opening, and allowed Caroline to pass through it before closing it behind her.

Inside, she noticed all the women were dressed in the same fashion, all white.

"I'll start with introducing everyone, give you the rules on workin' within the dairy, and then I'll let each woman tell you what they're doing, 'cause we rotate daily."

"All right." Caroline offered a smile that she hoped encompassed the three women.

"Well, you already know me. To my right, is Alice Lincoln. She's married to Chris, a hand on the farm." Rachel pointed to an older woman with straight red-hair that had more than a few grey streaks. She was plump with a warm smile.

"Oh, I met your husband yesterday. He mentioned that you managed the dairy."

The older woman's cheeks pinked a little. "That's just

Chris always ravin' about nothin'. I've been milkin' cows and makin' cream since I was off my ma's breast."

Caroline laughed. "Well, just so you know, Garrett thinks highly of what you do here as well. He said it was you who talked to him about settin' up the dairy years ago. I don't plan to take that away from you. I'm just here to learn, lend a hand where it's needed."

Alice's shoulders lowered some as if they had relaxed at her words. "As Rand's wife, it would be within your right to take over managing all this."

"Well, your position is safe from me." Caroline did want to learn all she could about the farm and dairy, but she wasn't plannin' to settle in any spot until she knew it was where she was supposed to be.

"Thank you." The older woman nodded.

"Next, you can meet Kimberly Hurst; her husband Jackson works over at the Spencer Pride Ranch." Rachel guided Caroline over to a woman who was younger than Alice but looked a few years older than she and Rachel were.

The raven-haired woman was slim and tall as she stood with a few wooden churns around her skirts. "Nice to meet you, Mrs. Rand."

"You too. Your husband is always kind to me when I've been over to Spencer property to pick up the fat scraps to make my soap. He usually helps load it into my wagon."

"That Jackson is one charmer. He had three sisters behind him growin' up so he can't help himself if he thinks for a moment a woman needs a hand."

"Well, I always appreciated it," Caroline declared. She enjoyed matching up the husbands and wives together. Being new to marriage, if she ever had a question, she'd know who to go to for a little advice.

"Lastly, this here is Merri, our newest addition. She's from

Oklahoma. It was just her and her pa there. She's sixteen and niece to the Grover's blacksmith. She came up to earn a little extra money for the summer, just in time, with me gettin' bigger daily and the babe due early fall, Doc says. We're hopin' she'll like us so much, she'll stay."

"Hi, ma'am. I-I mean Mrs. Rand," stammered the young blonde, her face turning as deep red as the base of the machine before Alice. In front of her, on the wooden table, were a few large balls of butter.

"Caroline works just fine, please, ladies." She placed a hand on the willowy beauty's shoulder to calm her. The girl was so pretty, Caroline wasn't sure if she'd end up stayin' because she enjoyed the work in the dairy, or if some man would snap her up with an offer of marriage. "Only women are hired to work in the dairy house?"

"Managin' and runnin' a dairy is considered to be women's work," Alice answered.

"Even though men have twice the arm strength to do it faster," added Kimberly.

"But no patience," Rachel injected.

"So, women do it better," Alice's voice rang out loud.

All the women, including Caroline, laughed. She liked the comradery of these women and hoped she'd be welcome as part of them, even when she wasn't working within the four walls. The small structure reminded her of the home she'd shared with her papa. Standing in it, made her heart ache with missing him.

"Is there a reason the walls are all painted white in here?" Caroline asked. The place appeared so stark, clinical even, like Miss Beadle had said the hospitals were in the big cities like Kansas City.

"Oh, yes. Because of the cream, it will absorb any strong scent or odor around it and that will come off in the taste of it.

So, we make it a point to work hard to keep it real clean in here, with our clothes, no shoes ever, because those attract dust, and we keep our hair covered." As Alice spoke, Rachel approached Caroline with a white cap and apron.

Caroline donned the dairy articles, even though she hated having anything on her head. She knew this was important for the sanitation of the Rand product.

"If you've noticed, the dairy is up wind from just about anything dealing with the cows and horses," Alice continued.

She had noticed that the house was situated closer to the growing crops than the barn, which she thought would have been better to just bring the canisters right over as they filled.

Alice waved her over, once Caroline had her apron secured at her back. The older woman stood beside a table with a machine of sorts that had a big silver bowl on top, with two spouts sticking this way and that with glass bowls below them, and a long, black handle that stuck out opposite of the spouts. "This right here, is the cream separator. It's the most important of what we do here, because it starts everything off for butter and those who ordered cream for bakin' or to feed to their hogs."

"I once had some of the best cream poured over some cornbread." Caroline thought about the treat Mrs. Morrison, Rachel's mom, would give out to the children in the afternoon to tide them over until supper. She'd fixed one for her too once, and it had warmed her belly and satisfied her sweet tooth.

"If it was here in town, it came from Rand Farms." The older woman smiled, pride showing in her eyes.

"That's good to know." Caroline meant that. She knew her husband was turning out to be special, but hearing how his employees praised his farm, warmed her heart. "How's it all work?"

"I'll pour milk in the top. Once that is done, you start crankin'." Alice lifted a large pitcher from the table and added it to the big middle bowl.

With a two-handed grip on the handle, Caroline started rotating it. She could hear the grinding and whirling of metal gears within the base.

"Nice and steady," Alice instructed. "Yes, just like that."

Soon, milk began to flow fast out of the wider spout, into the bowl beneath it while the cream came out at a steadier stream, as Caroline watched in fascination. She'd once seen her mama skim cream from the top of settled milk, but nothing ever as sophisticated as this process.

Alice poured milk from another pitcher one more time. Once both the large and small bowls were filled and the spouts were only dripping, did she tell her to stop turning the crank.

"Now the milk will go back into a different canister and those canisters will get picked up by one of the men and taken back to the pits for boilin' then shippin'. The afternoon milkin' goes straight there to the crew who makes the cheese."

Yesterday, Garrett had taken her to the far end of the farm where the large cauldrons sat and men boiled the milk and let it cool enough to place into special locked canisters that would hold up on the rocky train ride to bigger cities. There, the milk was refrigerated and sold. Garrett had said everyone in town who ordered milk from him got it fresh each morning without the boiling, what was called the pasteurizing process. It was a word she'd never heard, but Garrett said he'd learned how to do it from his father. It helped the dairy farms make a big profit and ship it safely.

"See this." Alice tipped the smaller bowl from left to right. "Notice how it's coatin' the sides." When Caroline nodded, she pronounced, "That's some good cream."

Picking up a wooden spoon, Alice dipped it in the bowl. "Taste that."

Claiming the spoon from the other woman, she placed it into her mouth. Her tongue was coated with the thick, creamy substance that was smooth as silk and sweet. "It's delicious."

Alice's smile was broad, a look of pride making her eyes bright. "Now, take that bowl to Rachel, and she'll show you what's next."

Following directions, Caroline gingerly carried the full bowl of cream to the foreman's wife.

"The first thing we do is pour the bowl of cream into another bowl." Rachel pushed a bowl before her that was covered with cheese cloth. "We do this to ensure that there is nothing that had gotten into the milk, like dirt, hair, debris."

Tipping the bowl over, Caroline poured the thick, smooth substance through the cloth slowly. Once she was done with that, she took the strained cream and added it into the churn.

Staring down into the churn, Rachel nodded. "Now there's enough cream in there. We don't churn it until there is plenty of cream at the bottom. It takes three bowls for each churn."

Caroline slid the plunger, a long pole with an X on the bottom, and lid onto the churn like Rachel told her. When the other woman handed her a wide strip of cheese cloth and told her to wrap it around the base of her pole, she did. "What's that for?"

"The extra moisture will start to rise up as the butter is forming and it will collect there instead of sliding back down into the churn, making the process take longer." Rachel gave a quick nod of her head.

"All right." Caroline realized it wasn't that it was complicated to make butter; it was more about the small details to get the job done efficiently and right the first time.

"Bring the churn and pull up a stool." Rachel went and sat behind another churn.

When Caroline grabbed a stool with a pillow affixed to the top, she sat and took hold of the pole the way Rachel was doing and began the up and down, circular motion. "How long does it usually take for the cream to turn to butter?"

"About an hour for each churn. So, it is all hands."

Sure enough, Alice and Kimberly both pulled up a full churn and they had all made a circle.

"This is where we spend most of our time," Kimberly said as she started pumping.

"When each batch is complete, we take it over to Merri to roll it and store it until it settles. The ones we do today, tomorrow, we will salt, rewrap in cheese cloth, and get it to the mercantile in the early morning, before the day heats up, weekly."

Plunging, Caroline frowned and looked around, just noticing something. "There are no windows in here. Why isn't it stifling?"

Rachel laughed and stomped a foot on the floor. "The winter ice is kept in the cellar beneath us. It's the best kept secret about this job," Rachel said with a laugh.

All the women joined in on the hilarity.

"In the winter, this is more of a storage. It's way too cold in the winter. So, we get a lot of butter stored up." Kimberly pointed to the many cabinets around the room.

After taking in all the things she had learned that morning in the dairy house, she looked back at the women and asked, "So, what is it that we do for the time all the churning takes?"

"Talk about our men, of course." Rachel winked.

Merri, who had joined them now, blushed to her roots and kept her head down as she began to churn.

As Kimberly started in on the antics of her husband,

Caroline thought about how she had enjoyed the time she spent at supper or how nice the meeting times in the brothel with the other women in the early mornings were. She had missed it over the last few days, but now she realized that she had another circle of women she could share in experiences with. She stared at each of their faces and realized that just like the Jewels had done, these women would go a long way in helping her settle into her new role.

GARRETT TOLD himself he needed to stop kissing his wife, that this was not the time nor place, even as he squeezed the nape of her neck with one hand while his tongue slipped further along her tongue. It was hard for his mind to operate when she continuously made the throaty mewing sound that even now was vibrating along his tongue. All he wanted to do was make her do it more, louder, until she was screaming out her need and pleasure. She tasted sweet and minty like the delicious orange mint marmalade she'd made from fruit their housekeeper had picked up earlier in the week. Caroline had popped open a jar that morning and slathered it onto her toast. He'd fallen for her beauty and sweetness but had been gifted with a wife who was a great cook. What she didn't know how to do in the kitchen, she threw herself into deeper to figure it out. It was that passion that she exhibited in every-thing she did, whether helping in the fields with the crops or in the dairy a few days a week with the women, Caroline never held back. Out of the two days he worked in the after-noons in his office, he found himself drawn to her in the kitchen and simply watching her work.

Just yesterday, she'd made a butter pound cake and brought him a slice with a glass of milk into the office. He'd taken the first bite and groaned. When she'd tried to leave the office, he'd dragged her into his lap and made her feed it to him off her breasts. He'd laid her out over his desk and dribbled the milk right from the glass onto her pussy where he'd drank it until she came, calling it Rand Farm's finest. She'd blushed to the roots of her hair as she'd lowered her skirts and left the room with the empty plate and glass.

Now, he inhaled as he glided his tongue in and out of her warm, wet mouth. Even in the fresh air, he could detect the rich, floral honey scent of her. He'd discovered she put jasmine oil in her bath water, and he loved the adventure of kissing and smelling along her body every night until he discovered the places where her natural musk combined with the sweet aroma—the side of her neck, under her breasts, behind her knees, and between her thighs. It pleased him to lick and suckle her pussy until only the humid scent of her ample cream was all that filled his head, while she came on his tongue.

Caroline gave him a reason to wake up each morning and a desire to crawl into bed at night. He'd discovered that his innocent wife had a head full of sexual knowledge that he'd more than enjoyed helping her learn to put into practice. His housekeeper had made it a practice to take care of her errands in the middle of the day, making it a point to keep out of the house while during the noon meal. Mrs. Copernic had said she was tired of coming into the house after pulling down the laundry from the line to see his and Caroline's heated stares practically burning the house down.

Garrett loved his housekeeper even more. Her absence allowed him just enough time to bring his wife to completion before he had to return to work. He made damn sure he did daily.

Now, he was trying to be good, attempting to keep himself

reined in, but when his wife started dragging her short nails over his nipples through his shirt all bets were off.

He groaned and sucked her bottom lip into his mouth then angled his head to the side for deeper access to her heavenly mouth. His cock stretched and pressed against the closure of his britches; it wanted out, and he wanted to set it free and slide inside his wife and make her writhe beneath him.

Her tongue circled his as she moaned.

Fuck, I need to feel her sweet ass on me. Dropping reins in his left hand, he reached for her and began to drag her into his lap.

"You know they make houses for that kind of stuff."

King neighed at the intruder and danced his hooves on the ground, rockin' the wagon.

Caroline squealed and shoved him away, her face crimson as a rose petal.

Garrett chuckled, feeling no shame to be caught in a passionate embrace with his wife. He released her before turning and meeting the gaze of the man bringing his black and white Piebald up alongside their wagon.

"Doc Clarkston," Garrett greeted his friend with a tip of his hat.

The man, who was about Garrett's size and most newcomers to town mistook for a rancher instead of the town doctor, brought two fingers to his own black hat and saluted him. "Your wagon's hoggin' the road there, Garrett. Hello, Caroline, you're lookin' lovely today. I guess marriage to the big lug agrees with you."

Garrett agreed wholeheartedly with the man. It was the way the sun showcased the natural golden highlights in her reddish-brown hair and how carefree she had looked with her head tipped back to the sun as she smiled sitting beside him that had him pulling the wagon to a halt and kissing her.

"Garrett has been kind to me." Garrett noticed how her gaze darted to him then away toward King. "Too kind."

His wife would just have to get used to being cared for and spoiled because he wasn't planning to stop, ever. Allowing her a bit of peace, he turned back to the doctor.

"Don't you have your own beautiful wife and daughter to spend a Saturday morning with instead of harassin' other townsfolks?" Garrett kept a hand on the small of Caroline's back, stroking along her lower spine with his thumb. There was tension there.

Takin' no offense, Doc Clarkston chuckled. "I do. But duty calls. Cary sent word that his wife is going into labor early."

"What? Isabel's having her baby? I wasn't sure if she'd already had it." That bit of news pulled Caroline's attention back around.

Garrett recalled his wife telling him about the years her papa allowed her to go to the schoolhouse and how close she and Isabel Reynolds, now Brown, had been at that time. The two friends had drifted apart when Caroline's father kept her close to his side and didn't allow her to visit with anyone. He hoped that now, Caroline would reconnect with someone who had been important to her.

"Babies. It's twins." Doc Clarkston held up a hand to keep her calm. "It's fairly common for them to come a good four weeks early; they just run out of room. The Browns have been prepared for this, reason I had Isabel on bedrest for the last two months. It's a good thing they lasted this long inside."

"Well, we won't keep you no longer. Pass our prayers on to both Cary and Isabel." Garrett heard the doctor's words, but like his wife, he felt a little anxious about the situation too. It was scary for a woman to bring forth one child, but two made it that much more dangerous. He was sure the soon-to-be parents were grateful for the physician's calming presence.

"And let her know if I can help with anything after the babies, lend a hand in any way, I'll be there."

"I sure will. With Cary's mom and her mother with them through this, they've got a lot of wisdom and support." With a sharp nod, he rode down the lane.

Garrett and Caroline waved him off.

He slipped his hand up Caroline's back then around her shoulder to pull her around to face him. "You all right?"

When she looked at him, her eyes were glassy, and her bottom lip was quivering slightly. "I guess I'm just worried. When we were younger, Isabel never talked about havin' babies, now she's about to bring two into the world." She shook her head. "She's bound to be scared."

Leaning in, he kissed her temple. "Thank the Good Lord she's got Cary's ma; Sunny had twin boys and she's half her size. They'll get through it."

"You're right." She rested a hand on his thigh and gave him a watery smile, but he noticed there were new clouds in her eyes as she turned away. "We'd better get on to town before the day is gone."

Garrett pressed the flat of his tongue to the roof of his mouth, making a clicking sound as he grasped the reins again and King moved down the road. He was no fool. All the talk about Isabel having not one, but two mothers at her side helping her in such a significant moment, had to have his wife thinking about the loss of her own mother. Whenever the Good Lord saw fit to allow Caroline to get with child, Garrett would make sure that his ma came down from Wisconsin for a while to help with the latter part of Caroline's pregnancy and support her through the birthing process. She wouldn't be alone, he'd make damn sure of it. Traditions be damned, he'd even be by her side.

"I'll leave you to what ladies do in a dress shop." Twenty minutes later, Garrett helped his wife down from the wagon before Mable's. "I've got the list of what you need from the mercantile, then I'll go 'round to the blacksmith, and finally, I'll make my way over with Ian, so take your time."

Smoothing a hand down her simple calico, one of the two she owned, his wife smiled up at him. "It shouldn't take me that long. I only need a few—"

"Caroline," he growled, still holding on to her waist as he waited for her to look up at him, ignoring the early day hustle and bustle of the town around them. This week, he'd seen how his wife kept things for herself simple. She usually washed her dress, shift, and drawers out in the bath and hung them up by the window in the room, leaving only his things for the housekeeper to tend to. Her eating had increased, but in the house, she had yet to put items on the list to add a woman's touch around their home. He saw his job as her husband to spoil her, make her comfortable with wanting things for herself. It wasn't just that he had the means to afford them, he enjoyed the surprise and wonder she tried to hide when he'd have Mrs. Copernic bring her back something like a new brush set from town.

When she finally did, he commanded, "Get a minimum of a handful of skirts and blouses you can wear around the farm. At least one real purty dress for the Founder's Day Dance, because I want to show you off at the event in a couple months. I'm sure there are plenty of underthings you may need."

She blushed and glanced away.

His fingers tightened at her waist and she glanced back at him.

Leaning in, he placed his lips right along the shell of her ear. "Get a nightgown all in lace, I want to suck your big, plump nipples through it and feel you writhin' beneath me from the sensation of my teasin' you through the delicate patterns."

She shuddered and let out a choked moan. "Garrett..."

When he stepped back, releasing her, he enjoyed the rush of color now filling her cheeks and the fire in her eyes, instead of the shadows of anxiety that had been there.

Givin' her a wink, he nodded toward the stairs leading up to the boardwalk. "Enjoy yourself, lovely bunny. Come to the office in a couple hours when you're ready, and we'll have lunch."

"All right." Her lips pulled up at the corners into a small smile before she turned and headed to the shop.

He watched her until she was inside the shop before he made his way around to his own errands. He'd lied to her, because the first thing on his list was getting to the livery and seeing about a horse for his wife. One docile enough, he could teach her to ride it, and sturdy enough to pull a wagon when she needed to get around. Over the last week, she had stuck close to the farm as she learned about all aspects of it, but he figured she missed her freedom to come and go into town. One night, over dinner, she'd talked about missing making soap. He wanted her to be able to do what she loved. As he'd told her, his farm and his life were both blessed to have her but didn't need her for it to continue to run efficiently.

So, he'd surprise her with a horse of her own that would provide her with a measure of freedom.

SEVENTEEN

"You look amazing. On some ladies, this design really does enhance what they have. That's true for you, Caroline." Daisy Mae, the youngest of Mable's daughters, now pregnant with her second child, kneeled before her and marked the bottom of the navy skirt with stick pins, to hem later.

"Wow. I am impressed with what you have done." Caroline would not have believed what the woman was saying if she wasn't staring into the fitting room mirror.

"Don't give me credit. We just enhance what the Good Lord has already given women. Every woman should be beautiful and well put together, no matter if they are sloppin' hogs or makin' lovely smellin' soaps." Daisy Mae winked up at her.

"Thank you." Caroline hadn't known how many women in town had liked and used her rose soaps. She had actually thought in the back of her mind that people just bought them to give a roundabout charity to the poor farm girl. It reminded her to bring up the subject again to Garrett. He'd supported her thoughts about her doing it again, but she hadn't really arranged anything. It had been more important for her to prove herself on the dairy farm and learn all she could.

Taking a breath to clear her mind, deciding to think about her little soap business later, she continued to stare in the tall looking glass. The pale-yellow, mutton-chop blouse, with its wide shoulders and fitting lower sleeve made her appear elegant, sophisticated even. Especially, once Daisy Mae had pinned it just so beneath her breasts. Even without a corset, it made her breasts sit up high, appearing a little larger. The colors were very subdued, so she wouldn't look out of place on the farm, where she would spend most of her time, but on the same token, she could run into town or go visiting and it would be perfectly fine. She turned slightly right then left to take in her profile but not disturb the woman below, working fastidiously. Caroline could not help but think about Garrett and how he would react at seeing her breasts displayed so fine.

Her husband loved touching and titillating her breasts, and she had discovered that she very much enjoyed his attentions, to the point of orgasm often. In the mirror, a wanton-faced woman stared back at her. Her eyes were glazed over and there were ample amounts of color in her face. The small curtained-off enclosure began to feel warm as heat sizzled through her body from her nipples to her core as her mind replayed Garrett's naughty suggestions an hour ago when he'd dropped her off.

"Well, there must be something wicked going on in your mind, Caroline. Your cheeks are redder than the stripes on a peppermint stick." Daisy Mae rose as she gave her a knowing smile. "Only thoughts of one's husband can do that," she whispered.

"Gracious." Caroline placed the back of her hands on her cheeks, trying to cool down the color in her face. "I don't know how my mind goes down such rabbit holes."

Because you're Garrett's bunny. His naughty bunny.

"I'd say all new brides who are happy with their match have the same vexation." Daisy Mae giggled.

"Perhaps." Lowering her eyes to her hands, Caroline couldn't hold back her own laughter. She didn't want to see her expression, evidence of her own audaciousness.

"Well, I'll help you out of all this, so you don't stick yourself." Daisy moved behind her on the dais and started unfastening the skirt. "The pink dress you wanted to wear home is on the peg behind you. Ma and I will get your things wrapped and let Connie Marie know you're ready to discuss your Founders' Day dress."

The skirt dropped and bellowed out at her feet. Caroline stepped out of it gingerly, careful of the pins. "Much appreciate it." Finished unbuttoning the shirt, she slipped out of it and handed it over to the other woman.

Holding her bundle, Daisy Mae moved to the curtain. "We should have this altered and the other two ready by week's end. You want them delivered?"

"No. If you don't mind, I'll send Mrs. Copernic around on one of her Tuesday shopping adventures." Caroline loved cooking, but she never cared for coming into town. Before, she had done it out of necessity, and early. She was grateful to have their housekeeper, who enjoyed it and used it as part of her visiting time.

"Then I'll send word 'round when they are done."

"Thank you." Caroline stepped down from the dais then grabbed the new carnation pink dress from the peg.

As she got into it and buttoned it, she blushed again. The dress' sleeves were also mutton chop style with three-quarter length, but the bodice was a triangle fashion. It came up to the base of the neck but instead of being a square cut, it started off narrow at the collarbone and wider at her bosom. It was cinched tight at the torso, not too tight to move, but just enough that once buttoned, it lifted the breasts high against the lower edge. It was simple, but just bordered on daring. There was a little lace embroidered at the edge to keep it modest, but if a man were standing close, he could just make out the shadow between the breasts. Garrett would be that close.

She wanted to wear something special for him for the ride home. She'd been grateful for his offer to get herself some new things, so she'd started with a selection of her more intimates when she first came in and the store had been empty. Hearing all the voices beyond the black curtain, Caroline knew it was a good thing she hadn't waited. Patting her hair, she made sure her simple chignon hadn't become mussed with all the dressing and undressing. Happy with her appearance, she walked over to the curtain and swept it out of her way.

The store was bustling. Caroline saw a lot of familiar faces, and as most turned in her direction, she could see the wide-eyed looks. She was sure most women didn't expect to see her in the dress shop. She'd only been in it once before, with Isabel and her mama. When Papa was alive, she'd followed a basic pattern and had sewn their things; they were nothing like the unique and sophisticated designs of Mable and her daughters.

"Hello." She stepped out of one of two fitting and alterations areas and spoke to those in the store front.

More than a handful of others smiled back at her or mumbled their own greetings from couches, shelves, metal dress forms that showcased originals, or flipped through the racks of patterns. Caroline was feeling comfortable and less nervous as she saw Mable and Daisy Mae working the area talking with the ladies and offering tea and sweet lemon water. She turned down refreshments. Garrett had mentioned that since they were in town, they would grab a bite at the

Drummonds' restaurant. Never having eaten there before, she was excited about another new experience.

Seeing that one of the books with the fashion dresses was available, Caroline moved through the crush of bodies to make her way to the back counter while she waited on Connie Marie. She wasn't sure what dress she wanted for the Founders' Day Dance. Not wanting to keep the woman longer than she had to, Caroline started flipping through the pages. Some of the dresses were so fancy, others, way too much material on a hot Kansas summer night.

A few things the women around her were discussing gained her interest. A few women, who must live in town because of the elaborate designs of their day dresses, discussed perfumes and fancy new soaps from Paris that the mercantile was carrying and the high cost. She was eavesdropping as she stared at a dress that she was inclined to request made, so it took her a moment to pick up on the loud whispers to the other side of her.

"You know a whore will always be a whore, no matter how you dress them up."

"Yeees, so true. It used to be that they would only come into town late in the evening or early mornings, before decent women had risen."

Caroline recognized the rude, biting voices but still hazarded a glance to her left to see who it was they were speaking about. Her heart sank when she realized Old Lady Bellmore and Widow Lawrence, who had just come in the store, were standing two feet away from her and staring pointedly at her.

Gasping, Caroline turned away, attempting to mind her business. Maybe she could pretend that they were discussing someone else.

"You could understand if a poor girl lost her pa and turned

to an old man or became a serving girl at one of the restaurants; there's some pride in that," crooned Bellmore in her high-pitched whiny voice. "But my son had taken pity on her and offered her to be my maid."

"Those would have been honorable...but to run over to the brothel willingly," the smooth sultry voice of the widow offered in a stage whisper.

Caroline's vocal cords seized, causing pain to shoot through her throat. She wanted to rage that her son had not offered anything respectable within her household. Caroline could hear the low whispers of the women around her start in, questioning 'is that Old Man Douglas' daughter' and 'was she really working as a whore', and 'was she at the little saloon; that place is so tawdry'.

Her stomach dropped and she thought she was going to be sick. Her new dress felt too tight and the soft cotton uncomfortable. Her hands were shaking all over and she could no longer see the pretty, sketched dress on the page because her vision had blurred.

"Poor Jillian Pettigrew, sweet and beautiful, got pushed over for the likes of her...Jillian would have been such a better match," Widow Lawrence tsked.

"But at least Garrett has the money to turn a sow's ear into a silk purse," the final cut came from Daryl Bellmore's mother.

Ladies gasped behind her as Caroline rushed out of the store.

"Mrs. Rand!"

Caroline ignored the call of her name. She couldn't stand there any longer and be mutilated before others by two vipers. She needed to breathe, and the store was closing off her oxygen and her lungs had seemed to stop functioning. It would humiliate her even more to have fainted at those two biddies' feet. The other women around would most likely laugh at her, the poor farm girl turned whore, because they would believe the vicious words of two prominent women in town.

Daryl Bellmore was one of the richest men in town, and his father had been one of the Founders before he died, making Mrs. Bellmore practically one step lower than the voice of God. Even a lowly farm girl knew this.

She fled down the boardwalk, the fastest route she could remember that would lead her to one of the alleys and away from town. Her core told her to go find Garrett, who should be at the Sheriff's Office by now talking to his brother, but she couldn't face him. Not right now. There were so many thoughts crashing into her mind, she just needed some time.

Right foot. Left foot. She just kept walking, down a path through the woods that would keep her off the main road. It was worn, well-traveled, and she'd been on it before, many times. It was where she could try to process some of the things she'd discovered that afternoon.

Garrett had another woman he was supposed to merry, Jillian Pettigrew. The lovely Jillian Pettigrew. Caroline knew the gristmiller's daughter. The girl had been two years behind her in school, one of Isabel's sister's friends, a group of young girls who always wore the latest fashions from Chicago or New York and carried lunch pails that had been painted in Paris. Jillian Pettigrew had been pretty and doll-like when they were girls, but she was breathtakingly beautiful now. Caroline had seen her a few times in town. Jillian had always been kind, but Caroline doubted it would be the same now that she'd stolen her intended.

Why did Garrett choose me? Caroline shook her head as she marched along the hardpacked ground, mindlessly dipping under low hanging branches. The mean women had been right; Jillian would have made a much better wife.

What man doesn't want a whore in his bed? Caroline reminded herself how often Garrett had told her he didn't marry her because he needed help in his household or his farm. *It was his bed.*

They had done things that would have been shocking or questionable to Jillian and other decent girls, but with Caroline having been trained at the brothel, she had learned things. Even though she had no practical experience, she rarely balked at her husband's suggestions. *A virgin whore,* that's what she had been.

She'd foolishly thought she'd been so insignificant to those in Grover Town, that no one even knew she had been missing and sequestered at the Harlot and the Hero. She'd kept herself around the property and stayed away from town even on her day off. People had noticed, and if they didn't, thanks to Old Lady Bellmore and the gorgeous widow, they did now. Word would spread from those in the dress shop to everyone in the town. Garrett Rand had taken up with a whore. Even if they'd had her placed at the little saloon, it didn't matter much, the taint on her, rather Garrett's reputation, would be the same. A whore was a whore was a whore.

Maybe if she'd been under Miss Kitty's tutelage longer, she would have been able to walk with her head held high and her chin raised like the other Jewels. They strutted around town on their day off with pride, daring anyone to say something out of place, lest they cut them down.

Even in that, she had failed. Perhaps she could convince him to let her go, so he could marry someone more worthy. Jillian would know how to be a woman of leisure like the other rich men's wives in town who had wardrobes full of dresses, wore the latest leather kid boots, and could pin a bonnet just right on artistic curls.

She swiped at the tears running down her face and neck

and stopped at the end of the long winding path. Miles away from town, she stared up at the small, familiar house. Her heart ached as she took the steps toward her home, her old home, but more comforting right now than the two-story place she lived in with her husband.

The silence echoed around the property, nothing moved, and the field was barren and dry, proof that even her papa's last crop didn't take. The pen, where Driscoll their goat had been, hung open and the barn leaned a little to the right now. She stopped at the pump and primed it. The water trickled out but still ran clear. She cupped her hand and took in a few handfuls of water to moisten her parched throat. With the last bit, she swiped at her face and neck, wiping away the sweat and dust that had gathered from her walk.

When she got to the front of the house, she saw her rose bushes were overgrown and dying early, from the lack of tending. She brushed her fingers along a petal, baked brown and withered under the hot sun. Even her light touch had caused it to break off and float to the ground, joining the others that littered the dirt.

Taking a breath, she went to the door and opened it. Nothing had been touched; it was as if time had stood still there as it had in her heart. She could almost hear the familiar sound of her father striking the unyielding ground behind her.

A loue ye. The words whispered through the room as she stared at her papa's rocking chair and the cot he slept on each night. He'd cry out those words often in his sleep. She knew those words of love, be they uttered in a nightmare or dream, were meant for her mother.

This was where she belonged, with the ghosts of her past.

THREE HOURS. It had been that long since he'd dropped off Caroline at the dress shop.

"I do believe your bride is cleanin' out Mable's," Ian teased from where he sat doing paperwork on his desk.

He frowned at his brother's words as he glanced from the clock on the shelf beside Deputy Nelson, the night deputy's, desk where Garrett sat with feet propped on the corner. "I'd have thought she'd been done by now. I ain't tryin' to rush her, but lunch will be about over soon."

"You know women can get forgetful when they're staring at all that lace and silk; they just want it all." Ian shook his head.

"Pretty much," Garrett muttered, but Caroline wasn't really that kind of woman. He'd practically had to drag her there to shop for herself. She never asked for anything for herself. He just couldn't see her going hog wild in a store unless it was a flower shop. The women loved talkin' about all the different kinds of soaps that could be made from combining the right herbs and flowers. He figured the place must have been busy, even with them coming out early. "I think I'll mosey on down and see if I can prod her along. She can come back in town."

He'd wanted to purchase her a horse, but at the livery, he'd found out that a horse man was due in town about a week before Founders' Day. So, he'd wait until then, to get her the best horse flesh.

"Good luck with that. It may be better for you just to get Mrs. Drummond to wrap you up a couple of her brisket and gravy sandwiches to go." Ian picked up his mug then started toward the small potbelly in the corner, only big enough to heat the pot of coffee.

"You're probably right." Dropping his boots to the ground, Garrett rose from the wood chair. "I'll at least let her know that's what I've done; maybe it will make her aware of the time of day."

"It's worth a try." Ian nodded.

"Come 'round one night next week with the wife, for dinner," Garrett reminded his brother as he swiped his black hat from the front edge of the desk.

"Now that your housekeeper ain't cookin' for ya, we will. See ya soon."

Chuckling, Garrett exited the office. He returned greetings of his friends and neighbors as he strutted the boardwalk to the dress shop.

"Afternoon, ladies." Garrett tipped his hat then removed it as he entered Mable's. There were a few women within, but not enough that it should have kept Caroline, whom he didn't see in the store anywhere as he scanned from left to right.

"Garrett, is there something I can do for you?" Mable approached him, as she came out the back with a little girl's pale orange dress with big white daisies embroidered on the skirt part.

He couldn't help but imagine what his and Caroline's little girl would look like wearing such a pretty creation. Shakin' the thought away, he asked, "I assume Caroline is still in one of the fittin' areas." He nodded his head toward two black, curtained off areas. "Can you let her know I'm out here?"

With large eyes, Mable stared at him. "Um, Garrett, I would have assumed your wife was with you. She left hours ago."

"What?"

The older woman stepped back, most likely from the harshness of his words. "Yes. Talk to Connie Marie. She never put in her order for the dance, and today is the last day. I think she even left some things. If you'll excuse me."

When he nodded at the shop owner, she continued to one of the fitting areas. He strutted toward the counter and waited a moment while Connie Marie completed a sale and handed the woman and her daughter the bundle.

He smiled at the two as they passed him and headed out of the store.

"Hello, Garrett, are you here to get your wife's things?"

Arching a brow, he stared at the women behind the counter. "Her things? Caroline didn't take her purchases with her?"

"No." The woman stared at him as if he had just sprouted another head. "There are quite a few things. If you all didn't bring the wagon to town, I can have them delivered to the house."

"I'll take them. Can you tell me where she was headed?"

"Honestly, Garrett, it was so hectic in here for the last two hours, I can't." Turning to the back counter, Connie Marie collected four large bundles wrapped in delicate tissue paper and others in brown paper, all held closed with ribbons in multiple colors. When she set them on the counter, she said, "I was headed to her where she was at the back counter looking at dresses in the book, but before I could make it to her, she just ran out."

Ran? Interesting choice of word. "Could something have upset her?"

Connie's face pinched as she seemed to consider his words. "I would like to say no. Honestly, now that you mention it, she didn't seem like the shy, cheery woman she had been the first hour she had been in here. Maybe there was a pallor to her face, like she was ill." Connie scrunched her face then shook her head. "It was a crush, so perhaps she had overheated. I thought it was strange, but I was needed to help other ladies waiting, sorry."

His gut tightened. He thought about Caroline in the shop, the place brimming with women from town. He knew from her past, she'd never been comfortable around a lot of people. He wondered if someone had said something to her.

"Not your fault. She probably went to the mercantile." He preferred to think of her perusing the soaps and seeing what had come in new, than her just running off. Either way, she'd disobeyed him, but one brought a heavier consequence then the other. He started to gather the packages but recalled something Connie's mother had said. "Today's the last day a woman can order her dress to have it ready in time for the dance?"

"'Fraid so. With Grover Town growing so rapidly, and people takin' the train in from other towns and placin' orders, Mama has had to hire part-timers to ensure she can fill the orders for Founders' Day."

He nodded understanding. One of his commands to his wife had been for her to get a dress for the event. If she'd disobeyed him, there'd better have been a good damn reason why. "Do you know what dress Caroline was considerin'?"

Connie Marie smiled. "I think so. Well, it was the one open on the page before she left."

"Show me." With bundles in his arms, he followed the woman across the store.

Once there, Connie Marie made quick work of shuffling her fingers through the book then stopped in seconds at a page. "Here it is."

Garrett leaned over and saw the design. It was simple but elegant, and he could easily imagine it would be something Caroline would pick out. It would complement her form just right. "Y'all have her measurements, right?"

"We sure do. There are a couple dresses and blouses we still need to finish for her."

"Then add this to the order in blue, one of those pretty light blue colors."

"Good choice, the shade will look lovely with your wife's chestnut tresses and soft golden skin." Connie smiled.

"Thanks." He returned her smile as he jostled the packages to get his hat on his head. With a nod, he left the store.

He went to the mercantile next door first and peered inside the large window toward the basket of soap cakes. There was no sign of Caroline there or anywhere else in the store. Shaking his head, he headed to the wagon to add her things to all the items already loaded in the back. Standing next to King, he pulled out his bandana as he wiped the sweat from his brow while he looked up and down the street, trying to see if he spotted his wife coming in or out of an establishment.

"Hey there, Garrett."

Turning his gaze from the boardwalk across the road in search of his wife, Garrett spotted Clive coming his way, hauling a crate on his shoulder. "Clive," he tipped his chin up. "That's some package you got there."

"Yup. Over the last month or so, my wife's brother has been shippin' things in." The foreman of the Spencer Pride Ranch had been married to Holly, the preacher's oldest daughter, for some time now. The pastor's youngest daughter had married a man of the cloth and moved to New Mexico territory to start a church, and their eldest son had left Grover not too long after. The boy had always been known to have a little wanderlust in his blood.

"Jacob?" Garrett watched the other man groan at the weight of the crate as he shifted it to the bed of the wagon.

Clive nodded as he shoved the crate forward. "There's at least two more of these today."

"What's in 'em?" Garrett shifted his gaze from the crate to peer down the road again.

"Not sure. I know one thing; we'll all sure be glad when he gets here." Clive took off his hat and swiped at the sweat rolling down his face as he raised his arm, using the sleeve of his shirt. "You lookin' for somethin'?"

"My wife." Garrett watched a loaded covered wagon roll by him and out of town, the single team horse guided by a woman with two boys on the boxseat next to her and three small girls staring out the back. "Is that the Langs, just moved into town about four months ago?"

Clive stepped up beside him. "It's at least the missus and their passel of young'uns. Shame what happened to the bookkeeper."

Garrett stared over at the man beside him. "Don't tell me...dead?"

"Yup. His body was found last night. Wife said he'd come in late last night and a few other nights, never would say what he'd been about. In the early morning, he was tossin' and turnin', just carryin' on and delirious, like then he was just gone." Clive shook his head.

"Ian was mentioning somethin' about another death. Says both spouses were clear. All their family money was tied up in the business, so their widows get nothin' but a hard road before 'em." Garrett recalled that was the same thing that had happened to the tobacco shop owner. Within two months, he was found in a field. There had been a few others too, over the year. "Doc thinkin' we got some epidemic that done come to town?"

"Nope. Spencer asked, makin' sure if we should keep the wives and children from town in case it's soemthin' that'll spread. He's the one who let the sheriff know it's arsenic poisoning."

"But how?" Garrett was asking more of himself then Clive. His older brother had been mulling over a few things, theories, but the only thing he could come up with that connected the men who died was Bellmore. Daryl owned all the land and storefronts of each of the men. However, he'd never been seen around any of them for any length of time or appeared to have an issue. But Bellmore was the only one who profited from the deaths, the widows forced to pay out bad business loans and surrender anything worth anything to clear the debt. Bellmore and his bad ass dealings.

Garrett thought about what had happened to Caroline after her father passed. His fists tightened as he thought about the asshole making her sell herself as payment.

"It's a bad situation for the Langs, but no reason to be mad; she's got family in the western part of Virginia, I heard." Clive placed a hand on his shoulder. "Did I hear you say you were hunting for your wife?"

The other man's hand on his shoulder briefly made Garrett aware of the tension in his body at the thought of Bellmore's antics. At the end of next month, when the council met, Bellmore was going to have some things to answer to. "Yes. She was supposed to meet me after her shoppin', but I figured she might have gone off to another shop."

"When I was headed into town, I was pretty sure I'd seen Caroline. I only recall it, because I thought she was a long way from home to be out for a walk."

"Where?" Garrett demanded.

"Deadman's path, over through the eastern woods."

Garrett wasn't sure if he even took the time to offer a thanks before he was in his wagon and headed out of town. Then only reason that walk through the woods was named so morbidly was because that part of Grover Town boundary was barren, no moisture for miles. If someone picked the wrong time of day to go out too far along the path, they could die of dehydration. There was only one thing that was out that far. Garrett prayed his wife had made it there safely, because he didn't want anything to keep him from tanning her hide when he arrived.

"YOU KNOW, wife, this ain't how I intended us to spend our day."

"Ah!" Caroline squealed as she whipped around and spotted him at the door.

Garrett stared at his wife in the new pink dress. Even the dirt at the hem of it couldn't detract from the sight of her that captivated him, the style of dress conforming to her body and showing off her narrow waist, the low line of the bodice show-casing the creamy swells of her breasts without being sala-cious. The desire to lick over her skin or tug it down just enough so that her nipples popped out had his cock rising.

"Um...Garrett...what are you doing here?" She licked over her full top lip, the sight of its odd fullness being wet by her delicate pink tongue made him think of things she could do with her mouth.

Later.

"That's a question I have for you." Garrett closed the door behind himself.

Her eyes grew wider as she stood in the center of the small front room, the space looking untouched by time, but Caroline had changed. She didn't fit in this space any longer and he wondered if she realized it.

She licked her lips again then continued along the bottom this time, as her hands fisted then released at her sides. "Well... I just wanted to take a walk, stretch my legs a bit."

"Thirty." He still stood close to the door as he watched her.

"What?" She frowned, tipping her head to the side. "Thirty what?"

Folding his arms over his chest, he informed her, "You've already earned twenty strikes by your actions, and you just tellin' me a lie added another ten. You want to try your answer again?"

Now her hands were twitching. They moved up to her waist, as she took in a shuddered breath, then down to her side again, proof she was more than a little agitated.

Garrett's position remained. "What are you doing here, lovely bunny?"

She stomped one foot then the other, apparently deciding to go for bravado. "It's my home. I have a right—"

"Forty. This place is Bellmore land. You live with me, *wife*," he growled.

"Forty! Forty. That's insane." She backed up. "Why not by single digits? Twenty-two is a much better number."

"Darlin' bunny, you should be thinkin' less about negotiatin' how many swats your ass is goin' to get and more about explainin' yourself."

She folded her arms too, mirroring his stance, except her position sent those luscious small breasts of hers higher above the bodice.

Fuck. His dick was heavier as it pushed at his britches. If his wife glanced from his eyes, she'd see the evidence of how much he wanted her.

"I shouldn't be the only one explainin' things, Garrett." She pointed at him. "What about you?"

He angled his head to the side and squinted at her below the brim of his hat. "What about me?"

She cut her gaze toward the single window beyond his

shoulder. "You were supposed to marry someone else, someone sweet and pretty. How do you think it makes me look when others think I'm a husband stealer, on top of being a whore?"

The growl rumbled up from his gut, through his lungs, and around his heart before it roared out of his mouth. He crossed the room in two strides then gripped her waist before dragging her against him. "First off, Caroline, there is no woman in this town as beautiful as you. Got that?"

She squeaked, "Yes."

"Second, I would damn well know if I had offered for any other woman's hand before yours, no matter what the Grover busybodies have to say about it. You hear me?"

He wished the best for Jillian, but she hadn't been for him. The mild-mannered young woman didn't have Caroline's beguiling fire.

"Okay," she whispered.

He wasn't yelling, but he kept his words clipped and harsh as he held her wide, brown gaze, ensuring that she understood every word he said. "Lastly, I warned you about callin' yourself a whore. That's fifty."

"No...Garrett," she whimpered, trepidation making her body shudder against his and her eyes to shine. She took a step back. With him still holding her, she couldn't go farther.

"Yes. It's not up for argument, but I'm willin' to tack on another ten for good measure."

She stilled.

Garrett chuckled. He glanced around the room for a moment before he spotted the perfect place. "Come here."

Taking hold of one of her hands, he walked her over to the small hearth. The stones were flush to the wall and the area swept clean before it. It would do nicely.

"What are you doin'? Garrett...Garrett?"

"Face the wall and raise your hands," he instructed.

Blinking twice, she stared at him for a moment before she did as she was told.

Removing his bandana from his pocket, he then took it by two of the four corners and pulled. The worn cloth stretched out longer as he twirled it around and around, the twists making it a stronger hold.

"Garrett, please don't," she pleaded as he reached up and cinched her wrists together.

"I told you, I'd ensure a disciplined home, wife."

When she started to lower her bound hands, he took hold of them and brought them up and over one of the empty rifle hooks.

"No. Garrett, no." She wiggled and pulled against the hook's hold, but it was solidly secured in the bearing wall.

He smiled. One thing he could say about Sam Douglas, besides his love for his only child, was he couldn't farm worth shit, but the man could raise a solid house. It was a shame Douglas hadn't realized his talent instead of burying his head in the dirt.

"Spread your feet wide," he demanded, still standing right behind her.

She shifted, her round ass grazing the front of his pants. When she gasped and shied away from the evidence of his arousal, he let out a laugh.

"One thing at a time, bunny."

"Umph! There's no way." Some of her spark was back as she eyed him over her shoulder, dropping her gaze low as if to indicate the area of his britches. She took one step out, barely parting her legs a foot.

"We'll see." He tapped the outside of one of her thighs. "Wider."

She huffed but still moved.

"Nice." He took hold of her skirts and began to drag them up her legs.

"What are you doing?" Her lids were round, making her eyes practically bug out.

"A good spankin' happens against bare skin. No need to do it if it can't be remembered, make the person uncomfortable for a while to sit."

"I'll remember. I promise."

"You sure will," he declared as he tucked the hem of her dress under the back of her fitted bodice. He stared down at her drawers. They were something else new. The material covered all her parts, but the cotton was so sheer, he could still see everything beneath it, the creamy skin of her backside and the shadowed cleft between it. He pulled his hands away and balled them into a tight fist to get his rampant desire under control. The urge to bend her forward and shove his cock between the slit of the covering he knew was between her legs and bury himself hard and deep in her tight pussy, had more than one trickle of sweat running down his spine.

After a deep breath, he slipped a hand around her waist and sought the ribbon or string holding them up. When he located it, he felt his wife tremble at his touch and heard her moan. She wasn't helping his resolve at all. With a swift hand, he undid the satin bow and watched as her delicate drawers drifted to the ground.

"Don't," he growled when she started to step out of them.

He enjoyed the depraved appearance of her with her dress rucked up and her underthings around her ankles, all her bare, pale limbs revealed to his hungry sight. He kneeled and caressed her stocking-covered ankles just above her boots. Lowered now, he could smell the scent of her musk melded with the sweet oil she preferred. It would take nothing for him to lean in and kiss along the curve of her pale ass until he reached the shadow of her center. Her taste would be heady and sweet, but now was not the time.

Glancing back to her feet, a crooked smile tilted his lips briefly when he saw that she still wore her worn boots beneath such a pretty new dress. In more than one way, she was still the young girl who lived on this farm. He knew she had other boots in her packages, he'd seen the boxes, but these dilapidated leather shoes were a comfort to her, a link to all that she had lost. Today, was a perfect example of her lack of trust in him to protect her, keep her safe, and care for her. She'd run to a home that was no longer hers instead of seeking him out. That chafed.

His chest burned with the acid from his gut, jealousy. He could be all things to Caroline, in the eyes of God and man, but he could never be her security until she trusted him more than a pair of damn boots. That trust, she would have to give to him of her own free will.

Rising, he dragged his fingers up her legs until he reached the snug ties digging into her thighs to keep the flimsy material up. Then there was the warmth of her soft, satiny thighs and the tremors of her body along his tips.

"Garrett...please." It was her words that brought him out of his own murky cogitations.

He palmed the two sides of her backside, squeezing and rubbing them, warming her flesh for what was to come. "I will, Caroline. You are my responsibility. It is my duty to ensure you are safe. That I know where you are, always. When you disobey me—"

"I didn't mean to. You didn't hear the hurtful words they —" she contradicted.

"Run away from me." He continued, ensuring she understood the danger of her actions. "When you failed to come find me instead of goin' off on your own, you showed you believe I don't have a care for what hurts you."

Hearing the truth of his own words hurt him. He leaned in, pressing his chest to her back, all the while inhaling her scent at the curve of her neck.

"I'm sorry..." she whispered.

EIGHTEEN

He felt the beating of her heart against his chest as the agony of her words told him she meant it, but it wasn't enough. Stepping back and to the side, with one hand on her waist and the other at his side, he said, "Angle your ass back toward me." Once she did it, her thighs wide and ass upturned, she was an enthralling view. Again, he had to grip his lust tightly to keep from undoing his britches and sliding his hard cock into her tight channel.

"Count them out, wife," he rasped.

She gasped as the first one landed. "One."

Then, the next one, on the center of the other cheek.

"Two." Her voice became calmer as she adjusted to each swat.

By the time he got to the fourth one, her voice was even and barely a vibrato. It didn't worry him, because he knew he was using the first ten just to prepare the virgin skin right. He made sure he landed hits all around her backside, from the swell to sit spot. His wife had never been spanked by him, and not by her pa as she'd confessed. He didn't want to injure her tender cheeks by starting in hard.

"Ten," she said, her tone matter of fact as she held her head raised and stared at the wall.

There was barely a blush to her ass. In less than an hour, that color would be gone if he stopped here. He pulled his hand back farther and let the next one sail. At impact, he felt the sting in his palm and the bounce and jiggle of her lush, round bottom.

Smack.

"Ow!" She arched forward, into the empty space of the hearth.

And another one went.

Smack.

"Garrett! Ow...no. That hurt." She danced to the right, pulling at her bindings as she tried to shy away.

"That's the point. Resume your position." He waited for her to shuffle back into place. "Now count, bunny."

"Twelve."

"Oh, no." He chuckled. "You missed countin' one, so that is just eleven."

She whimpered. "Eleven."

As he set off a volley of strikes, five directly in the same spot at the center of her right ass cheeks, then five on the same place of the other. He admired the hue of her ass; it showed two bright pink spots that rivaled the color of her dress.

"Twenty-one!" She was crying now, her voice wavered with emotions. Still, she held her position. "Plea-s-se...stop."

"Oh, love, we aren't even halfway through." The next four went to the sides of her right cheek, where the flesh was more firm. He landed the swats harder.

"Twenty-five. Noo...nooo...I can't." She clenched her cheeks and wailed.

"You can." He angled his body and took care of the other

side's cheek. "You're my wife. I'll be obeyed." *Smack! Smack! Smack! Smack!*

"Twenty-nine. Yes. Yes. All right...I'll be good. It hurts! Stop!"

He ignored her cries as he bit out, "You'll never call yourself a whore again."

He had to ensure that this lesson stuck. Earlier, his heart sank deep and his gut had curled in with fear when he discovered she had not only left the shop but town and was off alone. With death happening all around them and cattle wranglers caught over the winter who had threatened his foreman's wife, he dreaded the things that could have happened to Caroline. His older brother worked hard to keep Grover Town safe, but things still went on that even the badge couldn't stop.

He started on the lower curves and the tops of her thighs, ignoring the pain in his palm, which was smarting like he knew her ass was. With a hand still on her waist, he could not only see the trembling of her body but feel them in his fingertips. Her stomach was tightly clenched as she took in shallow breaths through her cries and whimpers. Her ass was a bright red, now overtaking the color of her dress and rivalling the neglected red roses bowing over the front rail.

Smack. Smack. Smack. Smack. Smack. He peppered each place with five.

"For-rty-e-i-ight." Her knees buckled, and for a moment, she hung from the sturdy hook. "No more, Garrett...stop...pleeassse. I need...I need—"

"We'll finish this, wife. Up." Standing back, he waited, feeling the throbbing in his hand.

She struggled to her feet, unaided by him. He watched her move back into place even as her body shook. Once she was there, in her original spot with her feet wide and her hips out, he commanded, "Come all the way back. Push your ass out toward me until you can't go any further. Offer yourself to me, to my discipline."

Without hesitation, she slid one foot back then the other, hobbling because of her drawers. Her body a plain, she was stretched and straining toward him.

He couldn't help admiring her apple red ass availed to him, her submission. As his gaze slid over her cherry bottom, with the pale crease of her cleft now revealed, he saw the winking of her puckered entrance as she clenched then relaxed before him. What shocked him was the sight of the cream coating the tops of her inner thighs and the swollen, glistening smooth skin of her pussy.

Garrett had known many widows and whores who enjoyed being spanked during sex, and his friends Spencer, Samuels, Clarkston, and hell, even Lyle, his foreman, had shared with him about how their wives had taken to discipline, but he'd believed their wives had simply been malleable after the spankings. What he was seeing before him wasn't evidence of acquiescence, but pure lust. A clear indication his lovely wife straddled the fine line of pleasure and pain. A true gift.

He was glad he had not given her a paltry twenty, a beginner's number. It was obvious his bunny needed more; she had to be pushed beyond the valley of pain and shame of her actions, to the pleasurable climb of her true surrender. His mind raced through her cries. She'd started out screaming about the pain, but at some point, she'd begun to whimper, 'I need...please'. Well, he had a need to, she'd soon discover.

"Tell me to do it, Caroline."

She shook her head, denying what they both knew.

"Tell me," he demanded. He not only wanted to hear the

words, he needed her to hear *her* words and recognize this was part of his caring for her. She was his.

"Spank me, husband. I'm yours."

It was the last part that had him raising his hand and bringing it down right between her gloriously spread cheeks, striking her at the only untouched place, her crease. *Smack.* His hand made contact with her tender rosette.

"Ow! Forty-nine," she panted but kept her frame.

Pausing, his own breath ragged, he slowly brought his hand up to his shoulder level and waited, letting both of their anticipations build. With a quickness, he brought it down to the same spot, the part now tinted the same carnation pink of her dress, complementing the dark shade of her round ass.

"Fif-ty," she cried, bowing her head.

"Good girl. My lovely bunny." He set his hands on her backside, feeling the pulsing heat of her skin. He caressed her slowly along her curves, down her legs and up her back, as he praised her. "You did well, darlin' wife."

She hissed and moaned at his touch, still in position.

When his touch shifted up along the inside of her thighs, through the slickness there, then brushed along her swollen lips, she shifted her hips as if seeking more of his touch.

Lowering himself to his knees, he continued to caress her heated ass, telling her how proud he was of her for taking her punishment. He stared at her fold, pink and wet, dewy with her cream pooled in every crease.

"You're so wet. Your cream is practically drippin' from your pussy, bunny." He brought his hands around, using his thumbs to stroke up and down her sex, playing from her opening to her clit.

She bucked and whimpered.

He pulled back her labia wide as he caressed, revealing her inner slit to his hungry gaze. Up and up he went, until he was at the tiny hole of her pussy. Once there, he pressed in, slowly, as he made her take both his thumbs.

"Oh...ooh. Garrett. I neeeed..."

"I know just want you need." In and out, he coaxed her walls to take him in, let him feel her. Even with both of his thumbs, the penetration was smaller than his cock, but it would continue to build her toward the release her body was begging for.

She smelled incredible, the rich floral musk of her beckoning him closer. He knew she'd taste even better. Dipping his head, he dragged the tip of his tongue along her delicate slit, collecting her cream and filling his mouth with the savory, sweet taste of her. He kept pumping his thumbs into her, readying her for what was to come.

He drank from her and licked along her pussy, keeping away from her plump, stiff clit.

"Yes...oh, yes," she cooed as she tried to wiggle her hips up, to get him to the aching place she wanted him. But her stretched position gave her little room to maneuver.

He smiled at her antics. Pulling out his drenched thumbs, he continued laving his flattened tongue over her sex. When he glided the thick digits up her part until he arrived at her tempting furrowed hole, she continued to shift and arch toward him. Once he was pressing them into her, she froze.

"Garrett...what are you doing? No. No."

Angling his head back enough to ensure his voice carried past the layers of skirts that hung between them, blocking his view from her face, he growled, "You are mine. My bunny to please you as I see fit."

"But...ahhh," she cried out, not completing her thought just as he latched onto her clit. He kept a steady push of his thumbs, her own cream gliding him inside her rear entrance, widening the snug hole beyond the first tight ring just through the border of the second. One day soon, he'd take her there, bury his cock deep and make her yield even that innocence to him.

He continued to suck and lick her clit. Thrusting his fingers into her ass, he stretched her, making her accept the pain, even as she begged for the pleasure.

She strained at her bonds as she bucked against his mouth, greedy for the attention he doled out to her clit which only caused her to fuck her ass with his thumbs. Caroline couldn't have one without the other. The small house became filled with moans and screams as she came, her body shuddering and curling inward as her climax struck her hard.

Garrett couldn't take it anymore, he needed to be inside her; his body demanded being one with her. He vaulted up, tore away his pants in seconds, before he shoved them down his thighs, then angled the head of his cock to her weeping pussy. His dick was so hard and stiff, he had to force it down from his belly. The bulbous skin of his crown was reddish purple, angry in its appearance as he brought it right against the apex of her thighs.

Even at the first touch, he could feel the quivering of her muscles as the waves of her orgasm still rolled through her. It was a naughty sight, making him wish he was an artist or a painter, that he could immortalize them together like this and it would stand beyond their time. Pressing forward, he entered her sweet haven. Tight and wet, her clenching body seized his head. He went farther, pushing deeper.

"Fuck," he groaned as her slick walls welcomed him in, accepting him, the man, the husband.

He rocked into her, half of him surrounded by the fisting heat of her sex.

"Yes. Please more."

Hearing her cries, he cupped her ass, squeezing the tender flesh and driving home.

"Ah!" she screamed, even as she creamed around him.

He pulled all the way out, seeing the evidence of her pleasure painted on his cock. Thrusting forward, he buried himself to the hilt, situating himself deep along her womb. Over and over again, he drew out and slammed forward, forcing her to take all of him. There was nothing gentle about his actions, no tempered thrust. He wanted her to feel his rage, passion, and unbridled desire for her.

"You're mine. You're mine." He let her feel the years of his want for her, how he'd come to this house in supplication for her hand, wanting her for his wife. "You're mine."

In and out. Harder and harder. His fingers dug deep into the reddened curves of her ass, turning the red white, his print on her.

His heart brought forth the weeks he'd searched for her, given up hope that she'd ever be his. "You're mine." He was growling now, his words barely discernable.

"Yes...Garrett."

Her words turned him into a mad man. Sliding his hand up to her bodice, he dragged it down until her breasts popped free. He cupped them, enjoying the warm supple skin against his palms as he squeezed her, stretched her large, sensitive nipples with his fingers.

"Ohh, bunny," he groaned, feeling her hot, wet pussy tighten around him even more. With every tug of her nipples, she clenched around him, milking his cock.

"Ah. Ah. Yes...please, Garrett. Pleaasse..." She wailed her need of him.

Answering her call, he used the leverage of his grip on her breasts to slam her back against him. The heated flesh of her ass a cushion to his thrusts, he took them both over the edge.

Her pussy was squeezing and flexing around him as she came, her body wild, her screams loud.

The groan that came from his lips was harsh, animalistic, and feral. An animal marking his mate. A man claiming his wife.

As the bottom dropped out from under them and the world ceased to exist for a moment, it was just theirs alone. Nothing but their heartbeats and ragged breaths filled space and time.

When he felt reality encroaching upon them again, he gingerly slipped his semi-erect cock from her. He inhaled then exhaled slowly, steadying himself as he drew up his pants and fastened them just enough to cover himself.

Still in position, he wife's body hung limp before him, trembling. He pulled down her skirts, before he scooped her up in his arms. When he moved closer to the hearth, he whispered, "Unhook your hands, bunny."

It took her two tries, but she finally was able to lift her bound wrists up over the large hook. When they dropped like lead in her lap, he felt like an ass. If he hadn't been such a horny bastard, he would have released her hands before fucking her. However, he knew when it came to his desire for his wife, he was never in his right mind.

Moving to the rocking chair on the side of the hearth, he sat with her slight form in his arms. She hissed as her sore backside contacted his hard thighs, but still, she curled against him with her eyes closed. He would have been concerned that he had pushed her too far if not for the satiated glow on her face and the small smile on her odd, plump lips. Her mouth was the same dusky rose as her nipples that still hung over her bodice. If he were a gentleman instead of a man who lusted after his fair wife, he'd have readjusted her dress to cover her, but he enjoyed the sight of her sensual surrender all too much.

"Garrett..." Her voice was low, barely audible.

"Shh, bunny. Rest." Keeping one arm around her shoulders, he used the other to untie her wrists. He caressed the skin, happy to see that there was some redness but no permanent marks.

Opening her eyes, she stared up at him. "I'm sorry."

He stared down into her swollen, red-rimmed eyes, evidence of her crying during the spanking. Reaching up, he caressed the side of her face. "I know. Sleep, lovely bunny."

Her eyes closed again, and her body settled into his as she drifted off to sleep.

Garrett sat there staring out at the barren land beyond the window as he held her in his arms and rocked her in the house Samuel Douglas had built.

"I'll take care of her," he vowed to the man. Caroline had been all that her pa had left, but she was Garrett's everything.

***

SHE PUSHED the marinated and covered brisket to the back part of the counter. It would need to sit for some time to allow the seasoning to set into the thick piece of meat. She could have the apple pie she was planning to bake for dessert in the oven be the time Garrett came in at the end of the day. Her husband told her that morning, he wouldn't be home for the noon meal because they would be repairing fencing. With Mrs. Copernic having the day off to help with the decorations for Founders' Day in a month, Caroline had some much-needed time to herself in the house.

"Now that's done. Time to start on the apples."

"Do you usually talk to yourself while you're cooking?"

"Ah!" she screamed. Turning fast, she saw her smiling

husband lounging against the wall of the archway. "What are you doing here?"

Lifting his right hand, he said, "Splinters. Showin' Timmy how to trim the wood to get the posts in right. He got at least one of them wrong. It's my spankin' hand." He winked at her.

It had been almost three weeks since that hand had reddened her bottom. Even now, she still recalled the pain of it all, how she had been sore and very uncomfortable on the wagon ride home. She'd felt every bump and sway through her hot tender flesh, and no matter which way she leaned, that area screamed. Did the man have to be so thorough in his spanking?

The shock of it had been that she'd found pleasure in the discipline method at all. She climaxed shamelessly more than once. Jade had tried to explain to her that pleasure could be found in the right amount of pain. Now she understood the woman's words clearly. Something else was clear to her as well, what Jade had been hinting at when she'd said Caroline was lucky. Garrett's skill had been what the Asian woman was referring to. Strangely enough, Caroline didn't find herself jealous over Garrett's time with the women of the Harlot. They provided a service, but Jillian Pettigrew could have his heart. Her own heart sank with the thought.

"Well, let's get that splinter taken care of and you back out to your work." She shook away the thoughts in her head as she exhaled and relaxed. She took a step. "I'll get the tweezers—"

She felt a shifting, and too late, she clenched and snapped her thighs together.

Thunk. Thunk. The hard sound was followed by a distinct rolling of something along the floor.

Garrett frowned as his gaze traveled from her face to the floor to locate the objects that had made the sound.

She closed her eyes and bit into her bottom lip, knowing what he would see.

"Caroline?"

Shamefaced, she wondered if she just turned around and started on peeling the apples if she could just pretend that nothing was out of order and Garrett would leave and go to work.

"Bunny." His commanding tone let her know he wasn't going anywhere without answers.

Opening her eyes, she saw her husband kneeling with one knee on the ground and two shiny, peach pit sized glass balls in his hand, the same one with the splinter.

"Um...I can explain." She swallowed, trying to moisten her parched throat.

Assuming his full height, he held her gaze. "I doubt there are a group of giant's children under your skirts playing with this size marbles. Since I can smell and see your cream coating them, it better be one hell of an explanation. Let's start with why they were between your legs."

"They're a type of weights."

He waited.

"Gracious..." She would have thought as worldly as her husband was, he would have known about them and she wouldn't have had to explain. "Women...some women...put them inside their...their..." She stopped and made a circular gesture around her private area, hoping he would fill in the word.

Instead, he just rolled the marbles around in his palm and stared at her with his intense cobalt eyes.

She saw the streaks of her juices leaving their mark there. Her entire face was now inflamed. "Pussy, Garrett. They put them in their pussy."

His crooked smile and the teasing light in his eyes was

proof he wasn't planning to let this go. He captured the balls between his fingers and lifted them toward his nose and inhaled loudly, taking in her scent.

Squeezing her thighs, she felt more wetness there, brought on not only by the balls that had aroused her, shockingly, from all the shifting around they had done inside of her every time she moved around the kitchen, but watching her husband enjoy her scent. She held out her hand. "If you give them back, I'll go put them away while I get the pinchers for your hand. I know it must pain you."

She attempted to remind him of the reason he'd come to the house.

"I'll live." He lowered his hand and looked at the glass objects again. "What would be the purpose of the *balls?*"

His inflection on the word made her think of her husband's balls, the heavy sac that hung at the base of his shaft and how he'd taught her to caress and cup them, firm but gentle. Her wayward thoughts were helping decrease the wetness between her thighs.

She glanced at the pitcher of water on the table and longed for a drink to cool her body and moisten her mouth. Deciding it was better to get the telling of the balls out of the way, she took on an educational tone as the midwife and Kitty had done to her often. "A woman has to learn to keep them inside her...sex, by clenching her walls. It strengthens them and teaches a woman control of that part of her body, to offer maximum pleasure to a man's...shaft during sex."

She heard him growl as he moved closer but didn't touch her. "Is this what you do all day, lovely bunny, insert glass balls into your tight pussy while you're cooking?"

Her breathing increased as he spoke to her in low, seductive tones. "No. No, just today. I wanted to try them. We gave

Mrs. Copernic the day off and you said you'd be in the pastures all day."

Lifting the balls, he rolled one of them over her top lip then the other, in the opposite direction.

The musky sweetness of her scent filled her senses before he claimed her mouth. His kiss was hot and hungry as he licked over her top lip and drew it into his mouth. She could hear him spinning and spinning the balls as he cupped the back of her head and deepened the kiss. His tongue was inside her and she suckled it. She loved kissing her husband; his passion sparked hers and made her feel uninhibited. Her nipples were drawn achingly tight, and they yearned for his touch.

When he pulled his mouth away, they were both panting. "Up on the table, wife. I want to see how wet your pussy is from your exercise."

She gasped. "But the fencing—"

"It can fuckin' wait." He gave her a small push toward the table.

Once she was there, she stepped up onto the chair at the end and sat on the smooth, polished oak wood. She saw Garrett had followed her over and was standing a couple of feet away as he watched her. Leaning forward, she took hold of the hem of her dress and brought it up slowly as she held his gaze. When she had gone upstairs to get the balls from the box in the cabinet of the washstand, she had removed her drawers so she could watch in her new cheval mirror as she put them in. She hadn't felt a need to put them back on. Once her dress was past her thighs, she spread her stocking-clad knees and revealed what she had been hoping to hide.

"Naughty girls walk around without drawers." His words were filled with pleasure, no censure.

The heat of her blush warmed her cheeks.

"Wider, bunny. I want to see it all." He grabbed the top of the ladderback chair and shoved it away so that her feet were now dangling above the floor.

Her body was shaking as she pressed her limbs out wide toward the corners of the narrow table end. Air kissed her wet thighs and pussy, making her blush heat her face even more. She knew what Garrett could see now, just how much the shifting spheres inside of her had aroused her. Part of her mind admitted that she needed this moment, hadn't conceived it would happen, that Garrett would find out what she had been doing with her time alone in the house, but she was so excited, she needed him to see her, touch her.

"Garrett." His name broke from her lips on a whimper.

"Oh, bunny, you are a lovely sight. Unbutton your top; I want to see those tight nipples."

She made fast work of the buttons, not feeling coy but achy all over. When her breasts were out, she felt liberated and sexy. Unable to keep still, she lifted her hand to her chest and fondled her taut tips the way he usually did. She moaned as a spark shot from her nipples to her core.

He watched her hands as he continued to spin the balls.

"Ah, my naughty bunny." His dark blue gaze rose to her eyes. "Does your touch please you more than mine?"

"No...never." She responded fast as she started to lower her hands, thinking he didn't like it.

"Don't stop. Pinch your nipples and lie back." He moved closer and reached by her.

She wasn't sure what he was doing until she saw the pitcher in his hand. He placed it out of the way on the seat of one of the chairs. Taking the puckered points between her forefingers and thumbs, she squeezed.

"Tighter," he commanded.

Compressing more, she whimpered at the pain her hold

caused in her nipples but couldn't deny that her core ached from the pressure.

Garrett leaned over her and swiped the tip of his tongue over each sensitive center. "Don't let go until I tell you to, wife."

"Yes."

He moved between her legs then placed his hands on her thighs and pushed her out farther. She felt the pulling at her center and the discomfort in her hips.

"So much cream, you're dripping with your own desire." He moved his fingers along the inside of her thighs, gliding through her wetness until he reached her bare, wet sex. When he circled her clit, she cried out, close to coming just from the brief touch, but then he stopped.

"No. Please, Garrett..." She arched her hips up, begging for him to keep up his fondling, take her to completion.

"Not yet, darlin'. I want you to show me how my lovely bunny has been studying to please me."

She stared up at him, her brow tight, wondering what he was getting at.

Smack.

"Ah!" She yelped at the sting of his slap against the wetness at the inside of her thigh.

"Don't let those nipples go." He arched an eyebrow and stared at her.

Unaware that she had relaxed her hold, she tightened her fingers again, not wanting to find herself at the end of another spanking again so soon. Evidently, the splinter wasn't hurting him bad enough that he couldn't still swat her. She licked her lips. "How do you want me to show you?"

Holding her gaze, he popped the balls into his mouth then lowered himself between her spread legs.

"Garrett?"

He didn't answer her. Instead, she felt the touch of his hands on her inner thighs, keeping them open. Next, she felt the distinct feeling of something rolling up her slit and around her clit. It wasn't his cunning tongue, but something warm and hard. She realized it was one of the balls he was swirling around her sex. When she felt him moving and spinning it right below the hood of her clit, she couldn't stop herself from writhing. It felt too good, hot from his mouth and her sex.

The tension in her core built and she felt the shudders deep in her body as everything inside of her tightened and she was coming. She was mindless, bucking against what she surmised was her husband's tongue and both the balls, all swirling around her and wringing her strong release from her. Even as she lay there dazed and glowing from within, from pleasure, she became aware of the tell-tale heaviness and shifting inside her. Garrett had managed to replace the balls.

"Oh..." The weighted sensation in her quivering sex kept her on edge.

"Nice, wife. I see you didn't let go of those tits." He reached up and flicked his thumb over one, admiring it. "Look at how dark and swollen they are now."

They throbbed between her fingers but had gone a little numb now, and she was glad.

He lowered his hand to the fastenings of his pants until his raging hard cock was revealed. Moving a hand beneath the bunched fabric of her skirts, he set it against her lower abdomen above her sex.

When he started pushing his thick length inside her, stretching her walls much more than the glass had done, she cried out, "Wait, Garrett...the balls."

"Yes." He continued sliding deeper.

"Ah..." She could feel the pressure and discomfort as his cock pushed the balls farther up her channel. Having her husband's large shaft inside her was already a great feat, but with the balls, it would be impossible. They wouldn't fit. "It's too much. I can't take it."

"Trust me. Just a little more, bunny." He went farther then stopped.

Peering down her body, she could see that he was barely halfway in.

"Now, show me," he commanded.

She realized this was what she wanted, needed. The short period of time she'd had them inside her, she'd thought about her husband, imagining it was him instead of the balls. She wanted his cock to feel her walls tightening around him. Biting into her bottom lip, she met his piercing gaze as she concentrated, focusing all her attention on clenching and loosening her sex muscles around him.

Flex and release. Flex and release. Flex and release.

Garrett's groan filled the room, and she knew he could not only feel the movement of her pussy around him, but the spinning of the balls circling his sensitive crown. She was manipulating both the balls and him.

"Fuck me," he growled.

NINETEEN

She wasn't sure if his words were a command or a statement, but either way, she gave him pleasure and took her own.

His thumb began to fondle her clit, keeping rhythm with her actions. He began pulling out and driving back in, bumping the balls but still not burying himself all the way in. The dual movement of his cock thrusting into her and the heavy glass brushing the bundle of nerves in her walls below her clit made her wild. Her body thrashed and arched on the tabletop as she was coming apart again.

"Garrett!" she screamed as her climax ripped through her, blazing a trail of fire along her spine.

He pulled out and yanked her body up in a sitting position, away from the table. With her thighs still spread, she couldn't keep the weights inside as gravity and her copious wetness drew them out.

The double thunking and rolling was loud, but she couldn't force herself to wonder if they had been damaged because her husband was shoving his cock back inside her. This time, when her back was pressed against the wood, her ass was hanging off the edge, and she felt all his thick, long length, forcing her tight, sensitive walls to take him. As he pushed her hands away from her breasts, blood flowed into each tip and she yelled as the white-hot pain shot through her.

Then Garrett's mouth was there as he hovered above her, sucking them, again manipulating the pain in her body to pleasure. The table scraped against the floor, while the edge dug into her backside as he rode her hard, pounding into her, proof that her sensual demonstration had made him wild for her. She loved it.

Just like with the massage, she was enjoying discovering how she could control her husband's body, just as he commanded hers, bringing them both to satisfaction. When he slammed into her one last time, so deep, it stole her breath, she toppled into another orgasm as he filled her with the hot, thick cream of his release.

She wasn't sure how long they lay there, their bodies shuddering as they gulped down air to fill their lungs. Garrett rested on her, his face buried in the side of her neck as his hands still cupped her breasts. When he squeezed them gently, she felt the scrape of the coarse wood along the bottom curve of her left breast.

"Your splinter." She lifted his right hand and stared at the shard of wood. It was pretty big, and she wondered how he'd been able to ignore it. "Gracious, you really are hurt."

He chuckled as he raised his head. Looking down at her, he shrugged. "I've had worse."

She accepted his swift kiss as he shifted away from her. She sucked in the wince as he pulled out of her sore center.

"You get cleaned up, and I'll find the first aid kit." He held out his left hand to help her down from the table.

Shaking out her skirts, she glanced around the floor.

"No worries, darlin'. I'll find your toys and get them put away." He swatted her backside. "Now get."

Nodding, feeling warm and tingly all over, she followed her husband's directive. This afternoon had not turned out at all as she had thought when she'd decided to try out the balls, but she found that she was pleased and incredibly so.

"THEY ARE ADORABLE, Isabel. You and Cary must be overjoyed." She stared down into the twin faces of the babies, now five weeks old, curled next to each other in the cradle. She wanted to ask to hold them, but it was often said to let sleeping babies lie.

"We are. Except at about two in the morning, when they are wailing for a feeding." Isabel set down the tray of cookies and tea on the table before the couch. "I swear, Caroline, one wakes up to eat and the other does it an hour later."

From her seat on the couch, she glanced over at the loveseat where her friend sat across from her. "I thought with them being twins, they would be on a similar schedule."

Isabel guffawed. "Evidently, no one told them that. Maybe because they are not the same gender."

She saw her friend shrug, before she turned back to the little bundles. One had a blue cap and the other, a pink knit cap. Caroline was right; they may have shared a womb but were very different. The boy was much bigger than his smaller sister. "I assume he eats more than she does."

This time, Isabel actually laughed. "The opposite. Cheyanne feeds from both breasts each time while Junior only nurses from one."

"I guess it works out that they aren't in sync. You may have a fight on your hands." Caroline smiled as she accepted the cup of tea. "I could have made us the tea. Shouldn't you be resting?"

"You know I've never been one to be idle." Isabel took a sip of her tea. "After more than a month, I've had enough lying around and staying in the house."

"Are you missing not being at the schoolhouse anymore?" Isabel asked, trying one of the lemon cookies.

"Gracious, no. Between all four children and the historian responsibilities, I have more than enough to keep my hands full. Not to mention an assiduous husband." Isabel's cheeks pinked.

"Aren't you still recovering?" Caroline whispered. She wasn't sure why, since the two older children they were raising after Cary's brother died over a year ago, and Sunny, Cary's mother, had gone back to her smaller house on the property, saying she was giving the friends time to visit.

"Trust me, Caroline. You discover various other ways to attend to your husband's needs until the weeks of your... confinement have passed." Isabel was blushing.

And Caroline's face heated as well. Before she was married or had lived at the Harlot, she would have had no clue what her friend was hinting at, but she was learning and practicing more and more bedroom techniques.

Caroline sipped her tea, hoping to cover the deepening of her blush.

"Before time gets away from us, I wanted to see if you minded sharing with me about your parents' journey to Grover Town. I wanted to add the history of the Douglas family to the recordings."

Lowering her cup back to the saucer, Caroline stared at the orange pekoe liquid. "It's not a cheerful story. There's no happy ending. I doubt anyone would want to hear it. Now, or years later."

"That is what can be inspiring to others. Yes, stories that end well are great, but to many who wonder if they are the only ones not to succeed at something, it will be a comfort to read." Isabel raised her cup and took another sip as silence filled the room.

Pondering the words of her childhood friend, Caroline thought about her life, if having read about someone else's poor and hopeless existence would have meant something to her on those lonely days. She surmised that it would have. She had felt as if no one in their town could understand her isolation.

"I wouldn't even know where to begin." Caroline wrapped her hand around the dish and allowed the warmth of it to fill her, settle her.

Isabel tipped her head to the side as she gazed off in the distance then smiled as she looked back at her. "When we were younger, I recall you telling me how your parents had a love match."

She couldn't help but smile wistfully at the memory of her parents. "Oh, yes. He loved her. Papa would say that he fell for Mama from the first moment he saw her. Mama stole his heart and he never wanted it back."

A loue ye. Caroline's heart felt heavy in her own chest. It was the kind of love she had always hoped for, especially on those depressing days on the farm. She would pray for a man to come and sweep her off her feet and express his love for her. The thought of her not having that all-consuming love from Garrett caused water to fill her eyes.

"Ahh, Ro," Isabel sighed, using her childhood nickname. "Tell me about them." Isabel spoke softly as she offered her a delicate linen handkerchief across the table.

Receiving it with a thank you, Caroline figured her friend believed the tears had to do with sadness over her parents. There was a shadow there for them, but most of her emotions were for herself. Deciding it was easier to focus on her parents, she took a fortifying drink of her tea then began.

"Well, Bel," Caroline forced out a smile as she responded with her friend's nickname. "Papa's parents booked passage from Scotland to New York for a better life, in hopes of carrying on the crofting tradition they'd had for generations before the Highlands were ravaged by war and famine."

"Crofting?" Isabel frowned as she set down her cup then reached for a journal at the end of the coffee table.

"A *crofter*," Caroline attempted to imitate her papa's Scottish brogue, but it didn't come across so well. She and Isabel both laughed. "It's basically a type of farmer. But *seanair* Douglas never made it as a farmer; he worked long years in turpentine distilleries. After Papa watched that work kill his father, he worked in a tap bar to save enough money to have that dream."

"Did your mother work there also?"

The girl baby made a small sound and began to wiggle in her sleep. On instinct, Caroline, who was sitting closest, reached over and stroked the infant's back until she calmed.

"Oh, no," she continued, "Abigail Benoit was the daughter of a successful French seamstress, when she simply walked by the bar window one day and captured Papa's gaze and heart, changing both of their lives forever."

Two hours later, Isabel closed her journal, ink now staining her fingertips. "Well, that is the start of one fascinating life story, Caroline."

"A start." Caroline shook her head. She hadn't meant to talk so long, but her friend seemed to know the right questions to ask to keep her going. She recalled things and stories about her parents' journey that she hadn't thought of in years. In the two hours of discussion, Caroline hadn't even made it to the part when they arrived in Grover Town yet.

"I've only spoken with a couple other families so far, before my confinement. Both took more than a handful of sessions to get their stories down."

"I never would have thought—"

"Trust me, neither did I, when I agreed to take the job. It was Cary who saw it in me. I have enjoyed every minute of it."

At that moment, baby girl began to wail.

"Oh, gracious me." Caroline placed a hand on her chest, startled at the instant high-pitched sound. "She has quite the lungs. How her brother continues to sleep through it at all, is a miracle."

Isabel chuckled. "True, because no one else in the house can. Well, except our two oldest. After the first few days they don't even stir. Do you mind getting Cheyanne while I wash the ink from my hands?"

"Not at all." Eager to hold the little one, Caroline got up and went to her while the new mother carried the tray of dirty dishes into the kitchen.

Caroline lifted the infant then pulled her in close to her body. Her heart melted as the girl curled right against her neck even as she continued to let out piercing screams. Cupping one hand under the baby's bottom, Caroline patted her back with her free hand as she walked around with Cheyanne and talked to her. It had been what she had done with her younger brother when he was fussing. Even though she was only a handful of years older than he, she followed instructions of her mama on what to do and how to hold him. It filled her heart with joy to have the tiny bundle in her arms. She and Garrett had spoken of children. They both wanted them, and she wondered if, even now, she was carrying. Her cycle was due in a matter of days, and part of her hoped that perhaps it wouldn't come.

Sunny and the two older children came in the house for a

late afternoon snack, breezing by with a smile and quick hello, just as Isabel came back in from the kitchen.

Caroline handed over the baby to Isabel, who was already rooting toward her mama's breast, smelling the milk. "Well, your hands are more than full now. I'll get going."

"You can see why I don't miss the classroom." Isabel settled in the rocking chair before the empty hearth as she nursed. "Come by next week. I enjoyed the visit."

"It has been good seeing you as well. It was nice." Caroline headed to the door. She meant her words. She'd missed being around her friend for so many years and was happy to discover they had not lost their amity.

"Very much so." At the door, she noticed a crate of books that she'd missed when she arrived. "Are you getting rid of your schoolbooks?"

"Yes, I am. Those were all the duplicates I had amassed over the years. I kept what I needed for my children."

"What are your plans with these?" Stooping down, Caroline flipped through the crate and noticed there were not only readers and arithmetic books, but some science and geography for various age levels.

"I was going to see if Miss Beadle needed them. Doubtful, because the town had the fund drive a few years back and it provided plenty in supply. It is how I got so many copies for the adult course." Isabel shrugged a single shoulder.

"May I take them?" Caroline stared over at her eagerly.

"If you have need of them, please do." Isabel's brow wrinkled, giving her a perplexed look.

"I know where they would be put to good use." Caroline hoisted up the crate just as the door opened beside her.

"Whoa, there." Cary's big frame filled the door, frowning as he watched Caroline stutter step from the weight of the books. Garrett was large, but Cary was massive, most definitely the biggest man in town. The mixed-race male, of Cherokee and Scottish descent, reminded her of her papa of old. Before hard work and low sustenance whittled him down in size. "Hand that over."

"I can do it." Caroline was used to pulling her weight when she was growing up.

"It's not a matter if you can, I don't plan on lettin' you. I'm pretty sure Garrett would have somethin' to say about not lettin' a man be a man around a woman." Cary arched an eyebrow at her.

At the man's words, Caroline allowed him to take the crate. The last thing she wanted was this big man reporting something to her husband that would only give Garrett a reason to express his opinion on her actions against her backside. "Well, thank you. If you would just set it in my wagon, I'll be on my way."

Cary gave a nod, then glanced over at his wife with warmth in his gaze. "Be right back, *Ayv adanvdo.*"

Isabel repeated the Indian words to him with her eyes filled with adoration even as she shifted their baby girl to the opposite breast to continue her suckling.

In the presence of such evident love, Caroline's throat felt tight. She was happy for her friend even as she was sad for herself. Her husband demanded she accept his care of her, but she wanted Garrett's love.

Unable to get words through the tightness, she simply waved and walked out of the house.

Once she was headed through the two large trees that bordered the end of the Brown drive, Caroline decided to take the road that led past the farthest end of town to drop the books off, so she wouldn't have to make another trip later in the week. Since her last trip into town a few weeks ago, she tried to keep away from the main thoroughfare when it was later in the day. The last thing she wanted was another run in with Old Lady Bellmore or the widow. For weeks now, she had avoided going into town by sending a list of things for Ms. Copernic to pick up, things she wanted to put around the house to make it feel more like a home. Garrett had taken her into town to pick out her cheval mirror, grandfather clock, and various wallpapers she had put up around the house. He never complained when she didn't want to go into town without him.

For a moment, as she stared at the late afternoon sun, she considered that it would be best to go directly home. When the message had come a week ago from Isabel, requesting her to come for a visit, Caroline had told Garrett she would only be away a couple hours. She'd spent longer than that with her friend.

At the fork in the road, she started to take the road that led home, not wanting to raise her husband's ire. However, she recalled that she had left her oils journal at the brothel, in her old room. She and Garrett had discussed many times about her returning to make soaps again, so she would need her notes to set a better plan of action. In a few days, she would meet with Spencer about buying scraps from his slaughter, as well as sit down with Gretchen and learn about buying some of her herbs and flowers too. It only made sense to retrieve it now and drop off the books.

"Getty up!" She snapped the reins, urging the horse to a fast pace as she took the direction to the brothel.

———

CAROLINE EXITED the backdoor off the kitchen of the brothel and stared up at the purple and blue coloring of the dusk sky. Clutching her journal in hand, she realized she had stayed way too long. She made it in record time to deliver the books to Donovan and the children, at the end of the school day. Being around the children with all their excitement and them wanting to tell her all the new things they were learning, she could not resist sitting and allowing them time to share. By the time she had made her way from the small house into the big one, she got caught up with getting Mrs. Morrison's ham and chive biscuit recipe to make for Garrett, while she waited on Miss Kitty to retrieve her journal. The main house was full of excitement as everyone prepared for the night's activities. There was already a new girl from Kentucky who had taken her place, Opal.

Now, that she was taking the path to the side of the house where she'd parked her wagon to keep it out of sight. Caroline was only partially happy she'd taken the detour. Yes, coming to the brothel had been a success in some ways, but it hadn't allowed her to avoid the two women she had tried to steer clear of. Caroline had forgotten that the back road that led to the brothel also went past Widow Lawrence's big house, right at the edge of town, a mile away from the brothel. When she'd ridden past, she'd seen the widow standing at her back porch with a red-headed man Caroline didn't recognize, but who was close in a familiar way to the pretty, voluptuous lady. His hands were pawing at her waist and breasts as he leaned in to kiss her.

Caroline hadn't meant to glance that way, but when the widow heard Caroline's wagon going by, she shoved the man back a few steps and shot Caroline a sour look. Quickly, Caroline had turned her head away and hurried her horse faster along. Who the widow chose to secretly entertain was none of Caroline's business, and the last thing she needed was the woman having a reason to antagonize her even more.

Riotous music kicked up and began to stream out from the

windows of the brothel, letting early clients who were most likely already forming an eager line out front, know that the house would soon be open for business. Glancing toward the evening sky again, Caroline was thankful that the summer months would give her more time to make it home before dark.

"Couldn't stay away, could you?" came a taunting voice.

Caroline gasped, shocked at the man now blocking her path to her wagon. Stepping back, she stared up into the face of the polished man, Daryl Bellmore.

"Wh-what?" she stuttered as she worked to strengthen her resolve. Lifting her chin, she boldly met his gaze. "What I do is no longer your concern. Excuse me."

When she made to go around him, he stepped to the side with her and continued to stand in her way. "Of course not, since your *husband*," he spat out the word, "paid off your debt."

"There are plenty of ladies inside to offer you attention. Please move." She tried to go the other way.

Bellmore took hold of her arm, squeezing it.

"Let go of me." She kept her voice low, not wanting to attract any others to peer around the corner. All she needed was for someone to see her here and it would validate the claims of Bellmore's mother and Widow Lawrence.

"Tell me, Pearrrl," he dragged out her old moniker. "What does all that money Garrett paid get him in bed? Does all that training you got at the Harlot let him fuck you whenever and wherever he pleases?"

She choked on her own breath at his insulting words.

"You must have a death wish."

Still with a grip on her arm, Bellmore slung her around with him as they now faced a pissed off Garrett.

She gasped at the sight of her husband, who strutted from King's side, appearing as an avenging angel.

"Rand."

"Garrett, it isn't what it looks like," she whispered, afraid he would see the situation wrong. Here she was, standing in the evening light with another man, on the side of the brothel.

Her husband's gaze was locked on the other man, and he didn't even spare her a glance. "Get your fuckin' hands off my wife, Bellmore."

"Rand." Daryl chuckled but released his grip on her arm. "You know how these things go."

"Caroline, get in the wagon," Garrett growled, standing a few feet away from them, but he still didn't shift his eyes to her, eyes she couldn't see in the dim light under his dark hat.

A shiver ran along her spine and raised goosebumps on her arms, and even though the evening air was warm, she couldn't feel it. Without argument, she followed her husband's direction and walked away from the two men.

"I told you to keep away from her," Garrett's voice rumbled, like thunder before a lightning strike.

At the wagon, she turned and glanced over her shoulder. She saw Garrett take a step toward Daryl, as the other man retreated.

"She came to me. You must not be pleasing her right."

She gasped, but it was only her own disobedience that kept her from rushing over and denying the crooked, fancy businessman's claims.

"It's your ass, Bellmore."

Holding his hands out, Daryl offered an innocuous grin. "Garrett, I warned you, a whore is a whore is a whore. I'd even pay you a Morgan Silver Dollar to see her pretty pink pussy—"

Garrett's growl roared into the night as his fist seemed to explode out of his shoulder milliseconds before it made contact with Daryl's face.

Daryl toppled back onto the ground and Garrett followed, still swinging.

"Garrett!" she screamed. Launching from the wagon, she started across the space, her shoes pounding on the hard dirt.

"Caroline, if you come any closer, your ass is going to be redder then it's already set for." Garrett straddled Daryl's chest as he barked his threat to her.

She skidded in the dirt at his words as she halted her forward movement and back peddled. She had assumed he was too focused on his assault and hadn't thought he was aware of her, but clearly, she had been wrong.

The night was peppered with whines and groans and the sound of flesh striking flesh, as Garrett pounded into the other man's face. It was the loud, boisterous music, the catcalls of men and teasing laughter of women that kept others from being alerted to the ruckus happening on the other side of the brothel wall.

By the time she was settled in the box seat again and staring over at them, she saw Garrett was on his feet.

"The next time you come near my wife, there'll be a pine box and cross with your name on it."

Wisely, Daryl kept his tongue as he curled to his side, spitting blood into the dirt. Woody came around the house at that moment, looked from Daryl to Garrett and quickly surmised the situation. He offered a brisk nod to Garrett then walked to the man on the ground. Woody didn't help the other man up, but just stood over him as if keeping him from doing anything else stupid.

Turning from them, Garrett stalked toward the wagon. He made a clicking sound that brought King toward him. Once he had his horse tied to the back of the wagon, Garrett made his way around the opposite side of where she was. The wagon rocked as he vaulted up into the seat beside her.

He took up the leads and leaned forward with his elbows on his knees as he snapped them, urging the horse to go. She saw the tension in his shoulders as they sat high below his ears, as he hunched forward. They had a long ride home, and she wanted to explain why she'd been at the brothel. She doubted it would keep her from receiving the spanking he'd hinted at, but she hoped giving him her side of the situation might reduce the number of swats of his hand. "Garrett, I—"

"Not a word, bunny."

Silenced, but comforted by his use of the endearment, she held her journal in her lap and stared straight ahead.

TWENTY

"Go upstairs and wait for me. Remove everything." He dropped his hands from his wife's waist then stepped away after he assisted her from the wagon.

Garrett had needed the quiet on the ride home to release the anger he'd felt at seeing Bellmore's hands on his wife and the taunting, crude things the man had said about her. Her was disappointed in Caroline for not coming right home after her visit with Isabel. When she hadn't arrived home after being gone for over three hours, he'd ridden over to the Brown farm expecting to see her still there. He'd been more than a little embarrassed to have to ask Cary if he knew where his wife had gone after leaving their home, only to find out she'd taken a crate of old children's books with her.

Since he hadn't passed Caroline on the way to the Brown's, he figured there was only one other direction home. She'd often spoken of the children who learned and lived at the brothel, so it didn't take him to be a genius to discover where she had taken the items. Figuring she'd gone to Kitty's hadn't worried him; however, it was the fact that she repeatedly had no care or concern for her own safety. If she would have come home first, he would have ridden out with her. In some ways, she was lucky that it was fucking Bellmore who had stopped her outside of the whorehouse at this time. Even in early evening, there were enough Grover Town outsiders and vagrants milling around the Harlot, eager for the first woman they could get their hands on. Last time, it was her own emotions that led her away. This time, it was her own good intentions. What would it be next time?

Shaking his head, as watched her climb the steps to the house before he led the horses and wagon toward the stables. He hoped this ass reddening would set, as a reminder in the future. He didn't only care for Caroline, but his wife had his heart in her hands. It tore him apart and set rage in his blood to see any man touch her. Bellmore was lucky he got away with his life this time, and there wasn't law or a man in Grover Town who would fault him for killing a man for that reason. Hell, even Pastor Morgan would offer a prayer for Bellmore's soul but wouldn't stop Garrett.

Once King and the other horse were fed, brushed, and settled for the night, Garrett made his way across the distance back to the house.

When he entered their spotless bedroom, the sky-blue mutton chop sleeve blouse, the indigo skirt, and the new kid boots his wife had worn that day were all put away, as Caroline stood naked beside the bed.

She stared at him.

He let his gaze slowly travel her lovely form. She was a sight with her big, doe brown eyes, full uneven mouth, small breasts with their large, dark pink nipples, curvy hips, almost too wide for her frame, giving her an A-shape. When his eyes rested on the smooth, puffy lips of her pussy, he had to stifle a groan. His dick had been on the rise since he started up the stairs, knowing what he would find waiting on him—a captivatingly beautiful sight.

"Take down your hair." He removed his leather vest as he crossed the room to his own wardrobe.

Out of the corner of his eyes, he saw her lift her hands without a single hesitation as she began taking out the pins that held the chignon at the crown of her head. He relieved himself of his shirt, toed out of his boots, then snatched off his socks and discarded them with his shirt in the hamper. He didn't trust himself to carry out her discipline if he removed his pants, so he kept them on.

Flexing his shoulders, he was glad he no longer felt the tension that had been there earlier, another sign he was in his right mind to spank his wife. He'd never strike her in anger. He watched her watching him, as he strutted to the washstand. Squatting, he turned to the cabinet and opened the small door. Reaching inside, he removed her special box.

"Um...Garrett. Husband." Her feet padded against the floor as she began to approach him.

Tilting his head in her direction, he arched a brow at her.

She froze, long brown hair in waves around her shoulders, longer now.

Standing with the box, he carried it across the room to the nightstand. "When I put your glass weights back in here, I was amazed at the items I found inside. The Jewels gave you quite the gifts."

Her throat moved as she swallowed, shifting on the balls of her feet, nervous.

"There are more than a few things I'll find handy tonight." Lifting the lid of the decorative painted white box, he peered inside. He didn't take anything out but, instead, met his wife's gaze.

Her coffee brown eyes were glassy as tears began to fill them.

"Are you afraid of me?" His breath burned his lungs as he stood there waiting for her answer. Maybe the fury he had released on Bellmore had scared her, made her think he would hurt her.

She shook her head. "No."

A tear spilled over the rim of one of her lids. He reached out and caught the racing droplet at her cheek. "Then why the tears already?"

"I'm sorry." She sniffed. "I know I disappointed you. I went to the brothel and caused Daryl—"

Taking hold of her shoulders, he dragged her to him. "No," he growled, needing her to understand. "You are not responsible for that jackass' actions. He wanted you, and he's bitter, but hear me when I say it gives him no right to touch you. Even if you weren't my wife."

"All right." She blinked and another tear rolled from the other eye.

The feel of her long, delicate fingers clutching his sides, her soft breasts, and the sharp points of her nipples against his chest, accompanied by the sweet jasmine scent of her was making his cock throb. He set her away, before he was tempted to toss her on the bed and take her instead of giving her the discipline she required.

"Why are you being spanked tonight, bunny?"

She licked her lips as she took a tentative step back.

He tipped his head and warned her not to attempt to run. The chase would probably have his cock splitting his britches, but her ass would pay for it with more swats, once he caught her.

Smart, she stayed put. Her lips trembled, but she kept silent.

"For every time I have to repeat the question, that is five more swats."

"Because I stayed gone longer than I'd told you. I went somewhere else without you knowing where I was going. I stayed out until it was almost dark and put myself in danger." The words came tumbling out.

Impressed she'd nailed each infraction, he reached over into the box and removed the paddle. "How many swats do you think your actions warrant?"

Seeing the object in his hand, she whimpered, "One."

He chuckled as he rubbed his hand over the leather covering the wood. "No. It will cover more area so there would be less, but more like thirty."

She shook her head.

He nodded his. Sitting on the side of the bed, he patted his thighs. "Come, bunny, over my lap." When she still stood there wringing her hands, he began, "All right, thirty-five then."

Diving across his lap, she pleaded, "Thirty, thirty...please."

Grinding his teeth to keep from laughing at her antics, he shifted his knees wide, situating her body so that her hips rested on one thigh and upper body over the other. The position and his size also kept her feet and hands from the ground; she'd be completely at his mercy.

He spun the paddle in his right hand as he caressed and patted the soft, firm curves of her backside with his left. "Thirty-five is the number, wife."

She whimpered and hung her head, her chestnut locks tumbling forward and sweeping the wood floor.

"I can't have you wanderin' around creation and puttin' yourself in harm's way because you didn't think. This spankin's got to stick, darlin'." He instructed her to spread her thighs to make it more difficult for her to clench and tighten her ass cheeks.

When he heard her sniffling again, he figured since he had yet to strike her once, it was her own shame that had her crying. He squeezed one ass cheek then the other, going back and forth a few times as he prepared her. "Count 'em out."

Whack. Whack.

He admired the view of her roundness as it flattened then bounced back.

"One! Ow...two!"

Whack. Whack!

"Three. Four."

Unlike with his hand, the weight of the wood and the sting of the leather already had the hue of her skin changing from blush to bright pink. The surface of the paddle was a little longer and wider than his hand, so it impacted both her sweet cheeks at the same time. It would do nicely. He'd leave his hand for sensual spanking and the paddle for when his wife needed reminding of his care.

Whack. Whack. Whack. Whack!

"Oh...Ooow. Five. Six. Seven. Eight."

Whack. Whack.

Her ass was rose red now, and he wanted to lean over and kiss it, feel the warmth on his lips.

"Nine...ten." She was crying in earnest now, as she kicked her legs out and flexed her ass, only to whimper from the pain of the movement.

"Be still, wife." He set the paddle down on the bed beside him. He wasn't near finished, but he needed to prepare her for what would come next after her spanking. Moving his right hand to her sensitive skin, he brushed along it lightly, allowed his fingers to tap her hot flesh. Up and down he went, until he reached the part of her thighs. The backs, just like her inner thighs were still a pale color, as he had yet to apply any swats to her sit spot. His gaze met the dew covering her wetness way before his fingers glided over it.

"Ah." Sniff. Wiggle. "Is it over now?"

"No, bunny. Not nearly."

She shifted so her thighs spread wider, arching into his caress along her slit. "Please, husband. I'm...sorry."

He knew she was trying to tempt him in another direction, instead of continuing with the discipline. Dipping a finger into the well of her pussy and feeling the tight heat surrounding him, made his cock throb beneath her belly. "Oh, no, darlin', we are goin to finish what it is we have started."

"Then why?" she moaned, flexing around his stroking digit again.

"Because before this night is done, your husband will have you, bunny. You'll feel my claim everywhere." He slipped out of her and dragged his cream covered finger up to the rosebud, then swirled around and around, coating the virgin entrance. Pressing in, he felt her bear down, squeezing her nether walls in an attempt to keep him out. However, her wetness allowed him to slip right past his second knuckle and her first and second ring. His middle finger went farther than his thumbs had, and his cock would go even deeper.

Her hands gripped his calf as he pumped in and out of her, feeling her submit to the wicked touch, even as she whimpered. As her body adjusted to the insertion and began to relax, he slipped out.

Whack. Whack. He struck the lower area of her ass, tinting her sit spot.

"Ouch. Ouch. Eleven...twelve."

He knew starting over again after a pause caused her ass to become more sensitive and to throb as it settled from the lack of attention. Even that heightened pain was part of her punishment.

Whack. Whack. Whack.

The numbers tumbled out of his wife on a cry.

He set the paddle down on the bed beside him again. This time, he fucked her pussy with two fingers, gathering more of her juices, only to shift those two to the creamed rosette and press in.

"No. Not again. Ohh... It burns." She tightened her hands on his leg and tried to use her grip as leverage to pull herself forward, away from his aggressive touch.

Smack. His left hand came down hard on her sore backside.

"Stop your antics, wife." He resituated her back into position even as he still thrust inside her, stretching the tight rings.

She shook her head. "I don't want it there. I'm not ready."

"You will be." He knew from the plug and cream inside her box that her training, if only in discussion, had included taking a man's cock in the ass. The wooden cock in the box with the flat base was a tease, a beginner's size, practically the length and narrow width of Caroline's thumb. It would be great for him to use as a daily reminder when she was in the house most of the day and he wanted to remind her of what was to come that evening. He smiled at the thought.

Tonight, he would give her practical application for all her knowledge. The image of him taking her in every way made his dick harder. After this first time, she'd soon learn he'd make use of this hole more often. Nothing could compete with the driving deep inside her pussy, but this would be a naughty treat at times.

Once he felt her body adjust and welcome him in, as a broken moan came out of her throat, he slipped out and resumed her swats. After the next five, he reached for the jar of cream that had sat nestled beside the wood carving in the box. He spun the lid, unscrewing it, then scooped out a liberal amount on three fingers, as he would need her well-lubed. Her own cream would ease his way for a few strokes, but it wouldn't last. He wasn't trying to injure his wife.

When the cool substance kissed her small hole, now winking as she reflexively clenched, her body's attempt to reclose the opening his fondling had created.

She sighed, her limbs and upper body settling into him as he rubbed the cold cream over her manipulated entrance.

As he pushed and worked three fingers inside, she balked.

"No. Aww...it hurts. It's too much, Garrett!"

"My cock is more." He pressed a hand on her lower back, keeping her in place as he thrust in and out, twisting his fingers. His thick digits together were about the width of his cock, if not the length. But they would widen her ass just right, making her rings submit. She may not want to take his cock in her ass, but it didn't take long before her whimpers and screams became moans and squeals of pleasure.

Her desire was building from his ministrations even as her lips denied it.

The room became filled with the pungent, sharp aroma of his wife's wet musk and the woody fresh camphor notes of the slick cream, meant to soothe and prepare her anus for fucking. When he felt her first shudders, he slipped his hand away. It would not be that easy for his wife to come tonight. For this infraction, she had a long road ahead of her.

He doled out another five firm swats and more stroking up her backside. Garrett kept the same rhythm until he hit his marker.

Caroline had ceased her thrashing and shifting on his lap. The only signs she was still feeling the impact was in the bite of her nails digging into his calf through his pant leg as she continued to cry, her tears making puddles on the floor and saturating the ends of her hair by his foot.

"That's it, lovely bunny. That part is all over with now." He set the paddle next to the box and jar on the nightstand as he caressed her hot, beet red ass and upper thighs and praised her with his words.

Her cries became whimpers and sniffles under his touch and voice.

Between her thighs, she was sopping wet, her labia swollen and spread, revealing the distended plump kernel at the top of her sex. Using one of his thumbs, he stroked and circled the stiff nubbin.

"Ohhh...Garrett. Please." She arched up and rotated her hips, needy and begging for satisfaction.

The desire to bury his face between her legs and lick all that juicy essence and suck her clit until she came all over his tongue had him locking his jaw, forcing himself to resist the temptation. Following a few more flicks of her clit, he pulled his hand away.

"Please...pleaaase."

"Soon." He palmed one ass cheek and squeezed.

She hissed.

"On your knees, love," he commanded. He gave her an encouraging push off his lap until she was kneeling on the floor.

Caroline groaned and twitched as her backside contacted her heels. Her face was red and blotchy and drenched from her tears as she stared up at him with puffy eyes. Her dark brown irises were luminous, docile in her submission. She was an exquisite vision.

Cupping her cheek, he met her gaze. "This night ain't over yet, darlin'. There's a bit more you'll submit to tonight, but I promise in the end, there'll be pleasure for us both."

She nodded and bowed her head, acquiescing to his words.

Leaning down, he tipped her face up to meet his. He set his mouth along her tempting mouth and kissed her. Burying his fingers in her soft, long tresses, he deepened the kiss. When he finally pulled away, they were both panting and shaking with need.

Rising, he stood before her and let her watch him shuck his britches, his last article of clothing. His cock bobbed before her face, hard and eager. Taking his length in hand, he glided his palm up and down, watching her as she stared, riveted on his shaft and movement.

He arched his hips forward until he could slide the tip of his cock over her quivering lips, swollen and dewy from their kisses. He used the pearls to paint her dusky pink skin and make her mouth glisten in the oil lamp light. "Open your purty mouth, wife."

Following his orders, she parted her lips.

Placing the crown right on the center of her tongue, slipping it to the back then to the tip, he made her taste him. His gut tightened, unable to take his own teasing as he commanded, "Suck it."

His wife didn't hesitate as she closed her mouth around him.

"Fuck, yes," he groaned as her lips drew tight around him and her tongue fluttered back and forth, licking the underside.

Closing his eyes for a moment, he enjoyed the feel of her mouth working him. There had been times during their love-making when she'd licked or suckled him briefly, but he was always too anxious to get inside her to let it go further. This time, he wanted her to perform this act on him until he spurted his cum on her tongue.

Her hands came up to his thighs, gripping him when he

began to thrust. He figured she was using her grasp to keep him from overpowering her. However, he didn't want to use her mouth to the point of injuring her, knowing this was another new situation for her.

He wrapped a fist around her hair, so he could tug her head back at an angle to take him a little deeper. The head of his cock was bumping the back of her throat, causing her to gag some around him. As a randy ass male, he couldn't help but enjoy the sound way too much. He stared down at her, his blood blazing and lust hazing his gaze as he took in the image of her full lips wrapped around his dick. He'd had months filled with dreams of her in this exact position, fantasizing and fucking his own hand as he tried to imagine it, her odd shaped mouth, red and stretched around his thick cock. It was nothing compared to the reality.

Then his virgin wife, trained by the best whores, turned the tables on him. He heard her inhale deep through her nose, seconds before she fully relaxed her throat, taking him in deep on his downstroke.

"Fuck!" he roared loudly, his rich baritone reverberating off the walls of the room and down the hall. He was pretty sure his crew in the bunkhouse heard him. He saw stars and everything turned to a heavenly white around him as he felt the head of his cock slip by the lower ring of her throat.

When his vision cleared, there Caroline Rand was, kneeling before him and staring up at him with her beguiling lips encompassing the base of his cock. Her throat worked along his shaft, once, twice, before she pulled back. Her tongue swirled around his crown a moment before she performed the same stunt.

He owed Miss Kitty and every Jewel in her house something spectacular—like real jewels. They'd trained her well. He didn't consider for a moment that Caroline had learned by mouth fucking other men during her month there, but somehow the ladies had found a way to teach her their craft. Caroline wasn't a whore, but his wife, and he was grateful for the years they had ahead of them.

Widening his stance, he let her maintain the lead for a while as she bobbed her head up and down his dick. When his sac became heavy and tight, drawing up along the bottom of his base, he couldn't hold out. Thrusting in and out of her lips, as she worked her tongue and throat on him, he laid claim to her mouth. He enjoyed feeling her hands slip around to the back of his thighs and clutch him just below his ass, urging him on. She hummed, an erotic vibrato in the back of her throat that sent white-hot heat shooting up his shaft, along his spine, and blooming in his core, destroying his restraint.

With a final thrust, he pressed all the way in until her lips were flush to his groin and her nose was buried among the dark hairs surrounding his base, coating her throat with the hot ribbons of his release.

Her throat worked, stroking his shaft as she drank him in.

He released the tight grip on her hair then stroked his fingers on her scalp to ease any pain. Grinding his teeth, he pulled out halfway and allowed her to continue sucking and licking his sensitive length to keep him hard. There were more tears in her bright, adoring gaze, and he knew it was a result of the act, taking him so deep.

"I can see, my little vixen, you studied well at the Harlot." He stepped away and smiled as he heard the sound of the bulbous crown popping from her mouth.

"Are you pleased, husband?" Her voice was raspy, sexy from the overuse and abuse of her vocal cords.

His groan was low. "Very much so."

Moving back until he was able to once again sit on the

bed, he then beckoned her up to him. "Come here, bunny. I need to finish claimin' your ass."

Staring up at him, her brow creased with trepidation. "Do we have to? I think we've done enough."

He took hold of her waist and pulled her up to straddle his thighs, plopping her down for emphasis. "I think your backside is sore enough not to have me spankin' it again because you disobeyed once more."

"Oh." Her swollen red lips pooched out as she pouted but stayed put.

Chuckling, he gave her a quick kiss on those tantalizing lips. "Don't worry, darlin', if you're real good, I'll let you come this time."

Sparks flashed in her gaze, but she remained silent.

"Place your heels down beside my hips and spread your knees wide," he instructed.

She parted them to the extent of his shoulders only.

"Wider."

Doing as she was told, she let her knees open further, the position giving him a clear line of sight of her from face to pussy. Her sex was even more swollen and wet since he'd touched her last, proof the oral performance had turned her on as well.

"Pretty, parted, and available. I could look at you like this all day, wife."

She blushed under his praise, as she pressed her knees out more.

"Ah, Garrett." Her arms flailed out as she lost her balance and began to topple back.

Not allowing her to fall, he tightened his grip on her waist. "I got you. Now, put your hands on my knees, then arch your hips up."

Sliding one hand to the center of her back to steady her as

she rose, he wrapped his other hand around his cock and angled it toward her center. He bumped the tip against her clit then circled it, coating himself in her wet heat.

Her moan was choppy as she undulated against him, her body trembling with need. His lovely bunny needed satisfaction.

He grazed along the blooming folds of her labia, down her slit, bypassing the opening of her pussy until he had his crown right against her cream coated rosebud. Using his thumb below the head, he guided just the tip in, then he stopped. Sliding his hand away, he held the lower half of his shaft. Meeting her gaze, he stared into her eyes, seeing the pull at the corners, apprehensive about what was ahead.

"You're going to do this."

"What?" She shook her head, doubting even as she asked.

"Yes, bunny. Just like you took the lead and fucked me with that delicious mouth of yours, you're going to submit your ass to me."

"I don't think I can." She rolled her bottom lip between her teeth.

Palming one of her hot cheeks in his hand, he squeezed.

She hissed.

"You will." He knew this wasn't the prime position for this act the first time. If he hadn't done such a thorough job of priming her ass, he'd have just bent her over and taken her. However, there was something exquisitely wicked about the idea of watching his wife fuck herself up her virgin ass on his cock.

He held her gaze, not rushing her. The rampant thoughts and emotions rolling through her mind were playing out in her beautiful, round brown eyes. Garrett knew the moment she gave in; he felt her shift, lowering herself just a smidgeon down, taking a little more of him in.

A rush of air came out of her parted lips as she exhaled and pressed down.

His crown was in now and he could feel the first tight ring's firm grip trying to keep him out.

"Nice and easy, darlin'."

TWENTY-ONE

She bit harder into her bottom lip as she let him in more. His head popped past the ring. She cried out, panting, and shaking.

He groaned. If it took all his strength, he would hold himself back and let her take her time. Understanding she needed a little assistance, he reached between her shaking thighs and started making slow circles around her clit.

"Oh. Oh." Her lids lowered halfway as she rotated her hips, grinding her clit against his fingers. As her focus shifted to the pleasure of his fondling, she unwittingly relaxed the walls of her back channel, and gravity took over. It pulled down her weight and drove his hard, thick cock along the slick cream and through the bundle of muscles.

"Ah!" Caroline's scream morphed into a broken sigh as her ass engulfed half of his shaft. "Garrett?"

"I know. Your tight ass feels so good." His grip on her hip was tight. She'd have bruises there the next day to accompany your red backside. He became more insistent in his stroking of her wet sex. "If we are ever going to find pleasure, you have to ride me. Come on, bunny, up and down."

She took to the command in his voice as she always did. Moving along his shaft in slow, short increments, she began to take him deeper, the ample cream making the glide of his thick shaft easier. He wasn't sure if she was concentrating on grinding her pussy against his hand, searching for her building climax, or finally enjoying his cock up her nether walls.

"Shit, you're takin' me, wife."

Her head bowed as she followed his gaze between her spread thighs and watched herself pushing his length in and out. Her mouth was gaped as she continued to moan and whimper. "It's so big. I'm too full. It burns, but—"

"Feels fuckin' good."

Up and down. Up and down. "Yes...oh, yes."

This was the part of his lovely, mysterious bunny who didn't want to admit that she got off on the right amount of pain that shifted into pleasure, but she couldn't resist it, even as her mind attempted to deny it. The evidence was in the wetness that covered her sex and inner thighs and his lap.

As her orgasm grew, her walls gripped him like a fist, pumping his length and pushing him toward a second climax.

Leaning in, he nuzzled her bosom, taking in one of her stiff pink tips. He sucked it hard in his mouth as he plied her clit with just the right amount of stimulation to push her over the edge.

"Oh. Oh. Oh. Oh. Ah-h-h-h-h-h-h!" Her scream was long and drawn out as she tipped her head back and bucked into him.

The ends of her hair brushed his inner thighs, her full mouth in the perfect O, her breasts bouncing, and her knees parted wide as she accepted his claim of her ass was a glorious sight. She began to come, her screams filling the room as her shudders fluttered up and down his shaft.

"Fuckin' lovely, bunny!" Unable to hold himself back, he rolled them until she was sprawled out beneath him.

She gasped.

Pulling her knees up over his arms, he pulled out, leaving nothing but his swollen red tip against the gaping raspberry opening between her cheeks. In one swift move, he drove all the way into her until her hole was stretched to a shocking white around the base of his cock. Drawing his hips back, he repeated the move again.

She arched against him and moaned.

Staring down at her, he saw and felt her response, and it broke the ties binding him to anything civilized and gave them both over to the hedonistic pleasure. He kissed her, feeding himself on her passionate cries and moans. His tongue pushed into her mouth, fucking her pretty lips as he ground deep into her.

Even as he claimed her, she offered him everything—all of herself—as she rocked up, thrusting, and taking from him as he gave to her. She wrapped her arms around him, holding him against her, taking on his weight.

He slipped a hand between their writhing hips then slipped down her slit and slid two fingers inside her pussy. The feel of his own cock pressing in and out of her back passage through the thin wall that separated him, sent a frisson of heat and power down his spine as he curled his fingers along the susceptible nerve bundle along the upper wall of her pussy.

Her thighs tightened against his sides.

Unrelenting, he branded every area of his wife's body that he had claim to. He brought her to a final climax as he filled her with his release.

Long moments later, when he had the sense and strength to move, he dragged himself up from the bed. One side of his mouth tipped up as he stared down at his wife, limp and in a haze of euphoric afterglow. He stumbled into the bathing room and started filling the tub with warm water. Picking up her bottle of jasmine oil, he added a few drops into the water, not caring if he carried her scent on him the next day.

Once it was filled, he returned to the room and spotted her now curled up on her side, her hands folded below her cheek. He couldn't help but enjoy seeing her bright red ass, a stark contrast to her pale back and limbs.

Moving to her, he scooped her up.

She groaned, even as she turned her face into his chest.

"Come on, my lovely bunny. I know just what will help all your achin' parts." He carried her into the next open door and continued his steps until he'd climbed into the clawfoot porcelain tub with her.

She hissed as the heat of the water greeted the tender skin of all parts of her well-used ass but settled between his knees with her head cushioned along his shoulder.

As he stroked her back, enjoying the feel of her sated and in his arms, he heard her yawn.

"I know it's not safe to fall asleep in the bath." Another yawn overtook her.

"It's all right, wife. I'll always protect you. Sleep."

Seconds later, she was out. Garrett thought about the day's events as he let his wife rest. When he thought about that man putting his hands upon Caroline, he became furious all over again.

"Garrett?"

"Yes, my love." He kissed her temple.

"What's wrong?" She glanced up at him, studying his face.

Refusing to allow anyone to encroach on what they shared between them, he shook his head. Reaching for a cake of soap, he began running it over one of her arms. "Nothin'. Tell me about the scents you planned out in that journal of yours."

As he knew it would, the conversation distracted her away from his wayward thoughts and allowed them to enjoy the rest of their night.

UNABLE TO KEEP the smile from her face, she didn't even try. She realized that she had a lot to smile about. She had a new horse, a pretty bay American Standardbred Garrett had bought for her from Jacob Morgan, when he showed up back in town. Garrett and Jacob, who returned to Grover Town to start up his own stud farm, said the horse had the perfect mild disposition for her, whether she rode him or used him to pull her wagon. Jacob had two of the males but had made Garrett promise that he could still use him as a stud when he needed. He also offered Garrett a fair price to have King sire a foal or two one day.

She couldn't say that in the almost two months she and Garrett had been married, he loved her, but she knew he cared for her and frequently showered her with adoration. She was happy for now with that and her love for him.

Caroline was more than happy she could sit on the wagon seat again. It had been four days since Garrett spanked her with the paddle and used her bottom thoroughly, or rather made her do it. Yesterday, her husband had taken her to the mercantile shop and had her help him pick out special bracelets that carried each of the Jewels stones in it for Miss Kitty and the women at the Harlot. Feeling more than a little jealous, she'd asked him why he was getting them all gifts. He'd leaned toward her and whispered in her ear in his rich, hypnotic timbre 'for the perfect useful box of gifts'.

She'd been shocked to a scarlet red right at the counter of the shop.

When she heard him place the orders for the bracelets with Mrs. Russell and request a single pearl on a twenty-two-inch chain, she waited until they were headed home to ask him why he'd gotten the chain so long.

"So, it can go around your waist, and every time I'm licking your pussy, I can watch it quiver as you climax." He'd then proceeded to slip a hand under her skirt and bring her to one orgasm after another all the way home.

Even now, her cheeks warmed at the memory. She stared up at the mid-afternoon summer sun. She was sweaty and dirty from working in the heat and wondered if she should have bought a bonnet weeks ago, when she ordered her new wardrobe. The night before, she and Garrett had talked about her plans for the day. She'd left the house right after breakfast to work with Gretchen Spencer in her flower and herb garden. Caroline had been impressed to learn so much from the pint-sized, red-headed wife and mother of two. Her journal was not only filled with more copious notes, but she had a basket of different flowers and fresh herbs, for her to study and work on at her leisure. She'd had a very full day, since she had discussed with Chance and Gretchen about them being sole providers of the soap line. Since she didn't have a space of her own yet to make or store a lot of her soaps, she'd have to start small. Perhaps a different soap each month. She mulled over options in her head as she thought about that and dinner plans that night. Garrett had said they would go into town and eat at the Drummonds' that night. He'd requested for her to wear her carnation pink dress.

Her husband's wink as he walked out the door after breakfast only made her understand he was thinking about the last time she'd worn it. Her first spanking.

"The man is incorrigible." She giggled as she brought Douglas, her horse, around the tree-lined glen following the creek around the Spencer property. She was now at the far end of it. This far down the road and at the far end of the cattle ranch, she would soon get to the fork that would lead into town or around it to the Rand farm, her home. There was a third extension of the crossroad, a rough path that led to her old home miles down the way. This time, she'd keep straight in time to take a long soak and get dressed. Tonight, she would not only wear the pink dress, but her new kid boots and she'd do her hair up real fine. Her husband didn't know it, but this was a special night tonight. She was more than a week late on her flow and she was fairly sure she was carrying a baby.

She knew the news would thrill Garrett. If she didn't know any better, she would say a lot of her husband's daily attentions probably were geared toward getting her with child. The other times, when he was taking her in places that clearly weren't avenues to her womb, she knew that was all for both their pleasures. She hated to admit that even the discomfort of him entered in her most naughty passage made her feel wicked, but she came hard with a chorus of nefarious pleas to her husband. She'd learned to give as good as she got. Last night, she'd met him after his bath with a drying sheet, and after she'd dried him, she'd then taken him deep in her mouth, using the skills Diamond had shown her.

Garrett's taste and feel was much better than the rubberized phallus she'd practiced on. Her husband had come so hard, he'd almost toppled back in the bath. He'd been quick to return the favor, laying her out right on the bathing room floor and takin' her to paradise three times with his mouth, only to roll her over on her knees and drive deep into her sex until they both needed another bath.

"Giddy yup!"

"Ah!" Caroline screamed as another wagon came careening around the road into the fork from the path that led to town and practically over the edge that led down to the creek bed, if Douglas hadn't acted quickly and trotted right instead of left.

A string of unladylike curses filled the air from the other wagon.

"Whoa!" Caroline pulled the reins, stopping him before the untended path. She turned around in her seat, not sure if the other driver had continued or not. "Is everyone all right—"

"You!" The vehement word came out harsh, like a slap.

Caroline stared at the faces of the two people she could have gone for months without ever seeing. "Ms. Bellmore... Widow Lawrence."

Their wagon sat across the road behind hers, almost completely turned around in the same direction they had just come.

"I should have known. You're like a bad rash that nothin' can rid of," Widow Lawrence sneered, her elegant diction and manners non-existent as she gave her a hard look.

Gasping at the vehemence of the two women, she was once again confused by their attacks toward her. "What did I ever do to the two of you?"

Old woman Bellmore cackled. "You're the prime example of the blight on Grover this town doesn't need. Another ignorant farmer and tradesman."

"It used to be this town was made up of landowners and clever businessmen. Now there are many races, inexperienced workers, and destitute families takin' from those with means. This place ain't even the same." Widow Lawrence folded her arms under her ample breasts. For the first time, she was wearing a worn gingham dress.

Caroline shook her head, too shocked to formulate words.

"I told my boy to kick your father off the land years ago. Another man who doesn't listen to good sense." Bellmore's thin lips curled into a sneer.

"Go on, get. Back to your *husband*. Somethin' else you didn't have no right to." Lawrence made a shooing move with one hand as she snatched up the fallen reins with the other.

Wanting to get away from the two malicious women, just as much as they wanted her gone, Caroline started to turn around in her seat when something caught her gaze. There was a tarp laid out over something in the back of their wagon. From their near accident, it must have shifted things around because Caroline found herself staring down at a gape-mouthed corpse.

"Oh. My. God." She slammed a hand over her mouth and the other over her heart. She glanced up at the two women, neither of them the town undertaker, doctor, or preacher, so they had no logical reason to be riding the countryside with a dead body. She was sure that man was dead. "What have you done?"

———

"RACHEL WANTED me to ask if you and the missus wanted to come over for dinner tonight. That is if'n you don't got plans."

Garrett stood at the bottom of the steps that led to the house, as he glanced up at the late afternoon sky, then back at his foreman. They were about to get started on the evening milking when he realized his wife hadn't made it back home yet. "We do have plans, but instead, we most likely will be occupied with another lesson for my wife. Since she's finding time a hard concept."

Her backside had just healed from the last paddlin' and it looked as if she was due for another one. *Fine by me.*

"A man's got to do whatever it takes to keep his house in order. Rachel's had to be reminded a time or two, even if I have to be creative with her advancin' pregnancy," Lyle added, removing his hat and swiping a rag from his back pocket over his brow to clear off the sweat.

Garrett nodded. On another day, he'd have to ask his foreman what those inventive things were, because he was pretty sure, since his wife hadn't had a flow but once in the two months they had been married, and that was well over six weeks ago, she was with child. He was planning to bring it to her attention at dinner.

He'd also wanted to tell her he was going to take some time off before harvest and after the Founders' Day events for a honeymoon. With Lyle being able to handle the place, he wanted to take Caroline up to Wisconsin to meet his family.

Mooing and the calls of the men on horseback, guiding the herd, drew both their attention.

Lyle started toward his black and white horse. "Looks like the men got the cows headed to the paddock, guess we should—"

His foreman's words were cut off as both heard the high stepping horse as he trotted onto the land, the wagon rolling behind it empty.

"That's Caroline's horse." Garrett raced across the land toward Douglas, fear's grip around his heart.

TWO HOURS LATER, Garrett was about to go out of his mind as he rode away from Spencer Pride Ranch with Lyle and now Chance at his side. Both men were riding their horses hell for leather as they broke through the wood gate with a large iron replica of Spencer's brand nailed into the center of it. Gretchen and Spencer had both confirmed Caroline had left hours ago and had stated she was headed home.

His wife's journal and the basket of herbs and flowers she'd gotten from working with Gretchen was proof that she hadn't made any other stops. He'd never been so grateful he'd purchased the clever horse from Jacob. If the well-trained horse hadn't returned home, he may not have gone looking for her until after they had the cows milked and moved to the next pasture, the whole while becoming more furious with his wife for going off on another adventure alone.

"I'll head down the creek and see if she fell in," Spencer called out.

"I'll take the opposite way around town. See if Kitty may have seen her. Maybe she was unwell and stopped by to get help from their midwife," Lyle confirmed. "We'll find her, Garrett."

Garrett felt sick to his stomach, afraid that somehow his wife had become injured, or worse. "I damn sure will. I'm going to alert Ian. See if my brother can spare his deputies to help us search."

Each of them on their way, Garrett headed around the fork to take the fastest road into town. Dusk was creepin' up on them fast, and it would be harder to find his wife in darkness if she was in a ditch somewhere.

In a flash, Garrett was reining in King before the Sheriff's Office, barely waiting for his horse to stop before he was slinging his foot over the back of the saddle and vaulting off the side in a dead run. He didn't pay heed to the stares he was drawing from people. Up the stairs of the boardwalk, he burst through the door. Before him, was chaos, as Ian and his two deputies were strappin' their gun belts while a pregnant, blonde woman, with two red-headed young girls clinging to her skirts, was crying and wringing her hands.

"This ain't like Jerry, Sheriff. Wouldn't be gone all day like this." The woman's face was blotchy, streams racing from her eyes and nose.

"We'll find him. You said he'd been actin' strange recently?"

Garrett shoved a hand through his hair, trying to be patient and not interrupt his brother, who was apparently in the middle of doing his job in helping a distraught wife and mother. Garrett wanted to have sympathy for the woman, whom he recognized as the new newspaperman's wife, but finding his own wife was too pressing of a matter to him.

"Yes, sir. We ain't been here but a few weeks, and two of them, I woke in the middle of the night to find him gone, or he came in late and said he don't want no supper." The two girls started crying, picking up on their mother's emotions.

"The last time you said you saw him was this mornin?" his brother asked the woman as he stared down on her.

"Yes, sir."

"And he didn't look well?" Ian followed with.

"Yes, sir. I told him that he was workin' himself too hard lately. His face didn't seem to be set right."

"Hm."

"He said Mr. Bellmore was trustin' him to get the new paper busines off the ground here or we would lose the year's money we put down for the lease on the business, and he didn't have time to sit around. Then he left." The blonde woman sniffed as more fresh tears rolled out. "When the girls and I came down an hour later, he wasn't even in the shop. We waited, but he's ain't never showed."

Fuckin' Bellmore, Garrett thought. *The man's name is*

always tied up in something when it comes to someone missing.

"You said that last night, he was complaining about chest discomfort, his feet and hands being numb." Ian turned to him, eyeing him as he continued to run through clarifying questions with the woman.

"Um-hm."

As he listened to the line of questioning, Garrett recalled that the last time he was in his brother's office, Ian had talked about the other wives of the dead men having a similar tale, only to have their spouses found dead in empty fields, no sign of how they got there. Dammit, of all the times he was in need of his brother's help, it looked as if Ian's hands would be full.

"What's goin' on, Garrett?" Ian hooked his thumbs in his low-slung gun belt. "You look like you just got some bad news."

"It's Caroline. She's missing?"

Ian's brows shot up high. "The hell you say?"

Garrett made quick work of the course of the day, telling him about her horse and wagon, her already having left Spencer's hours ago. "Lyle and Spencer are out looking to see if she's fallen, but I'm starting to think somethin' more serious is up."

"I agree. I'll help you look for her—"

"What about my husband?" the woman whined.

"Calm yourself, ma'am." Ian held his hands out to her. "I'll have my deputies start a search for—"

"Sheriff, you needs come quick. They goin' kill her!" Old Man Rivers came hobbling into the office next, with his gout-swollen feet, withered tanned face, and stringy gray hair as wild as his jaundiced eyes.

"Who?" Garrett and Ian asked together.

"That sweet Caroline, your missus," Rivers croaked as he

pointed a crooked finger at Garrett. "She goin' be just like the red-headed corpse they dragged out there, too."

"Jerry!" The woman screamed just as her eyes rolled back. Deputy Nelson moved quickly and caught the woman just before she crumpled to the floor in a dead faint.

"Mama! Mama!" the girls began to wail.

Garrett's heart sank as he gripped the older man by the shoulder. "Where is she, man? Where's my wife?"

"YOU TWO ARE NEVER GOING to get away with this. People are starting to suspect foul play. The sheriff is on to you."

Garrett squatted close to one side of the off-kilter barn next to his brother. Ian's two deputies were moving in on the other side. They'd left their horses two hundred yards away from Caroline's old home, so they wouldn't hear them coming. The wagon had been parked out of view behind the small house, but it had been empty. They could clearly see the body laid out in the middle of the field as if the man had just collapsed there. Doc Clarkston was hanging back by the house, waiting until they had the women in custody before he would check the body and confirm the man's death was the same as the others. The women would hang.

He had been shocked to hear from Old Man Rivers that it was Widow Lawrence and Bellmore's mother who had Caroline and the body. He and Ian had suspected Bellmore, even though he couldn't link any evidence to the man and he always had an alibi surrounding the times the men were missing. Even now, when they went by Bellmore's home, he was there knocking back whisky and in a card game with MJ Harvey.

Widow Lawrence's laughter fluttered through the old barn. "Men are stupid. Stupid, stupid, stupid. Wave tits and ass in their face and they cain't even see straight."

Gone was the woman's sensuous and elegant purring diction. Now there was a heavy twang to her voice. Garrett realized that the woman had bamboozled most of the men in town. If he had ever taken her up on her offer to go to her house for dinner and other things, he may have been as dead as the others.

"My husband was the same way. I got tired of living under his abusive thumb. Thinkin' he was so much smarter than me. Well, I showed them. And I raised my son to listen to his mother," Ms. Bellmore declared. "I taught him well how to lure people like your ignorant papa. The gullible, ready to throw all their savings in on a dream they're not fit to cultivate."

"You're a sick woman, to prey on hardworking people who want a better life for their families." Caroline's voice was filled with pain and disgust.

"Men think women are only good for spreadin' their legs and cookin' their food. So, I cooked them up somethin' real nice and took every paltry coin they thought they were being kind in givin' to some *poor, helpless* widow after a tumble. The cheats. I don't feel sorry for none of them. They all deserved what they got." Widow Lawrence laughed, then it cut off. "When you saw me last week with Jerry at my back door, I knew you had to be taken care of."

"Always you. You beguiled him beside that high-priced brothel, just to set him up to be attacked by your jealous husband," Old Lady Bellmore added. "It's because of you, a whore, that my son couldn't show his face in town for over a week!"

Slap.

Garrett heard Caroline's whimper and refused to wait a second longer. Dashing around his brother, he entered the wide rickety door of the barn.

"Don't move another step." Widow Lawrence aimed a small pistol at him.

Shit. He didn't suspect they had a gun, and now he'd possibly put his wife's life in more danger.

"Let her go, Daniella." Garrett held the gaze of the widow. He couldn't risk looking at Caroline; he had to keep his eyes on the woman with the gun.

"Well, well, well. Mr. Rand always comin' to the rescue of this chit of a girl. When you could have had a real woman." Lawrence's fake temptress tone was back as she wagged the gun from side to side.

"Drop it." Sheriff Silverman strutted in with both his guns out, one trained on each of the felonious women.

"If you come any closer, Sheriff, I'll shoot." Widow Lawrence shifted the gun from Garrett to the sheriff and back several times.

Now that his brother was at his side, Garrett shifted his gaze to Caroline's. From the dim lighting, he could see the redness on one of her cheeks but couldn't tell if it was swollen. His rage toward the older woman made him taste acid. He never would have thought he could feel so vengeful toward a woman, and one that was his elder at that.

"Are you all right, darlin'?"

She held his gaze and nodded from her position on the ground.

"You women are surrounded. It's best you drop your weapon and turn yourselves in. Maybe the judge will go easy on you," the sheriff attempted to reason with them.

"I have a better idea. The two of us are going to take the wench and ride out of town. If you don't follow, then we'll toss her off the wagon. Like any good bitch, she'll make her way back home. Look where she is now." The older woman cackled.

When the old woman reached out her hand to grab Caroline, Caroline ducked and kicked out hard.

Garrett watched the old lady go sailing back against the barn wall.

They were creaking and swaying, but the structure held as Caroline jumped to her feet and ran toward him.

"No!" Garrett yelled as he saw the movement and flash from behind her. He raced toward his wife, trying to get to her and shield her.

One. Nelson shot Widow Lawrence through one of the warped wood slats in the wall of the barn.

Two. Widow Lawrence's shot went wild.

Three. Ms. Bellmore pulled out a gun from the hidden folds of her skirt and shot Caroline.

Four. Sheriff shot old woman Bellmore in her wrist, holding the gun.

Shots rang out around them as he snatched his wife into his arms, shifting his body to protect her.

"Shit!"

Garrett wasn't sure who spoke; all he knew was that he was staring down into the pale face of his wife as she lay on the ground in his arms.

"Caroline. Bunny." He shook her. Unsure if the wind had been knocked from her on impact, he lifted a hand to her face when he saw the blood on his hand. "God, no. Caroline!"

Rolling her toward him, he stared at her back, the light green blouse covered in blood. He had no clue where it was coming from.

"Doc Clarkston! Come quick!"

She lay limp against him as he rocked her in his arms

while he waited for the doctor, whispering in her ear, "Please, love, please be all right."

"ARE YOU SUPPOSED TO BE UP?"

Caroline was across the room, standing before the cheval mirror as she tried to peel away the gauze. Guilty, she glanced over at the door and saw her husband standing there, his arms folded across his broad chest as he stared at her. He was wearing the green shirt with the navy-blue stripes that she had sewn for him, looking so handsome.

"Um, I..." When she saw his arched brow as he crossed the wood floor of their bedroom, she knew she was in trouble. "No."

She knew most people would not have to stay in bed so long after a small injury to the arm, but with the pregnancy and her fainting, the doctor wanted to ensure the baby was all right and that required rest and staying off her feet. As she suspected, Garrett had been extremely excited about the news of the baby, and she found out he had already guessed about her condition. The man was too observant.

The only bad news about the situation was the fact she would miss the Founders' Day events, but Garrett let her know he and Lyle had arranged for Garrett to take time off and as soon as the doctor cleared her, they were going on a honeymoon and she would get to meet her in-laws.

Once he reached her, he scooped her up in his arms, kissed her, then returned her to bed. "If you can't behave, I'll pay Mrs. Copernic extra to sit right here with you all day. Housekeeping and laundry be damned."

She poked her lip. "If you do, I'll ask her to show me some of her recipes."

"You wouldn't dare." His arms bracketed her upper body as he stayed close.

"Try me." She winced as she crossed her arms under her breasts.

His gaze lowered to the sight of her dark pink nipples pointing through her shift. "How's the arm?"

Thankfully, Mrs. Drummond, Mrs. Morrison, and Mrs. Livingston were alternating sending over meals for the week until Doc Clarkston cleared Caroline to resume her work around the house, and they didn't have to suffer their house-keeper's unique style of cooking. It had been only a couple days since she was shot in the back of her arm. The wound had only been a graze, but it had bled a lot.

"Still sore, but better today."

She'd only been out for an hour, but when she came to in her childhood bed, Doc Clarkston had already cleaned, stitched, and dressed her wound. It had only been the impact of the shot and her fall that had knocked her out.

"If you're a good girl, I'll carry you to the porch, where we can have our noon meal and you can get some fresh air."

Leaning toward him, she kissed his jaw, then followed it inward with more light kisses until she got to his mouth. "I can be really good."

He groaned. "Wife. Behave. You're in no condition to start somethin' we can't finish."

"Husband, it's my arm, not my—"

His growl filled the room as his cobalt eyes darkened.

She saw the spark of lust in his gaze mirroring the lust she always felt around him, but she leaned back against the pile of pillows. "Okay."

"I have something for you."

"You do? Is it a present?" She bounced in the bed, expectant. It was her husband's generous nature that had taught her it was all right for her to have special things and let him care for her, that she deserved good things.

"Yes." He reached back and pulled something from his back pocket.

She stared at the folded papers he held out to her. Frowning, she took them then opened the tri-fold.

DOUGLAS FAMILY FARM
Property Deed

HER HANDS BEGAN to tremble as she stared down at the paperwork, reading it. She saw her name.

"What is this?" Her gaze began to blur, making it hard to read all the words.

"It's the deed to your family home. It's yours."

"What..." She lost her voice. She swallowed then continued, still gaping at the papers in disbelief. "How is this possible?"

"Before Bellmore followed his ma to Topeka to face the judge, I got him to make things right for you." Judging from Garrett's peculiar tone, she figured there was more to the story but didn't ask.

"No..." Shaking her head, she folded the papers. "Are you through with me? Sending me away?"

"What? Hell, no." He grasped her uninjured arm. "Why would you think that, darlin'?"

"Then why?" She stared at his chest, afraid to look in his eyes and discover this dream of hers was short lived. "I thought my home was here with you." She placed a hand on her flat belly. "*Our* home was here."

"You bet your sweet ass it is, bunny." He slid his hand over hers, caressing the hand she used to protect their child. With his other hand, he tipped her chin up and looked into her eyes. "I love you. I know you have dreams of your own. You never got to plan and work toward somethin' that was just yours. I know how much you love dabblin' with scents and things, so I want you to take that place and make it whatever you want. Extend the house if you need to and fix it up any way you desire."

"You love me?"

He scowled at her. "Is that all you heard?"

"That's all I care about."

He cupped her face. "When I thought I'd lost you in that barn, I knew my life would end with yours right there." He inhaled as if to steady himself before he went on. "Of course, I love you, bunny. I've always loved you. I even asked your papa for your hand before he died."

She gasped. "You did?"

"Yup. He turned me down, but I wasn't going to give up. When I got back into town and discovered he had died and you were gone, I searched high and low for you. Then I saw you...even veiled, I *knew* you."

She gingerly lifted her injured arm to place her palm over his heart. She absorbed his warmth and the firm beat of his heart that matched hers. "I love you too, Garrett. I want to fill our house with love and babies. *A loue ye.*"

AUTHOR'S NOTE

If you would like to read Lyle and Rachel's story, Ruling Rachel, the novella is in Blushing Books' 12 Naughty Days of Christmas 2020.

Ruling Rachel

Rachel Morrison, the youngest daughter of a woman who maintains the local brothel, has always been a good girl, an obedient daughter, and a dependable housekeeper for her employer. However, as other young women in Grover Town are getting married, she feels as if she's always the one left in the wagon holding the bags. Until Lyle. Now she has one wish for this holiday that may place her on the naughty list.

Lyle Joseph, a farmhand who has big dreams of claimin' the foreman position. With all his hard work and determination, he hasn't given a blink to settling down. Until the first snowfall sets an angel in his path in need of rescue. The urge to tan her hide for breaking rules that placed herself in danger is only second to the petticoat blazin' desire he's got for her.

Can one night of passion destroy his plans or bring the true gift of Christmas?

YASMINE HYDE

USA Today Bestselling Author, Yasmine Hyde loves romance and writing it is one of her greatest pleasures in life outside of her daughter. Her belief in happily ever after began when she was sixteen and started reading romance books. Now as an erotic romance author, she tries to show that every woman, no matter color, age, shape or size, deserves a high level of passion in her life. She resides in North Carolina with her family and is a RomVet.

Visit her website here:
https://yvettehines.com/yasmine-hyde-erotica/

Don't miss these exciting titles by Yasmine Hyde and Blushing Books!

Grover Town Discipline
Guiding Gretchen
Handling Holly
Servicing Serenity
Educating Elizabeth
Instructing Isabel
Claiming Caroline

Anthologies
12 Naughty Days of Christmas 2020

BLUSHING BOOKS

Blushing Books is one of the oldest eBook publishers on the web. We've been running websites that publish spanking and BDSM related romance and erotica since 1999, and we have been selling eBooks since 2003. We hope you'll check out our hundreds of offerings at http://www.blushingbooks.com.

BLUSHING BOOKS NEWSLETTER

Please join the Blushing Books newsletter
to receive updates & special promotional offers.
You can also join by using your mobile phone:
Just text BLUSHING to 22828.